The Coil

Funded by the

**Itasca Lions Club
Light Up For
Sight Program**

Also by Gayle Lynds with Robert Ludlum in Large Print:

Robert Ludlum's The Altman Code
Robert Ludlum's The Hades Factor

This Large Print Book carries the
Seal of Approval of N.A.V.H.

The Coil

Gayle Lynds

WHEELER PUBLISHING

Published in 2004 by arrangement with St. Martin's Press, LLC.

Wheeler Large Print Hardcover.

The text of this Large Print edition is unabridged.
Other aspects of the book may vary from the original edition.

Set in 16 pt. Plantin by Liana M. Walker.

Printed in the United States on permanent paper.

**Library of Congress Control Number: 2004103279
ISBN 1-58724-710-0 (lg. print : hc : alk. paper)**

For my stepdaughter,
Deirdre Lynds,
who rides music and surf
with equal grace and joy . . .
showing the way for the rest of us

As the Founder/CEO of NAVH, the only national health agency solely devoted to those who, although not totally blind, have an eye disease which could lead to serious visual impairment, I am pleased to recognize Thorndike Press* as one of the leading publishers in the large print field.

Founded in 1954 in San Francisco to prepare large print textbooks for partially seeing children, NAVH became the pioneer and standard setting agency in the preparation of large type.

Today, those publishers who meet our standards carry the prestigious "Seal of Approval" indicating high quality large print. We are delighted that Thorndike Press is one of the publishers whose titles meet these standards. We are also pleased to recognize the significant contribution Thorndike Press is making in this important and growing field.

Lorraine H. Marchi, L.H.D.
Founder/CEO
NAVH

* Thorndike Press encompasses the following imprints: Thorndike, Wheeler, Walker and Large Pr int Press.

Prologue

As the State Department limousine sped through the wintry forest, Secretary of State Grey Mellencamp pressed the button to raise the soundproof glass that provided privacy from his driver. He stared out at the leafless trees and bushes, cold and black in the twilight. They formed a dark wall on either side of the Virginia road, almost a tunnel as they crowded together, lined with mounds of dirty snow. There was no movement out there in the shadowy timber, no sign of life.

With a sense of foreboding, Mellencamp sat back. He had just left his meeting with Liz Sansborough, where he had failed to get the information he needed. He was angry and disappointed but, as he thought about it, relieved, too, because she had been slated for sacrifice. Someone would be eventually. In the end, probably many. He hoped each was guilty, so their executions would be justified. He did not like any of it, and now that he believed Liz Sansborough

7

was innocent, he liked it even less.

He continued to stare out the window, forcing himself to relax, inhaling the scent of expensive leather upholstery. He had made thousands of successful deals around the world, first for his corporate law firm and now as secretary of state, and he recognized a situation he could handle.

He removed his cell from inside his coat and dialed Brussels.

Instantly, an English-accented voice answered: "Cronus here."

Mellencamp put authority into his words: "I've finished my interview with Sansborough at the safe house. She claims she saw no files, that it would've been out of character for her father to keep them. She never varied from her story."

"Bloody hell! He *had* to have files," Cronus said, his voice rising, the English accent crisp. "He must have kept track of whom he'd worked for and what he'd done. His contacts, for God's sakes. Who was secure, who wasn't. What worked. What *failed*. Addresses. Phone numbers. Aliases. No one can stay in business, especially one like his, without records. Certainly she's lying!"

The secretary of state bit back an irritated retort. "Sansborough says the Carnivore had a photographic memory, which means he had no reason to record details for himself. He told her he always destroyed everything that was on paper — plans, maps, timetables, that sort of thing — once he'd completed a wet job. Sansborough's mother told us the same thing when she was debriefed, and everyone knows the main reason he lasted so long was his hypervigilance."

The Englishman's tone was dismissive. "From all that's happened, they *must* exist. And Sansborough must know where they are. She's the only logical one, now that her mother's dead."

"Yes, obviously there are records, but her parents kept her in the dark. If she hadn't spotted her father in the middle of that wipe job in Lisbon, she might never have found out about their secret life, and we probably wouldn't have either. Ignorance was the best way to keep her safe, so what possible reason would they have to tell her about files? Besides, when she went over to them, they quit the business. She never actually saw them plan a hit. All in all, it makes no sense she'd know about files." He paused, and his heavy shoulders squared. "We'll find them, but it won't be through her."

"She must be playing you, Themis. She's capable of it. One of Langley's best."

Mellencamp was growing angry again. "Do you think that if she were holding back I wouldn't go after her with everything we have? *I'm* the one at risk here. This is a hell of a lot more important to me than it is to you. *You're* not being blackmailed because of what's in those damned records." He felt his heart pound. He was overweight and had a coronary condition, which frightened him when he allowed himself to think about it.

He closed his eyes and tried to get his emotions under control. Liz Sansborough was the only child of Hal Sansborough — the Carnivore, who had been one of the Cold War's most feared and elusive independent assassins. Despite competition for notoriety from others such as Carlos the Jackal and Imad Fayez Mugniyeh and the Abbot, the Carnivore was the real legend among those who knew about such things — hated, but hired by all sides. He had never made a mistake big enough to jeopardize his identity. No photos of him existed, and until near the time he killed himself, no one had been able to discover his real name. He had been a chimera, a chameleon in the world's soft underbelly of spies and international criminals, indestructible. The man without a face.

When Cronus spoke again, his voice was less accusatory. "Are you going to do what the blackmailer wants, Themis?"

"Never." The secretary of state's tone left no doubt. "We've got to find those records ourselves. I keep thinking about the three clippings I sent you. The answer may be in one of them." He removed them from his briefcase.

"If it is, I don't see it."

Mellencamp said nothing, studying them.

The Times, Great Britain

Sir Robert Childs, MP, was found dead in his bathtub today, his wrists slashed in an apparent suicide. His maid, who discovered the popular parliamentarian's body, says she found a note that relayed deep regrets to his family about his secret life with call girls. . . .

Bild, Germany (translated)

The nation awoke in shock this morning to discover Chancellor Hans Raab had resigned at midnight. Hounded by charges that he accepted illegal donations in return for political influence during his 16 years in power, he . . .

The Washington Post, United States

In yet another electoral surprise, the sixth congressman in as many weeks has announced he is dropping out of his congressional race. Jay White (D-OR) cited the birth of his third child, saying he needed to return to the private sector to earn a larger income to support his family.

That makes a total of three Republicans and three Democrats, each from the extreme right or left wing of his party, who will not run for reelection. None faced a serious challenge. . . .

"Take Sir Robert," Mellencamp said. "He bled out in a bathtub like some mad Roman senator, supposedly because he'd been discovered sweating up the sheets with a few whores. Ridiculous that he'd kill himself over such a minor matter."

"In certain circles around London, it was known he used call girls."

"Exactly. He must've been afraid something else would come out. Something huge, for him to commit suicide." Mellencamp sighed. "And now Raab's resigned with the excuse of financial shenanigans. It's unbelievable he'd resign at midnight like a run-of-the-mill thief because of some minor illegality like a slush fund."

"At least he can't ram through his choice for director-general of trade now. The environmental restrictions would've set back international markets ten years." The voice on the other end of the line hesitated and resumed thoughtfully: "Maybe that's it. Maybe Raab was blackmailed into resigning because of some appointment he was going to make, and the slush fund was just an excuse to give the public."

Mellencamp nodded. "But how does that relate to all the congressmen who've dropped out here before the election? Three from the far right, three from the far left. If we're correct, and the Carnivore's files are what the blackmailer's using —"

"Then something has to connect the congressmen, Robert Childs, Chancellor Raab, and you. Perhaps you should do what the blackmailer wants, Themis. After all, he threatened your life. It's not such a big request. A minor change in that new EU–U.S. agreement —"

Mellencamp erupted: "I told you *no!*" and then sank into stony silence. He had revealed to Cronus what was necessary about his being blackmailed, no more. He would not discuss it further.

But Cronus was already talking again, his voice intense as he pondered. "What is it that you have in common? You come from different countries.

Different lines of work, although all of you are involved in politics somehow. All of you are men. White men and in power. We know you hired the Carnivore, or your wife did."

Mellencamp snapped, "Leave her out of it." Ruth had died five years before, and he still grieved. She had made a misstep when she was young. With a boyfriend, she had gone to the Carnivore to stop a U.S. senator who had raped her younger sister. The senator and his powerful father, who had always protected him, died together in a yachting accident in the Mediterranean.

Cronus continued: "Our investigators found the Carnivore was connected to Raab and two of the six congressmen. The blackmailer doesn't seem to be after money. Is there some kind of overall plan, or is this simply a madman operating on whim?"

"Lord knows," Mellencamp said tiredly.

"Our people have come up with nothing but dead ends. They say it's like looking for a ghost in the fog. Whoever's got the files seems to know exactly how to remain beyond our reach. Which makes me ask again: Are you sure the assassin's daughter knows nothing?"

Mellencamp sat up, wary. "Almost completely certain."

The voice was cold, businesslike. "She's the last living link to the Carnivore. She must be eliminated before she can hurt us."

This was what Mellencamp had feared. "Each death draws a spotlight," he argued. "The greater the accumulation of light, the more attention is attracted. Kill her, and we increase the risk to ourselves that we'll be discovered. Instead, it'd be much better for us — much safer — to control her."

There was a surprised silence.

Mellencamp spoke into it, his tone now disinterested. He must not act as if he was asking a favor. Cronus would want to negotiate, and this was not negotiable. "If we arrange it right, Sansborough could turn out to be useful. Perhaps vital, if we can get a handle on who has the files, or if she remembers something that she doesn't realize is important. As you said yourself, she's our last link."

"Possibly," the voice from the distance admitted. "You have a plan?"

"Of course." Relieved, Mellencamp smiled to himself. "Consider the situation. Right now, Sansborough is at loose ends and probably depressed. Both her parents are dead, and her husband was killed long ago. She has no brothers or sisters, and because of the life she's been leading, she has no real friends, except her cousin in California."

"Sarah Walker, yes. I remember. And?"

"What she wants most is to go back to work for Langley, because that's what she understands. It's familiar, comfortable."

"Your DCI considers her a security risk."

"Of course Arlene does, and she's right. Arlene will continue to offer her the hope of contract work, just to keep her quiet. But there's nothing Sansborough can do to make it right with Langley. She's been keeping busy by working on

14

a graduate degree in psychology at Georgetown. I've encouraged her to continue. What we must do is create an opportunity for her in that field. Something irresistible. But we must move quickly, before she finds some other interest or gets in our way somehow. If we handle this right, she'll vanish into academia, just another woman with a past she'd like to forget. A cipher in some college or university. Small. Then as long as she stays quiet and out of the way, we can watch her. She won't be a danger to us. Or to herself."

Grey Mellencamp lived on a Thoroughbred horse farm some forty miles east of the safe house. The limousine had left the country road for the Beltway, where the nighttime traffic was thick and frustrating, normal for this hour. The moon was rising, casting a wash of silver across the speeding cars and the houses and the businesses, which spread in a vast ocean of winking lights everywhere he looked.

He returned the clippings to his briefcase, relieved Cronus had agreed to his plan. His mind wandered tiredly, avoiding the touchy parts of his past, but as soon as the limo paused at the farm's front gate house and the security guard waved the limo onto his land, he began to relax. Although he had not located the Carnivore's files, at least he had saved an innocent woman's life.

The limo pulled up to his front portico, where lighted carriage lamps sent a yellow glow across the brick drive. Chet jumped out from behind the wheel and ran around to open the door.

Mellencamp emerged into the cold, carrying

his briefcase. He nodded at Chet and climbed the front steps wearily.

"Six a.m. tomorrow, sir?" Chet called to his back.

"Yes, of course. See you then." Unaccountably, Mellencamp turned to add a final few words to his driver. "Have a nice night, Chet."

"Thank you, sir. You, too, sir."

The secretary of state walked inside, where the house was aromatic with the scent of a pine fire. He headed down the hall, shrugging out of his overcoat, and entered his den. Cherry wood wainscoting lined the walls, and heavy drapes on the French doors protected the room from the night's freeze. He dropped his coat onto a sofa and fell heavily into his chair beside the fireplace.

The flames licked up orange and blue. It was a real fire with real logs, none of that fake nonsense so many young people used now to avoid cleaning out the ashes. He leaned forward and rubbed his hands together, warming them, again nervous about who had the files and what it meant to his dead wife's good name and to his future.

His housekeeper called out from the kitchen. "I heard you come in, sir. Would you like a drink?"

He raised his voice. "Don't concern yourself, Gretchen. I'll fix my own."

He loosened his tie and pushed himself up, feeling all of his more than three hundred pounds and sixty-six years. He moved ponderously to the bar. He was measuring out a whiskey sour when chill air gusted from behind the drapes. He looked up and caught his breath.

A black-clothed figure stepped out.

Before Mellencamp could think, could react, the figure moved behind him and yanked back his forehead.

"No!" Mellencamp dropped his glass and grabbed for the hands, too late.

"You should have done what we asked, Themis."

The short needle of a loaded syringe pierced his fleshy cheek, where the mark would be unnoticed among the salt-and-pepper hairs of his evening shadow. As his head was released, a wave of dizziness swept through him, and he turned in horror, trying to focus, while the killer vanished behind the drapes. Pain seemed to crack open his heart. He realized with outrage that there was a human sacrifice tonight after all. His legs collapsed, and he pitched back, dead.

PART I

The rabbit snare exists because of the rabbit.
Once you have the rabbit,
you no longer need the snare.

— CHUANG TSU

One

May 2003
Brussels, Belgium

In one of his trademark conservative suits, Gino Malko strolled through the rue Sainte-Catherine area in the heart of the lower city, enjoying the cool sunlight of the northern spring as he swung his special ebony cane with the silver handle. From time to time, he threw back his head, shut his eyes, and let the sun warm his face, somehow avoiding the other walkers as if he had built-in radar.

Eventually, he turned into a café, Le Cerf Agile, and sat at an outdoor table covered in white lace.

The eager waiter bustled over. "Good morning again, monsieur. Another fine day, eh?" he asked in English. "Your usual?"

"Thank you, Ruud," Malko said, smiling, playing his role.

Malko was a heavy tipper, so the waiter returned quickly with café au lait and a Belgian pastry. Malko nodded his appreciation, poured from the two silver pitchers, stirred, and bit into

21

the pastry. He leaned back at his ease to watch the passing throng of locals, NATO personnel, businessmen, tourists, and EU staff members. It was early for tourists, but the fine spring weather had attracted a swarm.

He was on his second pastry when he spotted the target. He casually picked up his cane and moved naturally into the stream of pedestrians. Apparently, the density of the crowd forced him to hold the cane upright.

In the normal course of things, he bumped into one or two people, including his target, expressed his horrified regrets each time, and finally, as if the crush were too much, turned back toward the café.

A woman screamed. Everyone looked in her direction. Near her, a tall, slender man with a Mediterranean complexion had collapsed on the sidewalk, his hand clutching his chest.

As Brussels' thick traffic surged past, people converged. They shouted in French, Flemish, and English.

"Give him air!"

"Call the paramedics!"

"Can anyone administer CPR?"

"I'm a doctor — stand aside!"

Now back at his table at the café, Malko sipped coffee and chewed his pastry and watched as the doctor dove into the riveted throng. The spectators whispered into one another's ears and peered down. As Malko finished his pastry and dusted his fingers, a shiver of horror swept around the circle.

Almost immediately, a man in shirtsleeves

fought his way out, dialing a cell. His face was pink with excitement. "There's been a tragedy on the street in the rue Sainte-Catherine district!" he reported in French. "Heart attack — a doctor just said so. What? Yes, he's dead. Important? Hold your hat: It's EU Competition Commissioner Franco Peri! Get it on the air at once. Yes, the lead. Pull whatever else you have off!"

Gino Malko smiled, left euros on the lace-covered table, and headed off, cane swinging. He would be back in his hotel in five minutes. Checked out in ten. And in fifteen, taxiing to the airport.

July 2003
The University of California
Santa Barbara

It was after nine o'clock in the morning, and Campbell Hall was crammed with students sitting in row after row, rising toward the back of the amphitheater. Liz Sansborough studied them as she gave her last lecture of the summer term. There was something about their indifferent, interested, scrubbed, dirty, sleepy, alert faces that radiated hope.

They reminded her of her years at Cambridge, when she was their age and searching for a clue, too. She would probably continue to search until she keeled over from work and the occasional but necessary martini. The fact that they showed up class after class made her optimistic that they would not quit the hunt either.

23

"Marx claimed violence was the midwife of history," she told them. "But fascism wasn't created by an aristocracy any more than communism was by a peasantry. Both were the result of political ideologues, from Trotsky and Lenin to Hitler and Mussolini, and each political system was born in violence. They and their followers resorted to 'overkill' out of ideological intoxication — a substitute religion, if you will — to create a new world and a new human. In the cases of Stalin and Hitler, they used terrorism and violence not only against other armies but against civilians, including their own, just as dictators do today. Saddam Hussein, Osama bin Laden, the Taliban, and the al-Qaeda network are modern examples." She paused to let the summary sink in, then smiled. "All right, now it's your turn. Where do you think all of this fits in with what we've been talking about in terms of the psychology of violence?"

She watched their feet shuffle and their gazes lower. The hands of the usual suspects shot up, but she wanted someone else to show some mettle.

"Come on, brave-hearted souls," she coaxed. "Who wants to take a wild stab?" A few more hands rose. "All right, you look as if you'll have something interesting to say." She pointed a finger. There was no seating chart for such a large lecture class, and although she recognized the twenty-something, she was unsure of her name.

The young woman had a sheet of pale blond hair that hung straight, masking half her face.

She tossed her head to free her eyes and mouth, perhaps even to breathe. She said earnestly, "Adult aggression and violence can stem from early-childhood experience, Professor Sansborough, but that's not always the complete explanation."

"Go on."

"In fact, that explanation could be construed as too easy," she said, gaining confidence. "A cheap shot. 'Good' people sometimes get seduced into violence by situational forces. They . . . they get caught up in a violent moment, and their real selves sort of get lost." She stopped, groping for more.

Liz nodded. "In other words, their personal identities get suspended in a kind of moral disengagement. They use justification and interpretation to legitimatize their actions. Ergo, the 'herd mentality' and the 'power of the mob' and how an average person can wind up doing something despicable and violent and evil that they'll never forget and may never be able to forgive themselves for. . . ."

For Liz, the rest of the lecture sped past. When it was over, she was feeling wired. She gathered her notes and stuffed them into her briefcase. She was not supposed to have taught today. In fact, she should be in Paris right now, taking some vacation time with Sarah and Asher. But in the end, she had been unable to make herself leave this final lecture of the summer session to her assistant. It was too important. In it, she summarized everything her students should have learned, and if they paid attention and went back over their notes, each had a very good chance of not only doing well on the test but actually learning the material.

The lights dimmed in response to California's latest energy worries, and the auditorium emptied quickly. As they often did, a few stayed to walk with her across the grassy campus to her office.

"But shouldn't the 'good' person resist the power of the mob?" one asked.

Tall eucalyptus trees swayed in the ocean breeze. The air smelled fresh, of sea salt and sunshine. Liz breathed deeply, enjoying the summery morning, enjoying her life.

"Absolutely," she agreed. "But with that, we're getting into ethics."

"It's not an easy thing to do," another said quietly. "To resist, I mean."

"Right," said a third. "When the surf's up, sometimes you've just gotta dive in."

"And sometimes not," Liz reminded them. She liked their questions. They were thinking, which was the major point of an education, as far as she was concerned. "Ask yourselves what it takes to say no when everyone else is insisting yes. Once you start to consider how you'd like to behave, you begin to build up a savings account against the times when you face difficult decisions, and you will face them."

"I'm really glad you didn't get sucked completely into the TV thing," the youth who liked surfing said. "I mean, it's great you're still teaching."

"I can't imagine I'll ever quit," she assured

him. "Now that we've got a professional producer and crew for the series, I have more time for you."

They smiled and peppered her with questions about the new episodes on the Cold War that would be aired.

"You'll have to be patient," she told them. "I'm sworn to secrecy."

They liked that and laughed. When the small group reached the psychology building, she shooed them on their way. One young man was particularly sweet. He had a crush on her and was often among the group that stayed late.

Tongue-tied, he managed to mumble, "Great lecture, Dr. Sansborough," before shuffling off.

Liz pushed in through the door and climbed to the third floor. The building was faded pink concrete, utilitarian, without pretense, which she liked. The corridors bustled with staff and students. When she arrived at her office, Kirk Tedesco was inside, leaning back in her chair, his big Rockports propped up on her desk.

He was reading *TV Guide*. He lowered it and grinned. "Hi, babe. How was the howling mob?"

Her office was cluttered with books and papers. Kirk was the calm in the center of the research storm. She smiled in greeting. "Sharp as little tacks." She closed the door and dropped her briefcase onto the floor next to her gym bag.

"Right. In your wildest." Kirk was a psych professor, too, specializing in personality disorders. He was so easygoing that his scholarship was on the light side, but he was friendly and fun, and she had grown to depend on his companionship.

"No, really, Kirk," she told him. "This is a great class. They're interested in the subject. I'm glad I stayed for them. Paris can wait until tomorrow."

He picked up *TV Guide* again and waved it at her. "Nice article in here about you and the new season."

She took it from him, pleased. The first four shows for this new series were in the can, the next three were being filmed, and she was researching future ones. Her gaze ran down the story:

Sansborough's Cold War Series Is Back!

One word — and a simple image — said it all. Last month, posters that read "July 29" in scarlet red, with "Top Secret" stamped across in black, plastered New York City's bus shelters. No photos. No title.

But to aficionados, it was a code that sent shudders of delight that the wait for Dr. Liz Sansborough's sleeper hit, *Secrets of the Cold War*, to return was almost over.

A Compass network executive revealed that among the chilling Cold War situations to be aired was that of a leading CIA official's illegal tampering with presidential politics. Also on tap was a hushed-up FBI scandal that included a KGB defector who was a master of disguise.

In just three years, Dr. Sansborough's series has grown from a local cable show into an underground sensation.

As for next season, the psychology professor tantalized us with the prospect of
juicy details about some of the Cold War's
most elusive and deadly players — global
assassins such as the renowned Abu Nidal
and lesser-known, but many say mythical,
figures like the Carnivore and the
Abbot. . . .

"Good coverage," she agreed, and tossed it
back at him.

"It's more than that. Someday your face is
going to be as famous as Julia Roberts's. You're
already a hell of a lot prettier."

"And you're full of blue sky." But she grinned,
grateful, because he had been a reluctant sup-
porter of the series.

The window in her office looked back over the
campus, north toward the sawtooth peaks of the
Santa Ynez Mountains. She was high enough up
that no one else could see her. She peeled her
shirt over her head and stepped out of her trousers.

"Nice jogging bra," Kirk said. "Nice thong bikini."

She ignored him and stepped into her running
shorts. "Aren't you getting bored? You drop by to
see me do this three or four times a week, you
and your lame excuses. You've got too much time
on your hands, Kirk. Hey, you didn't even bother
with an excuse this time." She pulled her hair
back into a ponytail and slipped a band around
it.

"Definitely not bored. And I have a very good excuse." He lowered his feet to the floor and advanced on her. He was a square man, early forties, nice big shoulders, going a little soft in the middle, which she found endearing.

"Go away." She shook her head, amused, and knelt to tie the laces of her shoes. "This is my jogging time."

"So I noticed. You look much more appetizing in shorts than in that prison jumpsuit you wear for karate."

With his cheerful face, freckles, and red hair, Kirk was easy on the eyes. They had arrived at UCSB in 1998, the recipients of two brand-new chairs funded by the prestigious Aylesworth Foundation. In the same department, and single, they had gravitated toward each other and become friends. The rest had developed slowly.

"So tell me what your excuse is." She jumped up and lifted her knees, loosening her muscles.

"The dean's summer bash. This afternoon, remember? It begins at three o'clock. Want to meet there, or are you going to let me pick you up?"

"Let's meet." She patted his shirt and gave him a quick kiss on the lips.

He grabbed for her, and she dodged.

"You're going to get all sweaty," he warned, eyes twinkling.

"Looking forward to it, too." She found her sunglasses and visor.

As she locked her door and zipped her keys into her fanny pack, he ambled to his office. Eagerly, she ran down the stairs and out into the hazy California sunshine.

Paris, France

When it was ten o'clock in the morning in California, it was seven o'clock in the evening in France. As Liz Sansborough left for her run in Santa Barbara, some six thousand miles away Sarah Walker and Asher Flores strolled across the lobby of their Latin Quarter hotel, holding hands.

They were a handsome couple, somewhere between the ages of thirty-five and forty. He had curly black hair and a strong face, with the kind of sharp gaze that was never fully at rest. She was tall and lanky, with short auburn hair. A dark mole just above the right corner of her smiling mouth gave her a dramatic air, and the small finger on her left hand was crooked, hinting at some past athletic endeavor gone amiss.

They had arrived in Paris the night before and checked into her cousin's favorite hotel. Her cousin, who was joining them for just three days, had postponed her arrival until tomorrow. Neither Sarah nor Asher was the type to wait around. They had gone sight-seeing, visiting the Louvre and other traditional tourist places for which they had never had time, and returned to change for dinner.

The night *portier* caught sight of them through the glass lobby door. He pulled it open and bowed. "Mademoiselle Sansborough," he greeted her. "A pleasant surprise. I did not realize you were staying with us again."

Sarah shot him a smile as she headed out under the awning. "Sorry, but I'm not Liz

31

Sansborough. She was delayed."

Astonished, the doorman hesitated as if expecting the woman to laugh at her own joke. He quickly touched the brim of his cap. "Apologies, madame. Please forgive." He noted the gold wedding band on her ring finger.

"Don't worry about it," Asher Flores said genially as he followed. "They're cousins, and they look so much alike everybody gets them confused."

Sarah suddenly shook her head. "Oh, damn. I left my purse in the room. Do you have your credit cards, Asher?"

"A passel of 'em," Asher assured her. Then to the doorman: "Think it's going to rain? It's been threatening all afternoon." He stepped out from beneath the awning to check the sky. Layers of cumulonimbus clouds were roiling black and brown. Raindrops splattered down, and the metallic scent of ozone filled the air. "Well, that answers that." He jumped back under the awning's shelter.

"Allow me, sir." The doorman reached behind the door and produced a large umbrella. He popped it open and presented it to Asher.

Under its shelter, Sarah put her arm through Asher's, and they walked off jauntily just as the heavens opened and sheets of chilly rain pounded down. Drivers turned on their windshield wipers and headlights, while pedestrians ducked under awnings.

Sarah laughed. "So much for an easy, relaxing time in the Gallic sun."

"Do you think this is punishment because we

32

haven't been back here together before this?"

"You wish. We're not that important to the gods."

"We are to me." As traffic rushed past and the rain made a noisy tattoo on the umbrella, he impulsively pulled her close and kissed her.

Laughing, she threw her arms around his neck. Parisian horns saluted loudly.

Sarah had been reluctant to return to this city where so many ugly things had happened to them, but Langley had finally guaranteed Asher a month of uninterrupted vacation, and it was time to exorcise her demons. They needed to go away together, to renew themselves in each other, and what better place for romance than the two-thousand-year-old City of Light — and love?

She kissed him back eagerly, sinking into him, feeling warm and happy and carefree as they lingered in their private cocoon beneath the umbrella.

When he released her finally, she smiled into his eyes and said, "Let's find that bistro and have some dinner. I'm hungry."

Other pedestrians had disappeared into shops and stores, escaping the rising storm, and Sarah and Asher were alone on the sidewalk as they hurried onward. Thunder boomed, shaking the earth. Drivers continued at an insane speed, tires spouting dirty waves onto the sidewalk.

"Only one more block," Asher announced as they crossed a street. Their clothes were soaked.

"We can make it. I'm not totally miserable yet."

They jumped over a fast-moving stream,

landed on the deserted sidewalk again, and increased their pace. The sky turned black. The cold rain pelted so fiercely that it slammed back up from the pavement. They dodged and rushed, growing chilled and stiff. At last, Asher spotted the bistro's sign: ROUGET DE LISLE. It was at the end of the block. He was gesturing at it, about to tell Sarah, when a black van suddenly screeched to a halt beside them, hiding them from traffic.

Before its wheels stopped, Asher's internal alarm sounded. His alert gaze slashed from the van across the empty sidewalk to the dark alley on their other side. Two men wearing ski masks and armed with handguns jumped out from where they had been pressed against the wall, hiding. Asher hurled the open umbrella at them.

They ducked, and he gave Sarah a violent shove to get her safely past. He whipped out the small pistol strapped to his ankle just as the van's door slammed open.

As he swung his gun to aim, Sarah spun back to look for him. Her water-streaked face froze in horror as she took in the well-coordinated attack.

As he opened his mouth to bellow at Sarah to run, there was the muffled *pop-pop* of silenced gunfire. A bullet crashed into Asher's chest. Out of nowhere, a giant seemed to grab him roughly and hurl him backward. He landed hard. His arms and legs sprawled and his head hit the sidewalk. His gun flew from his hand. His eyes closed.

Sarah screamed, "Get away from me!"

Her voice barely penetrated his pain-filled mind.

"Asher!" she called frantically. "Are you all right? Asher! Let me go to him!"

There were the scuffling sounds of struggle.

"Merde!" one of the men swore.

"She's a tiger," another agreed in French.

Asher tried to open his eyes, to roll over, to get to his feet. Fight. *Save Sarah.* A massive cauldron burned in his chest. He raged helplessly, inwardly.

"Get Walker into the van!" one of the men shouted. "Hurry!"

"Asher!" Her longing cry stabbed his heart.

In a frenzy, Asher struggled harder. Felt himself move. His palms dug into the wet pavement.

Before he could push himself up, powerful hands smashed his shoulders back down. Someone cried out in pain. Him?

A voice spoke harshly into his ear: "If you want to see your wife alive again, Flores, get us the Carnivore's files. You and Langley have four days. No more. *The Carnivore's files.* Say it." This man's words were English, the accent American.

Asher tried to move his lips. He pushed out air. "Carnivore," he managed. "Four days." The Carnivore's files? *What* files? *"Impossible!"*

But the hands were gone. Car doors banged shut and wheels shrieked.

Wild with fear, he roared, "Sarah!"

There was no answer. The rain was unrelenting, pummeling his face, filling his ears as he struggled to get up. Falling back, he choked and coughed and grew icy cold. He pictured Sarah in his mind, went over each detail of her face, heard her melodic voice, felt her lips brush his cheek. Aching for her, terrified about what they would do to her, he felt weakness sweep over him, then darkness.

Two

Santa Barbara, California

Liz stopped on the lawn outside the psychology building to stretch. As she pulled one ankle and then the other behind and balanced freestanding, she admired the July sky and savored the soft ocean air against her skin. The temperature had been hovering in the low seventies, perfect, while the Weather Channel reported an oxygen-sucking heat wave blanketing New York and Washington. Moving to the West Coast had been one of her smarter decisions.

Her life was far different from that dark time when she had discovered her parents were assassins. She figured she was as happy now as she would ever be, and she had Grey Mellencamp to thank, because he had been right all those years ago. It was a pity he had died so soon after delivering his fatherly advice. She would have liked to tell him how much he had helped her.

As soon as she ended her stretches, she speed-walked toward the university's Marine Science Institute, feeling light and powerful, as if she were about to begin a match. Her other sport was karate-dō, one of the few leftovers from her previous life in intelligence. She gazed around, passing the usual sports cars with their tops down, the trash cans topped off with foam cups from the Mesa Coffee, and the students in their eye patch–size swimsuits, sitting out on dormitory patios, enthusiastically risking melanoma. Few palm trees decorated the campus. Instead, sycamores, magnolias, and exotic eucalypti stood here and there, country-club elegant.

When she spotted the squat marine lab building, she broke into a trot, running downhill past it onto a spit of sand that edged the university's big lagoon. She saw no one on the rocky cliff that towered ahead, which was just the way she liked it. Beginning to sweat, she loped up a sandy ridge to the dirt path that cut along the cliff's narrow top. The breeze whispered through her hair. Her quad muscles rippled.

Savoring the clean salty air, she looked right, where wild grasses and scrub trees and bushes welded the soil to the rolling slope that spread down to a blue lagoon so protected from the elements that hardly a wave showed. On the far side lay the campus, where a few students were visible. They disappeared into buildings, late for classes. Abruptly, the university was deserted — a perfect still life of simple modern buildings and manicured trees from some architectural photographer's prized album.

As she settled into her usual slow, steady gait, she gazed left at the ocean, which extended in a blaze of turquoise out to the Channel Islands some twenty miles away. Here on the ocean side, the vegetation was far different, not thick and upright and hardy as it was on the lagoon's slope, but sparse and gnarled from fighting to grow out of rock crevices where it was exposed to harsh sea winds. She could hear the roar of the surf far below — at least fifty feet — but she could not see it from the trail.

The cliff continued along the campus for miles. Every year, a handful of people died from falling off it during drunken parties or while bicycling, hiking, or running. The media would cover the tragedy, and people would be careful for a while. But as time passed, the sense of danger faded. They resumed old habits. Became careless. Until someone else was killed.

She tried to shake off a sudden feeling of uneasiness. There were still occasional moments when she felt as if her past were catching up with her, and she was overcome with despair. But that seldom happened out here, where the peaceful lagoon spread on one side and the timeless ocean on the other. Where the clear sky and the warm sun and the joyful calls of seagulls reminded her how good life was. She usually ran this high trail between the two bodies of water as if she were invincible.

But not today. She was nervy, wary. She did not understand it. Ahead, the path was empty, but she heard people behind. She glanced back, mindful of the rutted trail. There was another runner, tall and muscular, dressed in sunglasses, a baseball cap, and jogging clothes. Ordinary-looking. Behind him was a bicyclist, crouching low over his handlebars as he sped toward them, adjusting gears.

She listened to the rhythm of her feet, felt the measured beat of her heart, tested all her senses while she reminded herself to stay composed.

Soon the bicyclist whizzed past on her right, through the wild grasses on the lagoon side, off-trail. Relieved, she slowed to avoid breathing the billows of dust from his tires as he hurtled back onto the dirt track and roared onward. Next, she felt the movement of air that told her the runner was about to pass, too. She moved politely left to give him room. He did not move to the right.

Instead, he stayed directly behind, his speed increasing, his footsteps closing in. A chill shot up her spine, followed by anger. What in hell was he thinking! And then she knew. From the back of her mind, from a time and place she had worked hard to forget, she understood that she had been monitoring him all along, because he had been pacing her. He did not pass because he wanted something else.

She burst ahead, escaping. Her feet were light, her speed explosive. Her muscles sang. Vegetation passed in a blur, but his pounding gait told her he was fast, too. She dared not look back. She might trip, fall off the cliff.

She leaped off the beaten trail, risking tangled grass and loose rocks, aiming toward the gentle slope down to the lagoon. But with a suddenness that sent fear rushing through her, she felt his hard, hot exhalations on the back of her neck. Desperately, she tried to accelerate again, but she had nothing left. This was her top speed. She would have to fight.

As she started to turn, he slammed his arms around her waist, wrenched her off her feet, and swung her around toward the cliff's ocean side.

Above her, the sky tilted. Panting, she rammed her right elbow back. He grunted in pain. She had connected with his pectorals, muscular and resilient, but she had not hit him hard enough to really hurt. He was taller and far stronger. She twisted from side to side and briefly saw his face with her peripheral vision. Heavy jaw, hollow cheekbones, thick, short nose. Ray-Ban sunglasses. His lips were a thin, neutral line.

Frantic, she slashed her other elbow into his shoulder and punched a fist back over her shoulder at his throat. Too little, too late. Like a big, bored child, he flung her from his arms and staggered back to safety.

Her balance utterly gone, she sailed helplessly through the air. Her mouth opened, her arms windmilled, and a primordial scream erupted from somewhere deep in her belly. She did not recognize the sound, and then it was gone, lost in the roar of the surf pounding far below.

She landed at the cliff's edge. Unable to stop, she plunged feetfirst into a terrifying void of bottomless space. She jerked frantically around and grabbed clumps of pampas grass, which held for a moment on the sheer cliff and then pulled away, roots and all. But they slowed her inexorable slide, and she was not in free fall. Not yet.

Head spinning, terror threatening to paralyze her, she clutched at outcroppings and scrub while her feet scrambled for something to brake on. Nothing she grasped held for long, and sharp rocks jutting from the cliff's face ripped her T-shirt and shorts as her slide continued. Hundreds of cuts, scrapes, and puncture wounds riddled her hands, arms, chest, belly, and legs. The more she sweated, the more they hurt and burned, distracting her.

She almost missed it: a spindly tree battling to grow from a crevice. As her feet, legs, and waist rushed down past, she seized it with both hands. Miraculously, the tree held. She dangled there, trying to press into the rocks. There was nothing beneath her feet. The breeze was icy against her wet skin.

Time froze. She was in pain, discouraged, exhausted, and vividly aware that one misstep, one long, smooth stretch of cliff without handhold or toehold, or one second of inattention could lead to her death.

As she tried to fight the fear, to summon the energy to go on, a voice sounded in her mind: *You can do this.* She repeated the words, and then she knew: Yes, there was one problem she could do something about — herself. She needed to focus.

Her feverish nerves quieted. Concentrating, she dismissed her aches and bruises. She craned to look up but could not see the top of the cliff. There was no way she could climb back up anyway.

The tree gave an ominous creak, its roots loosening.

She forced herself to remain calm and gazed

down. It was a straight drop, some thirty feet now, and there was no one down there on the beach to call to for help. The surf was heavy, but at least there was sand directly beneath, not boulders.

She searched for a toehold and finally spotted a shallow lip about ten feet below. Focusing, she bent the scraggly tree over and patiently worked her fingers along the trunk as she lowered herself.

Finally, the toe of one running shoe found the narrow shelf. Almost immediately, the roots broke free in a shower of sand and rock.

She released the tree. As it fell, she swayed, caught her balance, and flattened into the sheer face, suddenly overwhelmed by pain. She hurt everywhere. Breathing deeply, she blocked it from her mind again.

There was another little ledge lower. Carefully, she eased her way down from outcropping to spindly bush to clump of grass. Progress came in inches. When she reached the ledge, she collected herself and saw a third place below where she could put both feet. With small goals, the impossible was achievable.

When she reached that ledge, she looked down again. Fifteen feet remained. A towering wave rolled in and crashed onto the sand, sending spray up against the cliff, almost reaching her. She decided that was too good a sign of a doable distance to ignore. She analyzed the drop, bent her knees, flexed her body, and stepped away from the cliff.

Heart pounding, she plummeted straight down

through the ocean air and landed in a crouch in the sand, sending seabirds aloft in flight. Their sharp cries of complaint rose and disappeared. She stayed there, fingers dug into the sand, motionless, panting.

Finally, as glossy white surf spent itself near her feet, she wiped an arm across her hot face and forced herself to think. It was illogical, impossible, that she had been a target of opportunity for some random madman. No, that bastard had been following her. He had tried to kill *her* — and had come very close to succeeding. But why here? Why now?

She shuddered, feeling again his steely grip around her waist, her helplessness at his well-planned attack. At last, she stood up, brushed the sand from her hands, and began walking back. Soon she was overcome by restlessness. Then a fiery bolt of outrage shot through her. Furious, she ran. Had the past caught up with her at last?

Three

In the psych building, Liz hurried down the hall. Walking toward her was a student with books clutched to her chest, her gaze far away, thinking. Then she saw Liz.

Her eyes rounded with surprise. "Are you okay, Professor Sansborough?"

"Had a little tumble jogging," Liz told her breezily. "Nothing to worry about."

Liz continued past. Students, books, academics. This was her life. A wonderful, stimulating world of the mind she had grown to love. She studied and taught about violence. She no longer lived it. That was finished. She was a different person now.

She unlocked her office, rehearsing what to say when she called the Sheriff's Department. But as she crossed the room, heading for the phone, she had the eerie sense that something here was not right either. She stopped behind her desk. Her office was a constantly changing mosaic of books, papers, newspapers, tapes, photographs — correspondence and research of all kinds. Dizzying to others, including Kirk. As she gazed analytically around, she realized with surprise that she could still reconstruct a scene with accuracy.

Nothing was out of place. Her imagination must be in overdrive. She swore aloud, reached for the phone, then stopped.

The red light was blinking on her answering machine. She punched the play button. "Message posted ten-thirty a.m.," the machine informed her.

It was Shay Babcock, her producer, in his unmistakable Hollywood mixture of insider whisper and con artist sweet talk: "Hey, Liz. Howareya? I've got some lousy news for you. Looks as if we're out of business for a while. Compass Broadcasting has postponed *Secrets of the Cold War* until next season. Maybe longer. Sorry, kid."

"No!" Liz fell into her chair.

With a rush of guilt, Shay continued: "I called and called but couldn't get a straight answer from any of those bottom-feeders. Personally, I don't understand it. But you can count on me to stay with this. None of the other programs I'm producing is as close to my heart. To my *spirit*. I mean, I'm really committed. The Cold War's *important*. The ignoramuses out there need to know it's still going on. Give me a jingle when you get a break from all those boys drooling all over you, and we'll talk. Love ya." The machine clicked off.

For a moment, she did not move. If someone had not just tried to murder her, she would be shaking with outrage.

She punched the replay button and listened once more. It made no sense for them to cancel the series now, at the last minute. The network had spent a fortune buying the rights to everything, including all of her old cable shows, and it had allocated another fortune to publicity. Everything was working — the buzz was spreading. She had been interviewed not only for the *TV Guide* story but for articles in *People*, *Entertainment Weekly*, and — surprisingly — *GQ*. Plus, the network had positioned the series to follow the hugely popular *60 Minutes* on Sunday nights. Although the two were on different channels, the time slot gave hers an extra push. Everything was in line to build on the series's cult success and explode it into TV gold. For her, what was most critical was she would reach millions of viewers.

"Good Lord, Liz!" Kirk stood in her doorway, the color draining from his face. He had, as usual, come in without knocking. "What happened to you? Are you hurt? Of course you are. What am I saying. *Look* at you!" He strode toward her.

She stared down. Her T-shirt was in tatters, and dirt and scratches covered her arms and legs. A bruise was turning purple on her midriff. She had no idea what her face looked like, but she figured it was not pretty.

"I'm fine," she announced. "I'll clean myself up in a minute. Right now I've got to call the Sheriff's Department. Some crazy jogger threw me off the cliff."

"What do you mean, a jogger threw you off the cliff? *What* jogger?"

"I wish I knew." She picked up the phone.

Kirk scowled, making a decision. "The sheriff can wait. First you're going to the doctor."

"Really, I'm okay. Nothing's broken." She began to dial.

With a surprisingly quick motion, Kirk snapped the receiver from her hand.

His face was turning pink, his freckles vanishing in the glow of his anger. Or perhaps it was fear. "I said *doctor*. You could be hurt a lot worse than you think. You're too damn bullheaded, Liz. I'll drive. When we get there, I'll phone the sheriff for you."

After her doctor examined her, cleaned her wounds, and pronounced her otherwise healthy, Liz followed Deputy Sheriff Harry Craine out to a wooden bench in the small park across from the doctor's office in Montecito. Kirk disappeared inside Tecolote Book Shop to pick up the new Covert-One thriller he had ordered.

Liz described the attack.

"How old was he?" Deputy Craine wanted to know. "What did he look like?" Craine was a large, gravel-voiced man with old eyes. He was only in his mid-forties, she guessed, but he had the demeanor of someone who had seen a long lifetime of bad people and worse deeds.

"He was white and had a snub nose, a heavy jaw, and prominent cheekbones," she told him. "His skin was taut, no sagging. Judging by it and his general muscle tone, he was in his early to mid-thirties. His hair was brown, a mousy color, on the short side. Inch and a half, maybe. He had a runner's build — muscled legs, lean chest. He was taller than me. I'd say maybe six-two. He wore Ray-Ban sunglasses, a baseball cap of some kind, light blue shorts, and a matching T-shirt. Regular jogging shoes, white, with dark blue stripes. Nikes. None of his clothes had any special logos or words. He was dressed to be unidentified."

The deputy looked up from the notes he was taking and studied her. "You don't miss much," he said mildly.

"Thanks. I tried to remember everything so I could report it."

"Most people couldn't have told me ten percent of what you just did, and I'd be worried about the accuracy of that. Most people are lousy observers."

She shrugged. "I wish I could give you more information. It all happened so quickly."

"I imagine it did." The same mild tone, but the eyes were suspicious. "I'm interested in your comment that he was dressed to be unidentified."

She had revealed more about herself than she intended. "I deduced that. It's one of the things I do — make deductions. I'm a college professor."

He nodded. "So you said. You also created a TV show. I've never seen it, but I think I've heard of it. What about the rest of your time? You haven't always taught college. You were born. You grew up. Anything in your past that might be coming back to haunt you?"

"No, Deputy Craine. The only angry people I have to deal with are the usual students who want better grades or the network execs who expect to change my show."

He nodded and closed his notebook. "I'm glad the doctor says you're not seriously injured. It's impressive you survived the fall at all."

She shrugged. "There was a tree, and I grabbed it." She added lamely, "It was just dumb luck."

"Uh-huh." He looked at his watch. "Where will you be the rest of the day?"

"At my office. The number's on the card I gave you. This evening, I'll be at a party at Dean Quentin's house above Mission Canyon. You have my cell number. I'd appreciate your phoning as soon as you learn anything. Anything at all."

He gave a curt nod and headed toward his car. "I'll be in touch."

By one o'clock, Liz was back in her third-floor office at UCSB. She stood gazing out her window, arms crossed, hugging herself. Sunlight shimmered across the low buildings and green trees and palms that sprawled throughout the fertile Goleta Valley. Her view extended up the lavender foothills to the towering Santa Ynez Mountains, where clouds haloed the ragged peaks. She was filled with melancholy as she studied the sweeping panorama. Usually, this lovely view gave her a sense of tranquillity, of time turned in her favor. Now, as she waited for her producer to return her call, she saw disquiet and uncertainty.

She stepped back and was about to return to her desk when she realized her reflection was in the window glass. She had a strange sense of déjà vu, seeing her face superimposed over her much-loved vista. It made her feel apart, again the outsider, always looking in. She was both deeply upset by the attack and annoyed that she was not taking it in stride as she once would have.

And, too, it threatened her new attitude about violence, which had grown with the years and her studies. All of it showed in the troubled look on her face. She studied her bold features — the high cheekbones, the flared nose, and the black mole just above the right corner of her mouth. Her brown eyes were wary, alert, and angry.

She noticed her hair. She had always liked the color — auburn, a dark brown with red woven through. This morning, it had been brushed and shiny, waving down to her shoulders, as free as her spirit. Now it was in wild disarray. Although she had changed back into the shirt and trousers she had worn to her lecture that morning, she had forgotten to brush her hair. At least her face was clean; she had washed it in the doctor's office. Even in the hazy reflection she could see her beach tan, her dark eyes, her upturned nose, which had once been unfavorably compared to a ski slope. She had a wide mouth, and she forced it open in a smile. But she did not feel like smiling.

The phone rang. She snapped up the receiver and sank into her chair.

It was Shay Babcock, and he gave her no time to question him. He repeated the message he had left earlier and added, "I've been on the horn ever since, playing phone tag with the knuckle-draggers. I know it's a big blow, kid. Hell, I was counting on parlaying the series myself."

"Tell me exactly what happened."

There was a pause, and she sensed outrage.

Their relationship had bordered on tempestuous. He disliked being questioned, while she continued to want to know why and how and when. He had wanted the Cold War series enough to put up with her, and she had wanted to reach a mass audience, which meant she needed a veteran like him. It had turned into a productive partnership but one not seriously tested, until now.

He finally said, "The usual. TV bosses aren't known for their badges of courage. But then, their jobs have all the stability of river fog. The word was sent to me from Bruce Fontana, the network entertainment director, that they'd decided last night. Of course, he had his assistant make the actual phone call, but not until this morning. I went right over to Bruce's office. He made me cool my heels for a couple of hours. When I wouldn't leave, he let me in. He was eating lunch and talking on the phone the whole time. The basic humiliation scene. When they don't bother to get off the phone long enough to tell you to get the hell out, you know the grave's been dug, the coffin's dumped in, and you're the corpse. After that, I went back to my office and made some calls, trying to crawl up above his head. Got nowhere. Hardly a surprise."

"We'll take the series somewhere else. Another network."

"No can do. We're locked into Compass. Sure, you could try to break the contract, but you'll have to foot the bill. I don't have those kinds of deep pockets. Man, the legal fees. Makes me hyperventilate just thinking about it."

"Who *did* you reach?"

He rattled off a list, and she wrote the names.

"Hell, Liz." He sounded drained, exhausted. "After them, there *is* no one else to go to."

"There's always someone else. The president of the company, for starters."

"Tried him." He repeated the name. "I'm telling ya, kid. Give it up."

"I can't."

"Fine. If you get the decision reversed, lemme know. Meanwhile, I've got to take care of my other projects. Don't want this to taint them. You understand?"

She grimaced. She did not want to be understanding. Still, she heard the fear in his voice. He really was worried about his other ventures if he pushed too hard for the Cold War series. The brutal world of national television had no time for troublemakers.

She put reassurance into her voice: "Don't get too busy, Shay. I'm going to need you when I turn this around."

"Right. Always the optimist. Good luck. Ciao, kid." And the line went dead.

Liz worked the phone, looking for someone to rescind the stupid decision. Her Rolodex contained names and numbers from when the series was a hot network acquisition, and she called every one.

"Liz! Nice of you to check in," said the head of development. "No, I hadn't heard. They actually canceled it? Why?"

The director of publicity groaned. "We're always the last to get the word."

No one could help. No one knew anything. She had expected to be stonewalled, but she also expected to figure out a way to get around it. Disgusted, she went on-line to research Compass Broadcasting and discovered its owner was InterDirections, the media conglomerate headed by the legendary Nicholas Inglethorpe.

That was interesting. She wondered whether the jet-setting tycoon knew he had idiots working for him. Obviously, she was going to have to enlighten him.

She found the phone number for InterDirections's world headquarters, which was in Los Angeles, and dialed, eventually annoying enough people that she was able to reach Inglethorpe's secretary. Again she encountered the same impenetrable wall, although politely expressed this time: "I'm sorry, Dr. Sansborough, but Mr. Inglethorpe is in Europe and isn't expected to return until next week. I'd be happy to take a message."

Liz left the message and leaned back in her chair again, this time stretching, rolling her head from side to side, trying to release the rage that was coagulating, distracting her. She needed the full use of her brain to plan her campaign to educate Inglethorpe. As she was thinking, her gaze landed on her filing cabinet. There were scratches on the built-in locks of two drawers. There had never been marks before.

Instantly, she was on her feet. In two quick strides, she crossed to the cabinet and knelt, studying the scrapes. Someone had broken into the drawers. She tried the bottom one. It was un-locked, although it should not have been. She pulled it open. Inside was her briefcase. She searched it. Nothing missing. She opened the second drawer, also unlocked, and read the file tabs. Heart sinking, she read them again. The folders that contained ideas for the future show about Cold War assassins were missing.

She remembered putting the files away just be-fore she left to jog and locking the drawer. She hurried across the room and yanked open her of-fice door. More scratches on that lock. Which would explain her uneasy sense that her office had been disturbed. She must have uncon-sciously registered seeing the marks.

Now she knew. Not only had someone tried to kill her, but at the same time, someone had broken into her office and stolen files.

She closed the door and marched back to the phone. With luck, she could catch Harry Craine at the Sheriff's Department. She remembered the calm experience in his gaze and his gravelly voice. Maybe he had learned something about the attack. When she dialed, she asked for him and listened with relief to the news that he was in.

"What can I do for you . . . Professor Sansborough, is it?" This voice was different. There was no sound of gravel or of experience. This man was young, high-energy, enthusiastic.

She asked, "Are you Deputy Harry Craine?" When he assured her he was, she said, "I re-ported an assault on me today to a sheriff's deputy. I thought it was to you. Whoever it was met me at my doctor's office in Montecito to take my statement."

"Haven't been to Montecito in a week. You must have the wrong name. Happens sometimes. I take it you didn't get his business card?"

"No." Dammit. She had forgotten to ask for one. Another mistake. She related the details of the assault. "At least two people may be involved," she concluded. "The man who pushed me off the cliff, and a second person who broke into my office while the attack was going on. He stole some of my research folders."

"I'll check our database," he said instantly. "When there's an attempt on a life, the information's entered right away. Don't worry. I'll straighten this out."

"Will your database tell you who took my statement, too?"

"You bet. And who the investigating officer is, if it's someone different."

As she waited on hold, she mulled the assault and break-in. It seemed to her the two events must be connected; the coincidence was too great. But what was the link?

"Professor Sansborough?"

"Yes?"

Harry Craine's voice had changed. It was edgy, distrustful. "I phoned the university, and they say you're one of their professors all right. Then I checked the number you're dialing from, and it's from your office. So I'm going to assume you're who you claim to be. Now, when did you say someone threw you off the cliff?"

"About ten-thirty this morning. That should

be in the initial call reporting the attack." What the devil was going on?

"Right. When did you make that call?"

"I didn't. A colleague, Professor Kirk Tedesco, did. He phoned while the doctor was examining me. It would've been about eleven-thirty, perhaps quarter to twelve. After that, your detective came."

"That's interesting. Especially since we have no record of ever receiving a call. It leaves me wondering. . . . Are you running some kind of psych experiment on us for your TV show or something? Is that what's going on?"

She was stunned. "You have no record of Kirk's call? Professor Kirk Tedesco?"

"No call. No record of any attack on you. Nothing — today or ever. I think it's time you leveled with me, Professor. What're you really up to?"

It took her breath away. "This is outrageous. Obviously, someone there either lost or ignored Professor Tedesco's report. Let me make this perfectly clear: *I was attacked*. If you check out my background, I think you'll agree I know an assault from an accident, and that I'm not some panicky college egghead! Talk to Professor Tedesco and to my doctor, Wendell D. Klossner."

"Did either see you go off the cliff?" Craine asked.

"No one *saw*, except the man who threw me."

"So all they know is that you were injured."

"That's right." Her voice rose. "Why would I lie about this?"

"I don't know, Professor Sansborough. Why

would anyone?" His tight voice told her he was working hard to control his exasperation. "We get crank calls all the time, and not just from nuts and drugheads. Regular citizens phone in, too. Maybe they've got to create an alibi because a spouse is getting suspicious. Or they could be thinking about collecting some insurance money. I'm not saying that's true of you, but even if Professor Tedesco and Dr. Klossner confirm your injuries, that still doesn't mean someone tried to kill you." He sighed. "I'll check into it. That's the best I can do."

Her voice was biting. "With that kind of commitment, Deputy, I doubt you'll do anything near your best."

There was a moment of silence. Craine said, "Say we did get the call about the alleged assault on you, and say someone lost the report or even dismissed it. Where did that fake Deputy Harry Craine come from? How did *he* know about Professor Tedesco's phone call, or about the attack itself, or even where to find you?"

Liz's hand tightened on the phone. How had he known? As an answer began to form in her mind, she felt herself go cold. She forced control into her voice and politely thanked the deputy. She hung up.

Trembling, she leaned her forehead into her palms, fighting fear. Perhaps someone in the Sheriff's Department was involved. Or maybe the killer had followed her to Klossner's office and somehow diverted Kirk's call. Either answer meant some organization was involved — a skilled, experienced, and efficient organization. One that wanted to kill her.

Four

Bratislava, Slovakia

It was after nine p.m., and the hot summer night was filled with the muddy odors of the Danube River. In the distance, a lonely barge horn sounded, while a boat's searchlight swept the black sky. Dressed in a tuxedo, Blase Kusterle stood hidden in the shadow of a tree at Hviezdoslavovo Square, where protesters were massing under the street lamps in front of the American Embassy. He rotated an unlit cigar between his fingers. He wanted to smoke the damn thing, but right now he had a situation.

The embassy was alight with a glitzy reception and formal dinner party for Stanford Weaver, the rich new president of the World Bank. Blase imagined the tasteful music, the clinking champagne glasses, and the inane small talk, enlivened only by the occasional drunk who blurted something truthful or insulting or both.

Outside was a very different matter. Far more demonstrators were here than he had been told to expect. They milled around the outskirts of the embassy grounds, avoiding the U.S. Marines standing sentry. Blase watched uneasily as fresh ranks of marines suddenly burst out from around the embassy, rifles up.

But the crowd merely fell back, watching the reinforcements take their places. Then another wave of protesters arrived — men, women, and a few older children — on foot, on bicycles, and pouring out of little Škodas and rusty Fords and a few Yellow Express taxis that rushed away like frightened rabbits as soon as their passengers emerged.

The new arrivals called greetings to old friends in Slovak and Czech: *"Ahoj!"* and *"Čau!"* In German, they were more formal: *"Guten Abend."* There was even the occasional retro American: "What's happenin', man?"

Dressed casually, they wore backpacks in which first-aid kits and plastic bottles of vinegar could sometimes be seen. A bad sign, those vinegar bottles. Anyone who carried vinegar expected trouble. They would soak their bandanas in the vinegar to offset the effects of tear gas.

The noise of their cumulative voices rose, rumbling, filling the muggy air, as they closed in on the embassy again, waving placards in many languages, but mostly in Slovak, German, and English:

GLOBALIZATION = STARVATION
SAVE OUR FORESTS & RIVERS
BUILD NATIONS. DON'T DESTROY THEM.

There were socialists, anarchists, and plain old-fashioned nationalists, all protesting globalization and its effects, but for different reasons. The socialists wanted a lot of state control over everything. The anarchists wanted no control at all. And the nationalists wanted their borders kept strong. Only something like globalization, which each faction considered an assault on its political beliefs, could unify them. Of course, environmentalists and unionists were here, too. But for them, party allegiance was less important than their cause.

From his hiding place, Blase spotted Tomasz and his wife, Maria. They were in their fifties, worried by the loss of Communist-era social programs in child and elder care. Tomasz was pumping up and down a sign that argued PEOPLE NOT PROFITS. Nearby was Lukas, in his early thirties, who had lost his job when globalization theories caused the mill where he was a machine operator to be privatized and sold. Within a year, it was bankrupt. He had found no steady work since.

Wherever he looked, Blase saw housewives, artists, writers, teachers, farmers — people he had met at antiglobalization meetings and demonstrations. Many had ardent democratic ethics and vigorous beliefs in a more perfect world. They were eager fighters for social justice and the environment.

All of this was normal, usual. What disturbed Blase were the nonlocals, at least five thousand, and still arriving. That was a shockingly large number for Bratislava, which was off the radarscope for most people — neither a top entertainment destination nor a regular site for major confrontations.

Judging by those he recognized and the conversations he overheard, these outsiders came mostly from the golden triangle of Central Europe — Vienna, Budapest, and Prague — and were organized in the usual "affinity groups" of five to fifteen people. Some were assigned to provide aid before a protest — such as finding out where anyone arrested would likely be jailed. Others were charged with helping during the protest — handing out water and snapping photos for evidence. And the rest had duties after the protest for the kids, cats, dogs, and plants of those who were injured or imprisoned.

He cocked his head, listening. A quartet of youths was discussing some big "direct action" planned for tonight. The only clue was that the speaker's group had been put through refresher sessions in nonviolence and Slovakia's legal rights, which was the norm when an event might turn dirty.

As he uneasily digested this new information, Blase spotted Viera Jozef. Her silky black hair was a cloud down to her shoulders, and she carried a covered bucket in one hand and a gym bag in the other. Wearing a light summer dress that brushed the tops of her knees, she was an appealing sight as she wound through the moonlit crowd, her gaze fixed on the austere embassy ahead. There was a look of hard determination on her pretty face. She was passionately opposed to globalization. He had slept with her before and was hopeful of more romantic interludes.

Trailing Viera was her brother, Johann, a thick-armed miner, glaring at any man who smiled at her. Smart and committed, Viera and Johann Jozef were the city's chief antiglobalization organizers. Johann was talking to a man who carried a giant placard that read NUCLEAR POWER KILLS. Blase did not know him. The two were deep in conversation, their shoulders together as they leaned into each other's ears.

Blase's gaze swept the masses, taking a reading. Tension was mounting. As he glanced at the double doors that fronted the embassy — they were firmly closed — and then back again, a Markíza television crew arrived in a van. Two cameramen hit the ground running, their cameras on their shoulders, already filming. Two reporters chased after, notebooks and pens poised, while three techs hustled out mikes, cables, and other equipment. The private TV station had sent a large crew, which meant they expected a juicy story. Which also meant more media would follow.

A minute later, squad cars and vans screeched to stops. But when the policemen emerged, they moved slowly, lethally. Communist rule had been gone nearly fifteen years, but old East bloc cops still gave off a sense of thuggery, and the Bratislava police were no exception. Clubs in hand, they glowered with that universal cop message of "Don't irritate me, blokes, or I'll break your skulls."

Riot police spread out methodically, trying to encircle and control, while other officers off-loaded cordoning ropes, hoses, and riot shields. A phalanx of uniforms pushed the crowds away from the embassy, back to the park.

Blase Kusterle liked none of it. Viera had told him nothing special was planned for tonight, just an ordinary demonstration against the World Bank and its wealthy new chief. Johann had confirmed that the usual small but outraged turnout was expected. If Blase needed to be someplace else, no problem.

Now he knew either they had been lying or were ignorant. If he were not wearing this damn tuxedo, which identified him as the enemy, he would be out there right now, where he belonged.

A sudden escalation of noise erupted from the edgy crowd. There had been no shouted orders, and he could see nothing to have provoked it, but, like a gathering storm, the throngs seemed to swell up into a single massive creature and sweep beneath the branching trees, around the parked cars, and toward the embassy. The noise was thunderous, frightening. The hot air seemed to crackle.

This must be the direct action, Blase decided instantly. Word must have passed mouth to mouth.

He threw away his cigar and ran. Someone near the embassy bellowed into a bullhorn at the crowds to back off. The agitators yelled back. Horns honked as the sea of demonstrators blocked cars. And just as quickly as it all had begun, those closest to the embassy abruptly braked. The rest of the crowd stopped, too, beginning at the front in a rippling effect like the deceleration of a centipede until the entire mob was uneasily stationary, angling to see what was happening.

Blase pounded around them, brushing past clumps of people until at last he stopped, panting. It was Viera. She was sprinting out into the open space between the agitators and the embassy, dress flying around her shapely legs. There was a moment of surprise: the police thinking they had stopped the crowd; the crowd transfixed by the daring young woman.

As Blase took a step forward, unsure, one of the embassy marines bawled at him in English, "Halt! Don't go any closer!"

He turned to tell the marine to bugger off. But then he saw the man's face. It was paling as he stared in the direction of Viera.

Blase whirled. He saw her lift the bucket she had been carrying, scale off the top, and pour some kind of amber liquid down over both shoulders so that her dress and body were soaked.

"Nie!" someone called in horrified Slovak. "It's petrol!"

"Viera!" Blase roared and bolted past the guard and toward her. "What are you doing? *Stop!"*

"Petrol!" The words echoed back over the crowd, changing languages, growing in shock, the voices unbelieving.

"Gas! Make her *stop!"*

As he ran, Blase's heart thundered, and his mind tried to grasp the impossible. She looked so small and vulnerable, surrounded as she was by the demonstrators, the police, the marines, the towering embassy. But there was that look on her angelic face, that look that said, This is me. I'm right. *This* is right.

"Stop her!" Blase shouted desperately in Slovak and then in English. "Someone *stop* her!"

But there was no time. She moved swiftly, as if she had practiced often. As he and others closed in, she pulled a small blowtorch from the gym bag, pressed a button, and a tongue of fire shot out. She turned it around toward herself.

"Viera!" he screamed.

"Stop her!" It was the frantic voice of her brother, Johann, shouldering through the crowd. "Don't let her do it! Help! *Stop her!"*

She exploded in flames. For a moment, it almost seemed like a fairy tale — the lovely princess was preserved forevermore in a glowing vase of fire. But then her skirt evaporated, a wisp of cloth turned to gas. Half-naked, she reached her hands out through the flames to the demonstrators, and her lips parted as if she were going to speak. She even cocked her head, and her face seemed puzzled.

Gray smoke burst from her open mouth, and her corpse toppled in the direction her head had tilted.

Blase was paralyzed, trying to comprehend what she had done, his mind so shocked that he did not immediately hear the noise or sense the pandemonium of the crowd's going wild.

Her body smoked. Flames licked around it. A breeze arose, carrying the awful odor of burned flesh across the demonstrators and into the sultry night.

In an instant, it was a riot. Protesters rushed the police and marines. Gunfire exploded as if shot from cannons. Riot hoses sprayed, and people shrieked in fear. One of the parked cars was toppled over, then another. Three cars were set afire, the conflagrations geysering red and yellow up toward the starry black sky.

It was the World Bank–International Monetary Fund battle in Prague all over again, but for Blase, it was far worse. Caught in the maelstrom, he tried to battle through to Viera's body.

As he pushed and shoved, Blase felt a hand slip deftly in and out of his back pocket. He grabbed the pocket and whirled, but no one stood out from the mob. Before he could think more about it, a fist flew past his ear, and a boot stomped the thin dress shoe on his right foot. Pain shot to his head.

He ducked, punched back, and pushed onward as the vision of Viera's appalling self-immolation shimmered before his eyes, erasing everything else. He had to get to her. Maybe he was wrong. Maybe he had imagined it all.

A deep ache settled into his chest. He was lying to himself. More police and media descended, and he was caught in another senseless fight. Along with scores of others, he was arrested and thrown into a packed police van. Guilty, grieving, he said nothing as the van drove off into the night.

Five

Bratislava's central police station still had the utilitarian furnishings and grim aura of its Communist past. Gray and harshly lit, by eleven p.m. it stank of sweat and resentment as it strained to accommodate the hordes of arrested agitators. After finally being booked, Blase was shoved into a tank cell crammed with angry men. Many had superficial burns and wounds on heads, arms, and legs, not yet treated. Doctors called in by the police were dealing with the worst cases first.

The heat in the tank was oppressive. There was no air-conditioning to relieve the hot night or the charged emotions. Everyone sat on hard benches or stood pressed together, still full of the adrenaline of the riot as they debated Viera Jozef's death. Some were incensed at her stupidity, while others were awed by what they considered an act of honor, of personal sacrifice. For all, her death had elevated their effort to stop globalization above the Neanderthal street fight that governments and the mainstream press presented to the rest of the world. The movement had somehow been sanctified, at least for a time.

Seething with grief and guilt, Blase searched through the milling crush, ignoring the stares at his mauled tuxedo, until he found Johann Jozef, Viera's brother. Johann was sitting on a bench, his back curved over, his face buried deep in his hands.

The bench was full, but as Blase angrily zeroed in on Johann, the older man sitting beside Johann took one look at his expression and scuttled away.

Blase dropped in next to Johann. "How could you let her do it?" he raged in Slovak, each word louder than the last. "Damn you, Johann!"

Johann jerked up. Burly and in his late twenties, not quite six feet, he radiated shock and grief from his posture to his grimy face.

"Because I damn well didn't know what she was damn well planning!" He groaned, and his lips peeled back in a grimace of pain. "We got separated. I shouted at her to stop, but I was too far away. Oh, God."

"You're her brother," Blase hammered, incensed. "You *should've* known! You planned the demonstration together. She *must've* said something. It was obvious she'd been practicing exactly how to pull it off."

Johann fired back, "Why didn't *you* know? She told me she'd be at your place last night. Dinner at the Korzo, then your apartment afterward. A celebration of today, she said. You're the one she would've told!"

Blase saw Viera again in his mind the last time they were together, alive and high-spirited. He felt her slim arms around his neck, smelled the natural perfume that seemed to infuse her skin. He could hear her voice clearly as she passionately recounted some new globalization evil — more jobs lost, more children starving, more natural resources sold off by corrupt governments and then turned into profit by greedy corporations.

She had liked him, and he had liked her, and the sex was explosive. Still, the truth was, that was all it had been — friendship, attraction, great sex. The casual cynicism of the relationship trivialized the parts that had been good.

"She canceled our date," he said woodenly. "I didn't see her at all yesterday or today."

A fresh wave of guilt engulfed him. He turned away from Johann. He no longer wanted to fight him. Viera had been dodging him all week, probably — he realized now — to hide her plans. Busy himself, he had hardly noticed. A fatal error.

Johann was staring at his clothes. "You're wearing a tuxedo! Like *them*. That's why you got so cozy with Viera! You're a fucking spy!" He lunged for Blase's neck.

As if splashed with ice water, Blase focused. Others in the cell had heard Johann's accusation. They stared with mounting suspicion. With both hands, Blase clamped onto Johann's wrists, holding the distraught man away from his throat.

"You're wrong," Blase told him between clenched teeth. "I had a plan. I needed a tux because I was going to talk my way into the embassy and corner that bastard Stanford Weaver. It would've worked, too, if the protest hadn't gotten out of hand. If Viera hadn't —" He blinked, regrouped, talked faster. "First, I was going to wait until Weaver was surrounded by the other bastard globalizers; then I'd ask him to sign our petition. He would've brushed me off, of course, but I planned to keep after him until someone called in the marines. There'd have been a nasty row, and they'd have thrown me out. The press would've loved it. They would've jumped on the story like a hound on a bone. I could see the headline — 'Chief of Globe's Richest Bank Refuses to Help Poor.'"

For a second, Johann smiled. "The coverage would've been just what we want."

Blase dropped his hands. "It was worth a try." His face twisted with anguish. "How could she hide her plans from both of us, Johann?"

Johann's shoulders slumped. "Viera could keep a secret," he said gloomily. He collapsed back against the wall.

The tension in the packed cell broke. Everyone watched the two men with sad sympathy. The brother and the lover.

"No one could talk Viera out of anything," Blase decided.

Johann nodded miserably. He peered down, flexed his fingers, then looked around as if hoping someone would explain the unexplainable, the unendurable.

Blase heaved a sigh. As Johann turned to talk to the man on his other side, Blase saw that everyone was settling into the role of detainees, organizing themselves to take turns sitting and standing. As the sharp edge ebbed from his rage and shame, he remembered the hand that had slipped into his back pocket.

He glanced around, reached into his pocket, pulled out a small crumpled paper, and read: "Sir Robert was murdered. If you want to know who did it, meet me." Blase inhaled sharply. There was no signature, but the message was followed by directions into St. Martin's Cathedral. The person would be waiting in a certain pew in a certain chapel at five a.m. The words were English, neatly printed in pencil.

The cell door clanged open. Blase looked up alertly, shoving the note back into his pocket. Everyone turned. The tank grew ominously quiet as four uniformed police guards pushed into the throng. Three grabbed two men who had been speaking German.

The fourth spotted Blase and advanced. "You! Yes, you. This way," he ordered in Slovak.

When Blase did not stand fast enough, the guard grabbed him by the lapels and hurled him toward the cell door. Hands reached out to steady Blase, keeping him on his feet until he reached the bars. The door rolled open, and the guard slammed a forearm across Blase's back, propelling him out into the corridor. Blase landed with a thud against the opposite wall. Pain ricocheted through his body. His head swam.

"Zatočte vl'avo," one of the guards commanded.

Blase and the two other prisoners turned left, as ordered. The group marched down the hall.

The guard who had spoken opened a door. "In there."

Blase was pushed again. As he plunged inside, he heard the same guard warn one of the Germans, "Your interview room is next."

The door closed and locked.

Ada Jackson, the British embassy's law-enforcement liaison, was sitting alone at a scarred table, drumming her fingers. She glared at him. "Christ Almighty."

She was small and compact, with perfectly coiffed black hair and wire-rimmed glasses. Dressed in a tailored skirt and suit jacket, she looked completely professional even at this early hour. There were two other straight-backed chairs in the room, plus a wire cage in the corner, no doubt for unruly prisoners too bad or too opinionated for the potential camaraderie of a tank cell.

But what he focused on was a second door, which, from the wall it was in, looked as if it opened onto the outside world. He inhaled with relief. The guards' taking him and the two Germans from the cell had been a ruse. His cover would remain intact.

He had almost been fooled, too. "You took your sweet time." He headed for the door.

She followed. "You're in one hell of a lot of trouble."

"With you or with Whitehall?"

She was also the local MI6 station chief. She unlocked the door. The thick night air rushed in, and they stepped out of the jail.

"With all of us, Simon. Get in the damn car."

With Ada Jackson driving, the nondescript embassy sedan headed through the old city's narrow streets, past medieval houses and Baroque churches, in the general direction of the Danube. Bathed in silver moonlight, the peaked roofs and soaring towers of centuries-old Bratislava were iridescent. Once a favorite of Magyar kings and Habsburg emperors, the charming city seemed asleep — innocent and untouched. Simon Childs envied it.

Aware he had again crossed some imaginary line with his higher-ups, he settled alertly into the front passenger seat, glad for the blast of the air conditioner. With a tight grip on his composure, he described the demonstration and Viera's awful death. He listed the protesters he recognized, repeated conversations, analyzed the overall organization, and hid his guilt.

As she drove, Ada queried every detail. He considered her profile, the glasses perched on her short nose, and the unchanging severity of her face. From her cap of smooth black hair to her pragmatic pumps, there was precision in her movements, the same sort of precision she brought to her thinking. Sometimes too precise and therefore inflexible.

He studied her hands on the steering wheel as she drove. She wore no rings. If she had ever had a romantic assignation or even an ordinary date, he had never heard. She was in her late thirties, very pretty, but she gave off that stay-away scent of a woman taken. In her case, he figured it was not a man on her mind, but her "career."

"You should never have left the embassy when you did," she told him, her voice severe. "It was the middle of the party, for God's sakes. Blast it, Simon, you had an assignment, and you didn't do it. Whatever possessed you?"

He had been walking a fine line; she was right about that. He was MI6's expert on antiglobalization groups in Central Europe, more successful at penetrating them than the Americans, Germans, or French. With so many terrorist fears, apparently no one had blinked when the World Bank chief, freshly anointed, requested a personal briefing from Whitehall with its mysterious antiglobalization source — him.

After all, the bank lent billions of dollars to governments in the region, and one of the major complaints across the protest movement was that the money went to destroying countries, not building them. So the plan was to disguise him in a tuxedo and slip him into the U.S. Embassy, where he would wait in a back room until Stanford Weaver could make time for him.

Simon pretended indignation. "I went outside for a few minutes to get a toss of fresh air. And I shouldn't think I was the only one. Those parties are numbing. 'Dull' is an enthusiastic description. I *was* bored, and that takes off the sharp edge."

" 'A few minutes' was all you needed to get yourself into trouble," she reminded him. "No one enjoys command-performance parties, but we take them in stride. What are you now, thirty?" That made him look at her. "Yes, thirty. It's time to quit acting like a boy, Simon. You're too handsome for your own good. Too charming, and too cocksure." Her small upper lip curled with distaste. "One wonders whether being in dark undercover with a bunch of borderline hoodlums is the only kind of assignment you'll ever be good at."

He closed his mouth before he uttered one of his whiplash retorts, settling on, "I don't suppose I should thank you for that."

"Wrong. Thank me. I doubt anyone's bothered to tell you the truth about yourself. Or maybe you just never listened."

She stopped the car at the waterfront, parking the nose downhill, toward the river. She turned off the engine and lights, and they sat in the dusky silence, alone in the parking lot, where no one would overhear their conversation or see through the darkened windows. To the left and right stretched the Danube — in Slovak, the Dunaj — magnificent and dark, tipped with mercury ripples, thanks again to the bright moon. To their left was the futuristic SNP Bridge, which stretched south from the old city to the sorry concrete-slab high-rises of Petržalka, where Bratislava's suicide rate was the highest. Those apartment buildings and all the other ugly, boxy projects on the outskirts of Old Town had been thrown up by the Communists — a stark cement legacy of the former Soviet Union.

"I mean no disrespect, Ada," he said, "but I shouldn't think it's the end of the world. I'll talk to Stanford Weaver whenever he likes. Name the time and place, and I'll be there. You know that."

She glared from the shadows. "It's too late. He's gone."

"Already?"

"The Americans got him out fast. But then, embarrassment's a great motivator. Viera Jozef's theatrical death is going to be the top news story at daybreak. It's duck-and-cover time for both the Yanks and the World Bank. Listen to me, Simon. Hear me clearly. Your behavior wasn't part of the plan. Tonight you were supposed to have had a very important conversation with a very powerful new ally for Britain. Not only did you basically flip him off, you created an additional mess for him and the Americans. Dressed in that tux, you stood out in that motley crowd like a robed priest at an orgy."

There was something to her complaints, but in the high-stakes world of MI6, both in the field and in the office, you could show no weakness, reveal no doubts, or you were dead — sometimes literally.

"What I learned tonight needs attending to," he insisted. "The police, the media, and the public always know in advance when there's going to be a big demonstration, because organizers abide by the laws and register. At the same time, they're usually so excited they can't keep their mouths shut anyway. But not last night."

"I'm listening."

"Somehow, more than five thousand protesters got past Slovakia's border guards. I heard not a whisper ahead of time, and neither did the authorities or anyone else. Add to that tonight's self-immolation — the first one, thank God, but you can bet it won't be the last. Viera was no religious-based extremist. No al-Qaeda killer in the making. She was a young schoolteacher who donated her free time to hospitals and soup kitchens. Her whole life was ahead of her, and she had the face of an angel. Perfect for front pages and the top of the news. She's a poster child for martyrdom."

"There's a point to this?" Ada said coldly.

"The point is, I may not have been holding some cheeky banker's hand, but I was doing my job. I was assigned to be a penetration agent because we were worried the antiglobalization movement could breed soldiers for terrorist groups. Right?"

She shrugged. "That was one reason."

"A bloody damn large reason. The zealousness I saw out there tonight was a wake-up call. Viera used violence to get attention for her group's grievances, and by morning, they'll see the headlines and know her sacrifice worked. It scares the piss out of me to think what would happen if every antiglobalization group figured that out and started to act on it. It wouldn't be long before they'd redirect their violence away from themselves and against the people they hold responsible for their problems. Then what happens if they actually figure out a way to work and plan together? If they unite, it could get worse than the sixties, and that almost tore apart Europeand the United States."

She shook her head angrily. "You're exaggerating. Those people are too weak, too happy to think of themselves as victims. Besides, existing institutions like the IMF and World Bank are one hell of a lot better equipped to deal with poverty and the world's other problems than the whining adults and ignorant kids we saw screaming and yelling out there tonight. If your agitators haven't convinced me, they sure won't convince many others either. So what if they nab a few headlines? They're still singing to the choir."

"That choir, as you call them, could explode. One should never underestimate the potential of the underdog. Especially if the underdog feels cornered."

She turned to face him. He did not like the look in her eyes. Her voice was arctic. "You excuse what you did by bringing me information. That's all smoke screen for your fucking up. I've sent my people to check the media film that was shot tonight. It's inevitable some of the photographers and camera people recorded you. I'll have to tap my contacts, which I don't like to do on something that should never have happened in the first place." She made a weary sound in her throat. "Even if I manage to find every scrap of film and get it scrubbed, remember you were protected only going into the embassy. It's possible somebody there saw you sneak outdoors and then costar in the riot. With so much press coverage, any witnesses will likely wonder about you. You're sloppy, Simon."

"I do my job."

"That's the problem. It's just a job to you. You like to pretend your work means something, but the truth is you treat it like a shell game. You haven't a real opinion about what these people you've been informing on for the past three years are doing. You don't think they're right or wrong. You don't think our government is either. Where's the real Simon Childs? Where's he hiding?"

God, she was annoying. "I care about Britain. I should think that'd be enough for you. Do you have anything else you wish to discuss?" Thinking about loyalty and Britain brought a dull ache to his chest, the same pain he associated with his father's death. Sir Robert Childs had been almost a national institution — member of parliament, beloved leftist, and respected by the other side of the aisle. Like Viera, he had died by his own hand. Simon had investigated thoroughly at the time, but he had been unable to find even a suggestion his father's death was anything but a suicide.

He kept his face neutral as he resisted the urge to look at his watch. He did not want to be late to the meeting with the nameless person who had written that note.

Ada Jackson fired up the car's engine. "I want a full report of everything you saw and your conclusions. I'll expect it at the bridge drop by eight a.m. The media's going to be sniffing for details about Viera and her life — the more intimate, the more spicy and gory, the better. Tell your friend Johann that you're so distraught that you're taking some time off. He'll spread the word, and the press will pick it up. I'll have a safe house lined up for you by the time you turn in your report. I want this whole thing to die down. Blase Kusterle must vanish."

Six

Santa Barbara, California

The twilight traffic was heavy on the 101 as Liz sped her Toyota sports car north toward the dean's party. Tense and wired, she was caught in fight-or-flight syndrome — that atavistic survival mechanism hard-wired into the subcortical region of the human brain. She was like a car whose driver had one foot flooring the accelerator and the other slamming the brake. The orderly, peaceful world she had created over the last five years had been abruptly shattered, and she was reeling.

She had left a message for Kirk, telling him what had happened and asking him to recall everything that was said in his conversation with the Sheriff's Department. Then she went looking for anyone who might have seen a stranger break into her office, a fellow jogger push her off the cliff, or the fake deputy who had interviewed her. After learning nothing useful, she canceled her vacation to Paris and left a message of apology on Sarah's cell. She must stay in Santa Barbara until she uncovered the truth.

Already late, she had driven home to dress for the party, where she had one of those nasty turns that stopped one cold. She had been attacked. Some powerful group wanted her dead. Of course, she needed a gun so she could kill them before they killed her. She had gone directly to her wall safe, removed her old 9-mm Walther, found it clean and well oiled, and loaded it.

Her movements were effortless, filled with the solace of relentless training. But they also brought everything back: Her three years of operating in the field for Langley — the long stretches of boredom, punctuated by the sweat-inducing peaks of danger. Her helplessness when her husband was captured and murdered by the Islamic Jihad. Being a shocked witness in Lisbon to the Carnivore's last bloody wet job. Then three perilous years underground, hiding and running with her parents while trying to arrange for them to come in from the cold.

She looked down at the pistol in her hand. Part of her wanted the weapon's security, no matter how superficial it might be. Violence could be so easy, such an inviting solution. But in the end, it fed off itself, until it became a mindless, self-justifying cycle that created far more problems than it solved. Violence corrupted individuals and societies.

She gave a rough shake of her head. *No.* She did not want to be seduced again. There must be other ways to handle these attacks. She unloaded the weapon, returned it to her safe, dressed, and went out to her car once more. She would be very late, but it did not matter. She needed to put everything out of her mind for a time and relax and find a new perspective. And she needed to talk to Kirk about the man who had pretended to be Harry Craine.

In the last faint light of day, the bloodred bougainvillea that grew alongside Dean Derrick Quentin's front porch was a tangle of radiant color against the white paint. Carrying only her shoulder bag, Liz walked past the bougainvillea and into the party. Greeting colleagues, she ordered a large, much-needed Belvedere martini and sipped it as she circulated. Almost everyone had heard about the attack on her, and she retold the story again and again as she watched for Kirk. Several people mentioned he was looking for her, too.

At last, her martini finished, she left the glass in the kitchen and pushed out through the screen door into the backyard. A dozen of the tenured and untenured stood on the deck, drinking and arguing about Freud and Jung and Rank as night settled in, but Kirk was not among them.

She walked around the porch. The martini had helped her relax, and she trailed her fingers over the bougainvillea. Tropical and lush, it climbed all the way to the three-story house's gables. As she admired it, she heard her name. Curious, she peered through the thick leaves.

Kirk and the dean were talking quietly in the side garden. Behind them, a taxi sped down the block and away, its motor purring. She strained to listen.

"I had to tell Themis about Liz first thing," Kirk was explaining. "What else could I do? You know he wants anything unusual reported immediately."

She frowned, puzzled. Who was Themis? Kirk was *reporting* on her?

"But lying to Liz about calling the sheriff was damned risky, Kirk," the dean said. "She's no fool, and she could still figure it out. That'd be a disaster."

Her rib cage contracted. Kirk had *lied?*

Kirk gave a low laugh. "She won't. She's in love with me. She trusts me completely. What really happened will never cross her mind. . . ."

Anger shot through her. Why that smug son of a . . . What? *What had he said?*

Kirk was still talking. "Besides, you saw how fast Themis sent that bogus deputy to interview her. The foundation obviously wanted the cops kept out of it. We don't want to shake up our arrangement with the foundation, now do we?"

She knotted her hands, keeping herself from exploding. Why were Kirk and the dean reporting on her? What in hell was going on! That bastard Kirk had betrayed her, and so had the dean. But what loomed even worse was that their boss, "Themis," obviously had tremendous power and resources, and, as she had feared, some larger organization — "the foundation" — was somehow involved, too.

She found a wider opening in the bougainvillea. The two men were standing close together under a peppertree. Kirk's posture was fully erect — no sign of the usual drunken slouch to which he quickly descended at parties. Compared to him, the dean was small and slight, but his gaze was sharp, like a rattlesnake's, and he appeared as sober as Kirk.

Kirk continued: "God knows how the Aylesworth people would've reacted if I hadn't reported it and the police *had* gotten involved."

"I still don't like it. Damned worrisome. Until now, our arrangement has worked so well. Everybody won, especially Liz. Five years ago, her credentials were short to be awarded such a prestigious chair."

Bastards! All of them! So it was the Aylesworth Foundation behind it — whatever "it" was. Yes, her credentials had been short, but her proposal . . . Liz stopped herself from justifying being awarded the chair. Right now, that was the least of her problems.

Worried and furious, she leaned closer. She did not want to miss a word.

"*We* won, that's for sure." Kirk's laugh was self-congratulatory. "I don't kid myself. I'd never have rated a cushy job at a big university if Themis hadn't hired me to watch Liz twenty-four seven."

The dean ruminated. "You're right. Two funded chairs didn't hurt me with the regents either, or with the departmental budget, for that matter. Still, I'd like to know why he wanted her here. I can't help but think this sudden assault on her and the theft from her filing cabinet are connected to our arrangement." He pursed his lips, frowning. "I'm concerned we might've been used for some dangerous purpose we haven't a notion about, and it's going to boomerang back and hurt us."

A string of oaths flooded her mind. Her funded chair, her special position at the university, her work — all had been arranged by this Themis, whoever the hell he was, and the Aylesworth Foundation. Not because her insights into violence and her work were worthy and important, but because some code-named asshole wanted to know where she was and what she was doing.

Outraged, she turned toward the flight of steps that led down to the garden. Words, sentences, whole paragraphs of disgust flooded her. After she told them exactly how despicable they were, she would find out everything they knew. Everything they had been told. *Everything.* What was Themis's real name? Had they ever met him? There must be at least a telephone number they had called to make their reports.

She stopped. Barely breathing, she stayed in the shelter of the bougainvillea, and her gaze shifted. Something had changed out on the sidewalk — a shadow had drifted when there was no cause for it. She traced it back to the silhouette of a man crouching behind a tree near the white picket fence that surrounded the yard. She glanced down again at Kirk and the dean. They were watching the house, not the street.

The shadow moved along the sidewalk, using the picket fence for cover as he studied the garden and house. The fence's upright slats made it almost impossible to see his whole face. But there was something familiar. With a jolt, she recognized him — the "deputy sheriff" who had taken her statement this afternoon.

Riveted, she made a decision. The pathetic duo in the garden could wait. The half-hidden man on the shadowy street came directly from Themis. He was the one who could lead her to Themis and perhaps to why she had been attacked. She turned and padded back the way she had come, continuing on around the long porch to the opposite side of the house, where she would have the best chance of being unseen. She slung the strap of her shoulder bag across her chest, so the bag hung off her back, where it would not be in her way in case she had to run. She kept her tread light.

At the front corner of the house, she peered around. The long purple shadows of early evening flowed across the Quentins' front lawn and out to the residential street, where old jacaranda trees lined both sides. There were a dozen cars in sight, but no sign of the sham deputy.

Liz sprinted down the steps and over the long walk to the picket gate, where she sat on her heels to watch again. Still nothing. She quieted her mind so she could hear more acutely. Behind her, laughter and conversation sounded faintly from the party. Then she heard a car door open and close softly from the left . . . somewhere up the street. She recognized another sound — an automatic car window was being raised or lowered.

She pulled open the gate and moved toward it. She passed a jacaranda tree and two cars, studying the shadows under the street lamps. A wind was rising, rustling leaves but leaving branches motionless, as if in limbo. The pungent scent of freshly cut grass infused the air.

She gazed back at the house, which was nearly out of sight now, and around at the deserted sidewalk and the quiet street that curled up into the rolling foothills. From somewhere high above came the sharp yips of a coyote.

Where had the man gone? She continued to prowl uphill, her gaze moving. And slowed, listening, feeling. . . . It seemed almost as if softly running feet reverberated through the sidewalk and into her consciousness. She whirled in time to see the bright flash of a knife in the left hand of a dark-clothed figure who wore a ski mask.

He was jumping silently toward her, intending to attack from behind.

Adrenaline shot through her. She dodged and turned to escape into the street, where the lighting was better, but her foot struck a tree root and twisted. She stumbled, her purse thudding against her back.

He was beside her in an instant. He locked his right arm across her throat and yanked her backward into the tree's shadow. He was the same size as the man who had thrown her off the cliff. Gasping for air, she reacted poorly, doing just what a trained attacker would expect: She grabbed at his arm with both hands and twisted and struggled, trying to pry it loose. Her one advantage was her years of athleticism. She was strong and flexible. She could feel him strain to maintain his balance.

But his arm continued to crush her throat. She

breathed in raw rasps, repressing the urge to keep tearing at him. Instead, she slammed back with both elbows in *ushiro empi-uchi* strikes. One elbow connected to his side, and she felt more than heard him bite off a grunt.

The grip on her neck loosened a moment. She tried to scream, but he quickly squeezed again. She fought harder, jerking and bending through the deepening night, battling for air. Lack of oxygen was making her light-headed.

When she saw the knife move and catch the light of the street lamp again, she had a brief moment of utter terror. He was going to stab up into her heart from the left side. If his aim were poor, her death would be slow and painful. She would bleed out. On the other hand, if his aim were good, she would die in seconds.

Inwardly, she cursed. Then she realized there was a small hope: His attention had shifted to the knife, and she had a weapon, too — her shoulder bag, still slung over her back.

Gauging carefully, straining to breathe, she watched him pull the knife back, ready to plunge. She must time her maneuver just right and take advantage of his concentration on the knife. . . .

Suddenly, he slammed it toward her. She gave an abrupt lurch to the right and threw all of her weight into wrenching around. For a second, she was free, and her shoulder bag swung.

With the impact of a hurtling fist, the knife rammed the bag and went all the way through. She flinched, but the point only nicked her. The arm across her throat loosened as the attacker cursed and tried to pull out his weapon.

Immediately, she reached up again with both hands. But instead of trying to pry away his arm as she had before, she gave a mighty push, raising it, and sank her teeth through cloth, biting into flesh. Blood spurted and dripped into her mouth.

He grunted and tried to shake loose.

Sweating, lungs burning, she hung on with her teeth, a pit bull at her enemy's throat. When his arm gave a tremble of weakness, she released him and spun free. At the same instant, his knife tore loose from her handbag.

He reeled, off balance. This was her chance. Maybe her only one.

She leaned back and slashed a foot up at his chin. His eyes widened in his ski mask as her blow landed. She had caught him at the right instant, when he was vulnerable, and he knew it. A glint of rage showed, then his head snapped back. He rotated helplessly on one heel and fell hard, facedown, onto the grass beside the sidewalk. His body lay twisted, showing the motion of his fall. He did not move.

She stood over him, panting, looking around for the knife. She massaged her throat and swallowed. *Where was the knife?*

And then she knew. Stunned, she focused on the downed man. His hips were at an angle, the left one raised, one foot under the other leg, and one hand under his torso. But his chest lay flat on the grass.

She swore and crossed her arms, hugging herself.

Almost immediately, she heard footsteps. She turned to run, then saw who it was. Ten feet away, the fake deputy emerged from between parked cars, lowering a 9-mm Sig Sauer. He nodded at her, holstered the gun, and strode to her attacker. Without a word, he rolled him faceup. The knife was buried in the man's chest, his bloody hand still gripping it.

Liz looked away. The violence and deaths of her past swirled through her mind. The attacker, a stranger to her, was dead because of her. He had tried to kill her, but she wondered whether that was really relevant. In the larger picture, his death had been as unnecessary as hers would have been.

The phony deputy looked up at her. "Nice work. Help me get him to your car."

"Who are you?" she demanded. "Who sent you?"

Seven

Liz studied his eyes, which had seemed old and wearied in the noon sunlight. Now, in the shadows, they burned like coals. Dressed in a sports jacket, open-necked gray shirt, and tan cotton trousers, his large size loomed toward her. He had a long face, broad across the cheekbones. His forehead rose up to a thick mat of straight hair. His chin was narrow, but there was a curved dimple in the center, giving him a faintly sultry air, as if when he was twenty years younger and had more kindly thoughts about the world, he had been a heartthrob.

"You know who I am and who I work for," he said.

"Yes." She was suddenly exhausted. "I know."

She supposed she really had known — at least in the back of her mind — from the moment the runner had tossed her over the cliff. Langley was back in her life — either the runner or the man she was talking to now, or both.

"We have a situation," he said. "A critical situation. Grab his feet. Help me get him out of here before someone sees us."

She remembered how Hughes Bremner's

92

rogue CIA group had tricked Sarah with a faked attempt on her life, making her believe the Carnivore had sent people after her who had "killed" her guards. A small but convincing movie.

"Not yet," she told him.

"There's no time —"

"Shut up. You wouldn't be here if you didn't need me. So just shut up while I check." She knelt and pressed her fingertips above the man's carotid artery. There was no pulse. His chest was bloody where the knife had plunged when he fell onto it. She pressed her cheek against the chest. There was no pulse there either.

"I told you he was dead."

She looked up. "Who trained you, sport?" She searched the man.

"I was going to check him when we got to your car. But hey, knock yourself out." He crouched beside her.

She said nothing. There was a small pistol holstered under the man's arm, his backup weapon. Obviously, the knife was intended to keep her murder quiet. His pockets contained no ID, just cigarettes.

She lifted her head, listening. A wave of laughter rolled out toward them from the dean's house. People were standing on the porch, saying their good-byes.

"Okay, let's go." She picked up the dead man's feet.

The man from Langley went first, lugging the shoulders. The corpse was light, perhaps 160 pounds.

"You know where I parked," she realized.

"I had a taxi drop me off," he told her. "When I didn't see you at the party, I went to your car to wait. I was watching for you in the rearview mirror."

"Then you saw him attack me."

He nodded. "Sorry I couldn't get there soon enough to help."

"Bullshit. You had plenty of time. You wanted to see whether I could still handle myself."

He did not deny it. She dropped the corpse's feet and unlocked her trunk. When the lid swung up, she spread the plastic grocery bags she kept there and helped him load the dead man onto them. She peeled up the stocking mask. She was not surprised — the same short nose, short brown hair, and heavy jaw.

"He's the one who threw me off the cliff," she told him. "Do you recognize him?"

"I didn't expect to. They're not going to send anyone who's readily identifiable."

"Who are 'they'?"

"We'd hoped you'd know." Scanning the neighborhood, he closed the trunk and used the heel of one big hand to press it down until it locked with a low click.

Liz was in no mood for anything less than answers. "What's your real name? What does Langley want from me?"

"Let's get into the car. We'll talk there." He peered down the street, where couples were heading toward their vehicles. "We've been standing here too long."

"That's not my problem. You've been in my house."

She had surprised him. He frowned, said nothing.

She told him. "You got inside my car and lowered the window. Since the only spare keys I have are in my kitchen, it's logical you got entrepreneurial and swiped them. God knows what else you took. Let me see your ID."

"They said you were good," he grumbled as he slid his hand inside his jacket and handed her CIA credentials and badge. The name was Angus MacIntosh.

"Thanks." She dropped them into her shoulder bag.

His eyebrows rose. "You can't do that."

She ignored him, examining the knife slice in the center of her leather bag. The blade had been two-edged — thin and sharp. A stiletto. As she lowered her purse, a crumpled scrap of paper on the ground caught her attention. She snapped it up.

"What's that?" the CIA man asked.

She smoothed the paper. "Dean Quentin's address." The address was printed in pencil, and there was an odd squiggle in the corner.

He looked at the note over her shoulder. "All that tells us is he didn't bother to memorize the address. Must've fallen out of his clothes. I'm surprised you missed it. Guess you're a little out of practice after all. Let's go."

"Langley's far from my favorite former employer, MacIntosh. I don't like your sneaking around, and there's no way I'll ever work for Langley again. Get that loud and clear, and get the hell out of my life." She jammed the paper into her purse.

He sighed. "Call me Mac. The sneaking around was just me trying to be subtle. Okay, so I'll cut to the chase. Like I said, we have a bad situation, but it's your situation, too. Your cousin Sarah Walker was kidnapped in Paris a few hours ago, and Asher Flores was shot."

"No!" She inhaled sharply. "Did Asher survive? Have you found Sarah?"

"Flores is alive. We're looking for her. The kidnapping happened about the same time you were assaulted on the cliff."

She worked hard to control her emotions. "Why should I believe you?"

He stuck a hand in through the open window of her car and came out with a CD player. "This recording was sent electronically from Paris." He pressed a button, and the CD began to spin.

"Liz, it's Asher." It sounded like Asher, but Langley had ways to imitate any voice. *"Some turd brains have grabbed Sarah. This is the real thing, Liz. They want the Carnivore's files. They've given us four days."* He coughed, and when he resumed, his voice was full of anguish. *"What in hell are they talking about? What files? They're going to kill her, Liz, and I can't get my sorry ass out of bed. I'm stuck in this damn hospital. If you've got the files or know anything about them —"*

MacIntosh pushed the stop button. "That do it?"

The Carnivore's files again. Her lungs tightened. "Get in. I'll drive."

Colorful and opinionated, Asher Flores was one of a kind. She had never heard anyone but Asher use the expression "turd brain," and the phraseology was his, too. Plus, there was the agony in his voice, the utter frustration that he was helpless while Sarah was in mortal danger. Like all undercover CIA officers, he was a good actor, but not that good. Asher's plea was just what he would have done, what he would have said, how he would have said it.

She opened her car door, her stomach knotting with fear for Sarah. They had grown as close as sisters over the years. Because of a rogue CIA plot, Sarah had been made to look like Liz, but that was only the beginning of their link. They had discovered they thought very much alike, even had similar tastes and interests. More than that, she admired Sarah's compassion and intelligence and her bullheaded dedication to the investigative pieces she sometimes labored over for months at a time. She had won a Pulitzer for an in-depth series on nuclear power plants in California.

Nothing would stop Liz from helping Sarah. Still, she had learned her lesson about Langley. She could not trust any of them completely, not even now. Especially not now.

As MacIntosh forced his muscular bulk into the passenger seat, she settled behind the wheel. They closed their doors quietly. She turned on the engine. "I assume you've made arrangements to fly to Paris."

"Langley sent a jet. It's waiting."

She did a U-turn, heading the car downhill. "You broke into my house. Did you pack a suitcase for me, too?"

"As a matter of fact, I did. Got your passport as well. All you have to do is drive us to the airport. My people will dispose of the body."

"Tell me what happened."

He described the strike. "Asher said it was over in minutes. Choreographed. The hotel had made dinner reservations at the bistro for them, so someone could've gotten the information, which would explain how the two men knew to wait in the alley. As for the van, it probably shadowed them." He shook his head, worried. "Now, the big question — the question we all have — is: Where are the Carnivore's files?"

Her voice was grim. "I don't think there are any."

"Then you haven't changed your mind since Grey Mellencamp debriefed you?"

"No. I looked into it afterward, but I never found a hint my father kept any sort of record at all." As she turned the Toyota onto Mission Canyon Drive, she stopped herself. Before this went any farther, she had to find out how willing he was to tell the truth. She said, "Is Langley behind the 'movie' here in Santa Barbara? Did they fund the Aylesworth chairs that brought Kirk and me here so they could keep tabs on me? Is one of your operatives code-named Themis?"

He gazed across at her. There was surprise in his eyes and a touch of respect. "You know about Themis?"

"Is he one of yours?" she repeated.

He nodded. "How did you find out?"

"That's beside the point. Why a movie on me?"

"If we'd heard the rumors about files, it was only a matter of time until others did, too. You'd become a natural target. Considering someone's already sent a janitor to scrub you twice today, I guess Langley was smart to be concerned. And maybe you should be grateful."

She snorted in derision. "Langley was — and is — concerned about the possible existence of those files, not about my survival."

His voice was apologetic. "We can't let the records fall into the wrong hands, Liz. You understand."

"Why should I believe Langley didn't send that janitor to kill me?"

"Doesn't make sense we would. If we want the files, you're still our best bet. That hasn't changed."

She nodded to herself. If Langley had sent the killer, they would've handled the fallout from the first attack much more smoothly. "You already must've been on your way to talk to me, or stationed close by, to get to my doctor's office so quickly."

He leaned back in the seat and crossed his arms. The top half of his face was in shadow, making his dimple appear darker, deeper in the sun's last rays. "I work out of L.A. I was heading north for an inquiry in Thousand Oaks when we heard about Flores and Walker, and then about you. Langley arranged for me to borrow the identity of Harry Craine so we could keep the locals out of it. The ID was waiting for me here."

"Have you covered it with the sheriff now?"

"Of course. Anyone who calls will be told Kirk's report has been found and the department is investigating thoroughly."

But already her mind had shifted. She had almost a physical feeling, a sense of being ill, of having an abrupt fever. Sick with fear for Sarah and Asher. "I can't believe Sarah and Asher are involved." She pressed the accelerator, speeding faster to the airport. To Paris, where they needed her.

"What did you expect? Once you let it be known you were preparing a national TV show about Cold War assassins, and the Carnivore was one of them, you were an inevitable target. Anyone who was threatened by the existence of records had already hired a killer at least once, when they hired your father. If they thought you might have evidence of what they'd done, your life wouldn't be worth an unpaid parking ticket. At the same time, anyone who wanted the files would come after you, too — any way they could. Including abducting your cousin."

"Why didn't you tell me all of this when we first met? Why try to fool me?"

"Asher was in and out of consciousness, not always making sense. We needed to be certain what happened, and that took time. But because Langley thought the attack on them might be linked to the one on you, I was sent to stand by."

She took a deep breath. "Did Langley order my TV series canceled?"

"We applied pressure," he admitted. "Now that

it's off the public stage, the threat against you may lessen. We want nothing to compromise our search for Sarah."

"Or for the files."

He shrugged. "Of course."

She turned the Toyota onto the Mission Street ramp to the 101 and accelerated west toward the airport. "Okay, so there are two groups involved. The first is Sarah's kidnappers, who demand the files as ransom. And the second is whoever sent the guy to kill me. Either they're afraid something incriminating in the alleged files will come out, or they've *got* the files and are worried I'll help figure out who they are."

"Yes, that's what we think."

"What's the situation in Paris now?"

"We've got it under dark wrap. The last thing any of us wants is headlines that one of the Cold War's top assassins kept records, and that the wife of a CIA officer is being held until we cough them up. To prevent leaks, we're working closely with the Sûreté, but only with the Sûreté. No other agencies inside or outside France. The hotel staff's been told Asher was injured in an armed robbery and that Sarah's been staying with him at the hospital. At the same time, the hospital's been informed Sarah's so overwrought that she's confined to her hotel room, medicated."

"What about the hotel employee who made the dinner reservations?"

"The concierge. We interviewed him but came up with nothing. He's being watched."

"And my purpose?"

"You're going to buy us time to rescue Sarah. Since the kidnappers were good enough to sandbag Asher and snatch Sarah, we figure they're smart enough to put their people out to keep tabs, but to do it in such a way that we won't spot them. When they see you, they'll think you're there to arrange the transfer, which means we're trying to fulfill their demands. That should relieve some of their tension. A lot of the time, kidnappers kill their victims because the pressure's gotten to them, long before it's time to collect their loot. They grow antsy and fearful and start imagining the worst."

Unfortunately, he was right. One more thing to worry about. "What exactly do you want me to do?"

"Visit Asher first, but pretend to be Sarah, so we can keep the cover story going. If anyone asks, you're over the terrible shock and want to visit your husband. We're hoping he'll remember more when he sees you. Then go to the hotel. You may spot a clue we missed in our search. We want you to use it as if it were your own room."

"As Sarah?"

"As Sarah," he confirmed. "That way, the hotel won't need any explanations. Of course, the kidnappers will know it's you."

"What are you doing to find her?"

"Our people are out on the streets, as well as making discreet inquiries among certain contacts we or the Sûreté have found useful in the past. Part of it is, as you know, a waiting game, but of course we're leaving nothing to chance. The truth is, we could use a break. Someone who wants something from us and is willing to trade. Or a rumor we can trace to a source."

All the usual protocols. "And the Carnivore's files?"

"We encourage you to find them."

"I've already tried and failed, dammit. They don't exist!"

"Try harder. Langley's been looking off and on since before you talked with Grey Mellencamp, but without any luck either. Still, somebody obviously is convinced they're real, or today wouldn't have happened." He hesitated. His voice dropped. "Of course, it's true they could be wrong."

Her brows knitted in worry, and her gaze swept the traffic uneasily. "That would be fatal for Sarah."

Eight

Bratislava, Slovakia

A cloying warmth settled over the dark city as night deepened toward morning. Simon was worried about the time. From the river, he rushed home on foot to his flat in Old Town, tore off his tuxedo, and threw on jeans and a loose shirt. He retrieved his 9-mm Beretta from a safe beneath his bed and checked it. He was eager to meet the person who claimed to have information about his father's death, but also wary. He holstered the gun under his shirt at the small of his back and grabbed a powerful miniature flashlight. He slid it into his jeans pocket.

But as he turned to leave, he glimpsed himself in the mirror over the bureau. For the briefest of moments, he did not recognize himself. Blase Kusterle? Simon Childs? He usually stayed in character and seldom reported to MI6 face-to-face. It helped his mental health to be just one person. But tonight everything had turned upside down, and he was abruptly, without warning, Simon Childs again.

He returned to the bureau and stared. Ada had called him handsome and cocksure, the opposite of how he thought of himself. He was a couple of inches over six feet, with wavy brown hair he kept on the long side, the way Blase Kusterle, the agitator, liked it. He needed a shave. His nose was big and lumpy. The reason for that came back to him in a painful burst, and he felt himself rock with it. Then he pushed it aside. His eyes were light blue and tired-looking, and there was something in them he did not like. He was unsure which of himselves — Blase or Simon — he had to thank for that.

He shook his head, disgusted at his self-indulgence. As he hurried out of the flat, he remembered the report he was supposed to write for MI6. It would have to wait.

Dawn was perhaps an hour away when he jogged along Kapitulská Street to St. Martin's Cathedral. The massive Gothic church, haughty and eerie, loomed just yards from the Communist-built Staromestká roadway, an elevated monstrosity that rumbled with traffic and exhaust even at this early hour. As he approached the cathedral, the area appeared deserted.

On high alert, flashlight in hand, he prowled around the grounds, checking courtyards, walls, other structures, and the adjoining Rudnayovo Square. A national treasure, St. Martin's had been the coronation church for Hungarian kings a half-millennium ago and still remained very much in use. It was kept locked at night. There was no one around, and Simon saw nothing suspicious.

Satisfied, he took out his Beretta and closed in on the door on the church's north side, which the note had told him to use. It was ajar. He inched it open. Immediately, he was assaulted by the earthy odor of dank stone. Lighted votive candles sat on wall ledges along the stone corridor ahead, although there were electric lights that could have been turned on. He listened. Pulse throbbing, he stepped inside. The air was a good ten degrees cooler here. He left the door cracked open, just the way he had found it.

The candles were set far apart, providing just enough light to guide him. He padded forward, gun sweeping from side to side. Large and confusing to newcomers, St. Martin's had a three-aisled nave, a presbytery reserved for the clergy, three Gothic chapels, an enormous Gothic narthex, and the Baroque chapel of St. John Mendicant. As he made his way to the end of the corridor, he listened to the deep silence, which seemed to emanate from the gray stone walls themselves.

As instructed, he entered the first chapel. He stood at the back, forcing himself to breathe evenly. As soon as he stopped walking, the air turned motionless. Nothing moved, not the candle flames nor the shadows they cast. The chapel appeared deserted. He studied the scattering of votive lights, the rows of pews, the old-fashioned tapestries, and the inky shadows. He wondered whether the person who had written the note was here. Whether he — or she — would appear at all. And realized he both feared that appearance and desperately wanted it.

He checked his watch. It was time. He walked to the third pew from the back and sat at the end, near an alcove. He tucked his Beretta under his right thigh, where it was easily accessible, and set the flashlight on the seat to his left.

He turned to look back at the alcove. In its shadow stood a white marble statue of the Virgin Mary that seemed to glow with otherworldly light. He found himself transfixed, remembering his days as a boy in London, when he regularly attended church with his mother, stepfather, and stepbrother. He was the younger of the two boys, the biological son of his mother, while his brother Michael — Mick — was the birth son of Robert Childs. He had loved his adopted father very much.

As he shifted to face the front of the chapel, thinking about his parents, he heard a sound so soft it seemed to come from his imagination. He started to turn.

"Stay where you are. Look forward again." It was a command in English but with an Italian accent. The voice was a man's, low and firm. "Be patient. With luck, we will finish quickly and each be on our ways."

Simon saw the silhouette of a man's figure but no face. "Who are you?" He turned away slowly.

The voice ignored the question. "Do you remember the Miller Street Killer? In London, when you were a boy?"

The man was a good ten feet behind, Simon judged. Out of reach, but close enough that his whispering voice carried easily in the silent chapel. Simon wanted to grab him by the throat and squeeze information from him.

Instead, he made his tone as hard as the man's: "You wrote that my father was murdered. Who did it?"

"Later. *Più tardi*. Patience. First, you must understand the beginning." The voice belonged to a man accustomed to giving orders, not to being interrupted or questioned. He repeated, "Do you know the story of the Miller Street Killer?"

Simon thought back. "Everyone believed he was a Londoner, because he left the bodies in some of the city's most hidden spots. One of the worst killers in London's history. I think the first corpse was discovered in an alley off Miller Street. I remember not being allowed to play outside because all the mothers were afraid."

"*Buono*. The killer was a monster. He kept the boys conscious for his *disgustoso* games, until they finally bled to death. After the eleventh mutilation and murder, the chief inspector was sure he had identified him — an aristocrat. Old money, old title. Then the evidence disappeared. Vanished. A clerk was chosen to be the scapegoat and was discharged. But at the same time, the inspector's assistant retired to the South of France with a sudden inheritance, while the inspector himself — he was the one who argued to pursue the aristocrat — was accused of gambling. When it was decided the suspect could not be charged, the gambling charges were also dropped." The voice related all of this with little inflection, as if he were reciting a memorized role. "But when a twelfth boy died, your father intervened."

"I remember he was outraged. Demanded a

government inquiry into police methodology in handling the case. But I don't recall anyone's ever being arrested. In fact, I don't remember anything more. The serial killer must've stopped."

"Partly true. What really happened was your father took care of it. Sir Robert had seen this sort of thing before — pressure applied, investigations dropped. But none was this serious. He felt something must be done to save other children, so he used discreet channels to hire an assassin secretly. The assassin killed the aristocrat but made it look like a motoring accident. Of course, by then, Scotland Yard was relieved. So was the family. In the end, no one bothered to look too deeply into the 'accident.'"

Simon was silent, surprised. Then surprised again when he realized he disapproved. Sir Robert had been a fighter for human rights. The idea that he would hire a killer seemed impossible, out of character. And yet . . . his informant was correct about one aspect: The Miller Street Killer had been a ghoul, with an apparently insatiable appetite for torturing little boys. And at the time, Sir Robert had two young sons and a frightened wife.

"Five years ago," the voice went on, "someone found out and tried to blackmail Sir Robert." The voice paused, then continued methodically: "That's when he slashed his wrists. He killed himself because he would have been arrested, and his reputation ruined. His political career and the only life he knew were over. Of course, he knew the scandal would hurt his family, too."

109

Simon felt his body go rigid. He said nothing while thinking that if his father had lived, his mother would have, too. She would have allowed a pacemaker to be implanted. She had died six months later. Simon knotted his hands, the old rage and sadness rushing through him. He had fought to give her a reason to go on, but in the end, her sorrow was too great. She did not want to live without the great love of her life. He had watched her grow thin, her skin yellow, her energy vanish, until she was a ghost. It was an image he carried always, no matter the name he used.

He changed the subject. "What did my father's blackmailer want?"

"His vote on a free-trade issue, which of course he would not give."

Simon nodded to himself. "No vote of his was ever for sale. Win or lose, he always took the high ground." He paused. That was untrue, he realized. His father was flawed after all: He had hired an assassin, and by killing himself, he had also killed his wife. Simon said gruffly, "Politics was everything to him. He would've been on knife's edge, waiting for the next time the blackmailer wanted him to change his vote. How could a blackmailer know about my father and the assassin? You said the arrangement was secret. Was the assassin himself the blackmailer?"

"Impossible. He was dead."

"Then who was the blackmailer?"

"Have you not been listening?" For the first time, Simon heard emotion in the low voice — barely controlled rage, but it was not directed at him. "No one knows. That's why I am here. You must investigate. Discover his identity. Stop him."

Simon's right hand was resting on the seat of the pew. He inched it toward his thigh and the Beretta hidden beneath. "Why should I believe you? Everything you've told me could be a lie. What do you *really* want?"

"Just what I said — to stop this barbarian. Nothing more or less. You were never trusting, were you, Simmy-boy?"

Simon froze.

"That was what your father called you, wasn't it? You must find the *bastardo* who provoked your parents' deaths. Man or woman, I do not know. I know too little." Again the voice was affected by emotion — frustration. "Remember your father's friend Terrill Leaming, the Zurich banker? He can give you more. But take my advice — tell no one. Neither of us knows the power of the forces you might provoke."

"More about what? How do you know any of this?"

There was no answer.

Simon spun around in the pew, but all he could see was wavering shadows. He jumped up and rushed out, clicking on his flashlight. He aimed the beam into every nook and recess, but the church was empty, as silent as death.

He stood motionless, thinking. At last, he walked briskly away, returning to the corridor that would take him out of the church. He considered the mysterious informer: The voice seemed that of an older man, sixties, maybe even seventies, with a light Italian accent but a sophisticated grasp of English. Simon thought about Italian friends and acquaintances from the past, but none seemed right for this anonymous messenger.

It was not just that the fellow knew his father's pet name for him — that information could have been learned from a servant or a family friend. But his claim about Sir Robert's stopping the Miller Street Killer had the ring of truth. So if the man were lying about Sir Robert, the killer, the assassin, and the blackmailer, at least he knew or had learned enough to make his story plausible.

As Simon approached the outside door, he saw it was still ajar. The scent of old stone was heavy here in the narrow corridor. He turned off his flashlight and blew out the candles. As he padded through the darkness, a sense of inevitability swept through him. Ada wanted him out of Central Europe for a while anyway. A trip to Zurich was not what she had in mind, he was fairly sure, but that was where he was going.

He flattened back against the wall and peered through the cracked doorway. The sun was rising, casting the open space around the church in pale golden light.

He looked for surveillance. For the anonymous man. The fellow was enormously skillful to have slid the note into the pocket of someone as trained as Simon without being caught. And there was something else: Simon had been working in deep cover for nearly three years, using a false name. As far as his family was concerned, he was far away and out of touch — in South America, employed by a British petroleum company. So how had the informant found out he was not only in Bratislava, but in the square last night?

Simon did not like any of it. Unsettled, wary, he slipped out into the dawn. He would write the report for Ada Jackson, and then he would fly to Zurich. For the time being, he would follow his informant's advice and say nothing.

Nine

Conference call from Brussels, Belgium

"Hyperion here. Is there news about the operation, Cronus?"

"This is Atlas."

"Prometheus. I'm on."

"Themis. Christ, what an ungodly hour!"

"Ocean here. Let's have it, Cronus."

"Very good. Then we're all assembled. This is Cronus. Atlas asked to be brought up-to-date. I should think you can blame him for the invigorating hour. The answer is that we've passed successfully through this critical stage. Sansborough was attacked a second time. Mac was there and witnessed it. She handled herself well. Her tradecraft is adequate for what we need. Afterward, he made contact. She's agreed to help. . . ."

Aloft, en route to Paris

The jet was a Gulfstream V, debugged and fully fueled, the luxury aircraft of choice for global

114

high rollers. The eight passenger seats were individual chairs that swiveled, each equipped with a multichannel telephone and an outlet for data services via satellite. Of course, there was a powerful onboard PC with wireless Internet connections, too, in a communications center aft. Since the pilot and copilot were busy in the cockpit, Liz and Mac had the rest of the sleek, fast jet to themselves.

At the miniature bar, Mac made a martini in a tall-stemmed glass and poured himself a Red Tail ale. "Belvedere vodka, just as you requested," he announced, pleased with himself. He gave it to her and settled into the chair beside hers, his hand wrapped around his beer glass. His sigh had the sound of relief in it.

She drank, grateful for the good alcohol and the simple concoction. It would be a long journey, close to eleven hours from takeoff to touchdown, although they were going over the North Pole, the fastest route. The pilot figured they would arrive in Paris no later than 2:55 p.m. local time, perhaps earlier, depending on conditions.

Mac was looking at her. "You're going to be a big help. You'll buy us time."

She was surprised by his earnestness. There was something about him she liked. Maybe it was all that experience that seemed to have tainted him in his own eyes but made him more palatable in hers. Still, he worked for Langley, was a veteran of that duplicitous world. In fact, she realized suddenly as she drank again that something he had said earlier was not quite right . . .

did not fit in with what she knew. But hard as she concentrated, she could not place what it could have been and when he had said it.

Then it was pushed from her mind by another disquieting thought. "What makes you think Sarah's still alive?"

"If they've killed her, there's a good chance we'd have heard. Corpses have a way of surfacing." He glanced at her and then away. "You're right. We don't know. But we're going to act as if she's alive until we damn well find out different. Look at it this way: Alive, they're working to keep the kidnapping buttoned down, too. That'd help account for the utter silence in the underground."

"Of course, even if you deliver the files, the odds are they'll kill her."

He shrugged and stared down into his ale. "We've got to work as if she's alive and as if the Carnivore kept files."

"Good."

Liz tried to settle back, to relax, but her mind kept fixing first on Sarah and Asher, and then on her responsibility for the trouble they were in now. Without a second of suspicion, she had jumped at the Aylesworth Foundation's invitation to apply. It had arrived less than a week after Mellencamp's death. That had launched her sham existence, and she never questioned the coincidence. It was her fault, her weakness, because she had so desperately wanted to be free of her past and find some way to live in an unfamiliar world. Perhaps even to be happy. Now Sarah and Asher were paying.

116

Mac pushed his table aside and stood up and reached into the overhead bin. "I've got something for you."

He lifted down a metal lockbox, tapped a numerical code, and removed a Sig Sauer like his, 9-mm and compact, much favored by U.S. intelligence operatives. A beautiful weapon, or so she would have thought back when a lethal machine was something she could call beautiful.

He held it out. "It's untraceable. I was going to bring your Walther —"

Her brows raised. She looked down at the pistol without touching it and then up at him again. "On top of everything else, you cracked my safe?"

"Couldn't find your gun anywhere else. You may need a weapon. Since I was already there, I figured I'd bring yours. But then I realized it could be used to identify you if anything happened in Paris, God forbid. That wouldn't be good for Sarah either. So I had Langley arrange for something untraceable to be waiting for us at the plane. This is it."

"Where's my Walther?"

"I left it in your glove compartment."

She sighed. "I don't want a gun."

"You almost got killed twice today. Don't be an idiot."

"Idiocy is thinking a gun can actually solve problems."

"In the right hands, a gun can save lives."

"That's a tempting appeal," she told him soberly. "If violence is for something good, then it's good. If it's for something bad, then it's bad.

That's what Mussolini thought — 'There's a violence that's moral, and a violence that's immoral.' And we know how he turned that philosophy into dictatorship and a partnership with Hitler. The problem is, violence isn't some kind of impartial raw material like butter or steel. It's not ethically and politically neutral. Just because someone thinks a cause is worthy, that doesn't mean the violence that's 'necessary' for the cause is worthy."

He frowned. "Let me get this straight. All violence is bad. Period."

"Now you're getting it."

"Even when it's used to stop worse violence? Mob violence, despots, genocide?"

"Look, the only reason the world has such a problem with violence is because we let it. We romanticize it by creating myths about killers like Bonnie and Clyde. We institutionalize it by forming military and police forces and intelligence agencies. You can see this mythologizing in all kinds of small ways. One of the saddest examples I found was the dying soldiers in Vietnam who used to ask medics for a last cigarette, although they'd never smoked. They were re-enacting heroic scenes they'd heard about happening in World War Two and seen in Hollywood movies. Romanticizing their own deaths. Heartbreaking."

"Thank you, Professor Sansborough."

"It's unimportant to me whether you think I'm reality-challenged. I'm not going to carry a gun. I know about violence. Been there, done that. Now I'm a scholar in the subject, too. I'll be damned if I perpetuate it."

He shrugged. "It's your funeral. Literally."

He studied her, but when her expression did not relent, he returned the Sig Sauer to the lockbox. The jet gave a shudder and small bounce as he pulled out a Nokia cell.

"This can't kill anyone." He held out the phone.

She took it. "Tell me about it."

"It's got special scrambler capacity hard-wired into it, and no numbers are ever recorded. I have one just like it. I'll be watching you in Paris, following whenever possible in case you run into trouble. If you won't carry a gun, you'll make my job harder, but my shoulders are broad. Since it'd be stupid to be seen together, we'll have our secure cells to stay in touch."

"I don't expect you'll have to rescue me. I was a pretty fair operative in my time. But you're right: There may be other reasons to talk. What's your number?"

He told her, and she memorized it. She would not program it into the phone, in case it fell into someone else's hands.

"One last thing," he said. "Asher told us you and Sarah hadn't seen each other in several months. Did you know she'd cut her hair?"

"No."

He handed her color photos that had been printed off a computer. In the first, Asher and Sarah were smiling widely, their arms wrapped around each other, standing ankle-deep in surf on a golden beach. In the next, they were chasing down the sandy shore, and in the third, Asher was tossing her into the ocean. Their delight in each other shone in each picture. A lump formed in Liz's throat.

"These give you different angles of her hair," he continued. "Think you can duplicate the cut?" He held out scissors.

She took the scissors. "Where'd you get the photos? From their house?" They lived in Malibu, about seventy miles south of Santa Barbara. Close, but distant enough that she and Sarah had not seen each other as often as they had intended.

He nodded. "One of my people broke in. They sent the pictures digitally."

"Figures."

To the Company, nothing was sacred, even the Constitution. One director once explained to Congress that the agency could not always honor it. That was another problem with violent men and institutions: They tended to destroy what they were created to preserve, the shell more important than the substance.

She headed back to the bathroom, where there was a mirror and good lighting.

Santa Barbara, California

It was nearly ten p.m., and Kirk Tedesco was angry, worried, and drunk as he sped toward home in his Mustang convertible. *Where was Liz?* They'd had a date, but she had disappeared.

After he and the dean finished their consultation in the garden, he looked everywhere. She was too damn skittish, always had been. He had not admitted to the dean that she thought their relationship was more about friendship than sex, and the sex was far from frequent enough. When he discovered her car was gone, he called her house, but only her answering machine responded. With luck, she was waiting at his condo.

Disgusted, he drank three stiff bourbons, a big improvement over the watered-down affairs he had been nursing all night. Terrible to disrespect Jack Daniel's that way. Still angry, he had stumbled out of the dean's house to his Mustang, lowered the convertible top, and, with a burst of acceleration from the big V-8 engine, took off down the dark foothill street.

Now he was cruising the 101, heading south to his beach place near Summerland. Traffic was light. More cars were going in his direction than north, which was the way it usually was at this hour. People were heading home to L.A., or planning to get there in time for a few hours of hotel sleep before morning meetings.

He was just thinking about that when he realized he had a faithful follower. He liked that — another driver who wanted to go the same speed as he. Both on cruise control, each watching for the Highway Patrol. The other car looked like an SUV, because its headlights were high. He glanced at his speedometer. He was locked in at seventy-eight miles an hour, just where he wanted to be, and so apparently was the other guy.

The wind whistled past, a warm night wind that tasted of the Pacific. The moon was shining out on the ocean, casting a silver funnel across the dark water and fading at the edges into gray. He liked that, too. Nothing should be black and white. It was too damn dull. He turned on KCLU, his favorite jazz station. But instead of music, a National Public Radio report was on, so he tried KLTE, his favorite rock station. Ah, yes. That was more like it.

He drummed his fingers on the steering wheel in time to Head Shear and again checked his rearview mirror. He did a double take. The SUV's headlights were closing in, bombarding his car with light. There was something unnerving about his follower — not just the sudden blazing speed but also the headlights, which were so close and high now that they seemed predatory.

He touched his accelerator, pushing out. As he passed eighty-five miles an hour, he checked his rearview mirror again. The SUV was even closer. *Unbelievable.* What in God's name was the guy smoking?

He forced himself to sober up, or at least to feel more sober. There was no traffic here as they climbed the long hill that would dip down into Summerland. Off to his right, the ocean shone quietly in the moonlight. With a rush of air, he moved his car out of the left lane and into the right. He did not bother to signal, and he did not slow down. Let the bastard pass at supersonic speed.

But the SUV did not pass; it followed him into the slower lane. Kirk's heart thundered, and his mouth went dry. Almost paralyzed, he stared into his rearview mirror as the headlights loomed closer over his open Mustang, until with an abrupt motion the SUV bashed his car's tail.

Kirk jerked and yelled. He slammed the accelerator and tried to move left, but the SUV swung around and paced him, cutting him off. He had been too slow.

As he shook his head, trying to clear the alcohol, the SUV abruptly crashed sideways into his convertible. Bellowing with outrage, he fought to control the steering wheel, but it ripped itself from his grasp.

Terror filled him. As the car hurtled through the guardrail, he realized he was going to die. Screaming his lungs out, he gripped the steering wheel as the Mustang shot over the high hill and crashed across the railroad track and down through chaparral, small boulders, and native oaks. One collision after another hurled him back and forth against his seat belt. As the car flew over a final precipice and nose-dived toward the shadowy shoreline, he let out one last piercing shriek. He felt one more moment of blinding impact, and then nothing.

Ten

Aloft, heading over the North Pole

Liz looked down at the pile of auburn hair in the bathroom sink. There was a lot of it, shorn like wool from a lamb. She gave herself a wry smile at the unfortunate comparison and combed her new cut around and out from her face so that it approximated the photos of Sarah — slightly wild, very modern.

She peered into her eyes and touched the dramatic mole near her mouth. Hers had arrived with birth, while Sarah's had been artificially given to her. She noticed the crooked little finger on her left hand, broken in a childhood skating accident. They had broken poor Sarah's finger so it would duplicate hers. She and her mother and father owed Sarah, who had gone through hell because Liz persuaded her parents to come in. Or thought she had. In the end, only her mother kept the agreement. Remembering it all, she felt a familiar hollowness somewhere in her chest.

She had wasted enough time. With a sigh, she left the bathroom and returned down the aisle. Mac was still in his chair, his head resting back, eyes closed, face relaxed. He had located a blanket somewhere. It covered his lap and legs.

She thought he was asleep until he said, "We need to talk about your parents. There may be something you've forgotten that would give us a clue about the files."

"I told Langley everything I knew when I was debriefed. And don't forget I was debriefed twice. No stone left unturned ad infinitum. Also ad nauseam."

He crossed his arms over his thick chest, and a smile touched his lips. Still he did not open his eyes. "Humor me. Think of it as small payment for this expensive private flight to Paris."

She fell into her chair. "Are there more blankets?"

But he was already handing one across to her. It had been on the floor on the far side of his seat. "Trade you for my ID."

"Fair enough."

She dug the CIA identification out of her purse and gave it to him. It disappeared inside his jacket as she took the blanket and spread it over her legs. It was warm and comforting. Comfort had a lot of appeal right now.

He opened his eyes. "Let's start at the beginning. The inner man. How would you describe your father? A sociopath? Maybe a psychopath?"

She felt herself stiffen. This was not a conversational path she liked. But Mac was right. By talking about him, she might recall something useful.

"No, Papa didn't fit either definition. He was remorseful, if you could get him to talk about it."

125

She turned her head to look at him. "Lack of remorse is the hallmark symptom for both psychopaths and sociopaths. They're indifferent to — or they simply rationalize away — anything from thievery and inflicting pain to murder. Both pathologies are defined by a basic lack of empathy, which is something seen most often in people who chronically lie or ignore the rights or feelings of others."

Mac frowned. "If I understand you correctly, there's no difference between a sociopath and a psychopath."

"Haven't finished yet. A psychopath has psychotic-like elements, too — usually paranoia or some kind of twisted, demented thinking, like believing people enjoy the pain he's inflicting, or that his victims deserve it."

He pursed his lips, thinking. "So if a guy does a contract killing and just doesn't care, he's a sociopath. If another guy does it because he thinks someone's out to get him, he's a psychopath."

"That's it. Adolf Hitler was probably a psychopath, while a businessman who ruins people for profit has touches of sociopathology."

"You just indicted capitalism."

"Did I? Well, at least you're still smiling. I remember one of my professors claimed if everyone were well-adjusted, there'd never be war again, and we'd have plenty of food, clothing, shelter, and leisure time to go around. We'd also be productive and creative. Pleasant to imagine a world like that."

"I used to hear that would happen when women ran things."

"Maybe it will. At this point, I don't care who's in charge. I'm interested in results. But let's get back to psychopaths and sociopaths. That will help you understand why Papa was different. They compartmentalize their lives. There's a great example in the movie *Analyze This*. Remember, Robert De Niro plays a mob boss?"

He nodded.

"There's a scene where his character's getting a blow job from a prostitute. While she's doing it, he's telling her he loves his wife but he can't let his wife give him a blow job, because it'd be with the same lips she kisses their children. De Niro delivers the line beautifully, and it's hysterically funny. But it's also revealing: His character has no idea how his wife feels about his seeing a prostitute, about fellatio, or about anything else. He's a sociopath. Who she really is, apart from being his wife, is irrelevant to him. Her only function is to play out the script he's created for her."

"Yeah, it's also classic mafioso. All of them want marriage. It raises their status in the family. Everything's about status in the mob."

"Exactly. Roles. In other words, more roles to be played that have nothing to do with the people themselves. That's why the De Niro character can behave like a loving husband without being loving, without actually knowing who his wife is. For him, appearing properly tenderhearted is probably self-serving, not empathic. Sociopaths keep up the appearance of caring, but what do they actually feel? . . . Who knows?"

"But your father wasn't that way?"

"I'm not sure." She paused uneasily. "I felt as if he loved us. Even though he was a killer, it still felt to me as if he loved us. When Mom and I wanted to come in, he said he would, too. That it was the right thing to do. At the time, I wondered whether he was just trying to please us." She shook her head. "His first kill was an act of passion. He was working in Las Vegas and was barely twenty years old, and he got away with it. But the Mafia figured it out. They identified him for his 'natural talent.' When the Mafia trains you as an assassin, the first people you're assigned to whack are usually in the mob, too, or working for the mob. He figured he was killing bad people."

"Was he a vigilante?"

"You like to put labels on things, don't you? Well, yes and no. He killed for money, but the line he drew was that his targets had to be dirty, and he was the one who got to choose whether they were dirty enough to deserve being hit. After the mob let him go independent, he could make that call without someone looking over his shoulder or second-guessing him. He always liked to be in control."

"What about your mother? Did she discover the truth about what he was really doing, or did he finally volunteer it?"

"She found out. She thought he had a mistress and started checking up on him."

In a flash, a painful old memory riveted her. Her mother, Melanie, was frantically searching through the clothes in her father's closet, fear on her face, her cheeks wet with tears. She ran to Melanie, and Melanie knelt in front of her, adjusting her play dress. *Don't worry, sweetie. It's nothing. Papa left a note, and I can't find it. Really. It's unimportant. Go outside and get your bike. We'll ride over to the park. Doesn't that sound like fun?*

Liz pulled herself back to the present. "But of course, even then he wouldn't tell her the truth. He said he worked for MI6, which he knew would appeal to her. She started helping him with the planning and the scut work of setting up a hit. After a while, she did wet work herself."

He gazed at her curiously, then suspiciously. "How do you know all this?"

"Years later, when I was living with them again, Mom told me everything."

He nodded. "Makes sense. I imagine the military background in her family helped."

She shot him a look, but his face was expressionless. Of course, Langley would have sent him all her personnel records, which included a complete — and now accurate — family history. While Melanie's father advanced in rank and her mother tended to the social and charitable demands made on an officer's wife, Melanie raised her three younger brothers. When Melanie's grandfather died, her father resigned his commission, and they returned home to Childs Hall in London, and he became Sir John Childs. After his death, Melanie's brother Robert inherited the title. When Sir Robert killed himself, the title and lands passed to his older son, her cousin Michael.

"Yes," Liz said, "she knew how to use weapons, and she'd grown up in an atmosphere where violence and death were woven into everyday life.

Later on, when she finally discovered Papa was really independent and killed for all sides, she was in so deep she couldn't stop, although she never worked against her country. But then, neither did he. When I found out what they were doing, she was able to quit completely, and he did, too."

She closed her eyes, leaned back in the seat. What came into her mind was a dark tenement in Madrid, one of their safe houses, where they had fled after his last job, in Lisbon. Her mother's face was white with shame and fury. *I hate you, Hal. You bastard. Look what you've made of us. Now Liz knows. You'll ruin her, too!*

Liz inhaled, refusing the memories. Hardening herself, because Melanie could have said no at any time. "Papa was tenderhearted when it came to us. He paid a lot of attention to me when I was growing up."

"You've hinted he was scarred psychologically. Injured. How did that happen?"

"It's complicated. Papa's father was a corporate lawyer, at the top of the West Coast pack. Apparently, he was such a ruthless SOB that not even his partners liked him. Sarah knew him. Her mother told me Grandpa was cold, distant, and particularly nasty to Papa. By the time he was a teenager, Papa was running with a wild crowd and getting into serious trouble. So his father sent him to an uncle in Las Vegas who was connected. What an appalling — and revealing — choice. He thought a mafioso was just the right kind of adult to control his son and act as a role model."

130

"I'm getting the picture."

Liz nodded. "That's where it gets even more strange. At first, Papa turned himself around. He got a job in a casino, fell in love, and married. But then his wife was murdered, and Papa went nuts. He was so trained to dominate a situation that he went into action, found out who did it, and killed him."

Mac's gaze darkened. "So that was his first hit. Of course, the mob found out. He was too close for them not to. That's when they would've enlisted him, and that's how he ended up like his father, a hired gun."

"You see that, too." She studied him. "You know the rest."

"Yeah," Mac nodded. "I know the rest."

For the next two hours, Mac continued to question her about the details of her father's and mother's activities, and she answered patiently. She had loved Hal Sansborough as a father but had despised him as the assassin, the Carnivore. She was torn between anger and love, between duty to country and guilt that she had set in motion the events that led to his suicide.

It was her unresolved war, and none of her scholarly understanding of the mind gave her peace with it. It was one more reason she had focused her study on the psychology of violence. In the end, she gave Mac explanations and insights but no new elements to help determine whether assassination records existed, and if they did, their location.

Santa Barbara, California

Shortly after midnight, a black Dodge SUV pulled into the driveway of Derrick and Dolores Quentin's white Victorian house in the sparsely settled foothills above the city. The driver was prepared for witnesses, just as he had been when he eliminated Professor Kirk Tedesco, but the isolation made his work easier.

The driver was alone. He stepped out of the SUV, carrying a flashlight and a 9-mm Browning with a noise suppressor. The house was dark. He had been e-mailed a floor plan and committed it to memory.

At the kitchen door, the driver broke a windowpane with the butt of his pistol, put his gloved hand in through the hole, and unlocked the door. He entered, listening. There was the sound of movement upstairs. It was important only in that it might make his job more interesting. He rolled up his ski mask so he could see better, turned on his flashlight, and padded through the kitchen, passing the messy remains of the night's party. The staircase was in the front hallway. He climbed it.

Upstairs, the dean was stepping from his bedroom, his sleepy face confused. The driver waited for eye contact. His target looked up and focused. Horror stretched his features, and he grabbed the doorway for support.

The janitor smiled and put a silenced shot into the target's forehead. There was a faint *pop*, and blood sprayed. The target reeled backward, hands reaching out helplessly as he slammed against a bureau and sank to the floor, blood pouring from his wound.

The driver watched longer, then went into the wife's bedroom. She was stirring under the quilt. He hoped the sound of the gunshot had penetrated her sleep. He waited, staring down at the face. Plastic surgery, he decided. She was nearly sixty but had been cosmetically adjusted to forty-five. Made herself beautiful for this moment.

Suddenly, as if she sensed his presence, her eyes snapped open. With satisfaction, he noted the terror. Her face twisted, and her mouth opened to scream. He fired into her mouth.

The killer checked all the other rooms. As expected, no one else was in the house. Next, he went into the den, where he located the floor safe. He shot a bullet into the lock, opened it, and cleaned out the jewelry and cash. After making certain both targets were dead, he strolled out to his SUV and drove away.

Aloft, heading south from the North Pole

Liz watched Mac sleep. Something was still bothering her, something he had said that did not jibe with what she knew. She went back over their conversations, trying to figure it out. When the answer came, it was with a burst of fresh anger. It had all started with her phone conversation with Shay Babcock, her producer. When he was describing the postponement of their series, he had said: *The word was sent to me from Bruce Fontana, the network entertainment director, that they'd decided last night.*

Last night. And Shay had left a message on her machine with the news while she was out jogging and was attacked. At about the same time, Sarah was kidnapped.

Still, according to Mac, Langley had applied pressure to make the network postpone the series, but *after* Sarah had been kidnapped. *We applied pressure. Now that it's off the public stage, the threat against you may lessen. We want nothing to compromise our search for Sarah.*

Someone was lying, and she doubted it was Shay. He had nothing to gain. But why would Mac lie? Or had Langley lied to him? She considered the awful possibility Langley had known in advance Sarah was going to be kidnapped.

Her throat tight, she studied him. He was breathing evenly, eyes closed, face smoothed in slumber. She waited patiently. After a half hour, she saw no sign he was faking. She crept to her feet, padded back to the business center, and quietly used the computer to log on to the Internet with the secure code Shay had arranged for her research. With it, she could erase her cyber trail.

In the unearthly glow of the monitor, she researched media baron Nicholas Inglethorpe, the man who had the ultimate power to postpone or give new life to her series. Born in Houston, Texas, he was self-made, starting with one broken-down radio station that he parlayed into a string of stations and ultimately an international empire of newspapers, books, video and music

134

stores, a film studio, and, of course, Compass Broadcasting.

As she read the details of his methodical rise, his business slugfests, and the feelers he was putting out for a possible run for governor of California, she gave a grim smile. A man who not only craved power but knew how to use it.

A *Business Week* article mentioned charitable works. She stared, shaken. Inglethorpe was the current chairman of the Aylesworth Foundation's board of directors. *The bastard.* Her fingers again flew over the keyboard, and she searched until she found lists of past board members. She focused on February 1998, when Grey Mellencamp had questioned her. She swore under her breath. Mellencamp was chairman of the board then, and at his death Inglethorpe succeeded him — just before the foundation solicited her to apply for the chair she ultimately won. Fighting fear and anger, she searched again, easily finding more boards and organizations to which both men had belonged, often at the same time.

At last, she sat back and crossed her arms to consider coolly what she knew. On the Aylesworth board, the line was unbroken between Mellencamp and Inglethorpe. It would be no great leap to assume Inglethorpe cooperated with the CIA in business — not unknown among tycoons who sought the occasional government perk. He did their bidding on the foundation board, and he cooperated again by canceling her TV series. Perhaps he, too, reported to this Themis, whoever he was.

This information did nothing to erase her unease about Langley. If anything, she saw even less reason for Mac to lie to her. She kept herself calm. What exactly was Langley up to? Was Sarah's life really a top priority . . . or was Langley following some private agenda she could not see?

Eleven

Zurich, Switzerland

Leafy and sedate, the legendary Bahn-hofstrasse was not only one of Europe's most elite shopping boulevards, it was the beating heart of one of the nation's most lucrative and famous businesses — international banking. Despite that, few of the shoppers and tourists who stepped into the costly boutiques and elegant shops to ogle the five-thousand-dollar watches and the five-hundred-dollar socks guessed they were literally walking on a street of gold.

To the Swiss, secrecy in banking was only one example of the delicacy to be expected in the conduct of one's affairs. Seldom did anyone mention that chambers — many five stories deep — lay beneath the Bahnhofstrasse, packed with ingots and the wealth of nations. In fact, this was the world's largest gold market. The banks that faced the street or hid out on side avenues were so powerful that they not only dictated decisions in Switzerland's capital but swayed others in metropolises around the globe.

137

Terrill Leaming was a senior executive at the Darmond Bank AG, located in a baronial building a block off the Paradeplatz. No windows faced the street. Only the address — not the bank's name — showed on a brass plaque beside the ebony door. A guard in a dark business suit, a bowler squarely on his head and a subtle bulge beneath his armpit, stood on the marble steps. Walk-in trade was discouraged at Darmond.

Simon told the guard his name, and the guard announced him on a walkie-talkie. The guard never smiled. Simon hardly felt cheerful himself as they waited together on the steps. He had tried to block the horror of Viera's death from his mind, but as the waiting stretched, it flooded back.

After his meeting with the anonymous man in St. Martin's Cathedral, he had returned to his apartment to shower, change, and pound out his report for MI6. He left it rolled up inside a crushed Coke can at the foot of a maple near the old bridge. At the same time, he casually picked up a rumpled McDonald's hamburger sack, advertising in Slovak, of course. Traditionally, public bathrooms were the most popular location for dead drops, but he had always favored the outdoors, where he could run if he had to. Once out of sight of the drop, he removed a tightly folded sheet of paper and tossed the sack into a trash can.

At a small café in the shadow of St. Michael's Gate, he fortified himself with a fresh hard roll and strong black coffee before opening the paper.

Inside was another sheet of paper. The first was a coded note from Ada, ordering him to a safe house in Florence, complete with street address and a curt message: *Viera Jozef left a statement for the world. Copy enclosed. Under no circumstances leave Florence until contacted.*

His throat tight, he took a long drink of the black coffee and opened Viera's last words. He read slowly. They were a plea for the rich to give as much as they took, to practice humanity, not worship profit. It was all very biblical-sounding, although Viera had been an atheist. In the note, she asked her brother and comrades to understand, to fight on, and to forgive her. No mention of him. Odd that he was surprised; odder that he was hurt. What had he expected?

For a moment, the sight of her fiery end filled his eyes. He blinked back moistness, tore the paper into fragments, and let them drop onto the table. As he brushed them into a tiny pile like the ashes of a dead fire, he reread his orders. Nice of Ada to send him to Florence. Stunning city, full of distractions, far from the action, and where he had no intention of going. He had ripped that message into bits, too.

Now it was three o'clock in the afternoon, and he was waiting on the steps of the swank Darmond Bank. His bag was checked into a downtown locker, and his gun was holstered at the small of his back, beneath his tan sports coat. He had been able to carry it into Switzerland courtesy of his MI6 identification.

It was time to put Viera and whatever mistakes

he had made with her behind him, although he did not know exactly how. As he thought that, there was a low beep from the guard's walkie-talkie.

The fellow lifted it to his ear. *"Ja?"* He listened, his morose expression unchanged, and turned as a quiet click sounded inside the bank's oversize door, indicating it was being electrically unlocked from somewhere inside.

The guard pulled it open, and Simon entered the hushed lobby. He repressed a whistle of appreciation. The lobby was three stories high, with Roman columns in white marble around the perimeter. The place was large enough for two cricket pitches and regal enough for a dinner party for the queen. A receptionist sat at a shamefully ornate desk a good twenty feet away. Above him, bankers and clerks rushed silently from office to office along open walkways lined with lacy black wrought iron. He imagined a rajah would feel right at home when he arrived to deposit his jewels and bullion.

"Simon?" To his right, a filigreed elevator door opened. Terrill Leaming walked out, grayer, more hunched, but looking sleek as an overweight otter. A worried otter.

They shook hands. "Good to see you, Terrill."

"Wouldn't have recognized you, Simon. How long has it been?"

"Dad's funeral. Five years."

"Yes. Yes, of course." He seemed to hardly listen, his mind somewhere else. "What can I do for you?" No invitation to go up to his office, where they could converse privately.

Simon kept his voice low. "I need to talk to you about Dad's death."

Leaming glanced nervously around, distracted, as if expecting wolves to attack.

Simon said, "It might not have been a simple suicide, Terrill. I've been told an assassin and blackmail were involved and that you have information I need."

Leaming's knees seemed to buckle. Simon grabbed his arm to support him.

Leaming cleared his throat. "My . . . my afternoon's full. Tomorrow. Yes, tomorrow! Come back tomorrow."

Simon leaned close. "You're afraid of something. Mention of Dad's suicide has increased it. Talk to me, Terrill. It makes no difference to me where. Or I can make one hell of a bloody scene right here."

The receptionist scowled, her gaze on Simon's hand, where he supported Terrill's arm. She probably spoke not only the usual German and French but also English and several other languages.

Smiling, Simon announced heartily, "A walk, Terrill? That's a splendid idea. A breath of the outdoors. Better than a stuffy office, what?"

Terrill finally looked him in the eyes. Simon saw the fear he expected but also an odd kind of acceptance and more — hope.

The banker gave an eager nod. "Yes, yes. Been cooped up here, that's true. There's a tea shop on the Paradeplatz you'll like."

Two minutes later, they were outside and walking fast. Gleaming Citroëns, BMWs, and

Rolls-Royces glided past, windows darkened. People strolled under the trees, intent on shopping. Terrill peered anxiously around, walking defensively, like a spooked deer, still expecting those wolves to attack.

"Has someone been following you? Watching you? Is that the problem?"

Terrill nodded dumbly, as if too frightened to speak.

Simon used the reflection of a boutique window to inspect the sidewalk and street. "I see no one suspicious."

"They're here." Terrill's voice radiated doom. He seemed to make a decision. "I've heard rumors you're MI6, Simon. Is it true?"

Simon studied the distraught banker. The first rule in intelligence was you revealed that to no one outside the life, no one at all, except your spouse, and not always to her or him. But Simon also believed there were times rules must be broken.

"Yes, it's true. But it goes no farther, understand?"

Terrill nodded anxiously. "Of course."

"What kind of trouble are you in?"

They were approaching Paradeplatz, where Zurich's blue-and-white electric trams rimmed the square, nannies pushed prams, tourists took photos, and young lovers swung shopping bags and exchanged excited, purchase-induced kisses in the sunshine. At the edge of it, the tea shop Terrill had suggested was an oasis of peace. They chose an outdoor table and ordered tea — delicate Formosa oolong for Terrill and strong, biting Lapsang souchong for Simon — and waited for the waiter to bustle away.

"I've . . . I've just arranged to put my entire estate in trust," Terrill told him. His eyes were red-rimmed, exhausted. "I'd planned to go to the police this afternoon, but you arrived first. I believe my bank has set me up, and I'll soon be arrested. Or worse."

"Or worse?" Simon repeated sympathetically, repressing impatience. "No wonder you're worried. I'll tell you what . . . I'll help you reach the police safely if you'll fill me in about Dad's death."

Terrill peered down at the lace tablecloth and nodded. "Thank you. Yes, thank you very much. What do you want to know?"

"Did he kill himself because he'd once hired an assassin and was being blackmailed for it?"

"I'm afraid that's true." Terrill looked up. "He wasn't proud of what he'd done, you understand, but he felt it necessary. He told me he'd accept the consequences in this world and the next. When the time came . . . when he was being blackmailed, that's what he did. A strong man, your father."

Simon's chest tightened. It had been *necessary?* Bullshit. Whacking a killer was a stopgap answer for an ongoing institutional problem of favoritism, irresponsibility, and dishonesty that invited heinous crimes, then covered them up.

"How is what Dad did connected to your trouble?"

They paused as their tea arrived.

As soon as the waiter left, Terrill shifted in his

143

chair, sipped from his cup, and checked out the *Platz*. "Do you know much about the Darmond Bank?"

"Old money, old social standing, quiet power. Infamously elite. I read that a would-be client with a net worth of less than a million Swiss francs tried to make a deposit once. Apparently, your bank declined, put him in its Rolls-Royce, and drove him to a crosstown competitor."

Terrill almost smiled. "The story's true. The Darmond Bank operates at a rarefied fiscal level. For thirty years, I worked closely with the chairman, Baron de Darmond, handling money matters for Europe's most prominent citizens." His shoulders slumped, and he whispered, "While serving these clients . . . the baron, the bank, and I barely eluded being swept up in some of the shabbiest financial scandals in recent times, everything from BCCI to Banca de Tebaldi."

"You were involved in BCCI and Tebaldi?"

"In other questionable matters as well. Some of our top Italian families wanted to evade Italy's capital controls and taxes, so the baron and I founded fake companies to hide the true owner-ship of their assets, and then we lied about it to the Italian courts. I'm not proud of this, but at the time it seemed to make business sense."

"Somehow, it always does," Simon said with barely concealed scorn. He drank tea and put down his cup. "Is that why you're afraid?"

"I wish it were only that. Do you know the name Giovanni de Tebaldi?"

"The banker found hanged to death under

Blackfriars Bridge back in '82?"

Terrill took out a silk handkerchief and mopped his face. A diamond ring — at least a full two carats — glinted on his thumb. "Yes. He was a criminal. A maverick who refused to co-operate with Europe's financial community. When the baron decided he had to be eliminated, I delivered a suitcase containing a half million dollars to a professional assassin. Now Italy's tax authorities are inquiring again, and this time the prosecutor wants blood. The baron's terrified something about Tebaldi's murder will come out. I think he's setting me up to be his scapegoat." His haunted gaze fixed on Simon. "And I'm being blackmailed about Tebaldi's murder, too, just like your father five years ago."

So that was why Terrill had nearly collapsed at the bank — blackmail. "You both hired the same assassin," Simon guessed.

"Yes. I told your father I was in a similar position, and he put me in touch with his man — someone named the Carnivore. I can't believe I followed through."

The Carnivore. Simon controlled his expression, showing no sign of the jolt that had given him. His father had retained his own brother-in-law. He wondered whether Sir Robert knew that.

Rage flashed in Terrill's eyes. "But I'm not finished. I'll confess everything and take the bloody baron, the bank — *everyone* — down with me." He had managed to avoid all references to ethics and morality. What propelled him were fear and revenge.

"I've heard of the Carnivore," Simon said cau-

145

tiously, since Terrill seemed not to know the relationship between the Carnivore and his family. "As I recall, he was something of a legend. But he's dead now. He can't be your blackmailer."

"True. But your father believed he kept files, and that the blackmailer had them. There was no other way anyone could have learned what Sir Robert had done."

"And what you did." Simon's mind moved quickly elsewhere, grappling. Christ! *The Carnivore had made a record.* That meant the highest level of names, dates, places. Perhaps not only who hired him but also the people around the targets — innocent people as well as those involved in embarrassing peccadilloes they wanted to keep private or felonies or even homicides.

Simon's voice was neutral. "So whoever has the files is the blackmailer. Did my father have any idea who that might be?"

Terrill shook his head. "No, but he thought he knew how the bastard got them."

Simon's brows raised. "How?"

"From the Carnivore's wife. It seems your father knew who she was. She died in an accident six months before he was blackmailed."

Aunt Melanie. "Dad thought she'd given the files to someone?"

"No, someone else in her family might've taken them. He suspected one of her brothers, but he refused to tell me who, because he had no evidence. He said it'd change nothing, and innocent people would be hurt. As I said, he was a strong man."

"How does the blackmailer contact you?"

"First, it was a whispering voice on my cell. Unrecognizable, naturally. The second time, just this morning, it was secured e-mail on my home computer. The prick had sent me what looked like actual entries from the Carnivore's records, covering everything from when I'd first hired him to when he hung Tebaldi under the bridge."

"Did you save the e-mail?"

"Are you mad? Of course not!"

"What did the blackmailer want?"

Terrill sighed heavily. "For me to go to Italy and take full responsibility for the bank's crimes. It'd be a far lesser sentence than if I were exposed as the man who set up Tebaldi's murder. In exchange, I'd get to keep the money I've earned, and there'd be no mention of my role in Tebaldi's murder."

"If you're right, the baron could be your blackmailer."

Terrill's voice was almost lifeless. "Yes, or they're working together somehow. I told you they were going to scapegoat me. My guess is they're arranging things so it'll look as if I were completely responsible for both." He peered at his watch. "Will you take me to the police station now?"

Simon wanted to walk away and let the self-serving coward find his own fate. Instead, he said, "Of course." Besides, Terrill's confession would put more pressure on Baron de Darmond and the blackmailer.

They left money on the table and pushed out among the shoppers and tourists. Terrill continued to condemn the baron, the blackmailer, Tebaldi, everyone and anyone but himself.

"I'll tell the authorities everything!" he raged. "The baron will be sorry he —"

They were moving through a mob of tourists off one of the blue-and-white trams, when Terrill's face tensed, and he stopped. His body seemed to shiver. He rose up on his toes and gave a gasp . . . a raw cough —

Simon stopped with him. "What's wrong, Terrill? Do you feel sick?"

But Terrill said nothing, his eyes wide as he slammed a fist against his chest once.

Simon grabbed him from the side, propping him up. He was a deadweight. Instantly, Simon pressed two fingers against the banker's neck, where his carotid artery was.

There was no pulse. Terrill was dead. In seconds, without warning, with no indication of feeling ill or weak or even uncomfortable, Terrill Leaming had simply coughed, pounded his chest, and died. Still propping him up, Simon scrutinized the throngs, sorting through adults and children, tourists and locals, off for business and shopping, until he focused on the back of a man dressed in a conservative dark suit. He was solid-looking as he walked off. Not hurrying. His step firm. Not looking back.

But what attracted Simon's attention was a black cane with a silver handle that the man gripped in his right hand, holding it out in front of him. As Simon watched, he let the cane slide down through his fingers until the tip touched the ground. At which point, he began using it properly, stepping rhythmically along, the tip tapping the pavement.

Simon dropped the corpse and tore after him. Behind him, he heard a muffled gasp, then a shout in German.

"What's happened?"

"Is he hurt?" someone else called out, also in German.

More shouts followed in other languages. The cries were taken up across the *Platz*.

"Stop him!" someone shouted at Simon's fleeing back.

But there was too much confusion — too many people, too many trams, too much fear in the few hands that clutched at Simon — to interrupt his headlong run.

The man with the cane, who should have reacted to the first scream as the rest of the crowd had, made a second mistake. He glanced back. As soon as he saw he was being pursued, he broke into a run.

The tall spire of the Fraumünster church rose ahead, sharp against the blue Alpine sky. Simon pounded alongside thick traffic heading toward the Münster Bridge over the Limmat River. As horns blasted angrily, the assassin suddenly darted among the vehicles, slapping fenders and dodging with the skill of a star soccer player.

Simon tried to follow, but a pair of bicyclists was pacing him. He dropped back, while the killer landed on the other side of the street. Simon sped after, also banging car fenders to alert drivers to slow as he ducked, dashed, and leaped. On the far side, he brushed past pedes-

149

trians and nearly fell over a low stone wall as he sprinted into a narrow medieval alley and pounded north, sweating.

The janitor was in superb shape, running easily, his strides long. But Simon was a runner, too. He was gaining, his lungs pumping air like a giant bellows. He chased him into a tangle of cramped alleys lined with stone houses that looked centuries old. The man dashed around a corner, but when Simon rounded it, the man was gone.

Four alleys met here. Breathing hard, Simon quickly took in the scene. A cat lay in an open doorway, licking its paw. Sitting next to the cat was an old man smoking a cob pipe, his feet on the cobbled intersection. Simon rushed to him, pulling out his wallet, showing euros. The solemn man did not smile. He slowly stuck out a finger, pointing up one of the alleys that disappeared around a bend.

Simon threw the money and raced off. As he wound around the curve, he spotted the assassin at last, this time a distant figure running up a picturesque street overhung by oriels — bay windows. The hill was steep, and he was slowing. But at last Simon knew the man's destination — the Lindenhof. He did not like it.

As he reached the top, the killer looked back again. His eyebrows raised in surprise over his sunglasses. Then he frowned. With renewed vigor, he leaped the last few steps over the crest and disappeared.

But at last, Simon had seen his face: long, closely shaved, sloping cheeks and medium-length dark brown hair, all dominated by military-style sunglasses.

His muscles straining, Simon tore up the hill, flagging, too, as he topped the crest. Panting, he slowed to look. The green, tree-dotted park spread before him, but he did not see the killer. Rimmed on one side with old houses, the Lindenhof overlooked the city in a vast panorama that was favored by walkers and lovers. It was also the oldest part of Zurich, where a Roman outpost once stood.

This was a workday, so few people were here. Beyond a fountain, two elderly women played chess on a gigantic board laid out on the ground. They stood, hands on hips, concentrating, staring down, inching from side to side, oblivious to everything. The kings, queens, and rooks were higher than the women's knees.

Simon was about to ask them, when he saw movement. Across the open space was a grove of linden trees, full of shadows. A dark figure was moving quietly through them and away, more a shadow than a person, cleverly blending into the grove. As police sirens began to wail, Simon took off again, running at top speed.

But when Simon reached the trees, the man was gone. At the same time, the police sirens rose in intensity, closing in on the park. Hundreds of people in the Paradeplatz would have seen Simon. Under normal circumstances, he might have gone to the police, identified himself, and let them sort it out with Whitehall. But not this time.

He did not even know for certain that Terrill

had been murdered. If he were, whatever had killed him had left no blood or bruises that he could see. Probably some kind of poison, administered through the head of the cane, where a hypodermic of some kind was hidden. An old tradecraft trick.

On top of everything, Simon was supposed to be in Florence or at least on his way.

Breathing hard, frustrated, he jammed his fingers through his hair and cursed loudly. He stalked along the rim of the long hillside, noting the web of trails that crisscrossed and plunged down in blind turns and vanished back into the city. There were too many trails from which to choose, and no one to ask. Gauging where the police cars would arrive, Simon ran down the hillside and away.

Twelve

Paris, France

Carrying a small box and a shoulder bag, Liz hurried along the hospital corridor, checking room numbers. It was Wednesday, a hot July afternoon, and the American Hospital had a drowsy air about it. Patients were napping, while nurses quietly filled out charts and sorted predinner medication. Liz had visited friends here before. Renowned for its English-speaking staff and high standards of medicine, the hospital had treated everyone from the Duke of Windsor to Osama bin Laden's stepmother, from confused tourists to penniless college kids, especially those with ties to the United States.

There was one misfit — a man sitting outside an open door ahead, reading *Paris Match*. From his casual demeanor to the covert looks he shot out when anyone approached, he had Langley written all over him.

When she got close enough, he stood, extended his hand, and raised his voice just enough so anyone within earshot could hear. "Hello, Ms.

Walker. I'm Chuck Draper. Asher's been talking about you. Glad you're feeling better." He was in his fifties, of medium height, with rat brown hair and blue eyes that matched the color of his sports jacket, probably on purpose. He had the air of a man who liked things to be exact and was inevitably dissatisfied with the world because of it. But he knew his role, and he expected "Sarah Walker."

"Thanks for taking such good care of my husband."

They exchanged a glance, acknowledging they were starting a movie. From her time at the Farm, where most Langley recruits went first for training, Liz had played numerous parts, but the vast majority had been fictitious characters created to suit a political need. Sometimes they had been real, a moment stolen from someone, as Mac had done with Deputy Sheriff Harry Craine. But now she was supposed to be Sarah, whom she cared about, to whom she owed a great deal.

Liz quieted her mind and walked into the private room. She was Sarah Walker.

Asher Flores swam toward consciousness. Through the grogginess, he remembered: *Sarah was gone.* He swore tiredly. *Christ.* And tried to jerk upright. Instead he fell back, disoriented.

A voice said, "Dodgers won today."

It was Liz. He opened his eyes and drank in the sight of her, feeling a little off balance because she and Sarah looked so much alike. Her voice was similar to Sarah's, too. That was what must have awakened him, he decided. For an instant, he had almost thought Sarah was back. But Liz's face was a few millimeters longer and her forehead wider. No two people were ever precisely alike, not even so-called identical twins, and not even when surgery was performed specifically to make them doubles. Still, he was one of the few people who would be able to tell them apart quickly.

"They're up another game?" he murmured. "Life's getting better again." What crap. Life would never be good until Sarah was safe.

She was smiling. He watched as she set down the box. She had the same large dark eyes, the same generous mouth, the same standout cheekbones, and now she even had the same short hair. *God, he wished she really were Sarah.*

She said, "I brought you a radio and the *Herald Tribune.*"

He nodded, but did not bother to take the newspaper.

She put it on the table beside his bed then opened the box, set a small Philips radio next to the paper, and plugged it in. "Do you like your gift?" she asked. "I thought you might be getting tired of TV."

She narrowed her eyes, and Asher frowned, then gave a subtle nod. He got the message: The room might be bugged, despite the CIA's precautions. The hospital was, after all, in France, and the French planted listening devices and hidden cameras even in Air France business class, hoping to pick up tidbits to pass on in the never-ending games of political, military, and economic espionage.

Asher made himself rally. "Turn it on, will you? Find me a good station."

Soon, some kind of unrecognizable rock music shook the room. Their only standard was that it be loud enough to cover their voices.

Her expression had softened, again like Sarah's. She spoke just loudly enough to be heard above the music.

"How are you feeling, Asher?"

"Not bad. Morphine helps. You still hurt like hell, but you don't care. Has anyone got a lead?"

"I wish. They're doing everything they can to find her. A man named Angus MacIntosh is my handler. Do you know him?" When he gave a single shake of his head, she continued: "Mac's keeping me posted. How bad's your wound?"

"Went clean through. Bounced off a rib but missed anything really important."

"Nice try. The story I heard was it also nicked your liver and intestine. You've had surgery, idiot. They had to sew you back together. Take my advice: Treat your internal organs with respect."

She dragged a chair close and sat, dropping her shoulder bag to the floor. She leaned forward, elbows on the bed. She was less than a foot from him, hoping to lessen the chances they would be overheard.

"Chuck dusted for bugs." He smelled her scent longingly. *Sarah.*

"Just pretend I'm paranoid. Have the kidnappers called?"

"They said they'd be in touch on day four. It's psychological warfare, making us wonder what they're up to. Focusing us on Sarah's life. Ignorance enhances pressure." It was a classic ploy that had been used before and would be again, because it worked.

She nodded. "You're actually looking pretty good."

"That's because I am. What's going on? You've got that 'They're all a bunch of turds' expression Sarah gets."

She studied him, and he gazed gravely back. He liked her, and he knew she liked him. A real friendship and trust that was always there, like oxygen, between them. Not something you ever really needed to talk about.

"You must be devastated," she told him.

"Looking at you is hard, you know? But I'm glad you're here."

"I'm sorry. I was afraid of that."

"Nothing to be done." His gaze was steady. "Let's get to work. You first."

Liz told him about the assaults on her in Santa Barbara, the theft of her assassin research, how Langley had arranged her life through the Aylesworth Foundation, and that yesterday's attacks here and in Santa Barbara had been precipitated by the publicity about the assassins show she was researching.

Asher listened in silence. There were times even he hated Langley. He hoped the damn files were real and worth the hell they had put Liz through. "Where's your gun, Liz? At your back, in your pit? On your leg?"

She returned his gaze. "You know I won't carry a gun."

"You've got to. Without one, you're pet food."

She smiled at his angular face, at the bushy black eyebrows and the thick black hair, curly and untamable, as he lay against the white sheets. His skin was its normal golden color. Her gaze swept over the tubes and wires attached to him, the machines that clicked and blinked behind and around, the LEDs that, in a rainbow of hues, related to the world all sorts of intimate information.

"You need a shave," she told him.

He rubbed his chin. "Commenting on my beard-growing talent is a nice attempt at a distraction. It doesn't change the fact that to go up against people who intend to use their weapons to stop you, you're helpless to defend yourself."

"Were Gandhi and Martin Luther King helpless?"

"No, but they were leading vast passive-resistance campaigns against governments and majorities, and a handgun was too small to make a difference. They were dealing with mass movements, but you're just an individual going up against people who have guns and want to stop you any way they can."

"Someone has to say 'enough' and take some risks."

"In the long run, maybe you're right. But this is the short term, and without a weapon, you can't do your job. There's no cause here. We're not proving a great truth. You're trying to save Sarah. Dead, you can't help Langley or Sarah. You put your life at risk, and you put Sarah's, too. And I'll be pissed to lose you."

"I'll think about it. But that's enough about me. You're in pain, you're probably ready for another nap, and I've got only one more thing to tell you. It's about Mac. He either lied to me, or Langley lied to him. That's why we've got to keep our conversations private. Turn on the radio whenever we talk, okay?" She described the inconsistency about when her TV series was canceled and what Mac had said Langley's role had been.

"If Langley's up to something, it'll become clear. They don't like to lose people, so my guess is Mac's just got it wrong. I've worked for Langley long enough to know it does a hell of a lot of good most of the time, or most of us wouldn't stick around. Tell me about the research that was stolen from your office. Was there anything useful in there about your father's files?"

She shook her head, the rock music beginning to annoy her. "No, of course not. But now I've been thinking about it. Do you remember when Grey Mellencamp died of cardiac arrest? It was just hours after he'd interrogated me. At the time, it seemed like a coincidence . . . a suspicious coincidence, so I looked into it. As it turned out, he had a history of heart disease, and the autopsy showed no sign of foul play. So who else would've known about the files?"

"Your mother."

"Right. After Mellencamp died, I investigated her death, too."

"When exactly did she die?"

"About six months before he and I met. Of

course, Uncle Mark was killed then, too. Bad luck for him he was visiting Mom."

"I remember there was an explosion. What caused it?"

"A gas line. There was a problem with it the week before. Mom told me she'd had repairmen in to fix it. So when I went back to dig around, I checked all the gas company's records, the fire-investigation report, and the autopsy reports on both Mom and Uncle Mark. There was nothing that hinted it might not have been an accident, and both bodies were conclusively identified." She looked away, missing her mother.

They were silent, uneasy with their thoughts.

Asher considered. "Langley's got better resources to find Sarah than you do. But you've got an inside track when it comes to your parents and family."

"You think I should look for the files. Mac said Langley also wanted me to look. Is your phone a direct line?"

On the table beside him, where she had set the radio, stood a simple black telephone. When he said it was, she told him about the cell Mac had given her. They exchanged numbers.

"Call me if you hear anything," she said, "I'll do the same. We shouldn't trust anyone but each other until we know exactly what's going on."

A thin smile played on his lips, and he turned away to look with yearning at the bathroom. "As soon as I can walk over to take a leak," he vowed, "I'm blowing this joint."

"Swell. Then you'll screw things up by putting us in the position of having to rescue you, too.

Do me a favor. Don't."

Asher tried to smile.

"Is the pain worse?" she asked.

"Naw. I'm just tired is all. And annoyed. Guess I'm not as good as I thought."

"No one is."

"But I should've known. I should've guessed the moment that van stopped."

"When you get clairvoyant, holler. I'll put you on my TV show." She patted his arm.

"Get the hell out of here, Liz. Find the files. Find her. Bring her back to me." His husky voice broke. "Please."

She kissed his forehead. It was moist with sweat. "Take care of yourself, and I'll take care of Sarah."

It was a big promise, full of potential for disaster, but she had to make it. Asher needed reassurance, and she wanted desperately to repay him for what he and Sarah had done to help bring her mother and her in from the cold so many years ago.

Outside the room, she said good-bye to Asher's CIA guard, Chuck Draper, who nodded politely. She stopped at the nurses' station to leave her cell number. In French, she asked to be informed of any changes in her husband's condition.

Liz spoke far better French than Sarah did, and she could put on a British accent in the wink of an eye, but then, she had been raised in England. She also spoke Spanish, Italian, and German, and had a flair for acting, an analytical mind, and a thirst for adventure, all of which she had translated into her black work for the Company and recycled again into her academic work. Now she hoped those old skills and talents would be enough for what she had to do.

Leaving the hospital, Liz walked out into the afternoon heat, making plans. L'Hôpital Américain was located in the heart of leafy Neuilly, one of Paris's swankest suburbs, on the boulevard Victor-Hugo, only twelve minutes from the Arc de Triomphe. She spotted Mac about ten feet away and slowed. He gave an almost imperceptible nod from where he sat on a bench in the shade of a plane tree. It was his way to let her know he was around if she needed him.

Casually, she surveyed the grounds and street, noting other people who were walking toward and leaving the hospital — older couples, young parents with children, men in suits and sports clothes, women carrying shopping bags and infants. Nothing appeared unusual.

She walked toward the curb and stopped. As she raised her hand to hail a taxi, she heard a sharp grunt directly behind. She whirled as a small wiry man sprawled onto the sidewalk, rolled, and kicked Mac's legs out from under him.

With a curse, Mac lost his balance and fell, while Liz lunged for the kicker.

But the man turned and jumped to his feet, free. As he started to run, Liz heaved her shoulder bag. His foot slammed into it. He staggered sideways and went down hard on his left knee. The knee's impact with the concrete made a dull cracking noise. His eyes went wild with pain and fear.

As Mac scrambled up and Liz got to her feet, the man gritted his teeth, leaped up, and frantically half-ran, half-limped along the sidewalk, thrusting startled pedestrians aside.

Mac pounded after, and she scooped up her bag and followed. The fugitive cast a panicked glance behind. He was injured, and Mac was closing in. There was no way he could outrun Mac. He windmilled his hands above his head and turned into the speeding traffic. Brakes screeched and horns screamed as he bolted safely between two cars.

Frowning, Mac halted at the curb as the fellow continued his suicidal run onward into a second lane, where a black Citroën was unable to stop. The shriek of the tires and the sickening thud of the impact echoed through the summer air. Cars slewed and skidded to avoid where the man lay in the street, but two more ran over him before all of the traffic came to a shuddering halt.

Mac and Liz stood far apart on the curb, silent witnesses to the chaos. People jumped out of cars and converged from both sidewalks to help. Soon a man broke free of the crowd in the street and looked across the halted cars at Mac. He shook his head, clearly signaling Mac that the attacker was dead.

As police Klaxons wailed and an ambulance alarm screeched, the spotter slipped away into the crowd.

Mac hurried to Liz. "We'd better get out of here. Separately."

"What happened? Who was he?"

In answer, Mac opened his hand. On his large palm lay a cigarette lighter. He flipped open the cap. Instead of a flame, a miniature hypodermic syringe appeared. "This was in his hand. He was about to inject you with something. Probably poison. I'll have the lab analyze it."

Her heart thundered. "My God. How did you know?"

"I didn't, not for certain. But he was watching you while pretending not to. When you stopped to get a taxi, he closed in. That's when I acted. It might have been nothing, but after Santa Barbara, I was taking no chances."

She could feel the sweat trickling under her clothes. "Thank you. Thank you very much."

"You're welcome. Nice job with your bag. If he hadn't hurt his knee, he might've gotten away to try again."

"I'd rather have been able to interrogate him."

"Me, too." He lifted his head and turned toward the sound of the ambulance. Its siren was screaming as it bulled its way through the stalled traffic. The police would be close behind.

"We'd better separate and disappear." He walked away.

It was then she saw a woman she had noted earlier. When Liz had left the hospital, the woman was holding a Galeries Lafayette shopping bag and standing near the hospital's door, as if waiting for someone. She was still alone but apparently had given up waiting. She had an aristocratic nose with a small bump in the center and a light dusting of powder to even out the color of her skin. Her lipstick was a faded red, almost brown. There was a middle-class look about her, from her simple haircut to her button-down shirt tucked into inexpensive trousers. She also wore a loose, lightweight jacket in the warm sun, when nearly everyone else was in shirtsleeves or simple summer dresses.

What made Liz notice her was that she seemed connected to Mac, too, another spotter. The woman glanced at him and wound off among the stopped cars. Her movements were light, adroit, despite her heavy size. She had been trained. Liz studied her as she disappeared into the throngs still gawking at the fatal accident. There was more than clothes beneath her unseasonable jacket.

Liz hailed a taxi, climbed into the back, and told the taximan to drive away.

"But where, madame?" he asked in French.

She kept her voice neutral. "Just drive."

She was supposed to go to the Hôtel Valhalla to check Sarah and Asher's room. Instead, her mind raced as she grappled with the power of the person with the files. First, he — or she — had sent people to kill her in Santa Barbara. The problem was, that person had also arranged to have another attacker waiting in Paris.

Only Langley knew she was flying to Paris. Only Langley knew when she would arrive and that she would go straight to the American Hospital to visit Asher. She felt a sudden chill. How could anyone else — even the person with the files — have found out she was here, unless Langley had a leak, a traitor?

Thirteen

Call to Brussels, Belgium

*"What did Flores and Sansborough talk about?
Why do you sound amused?"*

*"She took him a radio and turned up the volume
so high I couldn't hear. Whether she knows it or not,
she's getting back her chops."*

*"I suppose it doesn't matter what they said. If
Flores knew anything, he would've told us long before
now. She would have, too."*

*"Exactly, Cronus. In any case, that's not the reason
I'm reporting. We have a new situation. Sansborough
was attacked again —"*

"What!"

*"— after she left the hospital. Mac was waiting out
front with his people. One of them noticed the man
and signaled Mac. There was a struggle, and Mac
took him down. He found a syringe in his hand,
hidden inside a jigged cigarette lighter. Mac's sent it
to the lab. We'll know by tomorrow what he was
going to inject, depending on how many and what
kinds of tests have to be run."*

"And the janitor?"

"Dead. He fell and injured his knee when

166

Sansborough threw her bag to trip him. He leaped into traffic to try to escape, but he was hit and killed. One of Mac's spotters frisked his corpse, but he was carrying nothing but cash."

"Damnation! Would've liked for you to have had a conversation with the bastard. Who have you told?"

"No one. I take my orders from you."

"You know why I ask?"

"Of course. First Santa Barbara. Now here. He knew where she'd be. They knew where she'd be. That's insider information. At best, we have a leak."

"And at worst, we have a blackmailer in our midst. Dammit all to hell! I should've guessed! Isolate Mac's unit. This information has to be contained while you and I investigate. Tell no one else about the incident. Let the bloody blackmailer wonder. We'll make him reveal himself."

Paris, France

In Les Halles, a yellow taxi sat parked in a shadowy alley, its motor idling and the white signal light on its roof unlit, indicating it was unavailable for fares. Its windows were rolled up, and its doors locked. The driver leaned back in the draft of the air conditioner. His cap was pulled forward over his sunglasses as if he were catching a quick nap. After all, it was a hot afternoon, and a working man grew weary.

But this working man was neither weary nor sleeping. He turned off his cell and put it away, continuing to surveil. He had positioned the taxi, the taxi's mirrors, and himself so he had no blind spots. In his early sixties, he was muscular, with a quiet, untroubled expression. He had no distinguishing marks, although he was completely bald under his cap.

His name was César Duchesne, but behind his back, he was called Le Boiteux, the Cripple. To his face, no one dared call him anything but Duchesne.

When a second yellow taxi pulled into the alley and parked some distance behind, Duchesne picked up an old companion, his 9-mm Walther. It was untraceable, and so was he. He climbed out and tucked the weapon into his crossed arms. He walked with a noticeable limp, his right foot toed in.

"Come along, Guignot," he called softly in French. "Don't waste my time." Paris's heat clung to him like an unwelcome woman.

The second man, Guignot, stepped out into the shadowy alley, his head turning nervously as he peered around. He hurried to Duchesne. *"Bonjour, monsieur."*

"Report."

Guignot worked to keep his voice professional. "I missed her at the airport. She queued up too quickly and got in front. I could not break into the taxi line with the police right there." He stopped abruptly, having caught sight of the weapon in Duchesne's arms. He stepped back. "Is that for me, Monsieur Duchesne?" His voice was breathless. His dirty fingers picked at the front of his denim shirt. *"Non, non.* Trevale said you were a hard man but honorable." He glanced back at his vehicle.

Duchesne knew the fellow was gauging the risk of running for it. "Honor can be expensive." He stared through his sunglasses. He had learned with the years to impress upon all new employees the seriousness of their work. "Can I afford you, Guignot?" He moved his hand, and the Walther abruptly pointed at the Frenchman's heart. "Can your wife and children?"

Guignot took a step backward, his face tight with alarm. "*Oui. Absolument.* On my mother's grave!"

"Where's the woman now?"

With shaky fingers, Guignot wiped sweat from his upper lip. "At her hotel. That's the good news. There was a terrible accident at the Hôpital Américain. What a snarl! But I watched and managed to reach her when she raised her hand. At the hotel, she told the doorman she was Sarah Walker. She's staying at the Hôtel Valhalla, near the rue de Buci, as you said she would."

Duchesne studied his new asset, who was shifting from one foot to the other, his gaze downcast. "*Bon,*" Duchesne decided at last. "I'll tell Trevale you're satisfactory, and I'll continue to require your services along with the others." He reached into his shirt pocket and handed over a fat roll of euros. "This will help with your debt to him."

Guignot's face spread in a brown-toothed grin. With an expert flick of his wrist, he undid the roll, fanned out the bills, and ran the tip of his little finger over them, his lips working as he toted them up.

Duchesne told him where they would meet next. "You know your assignment?"

Guignot was already heading back to his cab. "*Oui*. I will make another full report."

The Hôtel Valhalla was an unpretentious but comfortable Latin Quarter establishment, boasting upper-floor bay windows with views over the intersection of two cobbled streets. A centuries-old market was nearby, from which the aromas of country cheeses and freshly baked breads perfumed the air. People sat outdoors at small café tables, where they sipped *vin ordinaire* and watched the passing parade of women in swinging skirts and men in polo shirts and trousers.

At first, Liz had been reluctant to continue with Langley's plan for her. Every time she thought about the janitor outside the hospital, she was more convinced that Langley was soiled. Was the woman she had spotted there the Judas? Maybe even Mac? Perhaps someone had paid off the pilot, and he had relayed her flight information, and then the killer had followed her from de Gaulle. It could easily be someone higher up in Langley, or another of Mac's spotters or colleagues, someone about whom he had no suspicion.

The bottom line was, she could no longer trust Mac. Even if he were not the informer, someone close to him was.

She had decided to continue with her role anyway and check into the hotel. There might be some clue in the room, and she did not want to alert the mole to her suspicions.

At the front desk, there were no messages for Sarah or Asher. Liz picked up Sarah's key from the desk clerk and headed for the elevator. The room was on the fourth floor. She entered cautiously, but the place appeared undisturbed, as if Sarah and Asher had just stepped out. She found her suitcase sitting on the large bed — Mac had seen to that. A small room, a large bed. Very French.

As she looked around, she felt like an intruder; she did not belong here in the middle of someone else's love affair. For a few seconds, she allowed herself to think about Kirk, about herself, about his betrayal, about what sorts of intimate details he had told Themis. What a damn fool she had been.

Then she put it out of her mind. She had life-and-death problems to deal with now.

She searched the room thoroughly, from the laptop on the table to the clothes in the closet, as Mac had asked, but saw nothing that hinted at Sarah's kidnapping and Asher's shooting. Satisfied, she opened her own suitcase. Waiting on top was the Sig Sauer that Mac had tried to give her on the jet. It made her smile, because it was evidence — not necessarily proof — that he was not the mole. Otherwise, he would not go to such lengths to arm her. Still, despite what both Mac and Asher had said, she would not carry it.

Again she studied the room. This time her gaze settled on the wall heater. She hid the weapon behind its metal grille. The city steamed like a teakettle; no one was going to turn on the heat.

Steeling herself, she opened Sarah's purse and found her driver's license and passport. She adjusted the strap, lengthening it so she could use it as a shoulder bag, always more efficient. She did not want to carry her own, now that it was marked by a knife's slice. She went through the remaining items in Sarah's bag, noting the pen, pencil, makeup, comb, and wallet. She checked the wallet and returned everything to the bag and added her own wallet and lipstick.

Carrying the cell Mac had given her, Liz headed toward the window, flattened against the wall, where she could not be seen easily, and peered down four stories. The view was of one side of the lively intersection. She saw no sign of Mac. Still, she knew he was there somewhere, watching. It gave her a strange feeling to be protected. It had been a very long time. And yet she could not quite trust him.

She scrutinized the pedestrians, the people sitting out at the little sidewalk tables, the two women on a bench at the bus stop, the crowds standing at the intersection waiting for the light to change . . . and her gaze returned to the bench, because there was that woman from the hospital again, her Galeries Lafayette shopping bag at her feet. She was sturdy and plain, very well behaved in her red-brown lipstick. It looked as if Mac had a good agent there.

At last, Liz dialed her cell. It was time to confront Kirk and wring out of him everything he knew about Themis and why she had been watched. She had a strong hunch there was more to the story than Mac had related. Besides, Kirk might know something that would point to the mole. It was after six o'clock here, which meant it was past nine in the morning in California. Kirk taught no classes Wednesday mornings.

When his answering machine picked up, she hung up and phoned his office. Again, his machine answered, and she ended the connection. She considered. There was still Dean Quentin. She dialed again.

His secretary's voice shook; she sounded near hysteria. "He's . . . he's *dead,* Professor Sansborough. I can't believe it. *Murdered!* A burglar broke in and killed both him and Mrs. Quentin. She had lots of beautiful jewelry, you know, and that evil bastard took all of it. But why did he have to *kill* them, too?"

Liz's chest tightened. "Murdered? My God, Chelsea. Can you tell me what —"

Chelsea's voice was tentative. "You . . . haven't heard about Kirk, have you?"

She struggled to breathe. "Kirk?"

"I mean, you and he were close, so maybe —"

Liz steeled herself. "Tell me."

"It was a car accident. You know that beautiful Mustang of his? They found him in it at the bottom of a cliff near Summerland. He loved that car a lot, didn't he? Now it's like a coffin. Isn't that ghastly? People who went to the party said he'd been drinking a lot at the end, like he did sometimes. I guess no one's surprised he finally had a wreck. But on the same night as the dean and Mrs. Quentin were robbed and killed? It just makes it so much harder for everyone. We're pretty much a mess here. Will you be home

173

soon? Kirk's sister is flying in from Hawaii. Oh, it's all so *horrible*."

Liz closed her eyes. She had stopped listening halfway through Chelsea's lament. Both Kirk and the dean were dead. Dolores Quentin, too. She was an innocent, in the wrong place at the wrong time. But the two men had been working for Langley. There was no doubt in her mind that they had been deliberately eliminated. More dirty work from the people who had sent men to kill her.

"Professor Sansborough? Are you still there? Are you okay?"

Liz cleared her throat. "I haven't fainted or had a heart attack, but I am shocked. It seems impossible. Are the police sure it was an accident and a burglary gone bad?"

"Why?" There was an almost eager leap in Chelsea's voice. "You don't think —"

"I don't know what to think. All three of them on the same night?" They had pretended to be her friends, colleagues, all the while spying and reporting the details of her life. But at the same time, they had lived and breathed and laughed and felt pain, part of the human experiment as much as she was.

"It is . . . unbelievable, isn't it. Maybe —"

Liz sensed danger. Chelsea was impressionable, and the deaths were probably more disturbance and unfortunate excitement than anything she had experienced. It was not a good idea to stir up the Sheriff's Department to investigate more thoroughly.

At least not yet. "I suppose fate can't be explained," Liz said kindly. "It simply happens, doesn't it? Right now I'm numb and a bit confused. How about you?"

"Me, too," Chelsea said solemnly. "I feel the same way."

"I'll try to get back for the funerals. Let me know when they're scheduled, will you? Here's where I can be reached. If I don't answer, leave a message." She repeated her new number. "Please let Kirk's sister and the dean's family know I'm sorry."

"I will, Professor Sansborough. Thank you."

Liz pressed the off button and sank back against the wall and closed her eyes. A wave of fear swept through her. Her skin felt hot. Someone had not wanted her to question the two men. Kirk and the dean had paid the ultimate price for what they knew, what someone did not want her to find out. But killing them would not stop her.

More determined than ever, she put Santa Barbara from her mind and mulled what she should do first. Her mother was the one who would have been closest to the records. Still, if she would not reveal them to Liz, she certainly would have told no one else. . . . Except, perhaps, a brother. Yes, perhaps Mark Childs, who had died with Melanie. She could not imagine Melanie would have given up the files to anyone while alive. But in death . . .

That was when the files could have fallen into someone else's hands. Mark had lived in London, and as far as Liz knew, his ex-wife still did. Liz dialed information and asked for the phone number of Patricia ("Tish") Warren Childs. There was none. Surprised, Liz asked the operator to try again, but the response was the same.

She peeled away from the wall and turned on Sarah's laptop and did an Internet search. Still no phone number, but an address in London's East End. A bad address. Had Tish Childs's fortunes fallen so low?

The answer was that she would soon find out, but she needed a disguise so she could slip out of the hotel without Mac or the woman noticing. In her suitcase, she found a boxy brown pantsuit Mac had packed for her. It had been a mistake to buy; she had never liked it because it did not fit right. Now it was exactly what she needed, because it made her look shorter and heavier. She put it and a pair of Sarah's lace-up shoes on, removed her makeup, and added Sarah's large round computer glasses, which had plain lenses coated against screen glare. In Asher's things, she found a beret, which she pulled down over her short hair.

At the mirror, she rounded her shoulders and curved in her hips. With the glasses, beret, and square body shape, she looked like a timid schlump, unthreatening to anyone. But was it enough?

There was only one way to find out. She grabbed Sarah's shoulder bag, dropped the cell inside, and left, preparing herself psychologically to begin another movie.

From the hotel lobby, she slipped into the connected restaurant, which was quiet and unoccupied. Too late for lunch; too early for dinner. Her pulse pounded in her ears as she walked purposefully through to the kitchen and gazed out the round window in the door to the alley.

She did not like what she saw: A burly man was moving garbage cans, working with little enthusiasm. She studied him. He was either lazy or surveilling for someone . . . the Sûreté, the CIA, the kidnappers . . . the killers?

She did not want to leave by the front door. The woman on the bench would spot her. There was a garage under the hotel, and she could walk out of there. But if there were surveillance here, there would be surveillance there, and she saw nothing to be gained by delaying the inevitable.

Either her disguise worked or it did not.

She composed herself, shifted her jaw back to make it look smaller, went into her schlump posture, and cracked open the door. A timid mouse, she slid out. With her peripheral vision, she saw him pause, stare.

The hairs on the back of her neck seemed to stand on end as she waited for him to call, to chase, to shoot. . . . And then she heard a scrape behind her. She looked back. He was moving another garbage can across the cobblestones, his interest in her ended. The disguise had held. Silently she cheered, feeling more confident. This was a decent start to getting back her chops.

As she stepped from the alley, she turned away from the intersection, passing posters slathered against a wall. She did not pause, although one caught her eye. It announced the arrival of the Cirque des Astres — the French traveling circus she and her parents had used for cover years ago.

A flood of memories threatened to engulf her. She pushed them aside, saw a taxi, and rushed toward it.

"*Je voudrais de Gaulle, s'il vous plaît,*" she told the driver.

As she climbed in, she looked back carefully. There was no sign of the woman or of Mac. Still, she was uneasy. She settled at an angle against the seat as the taxi hurtled into traffic, watching for a tail.

Fourteen

Call to Brussels, Belgium

"This is Hyperion."

"At this early hour? Has something happened? Where are you?"

"En route to my château. I've an arrangement to discuss that would be advantageous to both of us, Cronus."

"You sound certain."

"Of course. It appears I may be able to tell you who the blackmailer is."

"Ah! You have my complete attention. Who?"

"Not yet, Cronus. But if things work out the way I expect, I'll pass along the name soon. There's a condition, though."

"And that is?"

"Utter secrecy. No one must know I'm the source. Are those terms agreeable?"

"Interesting. Are you being blackmailed, Hyperion?"

"That's beside the point."

"Is this blackmailer someone we both know?"

"I'm not going to discuss it. Do we have an understanding? . . . Cronus? Are you still there?"

"Yes, of course we have an understanding. Looking forward to your call. Be careful, Hyperion. The man with the files is a killer. But then, I don't have to tell you that, do I?"

London, England

Never a wealthy area anyway, London's East End had been backhanded by globalization. The economic readjustment that was decimating middle classes everywhere showed here in the worn buildings and shuttered shops. Liz hurried past five stores in a row that were boarded over. Nearby, men and women stood outside pubs, pints in hand, smoking cigarettes down to the filters. Cars cruised the streets, and people with tired faces ambled home.

Liz had felt as if she were being observed during her entire journey here, although she had been unable to spot any surveillance. In a bathroom in Heathrow, she altered her appearance so she would no longer look precisely like the woman who had left Paris. She still wore the trousers of the ugly brown pantsuit, but she had put the beret, the jacket, and Sarah's glasses into her shoulder bag. Her hair was combed, and she wore mascara and dark red lipstick. With her sleeveless top and normal posture, she would be easily recognized by Tish, despite the passage of years. But at the same time, she could quickly drop back into a deeper disguise if need be.

She covertly scanned the twilight street as she watched for the apartment building where Tish

Childs lived. A block later, she found it. The door was on the alley. With a final glance around, she climbed the staircase and knocked. The odors of rotting vegetables and fruit floated up from the greengrocer on the ground floor.

Tish cracked open the door, her face brightening with surprise. She was a tired-looking woman in her late fifties, with a jaunty red scarf around her throat and carefully applied black mascara.

"Well, come in then, Liz. Mustn't stand on the doorstep. A cup of tea? The kettle's on. Won't take half a sec. How did you find me, girl?"

She wore a threadbare dressing gown and slippers. She smoothed the gown and turned back into her room, walking carefully, but with the same pride Liz recalled. The bed was in the corner, and a sitting area was across from it. In between was a kitchen nook. There was no phone. Probably too expensive now.

Liz stepped in and closed the door. "I found your address on the Internet. How have you been, Aunt Tish?"

"Oh, my. The Internet? A world I'll never know. But *do* stop the 'aunt' nonsense. Makes me feel ever so old. I'm not really your aunt anymore anyway."

"Of course you are. Once an aunt, always an aunt."

"That's very sweet of you, dear. Mind sitting over there? It's clean at least."

The indicated sofa was lumpy and faded but neat. Liz sat and watched Tish turn up the gas under a teakettle. The low rays of the sun streamed in the single window. The room had grown cool, the only warmth radiating from the stove, where a large coffee can, both ends removed, holes punched in the sides, sat atop a lighted burner. It was not an efficient heater, but it was cheap: Britain's energy costs were astronomical again.

Liz talked about other things as the water boiled and Tish made tea.

"Only orange pekoe, I'm afraid," Tish told her, "but I'm rather fond of it."

Liz suspected it was her only tea — ordinary and cheap. "One of my favorites," she assured Tish. "Would you like some help?"

"Don't fuss, girl. I can manage."

Tish covered the teapot with a crocheted cozy. She set the pot, a small pitcher of milk, and two teacups onto a butler's tray and carried the tray to a wooden coffee table framed with piecrust molding. She moved stiffly, seeming to judge each step. Very erect, she sank into a tattered wingback chair and leaned forward to set the tray on the table. Hanging inside the back of her chair was an electric heating pad.

At last, Liz said, "Please forgive me for prying . . . but didn't you get alimony or some kind of financial settlement from Mark in the divorce?"

Tish hooted. She sat back against the heating pad, laughing, wiping her eyes. "Oh, that's rich, that is. Mark never had a spare farthing, love. Why d'you think we never had children? I was raising a child already. *Him!*" She reached to her side and pressed a switch. "Heating pad for my wonky back. Pour the tea, would you, dear?"

"Happy to."

The tea cozy had been elegant once, hand-crocheted with little tucks and ruffles, but it was shabby now. Liz poured milk into the cups and then tea through a strainer into the milk. The tea was thin, saving the cost of leaves. But the cups were real bone china decorated with delicate yellow roses, a classic pattern she had not seen in years.

Liz picked up her cup. "Mom never said anything like that about Uncle Mark. I mean, he was very charming. Handsome. I didn't realize —"

Tish's laughter had calmed into a knowing smile. She cradled her cup, as if warming her hands. "Of course he was. An appealing scamp. He worked ever so hard at it, didn't he just. The only thing he *did* work at. I was a twit of a girl, took me in properly. Oh, we had money much of the time, I admit, and I could be as big a spender as he. Looking back, Lord knows where it came from and where it went. He wouldn't tell, and after a few years I didn't want the answers. So I went back to work just to be sure I had a few shillings for food and a roof over my head." She gave a ne'er-do-well shrug Liz had seen Mark use. Her voice lowered. "Can't work anymore, though. Touch of arthritis in the spine. Nasty bit of luck."

"I'm sorry. I had no idea about your health problems. You should be getting help from the family." She gazed at Tish. What a terrible time she'd had. Liz would call her cousin, Sir Michael — Mick — the most recent Childs male to

183

inherit, and see that Tish got help. "Didn't anyone realize what Mark was like? I mean, surely Uncle Robert would've done something. I know Mother would've."

"Robbie did. After all, Mark was his baby brother. Robbie tried to get him jobs, but that's not what Mark wanted. He was after money, pure and simple. The cash for the main chance. So Robbie doled it out for years, until he got fed up, and I didn't blame him. He told Mark it was time to grow up, and that was the end of what I always called Robbie's guilt money. I expect no one else really knew how bad it was, not even Melanie. After all, Robbie was a good politico and could keep his mouth shut, and Mark was certainly not about to tell anyone." Her voice took on a bitter tinge.

"What do you mean about Sir Robert's 'guilt money'?" Liz asked.

Tish sipped tea and was silent. "I loved Mark, Liz. But as time passed, he got more and more sour that the baronetcy and fortune went to Robbie. It was the way things were and are, and Melanie and Blake understood that. They adjusted, made their own lives as daughters and younger sons have done for a thousand years. But for those same thousand years, many didn't adjust, and Mark was one. He could never get past the conviction that his birthright was to be landed gentry, without the need to work — like a common drudge, as he put it. So he drank, took beastly drugs, gambled, and played the charmer, as if he were always going to be eighteen and inherit the world." Her lips tightened.

"On the other hand, I think Robbie was ashamed he'd been given everything while the rest of the family got little. That's why he subsidized Mark, and it didn't help poor Mark one whit. The time came when I couldn't live with him anymore."

"That's such a sad story, Tish."

"Yes," she nodded, "it is. For Mark and for me." She seemed to brood for a moment, perhaps remembering the good times. Then she brightened. "Well, enough of that. One goes on, doesn't one? More tea, dear?"

"Thank you. I sometimes forget how good English tea is."

Liz poured Tish a fresh cup, then refilled her own. Liz put the cozy back on and reached for the milk. "I know you and Mark were divorced by the time he died, but did you ever talk to him before he went to see Mother in America about why he was visiting?"

Tish seemed astonished. She frowned as she stirred her tea. "Now that's odd. That you should ask, I mean."

"Why, Tish?"

"Well, someone else put the question to me. I recall it, because he was such a posh chap and seemed embarrassed to pry, as well he should have been. Can you imagine? A perfect stranger asking about family matters? I mean, Mark and I may have been divorced, but I still wouldn't discuss Childs family business. The very idea."

"He wasn't from the police?"

"Police? No, nothing like that. That might've been different, though he'd have had to give me a bloody good reason and show his credentials and all."

"Then you told this person nothing?"

"I should think not!" She gave a sly smile. "Well, not exactly. I said very firmly that of course Mark and I discussed it. He had only one sister, and it was high time he visited her, even if she was out of the country and plane tickets were a fortune. He asked a few more questions, of course, but that was my answer, and I stuck by it."

"When was this, Tish? Exactly. It's important."

Tish thought. "Well, five years ago, I should think. Yes, five or six months after Mark and your poor mother died and quite soon after poor Robbie. Such a terrible time for the family."

Almost the exact time Langley had called her back in for a second interrogation, this time about her father's files. "So Uncle Mark did talk to you about the trip?"

"As a matter of fact, yes. He was always ringing me up when he was in his cups and feeling sentimental. But this day, he showed up here, out of the blue. Sober as a deacon. Cleaned up nicely, shaved, handsome as the groom on the top of a wedding cake. Talking about a second chance. He'd slapped his boots on straight, he said. He'd soon be out of debt, and we could be together again." Her eyes misted. "He begged me. He said your mother was going to help, and it'd all be fine and dandy."

Liz set down her cup and leaned forward. "Mom was going to help? How?"

"I asked him. I can still remember how his eyes

gleamed. So revved up and hopeful. Said he couldn't talk about it yet, but he and Melanie had a deal that was going to make him rich. Something about 'Great Waters.' It was as good as wrapped up in a red silk ribbon, he said."

"He told you nothing else about this deal? Where Mom fitted in?"

Tish stared into her cup. "No, but he left what little he had to me. When he and Melanie died, I went through his papers and found the file. There were only notes and didn't make a whit of sense. I always thought Great Waters must be some kind of pot-of-gold resort. But even if Melanie had given him money, I couldn't see how it'd possibly be enough to buy an entire resort."

There was a file. Liz controlled her excitement. "What did you do with it?"

"Oh, it's still with his things. Can't turn out an old dog now, can I? Everything's in a lockup in Fulham. Lawrence Storage. Would you like to see them? That's nice of you, dear. Perhaps you'll find some things you want to keep. Little treasures, you know. I hate it that Mark's been forgotten. I'll give you the address and key."

Two hours later, night was in full swing in London's East End. Street lamps cast pools of light on the dirty pavement, while shiny Jaguars and Bentleys ferried drug lords. Girls, boys, and women stood on corners in tight wisps of clothes, hoping to feed their habits. Little attention was paid to a silent figure dressed in a black jumpsuit, who pulled open the alley door that led up to the

187

rooms above the greengrocer.

Once inside, he rolled a ski mask down over his face and walked soundlessly up the stairs, not hurrying. He tapped on Tish Childs's door. The instant he heard the dead bolt unlock, he rammed the door open with his shoulder.

"Where is she?"

He shoved Tish Childs back into the room and locked the door behind. The dark makeup around her eyes made her look like a cornered raccoon.

"I don't know what you're talking about."

Her voice was low and strangely controlled, not as frightened as the intruder had expected. He decided she had been questioned by other professionals over the years and was waiting to see how serious he was. He pulled out the stolen Walther and held it up. That got her attention. Her eyes turned into faded agates but remained hard.

"Liz Sansborough," he told her. "Where did she go?"

Rebellion flashed across her face. "Liz wasn't here," she said triumphantly.

He gave a cold chuckle. Of course she resisted. He had known she would, from the moment he saw that spark of mutiny and heard the triumph in her voice. He liked that. He beat her until, bloody and whimpering, she told him. It did not take long. With women, it rarely did. Not with ordinary men either, and most men were ordinary.

Finished, he screwed a sound suppressor onto the Walther and killed her with two shots — one through the belly and the other through the heart. He ransacked the room, left a dusting of cocaine near her corpse, and trotted downstairs and out into the alley, where he dropped the Walther into a Dumpster.

His people had sent the weapon all the way from Santa Barbara, from the glove compartment in Sansborough's car. The corpse and Sansborough's gun would be found as soon as he phoned a tip in to the police.

South of Brompton Road in Fulham, Lawrence Lockup & Storage was a large complex with walk-in lockers that rented by the month or year. Traffic on the major arteries nearby was heavy as Londoners returned to the suburbs after late meetings and shows, but this street of warehouses and light manufacturing was quiet and dark, black shadows impenetrable between the distant lampposts. In his rental car, Simon Childs cruised slowly, noting no lights showed inside the facility's office. It was a freestanding structure, while behind it stood a line of parallel buildings — the storage units.

He parked and got out. In the distance, tall stadium lights blazed, and young people shouted as they practiced soccer. The night smelled of dust and cooling asphalt.

When Simon had arrived in London, he met with the Childs family's solicitor and discovered he had handled Tish Childs's inheritance from Uncle Mark. There was little, just a few pounds and some belongings in a rented room. Tish had rented a locker, he had told Simon, where she ordered everything sent and apparently visited periodically. The attorney clearly disapproved. Why drain her little bit of money on useless things that had no value other than sentiment? Simon liked her for it.

The gate was locked; the facility closed. Given the late hour, this was not unexpected. He studied the wire mesh fence that surrounded it. About eight feet high, it was topped occasionally by closed-circuit cameras, which meant somewhere indoors was a security room with monitors and, with luck, a bloke who had been doing this so long he was bored and paying little attention to the unchanging views on the screens.

With a swift motion, Simon leaped up, grabbed the fence, scrambled over, and dropped into the complex. Immediately, he raced for the office building and pressed back against the wall, where he was out of range of the cameras. The concrete yard remained quiet, and no lights blazed on. After ten minutes, he headed quietly around to the back, passing a pickup truck that had the lockup's name painted on the side.

Tish Childs had rented G-3. "G" turned out to be the sixth line of buildings after "A," and "3" was the third locker in. The door was labeled clearly G-3, but the padlock was broken and hung open. No light showed around the door.

Simon drew his gun, yanked open the door, and jumped inside.

Before he had time to settle his balance and decide whether he had been unnecessarily cautious, he had his answer: A massive impact exploded inside his skull, and his gun fell from his hand.

Fifteen

Simon sprawled flat into cardboard boxes. Top-heavy, two toppled onto him. His head rang where he had been kicked, and his shoulder and chest ached where the boxes had landed. As he shoved them off, the glaring light of a flashlight blinded him.

"Who are you? Why are you here?"

It was a woman's voice, vaguely familiar. "I'm Mark Childs's nephew," he said indignantly. "Simon Childs. Who in bloody hell are you?"

Simon? What the devil was *he* doing here? Liz stared. Not that she recognized him easily. The last time they met, he had been a teenager. In the bright beam of her flashlight, she saw that the scrawny boy had grown into a man — but still lanky, still brown-haired. His face had filled out and was on the square side, with clenched jaws and one of those good chins people noticed. The best thing about him was his nose — it was misshapen, probably rearranged in some fight, which told her he might not have changed all that much. He was dressed in a tan sports jacket, an open-necked shirt, and blue chinos belted tightly over a flat waist.

She turned off her flashlight and switched on the overhead fluorescent bulb. "Get up, Simon," she said brusquely.

"Liz?"

He was already rising, staring, as she stood hands on hips, one holding his unaimed Beretta, the other the flashlight. Once he'd had a crush on her. He drank in the high cheekbones, the wide shoulders, the big breasts, the long legs. She was less beautiful than he recalled but far more tantalizing. Or was that simply the lingering effects of long-ago testosterone fantasies? The romantic notions of a boy in heat?

"My God, it's been years," he said.

Liz did not know this grown-up man. She *did* know he was MI6, and Mac had emphasized that Langley had brought in only the Sûreté, not the Brits. So what was Simon doing here? He would remember that she, Liz, had been CIA. Until she knew more about MI6's interest in Mark's affairs, she would have to play it close.

"Close, but no blue ribbon," she lied. "I'm not your cousin. I'm Sarah Walker."

He stared harder. "You're *Sarah?*"

"You think you'd have gotten off with just a kick in the head if I'd been Liz?"

"I heard you two looked alike." He stared longer, then dusted his jacket and trousers. His skull throbbed where her foot had connected. "I suppose you're right. With all that Langley training, she'd have jammed a gun into my carotid artery until I gave proper answers." But what had brought Sarah here? He asked casually, "Are you still married to . . . what was the chap's

192

name? Yes, Asher Flores. The CIA man."

"Don't get creative, Simon. You haven't answered my question. Why are you here?" As a boy, he had been fast on his feet, fast with his mouth, and fast into trouble.

He raised his brows. Not only did she look like Liz, she acted like the Liz he remembered. "I'd say that's my question, too, eh?" He glanced pointedly around at the clutter of old pictures, cartons, and stacks of memorabilia. A banker's box stuffed with file folders was open. He nodded at it. "Looking for anything in particular?"

"No," she said dryly. "I'm the tooth fairy, digging for molars and canines. Shall we play nicely, Simon? Logically, we're both here because of Mark Childs. I asked first, so if you set a good example and come clean, I will, too."

He studied Sarah. In the aftermath of the CIA mess in 1996, he had run a discreet probe, because Liz seemed to be involved. One thing led to another, a favor exchanged, a contact, two contacts, a cabinet left covertly unlocked, a computer code discovered . . . and he pieced together a lot of what had happened when Liz and Sarah had tried to bring in the Carnivore — Liz's father. Uncle Hal, as it turned out. A shocker.

What was important now was that Sarah had been with the Carnivore at the end. She might know something useful about the files.

"How can I refuse?" he said. "Perhaps we can help each other. Let's start with my gun." He put out his hand.

Hesitating, she looked into his eyes. They were

193

the same deep blue she remembered but more contemplative. His expression was somber. She handed the weapon to him, butt-first.

"Thanks." He holstered it. "Put simply, I'm looking for a connection between Mark and our mutual uncle, the Carnivore."

She did not allow herself to show surprise. "Why in heaven's name would MI6 care about the Carnivore? He's long dead."

"This has nothing to do with MI6."

"Are you off the clock, or are you AWOL?"

"Doesn't matter. This is private, and I'd appreciate your keeping it that way."

That sounded like Simon — fast into trouble. Still, he seemed as eager as she that word not leak. She fit the lid back onto the box of files she had just searched and sat on it.

"I'm game," she said. "Let's hear what's happened."

"I was in Bratislava yesterday on business — and no, I'm not going to tell you what it was." He sat on another carton. "Late that night, someone slipped me a note. It sent me to a cathedral, where a man met me. I never saw his face. He claimed my father was driven to suicide by a blackmailer."

"Was he?"

He thought about Terrill's confession. "From everything I've learned, yes."

"Poor Sir Robert." She had always liked him. He was one of those solid British types whose word was his bond, while at the same time he was jaunty, as if he secretly thought of himself as a long-ago pirate the Crown relied upon to steal fortunes in doubloons. The stories about his affairs had never been confirmed, and she long ago had decided to assume they were groundless rumors.

Simon described his father's hiring of the Carnivore to eliminate the Miller Street Killer. "A couple of decades later, someone tried to blackmail Dad about it." Simon told her about his trip to Zurich, where Terrill Leaming revealed that he, too, had hired the Carnivore and was being blackmailed.

Liz was silent. So that was why whoever had the files was protecting them — they were being used for blackmail. She remembered Terrill Leaming as one of Uncle Robert's friends from university, and she knew Claude de Darmond's name. There had been a de Darmond listed on the board of the Aylesworth Foundation — *Alexandre* de Darmond. The two were brothers. Theirs was a large banking family, a dynasty like the Rothschilds'.

Simon continued, "According to Terrill, Dad believed the blackmailer was working from the Carnivore's files. Terrill did, too, especially after he got a threatening e-mail that included what looked like a record of the job the Carnivore did for the bank."

"What did the blackmailer want from them?"

"A vote on trade from Dad. And he demanded Terrill take the fall for Baron de Darmond."

"The fact that he didn't ask for money is interesting. Instead, one was for something political, and the other was to clear up a crime."

"That's the way I see it. He seems to have

plenty of disposable income, certainly enough to hire janitors. In any case, my goal's simple. I want the bastard who provoked Dad into killing himself. One of the most direct routes to him is through the files."

"Why are you wasting time here? Talk to Baron de Darmond."

"Can't. He's on the road, traveling from Zurich to his estate north of Paris. No point twiddling my thumbs until he lands. So I followed another lead Terrill gave me." He recounted Terrill's story that Sir Robert suspected one of Melanie's brothers had stolen the files. "Since Uncle Blake died in that chopper crash in Bosnia, that left only Uncle Mark."

"So you want to find out whether Mark got the files, and if he did, what happened to them after he died."

"Right." Every time he looked at her, he felt unsettled. Those dark eyes, the extraordinary face. She even had the same melodic voice as Liz. "Your turn."

Could she trust him? Mac was adamant no one hear about the Carnivore's files or learn that the wife of a CIA operative had been kidnapped. At the same time, the files might be necessary to save Sarah. Fear for Sarah gripped her, but she pushed it quickly away. Simon already knew about the Carnivore's records, so that left only the kidnapping to be kept secret.

"I'm here for the same reason — the Carnivore's files," she told him. "I didn't ask what you were doing in Bratislava, so you can't ask why I want them."

He hesitated. "Fair enough."

She described her visit with Tish Childs. "According to Tish, Mark's last 'big deal' involved Melanie and some resort named Great Waters. She said he kept a file on it, so that's what I've been looking for. I've checked these." She tapped the banker's box on which she sat and indicated five others. "What say we look together?"

"I thought you'd never ask."

There were at least twenty file boxes amid the jumble. He rose and opened the one on which he had sat. It was packed with dusty file folders. He thumbed the tabs, reading carefully for any reference to resorts or spas, specifically Great Waters. Nearby, Liz opened another box. She searched through it, too, stopping to check inside several folders. They finished almost simultaneously and moved to new boxes.

"Despite his being such a washout," she ruminated, "Mark's records are amazingly tidy. What's odd is that some of these folders date all the way back to the 1970s, even though they're empty. Pristine. It's as if he stuck on labels because he was hopeful, but when nothing came of a deal, he still couldn't throw out the file. That certainly fits Tish's description of him as an unrealistic dreamer."

"I'm finding the same thing. Encourages me he kept something that'll help us." As he worked, he remembered, "Speaking of searching files, did you notice the FBI's named its killer wiretap program 'Carnivore'?"

"I read about it. It's probably just a coincidence."

"I couldn't help but wonder whether it was a tip of the hat to dear Uncle Hal."

She smiled. "Anything's possible. Why don't you phone some of your chums at the Bureau and ask?"

"Right. I'll do that."

"Sure."

They exchanged grins and resumed their search. An hour passed. The storage locker grew stuffy. Liz's back began to ache from the cramped position.

They were well into the second hour when suddenly Simon shouted, "Great Waters!" He whipped a folder from his box. "Here it is!"

She was at his side in a heartbeat, crouching as he opened the file, her weariness gone. Inside were lined pages from notebooks, typing paper, even a napkin — each listing a time and a date and sometimes a place for what must have been meetings.

They read through the notes quickly, but there was nothing about the deal itself.

"At least they're in chronological order," she noted, discouraged.

He pulled up the last piece of paper.

> Meet Great Waters
> Thursday next with goods.
> Payment 1 mil sterling.

She took the scrap of paper. There was no date and no signature. "What 'goods' does he mean?"

she wondered. "The Carnivore's files? They could be worth at least a million pounds to the right person."

He looked away, his gaze unfocused. " 'Meet Great Waters.' " He shook his head. "Meet *at* Great Waters?"

"Which takes us right back to what in hell *is* Great Waters? *Where* is it? I've never heard of it, have you?"

He shook his head. They stared at the note.

She frowned and free-associated: "Maybe he really did mean to meet Great Waters. Maybe it's a person or an animal or a character in a play or a code name —"

"That's it!" Simon stood up, pulled out his cell, and punched buttons.

"Who are you calling?"

He pressed a finger to his lips and spoke into the cell, "Hey, Barry, old boy —"

Before he could say more, the voice on the other end of the line growled, "What is it with you, Simon? Your boss wants your gonads for her fish tank!"

Simon was surprised. "Care to enlighten me?"

"Why aren't you in Florence, where you're bloody well scheduled to be? You're sure as hell not supposed to be calling HQ. Where *are* you?"

Ada's safe house. Dammit. He had forgotten. "It's a small miscommunication. I'm on the job, and I need information."

"Wrong. I'd say you need to call Ada with your excuses, lame as they may be."

"Sorry, Barry. Didn't mean to cause aggravation. I'll head for Florence tonight," he lied. "Before I go, I have one small loose end to tidy up. Do you or Scotland Yard have any gangsters in the data bank named Great Waters?"

Without another word, Barry Blackstein put Simon on hold.

Liz stood up, her expression questioning.

"I'm on hold," Simon explained. Dammit, something about her made him feel nine years old again. "What?"

"You're in trouble, aren't you," she said. A statement, not a question.

"I see you're a journalist, right enough," he said. "I can tell by your nosiness."

"And the accuracy of my deductions. You're supposed to be in Florence. Are you really going tonight? You haven't changed much after all, Simon."

"Florence is a little vacation I don't want to take. It seems rather crucial to discover whether my father's suicide was provoked."

He had her there. Reluctantly, she nodded. "You're right. Sorry."

He held up a hand and whispered, "Apology accepted. Hold on."

Barry was talking in Simon's ear: "Great Waters is the nickname of a London hood named Gregory Waterson. That's straight from Scotland Yard gang control. Waterson was murdered in June 1997."

Simon shot a look at Liz and said to Barry, "So Great Waters was a hood. The name had the sound of it. Murdered? In June 1997?"

Liz went rigid. The same month and year her mother and Uncle Mark had died.

Barry continued. "He owned a gambling club and was into prostitution, outside betting, extortion, whatever he could find. He was a small-timer, but ambitious. His turf was taken over by Donny Mester. Word is Mester killed him for it, thereby doubling his own territory. My question is, Why should this interest a penetration agent such as yourself?"

"Now you're getting the point," Simon said with sincerity. "That's what I'm trying to ferret out."

"What possible good will gang wars here do you there? Oh, no. Simon, no. You're not in London, are you? Ada will be apoplectic. You're supposed to keep your head down and fingers clean. I'm going to have to report this —"

Simon sighed. "Come on, Barry. I may be a tad incomprehensible at times, but I'm not the queen's fool. Of course I'm nowhere near England. The British Isles are safe. Soon you'll have to worry about what I'll do to Italy. But first, my contact needs to find out what happened between Donny Mester and Great Waters. Then he'll tell me what I want to know to do *my* job. Does Mester have a rival I can send the chap to?"

There was a sigh of exasperation. "All right, your contact should probably chat up Jimmy Unak. He was a close pal of Great Waters. But when Donny Mester took over, Jimmy prudently switched loyalties to Mester. Now the street is saying Mester thinks Jimmy is plotting a coup d'état. In return, word is that Mester's scheming to kill Jimmy before he can pull it off. Business as usual on the left side of the law." He relayed the

201

address of the gangster's club, threw in a few more details, and hung up with a final warning: "Get your arse to Florence!"

As soon as Simon touched his cell's off button, Liz said, "The gas explosion and fire that killed Melanie and Mark was in June 1997."

"I'd guessed that. Nasty business." He told her what Barry had said. "I'd say a visit to Jimmy Unak is in order."

"I agree. Let's go." She headed toward the door. "Turn off the light, will you?" She pressed her ear against the door, listening.

Simon cut the light and stood behind her. Her hair smelled nice. She pushed outside. He followed and closed the door while she sped toward the office building. He loped after, enjoying the view. She slid to the left of the structure.

Scanning for a janitor or security guard, he caught up with her. "How'd you get in?" he whispered.

"Over the front fence. How about you?"

"Same way."

As they hurried around toward it, he surveyed the facility, concerned about this open area, where the high cameras could record them. The second they reached the gate, he punched the electric lock, which had been impossible to reach from outside.

As the tall gate creaked inward, Liz glanced back at the office and saw a silhouette move across on the other side of the blind.

"Hurry!" she whispered.

Simon gave the gate a pull. It resisted, still moving slowly. Spotlights flashed on from the office's roofline, illuminating the concrete drive, where they were trapped in bright light. Simon cursed.

Liz turned sideways, slid through the opening, and almost immediately slipped back, pushing the gate shut.

Her voice was tight. "We've got a visitor. Dressed all in black. He was getting out of a black SUV — no interior lights showing. Looks as if he's carrying a silenced pistol."

"Did he see you?"

"Of course not. And yes, I got the license plate number. No one followed me here. There was a woman in Paris who might have been surveilling me, but I lost her there. He must've followed you."

"Don't see how he could've. Let's lose him fast."

As they tore away from the gate, a security guard stepped out of the office and yelled, "You'd better get out of here! I've called the police!" He wore a drab gray shirt and matching trousers, the name of the storage facility emblazoned on his shoulders and the front of his flat-topped guard's cap. He was unarmed and had a pendulous belly and a resolute face. Hardly terrifying, even to the under-twelve crowd.

Simon whispered, "Keep me covered. I'm going to requisition that uniform."

He pulled out his gun and ran straight at the man, who made a frightened sound in his throat and turned. Simon was on him instantly, pushing him inside at gunpoint.

Liz sprinted past and along a hall, where doors

opened onto dark offices and through a doorway where light showed. It was the security office; monitors lined one wall. She threw herself into the chair in front of the console and studied the control panel, locating the switches for the closed-circuit cameras that recorded the front entrance. She pressed all buttons marked ERASE.

When she emerged, Simon had blindfolded the guard, who was now in his undershirt and trousers and tied to a secretary's swivel chair. Simon wore the man's cap and was buttoning the oversize shirt over his own. With the guard's keys in one hand, Simon grabbed his sports jacket with the other.

He hurried toward the side door. "This way." Without checking whether she followed, he pulled it open. If he remembered correctly . . . yes, there was the facility's pickup.

Understanding immediately, she ran out into the night after him. They must move fast, before the intruder climbed the fence. "I'll get the gate." She dashed off.

Simon jumped behind the steering wheel, turned on the engine, hit the accelerator, and spun the truck around, heading toward the front.

Liz smacked the big gate's electric opener and stepped to the left, so she would be on the passenger side. She could hear no noise on the other side of the fence; the approaching pickup's engine was drowning out everything. As soon as Simon slowed the vehicle, she leaped in beside him and dropped to the floor.

"Good show." He did not look down. "Gate's wide open now, so here we go." He drove out sedately, looking official in his guard's shirt and cap. "Which direction is the SUV?"

"Right," she told him from the floor.

He turned left.

"Do you see him?" she asked.

He checked his mirrors and gave a slow smile that widened his jaw and made his smooth cheeks rise toward his eyes, making him look particularly young and carefree, just the way he often had been. He gave a deep chuckle.

"What's funny?"

"The guy just slid in through the gate, looking appropriately sneaky. He's got a ski mask pulled down over his face. Probably congratulating himself for being so quick-witted, he didn't have to crawl the fence. We'll double back and pick up my rental car. He's busy enough to give us no trouble."

Liz climbed onto the seat. "For now."

Sixteen

Well after midnight, the streets of London's lively Soho district radiated a boisterous carnival atmosphere. Cigar smoke and music flooded from the open doors of pubs and clubs while the young drank and danced and smoked and sniffed. Gangs of girls sat at outdoor café tables, gossiping and ogling boys. The summer night was garish with streetlights and illuminated signs, and the sidewalks were jammed as always.

Inside Simon's car, the radio droned about the meeting of G8 leaders who would be in Glasgow next week for high-level talks and global photo ops. As he and Liz cruised along, looking for a parking place, the news items changed.

When Liz heard the name Tish Childs, she turned up the volume. ". . . found dead of a gunshot wound in her East End flat," the announcer said, "with traces of cocaine beside her. She was beaten badly before death."

"Oh, my God! *Tish!*" She leaned closer, listening.

". . . and a Walther with a sound suppressor was located in a trash bin in the alley below her flat. It's being tested to determine whether it's the murder weapon. One witness reported seeing a tall woman with short auburn hair visit Mrs. Childs tonight. Another witness described a suspicious-looking man in a black jumpsuit, wearing a black cap pulled so low his face was hidden. . . ."

"Damn!" Simon exploded between clenched teeth. "Mark gave her a crappy time, and now this."

Liz's heart pounded. "It's horrible." The person with the files had ordered Tish killed, too. Just as he had tried to kill her twice in Santa Barbara and then outside the hospital in Paris and at the storage locker tonight. She looked out at the busy street, and for a moment it seemed as if behind every car window a janitor lurked. Poor Tish. She had deserved so much more from life.

"You think all of this is about the Carnivore's files?"

"What else?" She watched the traffic as if she could find answers in it. "The first witness described me, but the second described the gunman who came after us at the storage locker. Which means he didn't follow you or me. Instead, he beat Tish into telling him where I'd gone. Monster!"

"So he went to Tish's looking for you. How did he know you'd be there?"

"I wish I could figure it out." Her mouth was dry. Although she had sensed surveillance, she had seen none. Her skills must be far weaker than she thought.

"Fill me in," he urged. "Maybe it'll make sense to me."

She looked at him sharply "Are you ready to tell me what you were doing in Bratislava?"

"I can't."

"I can't tell you any more either."

They exchanged a look. As he gazed away, he said, "Now the police are after you, too. We'd better count on their description being a lot more detailed than the radio broadcaster had time to relate."

Liz lapsed into silence, thinking about Sarah. Trying to imagine where she could be, trying not to worry about how she was, what they had done to her, how afraid she must be. Trying to get her mind off the people who had already been killed. She would do no one any good if she allowed herself to dwell. All were victims, even her. But this victim had teeth.

Simon found a parking spot on a narrow street, cut the engine, pulled a black gym bag from the backseat, and sorted through an array of identifications.

"Are any of those IDs real?" she asked.

"Hope not."

"Private or MI6?"

"Bit of both." He found his cell and dialed. "Give me Michele Warneck. That's right. Simon Childs calling." As he waited, his fingers drummed the steering wheel. "Michele? Yes, the same. As usual. Right, and thanks." He punched off.

"What was that all about?"

"A precaution. Shouldn't be giving away

Whitehall's secrets, now should I? Let's see whether we can learn something useful from Jimmy Unak."

Jimmy Unak's headquarters was a nightclub called the Velvet Menagerie. The large neon sign was small and tasteful for Soho. The doorman had a heavyweight wrestler's build and wore an expensive black silk sports jacket. Two gold pegs pierced the skin between his nostrils, and a single black braid hung down his back. From the way he moved his shoulders, Liz judged he had a gun in a harness in his armpit.

Simon flashed his fake ID, and the doorman grunted ominously, which evidently was permission to enter. Inside, old-fashioned disco lights flashed vertigo-inducing colors across the enormous dance floor, where couples gyrated to the ear bleeding sounds of Split Lip. The banner that hung from the ceiling proclaimed the band to be the hottest act on the city's club scene. Despite being long past midnight, the air was ripe not only with sweat and alcohol but with enthusiasm.

"My turn," Liz told Simon.

Before he could object, she shouldered through to the bar and crooked her finger. Optimism in his eyes, the bartender arrived at the same moment as Simon. He glanced at Simon but settled on her. She gave him her best smile and inquired over the din where she could find Mr. Unak. He directed her to a carved door guarded by an unobtrusive man in a dinner jacket.

When he left to help a real customer, Liz noted the protrusion at the small of his back, under his white apron. She turned, saw Simon's line of sight, the grim set of his mouth. He had seen the gun, too. They circumnavigated the dance floor, heading toward the dapper guard at Jimmy Unak's door. He would be armed, too.

She spoke into Simon's ear: "If you go into Unak's office, they're sure to search you." He was still carrying his Beretta.

"Don't believe so."

"You're not going to do me any good in the hospital or dead."

"Have faith. It's handled."

"You worry me, Simon. This isn't a lark."

He sighed. "That's what my boss says. Trust me, I know what I'm doing."

"I can do this alone, you know."

"No, you can't, Sarah. With luck, they wouldn't hurt you, but you'd get nothing. Just keep quiet and follow my lead. This is my territory. Liz would understand."

She frowned. She would let him lead but keep a sharp eye on him, too.

At Unak's door, Simon flashed his ID to the meticulously dressed sentry. "Inspector Scott Anderson. Here to see Jimmy Unak."

The man caught Simon's wrist in midair and studied the ID carefully. He cocked an eyebrow. "Manchester? A long way from home, aren't we, Inspector?"

"By God, you can read. Now, if you don't mind?" Simon jerked his wrist free and glared.

With the flat eyes of a great white shark, the gangster returned the glare, lowered his chin, and spoke into a lapel microphone. A small receiver showed inside his ear.

After a moment, the eyes flickered. The sentry opened the door, touched his forehead with thumb and forefinger as if humbly pulling a lock of hair, and announced in a low, mocking voice, "Second door to the left, guv'nor."

Liz felt her adrenaline rise at the sneer in the man's voice. She had to admit Simon's control was impressive. The door closed with a solid *thunk,* like the closing of a vault, and the music and noise vanished as if cut off by a knife. State-of-the-art soundproofing, and Liz guessed the door and corridor would be bulletproof as well. Waiting for them was another guard, this one heavily muscled. He led them down a well-lit corridor.

He knocked on Unak's door once and opened it.

Jimmy Unak was standing behind a long desk that could have belonged to the CEO of any blue-chip corporation. Small, tastefully framed Impressionist paintings that could be originals hung on the walnut-paneled walls. Unak was a huge mound of a man, but his elegant tuxedo fitted so well he appeared only mildly overweight. He used his remote to turn off a political debate on BBC Television, eased down into an enormous desk chair, and waved Simon and Liz to a pair of fine leather side chairs.

As they sat, the muscular guard took up a post against the door. Behind Unak, another man sat in a simple straight chair tilted back against the wall.

Unak scowled. "Manchester, is it? What could

Manchester CID want with me, Inspector — what was the name?"

Liz saw a tight wariness in Unak's face. Perhaps because of what MI6 had passed on — that Unak's rival, Donny Mester, had put a contract out on him.

"Anderson," Simon said pleasantly but as if speaking to a child. "Inspector Scott Anderson."

Unak gave a small nod. The guard at the door opened it and left. He would check with London's Scotland Yard, where a Manchester CID inspector would have made his arrival in town known. Liz realized now that was why Simon had phoned one Michele Warneck. Warneck would cover him at the Yard.

"Never did have a head for names." Unak laughed. A cold laugh, yet hinting at nerves. "So, what brings you here, Inspector? I ain't been north for years."

"We need a chat about some news we recently turned up," Simon said, crossing his legs, sitting back at his ease, but keeping his gaze firmly on Unak. "Might be better if we spoke in private. Doubt you'll want this to go beyond you and the two of us." He never looked at the bodyguard tilted against the wall.

Neither did Jimmy Unak. Instead, he turned a tight smile onto Liz. "Who might the lady be, Inspector?"

"Detective Phyllis Roan," she told him, making her voice flat and cold.

Unak gave her a slow look of sexual approval. "Might be I should get up Lancashire way more often, luv."

Liz curled a lip in disgust, playing out her role as the contemptuous CID detective from the tough north.

Unak picked up a letter opener and cleaned his fingernails. "Nothing my old pal Packy can't hear, Inspector." He gestured at the bodyguard, whose name was obviously Packy. "So then, what's this 'news' you think I'd want to talk about?"

"Your former friend, the deceased Gregory Waterson, and your competitor, Donny Mester."

The scowl returned. "Don't quite fancy talking about the past. Nothing to be done about what's over, is there? No point nattering on about it."

"Unfortunately, Jimmy, we *do* want to talk about it, and we *are* going to talk about it."

Unak's eyes flashed, and he rose behind his desk, the *Titanic* cresting a mountainous wave. "Unless the pair of you brought an arrest warrant, Anderson, I really don't give pigeon shit for what you want, do I now?"

"*Inspector* to you," Simon snapped, the superciliousness still in his tone. He did not move from his chair. "And actually, you do care what I want. You see, we have the complete description of a chap who's been sent to kill you."

The gangster's expression did not change, although for an instant alarm replaced the anger in his eyes. "Who might that be?"

"First we discuss what we want from you. Call it a trade."

"A trade? What bloody trade?"

"A deal, Jimmy, as they say in America. Quid pro quo. You do know what that means, don't

213

you? An important man like you."

Liz tensed. Simon had been doing well, but now she worried. The most powerful psychological cause of violent behavior was the feeling of being shamed, humiliated, insulted, slighted, rejected — any of which could convey the ultimate provocation: The other person was inferior, a nobody, insignificant.

Simon was deliberately provoking Unak. There was a thin line between a gangster not wanting trouble with powerful Scotland Yard, and a venomous and volatile man, probably with an inferiority complex, who could easily act irrationally and against his own interests. The danger was palpable.

Unak's face turned red. "I know what the fuck it means, copper, and I don't give a piss about your goddamn trade!"

The bodyguard, Packy, let the front two legs of his chair slam to the floor as his right hand reached inside his tuxedo jacket. Liz shifted, ready to act or dive. Only Simon remained unperturbed, as a CID inspector should.

"A trade," Simon repeated. "Figured you'd like to know who your executioner will be."

Unak blinked. With a dismissive wave of his big hand to Packy, the tension broke. "What's the bloke's bloody name? I'll kill the bastard myself!" He had focused on what was critical — his life.

Simon shook his head gently, as if chiding the big man. Liz forced herself to breathe normally, maintaining a stony expression. England was a different country, a different world, from the States. The police-criminal balance here was weighted far more toward the authorities. Simon had been playing good cop/bad cop all by himself — angering the gangster to the edge of doing something he would regret, then offering a trade that was not only no threat but a relief.

Simon said, "Remember that trade? It involves a couple of questions about Mark Childs."

When he heard the name, Jimmy Unak nearly smiled. He snapped his fingers at his silent bodyguard. "Give us five, Packy."

Without a word, Packy glided to the door. It closed softly behind, like a whisper.

The gangster settled back into his chair, visibly relieved. "What about Childs?"

"We've been told Donny Mester killed Gregory Waterson," Simon said. "What interests us is that everyone thinks the reason was to take over Waterson's territory. We believe there's a good deal more to it than that, and that it involved Mark Childs."

Jimmy Unak's big head gave a single nod. "You could be right. Now, you hand me the name of the bastard who's planning to off me, and I'll fill you in about that sucker Mark Childs. With pleasure."

"I don't have a name, but I can give you his description, where he was last seen, his license plate number, and details about his SUV, which is surely stolen."

Liz realized what Simon was going to do a split second before he described the gunman who had killed Tish and traced her to the Fulham storage locker. Jimmy Unak carefully printed what Simon told him on a piece of paper. Then he sat back and favored them with an almost paternal gaze.

"Right, then." Unak got to business. "What happened was, Greg ordered Childs wiped, because he controlled a Zip disc supposedly worth at least a million quid. That was one right bigger chunk than Greg's whole damn business was worth."

Liz's pulse raced. The Carnivore's files were on a Zip disc! And the confirmation was Mark's note at the storage locker: *Payment one mil sterling.*

"This was in the United States?" Simon said.

"Sure. Like I said."

Liz asked, "Did Waterson kill Childs's sister, Melanie Sansborough, too?"

Unak glanced at her. He shrugged. "Had to. She spotted him."

She bit back rage. Her mother. The bastard had killed her mother!

Simon was already talking. "Tell us just how he did the job, Jimmy." His words implied that he, Simon, already knew, so Unak had better get it right.

"Blew up a gas line and made it look like an accident."

"And he took the disc?"

"That's what he claimed. But then that pisser Mester killed him for it and turned around and sold it for the whole bag himself." He swore loudly.

Liz fought to control her emotions. Her mother had had the disc, and somehow Mark found out about it. She remembered Tish's words: *He said your mother was going to help, and it'd all be fine and dandy.* It was another of Mark's wishful lies. Liz could see a violent argument between Melanie and her brother. Melanie would not give up the disc, while a desperate Mark would do anything to change her mind — even bring along his new friend, Great Waters, to "convince" her.

And Great Waters had killed her. Melanie, with her delicate features and large smile and the bad past she was trying to rise above, had finally lost her life, not in the dangerous work of an international assassin, but in her safe new home in Virginia, while her adored younger brother was visiting.

Liz breathed shallowly as she tried to keep her face impassive.

"Do you know what was on the disc?" Simon asked. "Who bought it?"

"Don't know who put up the bundle, but Greg said there was nothing but a bunch of files with names, dates, and like that on it. He had to hire a hacker to crack into it. Worthless, if you asked Greg." The gangster leaned to an intercom on his desk and bellowed, "Packy, get back here now." He looked at them. "Best you split, right? I got a black SUV and a hit man to find, and you don't want to know nothing more."

Simon stood. "It's been a pleasant visit, but I suggest you don't return it, eh? I doubt you'd prosper in the north."

With that final warning to stay away from Manchester, they left as the guard reentered. Lost in thought, Simon passed him as if he were invisible, nonexistent. As they skirted the noisy chaos of the dance floor, Liz could feel eyes watching.

Outdoors, Simon stuck his hands deep into his trouser pockets as they hurried along the sidewalk. He glanced up at the stars.

"Now we know," he said gloomily.

She nodded. Her voice was brittle. "The files exist. And Liz's mother was murdered for them."

Side by side, they continued silently on, while the clamor and excitement of the vibrant global city swirled around them. Liz watched everywhere, uneasy, her gaze never at rest.

Seventeen

Call from Brussels, Belgium

"*Has Sansborough found the files?*"

"*Not yet, Cronus.*"

"*Was she attacked again?*"

"*In a manner of speaking.*"

"*Tell me everything.*"

"*First she went to see a woman named Tish Childs.*"

"*I remember her — Mark Childs's ex-wife. We tried to get information from her five years ago, when this filthy business with the files erupted. She was ignorant as a stump. Did Sansborough do any better?*"

"*Yes. Sansborough got a lead that sent her to a lockup in Fulham. Simon Childs showed up there, too. He's her cousin, but you must know that.*"

"*He's also MI6! We don't want bloody MI6 to get the files!*"

"*He claims it's a private matter. Personal, because the blackmailer provoked his father's suicide. From the lockup, they followed the lead to a nightclub in Soho. They learned there that a local gangster took the files from Melanie Childs and her brother Mark*"

219

and killed them. Then the gangster turned around and sold the files for a million pounds to some unnamed individual. Since the price was so high, and there was no problem associated with the payment, I think we can assume the buyer is wealthy and wanted them for his own purposes."

"The first round of blackmailing began shortly after that. Why didn't we find this out then? I sent your predecessor to interview Tish Childs."

"She said someone had visited her and asked about Mark. But she told Sansborough she never revealed family business to anyone under any circumstances. She'd been knocked about enough that she was tough about such things."

"Was tough?"

"She's dead, murdered. Probably within two hours of your conference call to alert everyone to what Sansborough was doing."

"The blackmailer sent a janitor to the address in the East End to find Sansborough?"

"Yes, Cronus. The address I told you that Sansborough gave her cabdriver. The janitor beat Mark Childs's ex-wife to find out where Sansborough was going next, then he killed her."

"The trap worked. Hell and damnation! It is one of my people!"

London, England

In the bleak hours before dawn, Simon drove Liz quickly away from the Velvet Menagerie nightclub. They watched for police as he turned the car southeast, in the direction of

Waterloo Station. Both were returning to Paris, where Simon would look into Baron Claude de Darmond.

"What about you?" he asked. "What will you do there?"

"Go to my hotel and take stock," Liz told him.

Not exactly true. Her cell had not rung, and there were no messages from Mac, which meant the situation with Sarah and Asher was stable and he did not have the lab report on the contents of the syringe yet.

She said, "I'd like to know what you find out from the baron."

"Sure, as long as it's about the Carnivore's files. That is, if you'll reciprocate."

"Done."

After they exchanged cell numbers, she phoned ahead to reserve tickets on the Eurostar. The first available seats were on the 7:40 a.m. train, arriving at the Gare du Nord at 11:47.

She put away her cell. "Do you think Unak's people will find Tish's killer?"

"On his pitch? Bet on it."

She thought about Simon's "trade" with the gangster and felt an odd uneasiness, a certain confusion. The killer had brutalized and murdered Tish Childs and then driven to the lockup, no doubt intending to kill her, too. But now the killer was as good as dead, and one threat to her was erased. Simon had cleverly set him up, but that did not take away from the fact that what Simon had done was vigilantism.

She considered Simon, who was surveilling as he drove. In profile, his chin jutted forward, and his mouth was full and tense. He had a taut and angry look, and all at once he no longer seemed young and callow. His work in the nightclub had been solid. However, it was difficult to get past the sense that he was too impetuous, which made him a risk not only to himself but to her and to Sarah. She wondered how much of that was prejudiced by her memory of his reckless childhood.

"We're here." There was relief in his voice.

She stared up at Waterloo's landmark station, looming like a phantom against the stars, as he drove around and down into the garage beneath the international terminal. The subterranean building was like a sarcophagus — a drab, reinforced-concrete box that was a foundation over Underground train lines as well as a support for the rail structures over their heads.

Simon found a remote corner and turned off the motor. They checked their watches. They had a little more than four hours until their train left for Paris.

"No one knows this car, right?" she asked.

"Right," he echoed. Weariness showed in the circles under his eyes. "We should be safe for a while. Do you want to sleep first, or take the first watch?"

"You sleep. I'm too wired." She scanned the silent cars, peered into the shadows.

He nodded, reclined his seat, adjusted his shoulders, and was snoring within seconds. She continued to stare out into the garage as a car drove off somewhere, thinking about the busy international station upstairs, planning what to do if police or janitors were waiting.

In the business, he was called Friar, and he worked alone. His reputation was solid in the shadowy circles where it counted. Sitting in his stolen SUV outside the storage lockup, he reported on his cell to the confident male voice that had hired him through intermediaries.

Friar maintained his iron control, although he was furious. He had failed, and it was his employer's fault. "The Walther arrived at Heathrow too late for me to catch her at the flat. When I got there, the Childs woman was difficult. I lost even more time."

"You followed the backup plan?" The voice was coarse and whispery, obviously using some sort of disguise mechanism, but it did not hide the tone of superiority.

"Of course. I killed Tish Childs and planted the cocaine and the weapon."

"Then there'll be police pressure. I'll find out where she is. If she's still in London, I'll contact you to finish the job. Your pay will be waiting at the post office." He hung up.

Don't do me any favors. Disgusted, Friar started the SUV and slid it into gear, thinking of a good pint and a ham sandwich. But he had driven less than a block when he spotted a truck ahead, slewed sideways across the deserted road. He slowed. Barely visible to most people, but clear as day to Friar, two men hid in its shadow. A side street entered conveniently on his right. Too conveniently. An ambush.

Friar felt an excited thrill. This was more like

it. He hit the SUV's brake, threw the gear into reverse, floored the accelerator, and yanked the steering wheel left. As the vehicle skidded to his commands, he swerved it up onto the sidewalk, seized his Mauser, and excitedly reached to open his door.

A silenced bullet shattered the passenger-side window. For a fraction of an instant, he heard the noise, like the crack of a whip. And then nothing. The bullet arrowed through his brain, exited through his ear, and burst out the driver's window. He pitched out, dead before his head struck the concrete.

The bouncer walked around the SUV. A black braid hung down his back, and two gold pegs pierced the skin between his nostrils. With his heavyweight wrestler's build and black silk sports jacket, he would appear out of place to any observer, even if he had not just committed murder. But only his own men had seen him, and his target was dead. He holstered his pistol. In minutes, he would be back on the door of the Velvet Menagerie.

Liz was sleeping uneasily. When she awoke, her limbs were heavy as lead, and she felt disoriented. She did not open her eyes. Instead, she noted the quiet of the subterranean garage, the distant scent of petrol, the firm car seat that supported her.

At last, she slitted open her eyes. Simon was staring at her. She remained motionless, as if still sleeping. His blue eyes were dark with intensity, and his arms were crossed, his Beretta showing in

224

his right hand, while his left hand was hidden in the crook of his elbow. He looked away to give the garage an alert scan.

From his fluid movements to his smooth good looks, there was an artlessness about him that she enjoyed, a contagious sense of life as an adventure. Women's gazes had followed him wherever they were. It was not just that he was handsome in a different sort of way, it was the aura he carried. A little predatory, very confident. He was the kind of man who had an easy time with women.

At first, she was curious and slightly amused that he was studying her as she slept. But now, as he focused again, his fierceness unsettled her.

She opened her eyes, blinking as if just awakening. "Any trouble?"

He looked away. "None. A security patrol passed through twice, but they didn't bother with our corner. How are you feeling?"

"Better. It must be time to get our tickets." She wondered what awaited upstairs.

"Almost. Will anyone meet you in Paris?" His expression was concerned.

You're Sarah, she reminded herself. *You must think like Sarah.* She was struck again by the duplicitous nature of the work, at how smoothly one slipped back into hiding the truth and living the lies.

"Asher had planned to," she explained with a fond smile, as if thinking about him, "but he's on assignment. It's not a problem. I like the city, and I have work to do."

"Do you expect more trouble?"

"Like Tish Childs's killer? Certainly not."

He appeared not to believe her. "Are you carrying a weapon?"

"No, and I don't intend to."

He uncrossed his arms and opened his left hand, displaying a pistol, small and snub-nosed, an unusual .22-caliber. "You should. Assuming someone hired him, that same person will hire more. You can have my backup gun."

"That's kind of you, Simon. Really, it is. But no. I won't carry a gun. I gave them up several years ago. End of discussion."

"Not even if it saves your life or someone else's?"

"There are ways to solve problems other than violence. I'm working on that." She changed the subject. "What will you do after you go to the baron's estate?"

He considered, seemed to make a decision. "Depends on what I learn." He pulled up his pant leg and snapped the gun into a calf holster.

"Or *if* you learn anything." Espionage was as much art as laborious craft, but she sensed evasion. "Simon, why are you being sent to Florence?"

His mouth tightened, became guarded. "Italy really is a sort of vacation." He gave her a mischievous grin. "Mildly enforced."

Liz smiled back, hiding a sudden perception. This was his act: Boyishness, impulsiveness, even arrogance were tools Simon used to encourage people to think he was a lightweight. He was harder-nosed and more substantial than he liked to reveal.

"Then I'd suggest you forget about Paris and go to Italy," she told him. "If MI6 doesn't know about the Carnivore's files, and you bring them down on us, things could get mucked up not only for you but for me. You might lose us the blackmailer and the files."

"I can handle my boss," he said breezily, concerned whether she could handle whatever trouble she was in.

"That's exactly what worries me. That damn flippant cockiness. It makes it hard to believe you know what you're doing. Are you reliable? Are you going to go off on some ego-boosting tangent to right some childhood wrong?"

Anger crossed his face. "Hold on. You're the amateur here. If you don't want to work with me, fine. I'm not sure you can bring anything more to the table anyway. But if you think you might, I'd like to stay in touch." And help her again if she needed it.

She considered. He had been creative about escaping from the storage lockup as well as successfully manipulating Jimmy Unak. He had found a clever way to eliminate the masked killer. In the end, he had given her no operational reason to doubt him. And later, if she changed her mind, she did not have to tell him what she had learned.

"I'm in," she decided. "But we'd better have a backup message drop. There's a restaurant off the Champs-Elysées, on the rue de Bassano. It's called Chez Paul — near the Arc de Triomphe. Across the street from it is a parking garage and a phone booth."

"I know the area, but I don't remember a phone booth."

"You'll find it. It's an especially good message drop. A young woman, a poet, used to leave love notes there, written to an older man she saw eating breakfast at Chez Paul every day. She was poor and too shy to introduce herself, so she slipped anonymous messages between the phone and the wall, never expecting him to read them. At the same time, the man had taken a liking to her. One day, he decided to wait at the booth for her to come out. Instead, he saw her leave a scrap of paper. That worried him. So instead of speaking to her, he walked off. But later, he returned to find the note. There were a dozen."

"Was he an operative?"

She shook her head. "A book editor. When he put the notes together, he realized they were part of a long narrative poem written in homage to an unreachable lover. It was called 'In the Wrong Heart,' and —"

He quoted: " 'We are alone in a glass a bubble a tear.' I remember the story now. They fell in love, she finished the poem, and he published it."

"Yes, that's it. Anyway, locals leave messages there for each other now. It's supposed to bring good luck. You know the French and unrequited love."

"I like it. There'll be people around to cover us." He set his weapons in his lap and raised his arms over his head and yawned. "You were sleeping on my shoulder for a while."

"You didn't like being a pillow?"

He grinned. "Actually, it was pleasant."

He could not get over how much she looked like Liz. It was strange to realize that everything his memory and emotions said was wrong. Despite his tiredness, he was infused with that restless feeling he remembered from his youth, of the hormones that had controlled his life and still played a profound role. But it was more than that. Liz had been an untouchable icon, older, imbued with the wisdom of active sexuality. Utterly desirable, and completely out of reach.

He remembered the jerk she had married. Garrett something. CIA. There were rumors in the family she joined the Company to be able to spend more time with him. But then Garrett was sent to the Middle East, where terrorists nabbed and killed him. The last Simon heard, Liz was living in California and teaching at university.

He cleared his throat. "I have a confession to make."

Liz hedged: "I'm not sure confessions are a good idea right now." She had an uncomfortable feeling what it would be.

Simon swore silently to himself. *What was he thinking?* Guilt washed through him. She was not Liz. She was Sarah Walker, and he knew little more about her than what he had read in her dossier.

Still, he had started. "Maybe not, but you should know that if I've been acting a bit strange, it's because you remind me so much of Liz. I apologize."

"No apology necessary."

"No, really. I am sorry. You see . . . the truth is . . . well, I suppose I should just come right out and say it. I had a horrendous crush on Liz when I was growing up. Now you're really smiling. I'm sure you think it was complete idiocy, the age difference and all, but I worshiped her. Yes, I really did. I used to sneak around, following her, when she'd come home on holiday from Cambridge. Can you believe the bastard she married? Garrett something, wasn't it?"

"*Garrick.* Garrick Richmond. You thought he was a bastard?"

"Didn't you?"

"Never met him. But I think it's safe to say Liz eventually realized he was rotten husband material."

"You're tactful, like her."

"You thought Liz was tactful? My goodness, you were deluded." Strange to be speaking of herself in the third person. "Weren't you the one who said just a few hours ago that Liz would've shoved a gun into your carotid artery? Since when is that 'tactful'? Okay, you've made your confession, only it's Liz you should tell, not me." Uneasily, she looked around the garage and checked her watch. "It's time to go." She opened her shoulder bag. From it, she took out Sarah's glasses, Asher's beret, and the brown jacket.

As she put them on, Simon watched, assessing. "*That's* your disguise?"

"It'll do the job."

He was dubious, but stopping her was like stopping a force of nature. "We'll find out soon enough."

"I'll go first," she told him. "We should get our tickets separately."

"Agreed. And we'd better not sit together on the train."

"Good idea."

Liz climbed out of the car. Lights high on the walls glowed through the concrete gloom. She adjusted the ugly jacket and walked toward the escalator, changing her posture with each step. She felt heavy with the weight of her mother's murder. Even though her mother had escaped her clandestine life, she had still been killed because of it. Maybe no one escaped.

Simon followed, watching with surprise. Sarah appeared to be sinking into herself, growing shorter, softer, almost beaten, but defiant about it. He wanted to compliment her, to tell her he admired what she could do, but she was pulling farther ahead, scurrying like a timid mouse. By the time they entered the international terminal, he saw little in her that looked like Sarah Walker. It was a good thing, and not just because of the police. If one killer had been sent after her, others would be, too.

The lobby's vast open space rang with voices, moving feet, rolling suitcases, and announcements. Liz forgot Simon and his assumptions, because as she advanced toward the ticket counter, two helmeted bobbies appeared. Her pulse raced. She ached to turn away, but such a move might attract their attention.

She forced herself to breathe evenly as the men's gazes swept the airy lobby. Almost in unison, they settled on her. She hunched deeper into herself and continued her awkward gait, peering through Sarah's glasses, pretending des-

231

perate nearsightedness, while she watched the policemen covertly with her peripheral vision.

To her far left, Simon showed his MI6 credentials at one of the windows and disappeared behind to get clearance to carry his Beretta onto the Eurostar. That could take seconds or a very long time, if they decided to get official.

As she stepped up to another window, the policemen separated and continued their patrol.

"Gare du Nord, please." She gave the name in which she had made her reservation — Sarah Walker.

"Your passport, ma'am." Gray-haired and serious in his pressed uniform, the ticket agent peered at her over rimless glasses. Age lines crosshatched his forehead and cheeks.

"Yes, sir," she said softly, maintaining her shy persona. She opened Sarah's passport.

As he bent over it, turning pages, she saw a uniformed employee step out of a door and into the long cage in which the ticket agents worked. He marched behind the agents, setting a flyer on the counter next to each. Liz gave the flyer at the elbow of her agent a sharp look. Her heart seemed to stop. The flyer was upside down from her vantage point, but she could see it was official — from Scotland Yard.

Her mouth went dry as she saw the words *Patricia Warren Childs* and *murder* and *East End*. The drawing resembled her, the potential murderess, but it was not perfect, and she looked even more different because of her glasses, beret, and timid character. But if the ticket agent were to connect the drawing and the passport photo, it would be too much of a coincidence even for a casual inspection. If he summoned the bobbies and they searched her purse, they would find two passports in two different names, but apparently with the same face on both. For that alone they would arrest her, and detention would end any chance she had to find the Carnivore's files and save Sarah. Inwardly, she cursed herself for not hiding her own passport.

The agent stopped flipping pages and studied her photo.

She had to do something quickly, before he checked the drawing. Quickly, she noted his gray hair and deeply lined face. He was at least a hard-lived sixty. That gave her an idea. . . . It was human nature to worry about one's health, especially as one grew older.

As he looked up from the photo to her and back down again, she shoved a hand into her shoulder bag.

"Here's my California driver's license," she said apologetically, opening Sarah's wallet to show him and confirm she was the woman in the passport photo. "This photo and the one in my passport were taken before my macular degeneration got so bad." She leaned forward and touched the large eyeglasses she wore and whispered, "I see you wear glasses, too. I hope you don't have anything seriously wrong with your eyes."

Without thinking, he pushed his wire-rimmed glasses higher on his nose. "You don't look like either of the pictures," he accused.

"I wish I still did." She gazed around

unfocused. "I was going to ask you which direction the trains are. I'm not blind yet, so I don't need a cane, but distant signs are hard to read. Some directions would help — if you wouldn't mind."

She hid her nervousness as she glanced at him. His severe expression had softened a fraction. Now was the time to push him, despite the risk he might balk and call in help.

"I'm going to have to give up my driver's license when I go home," she explained. "I can't really see well enough to drive anymore. Going blind's shaken my confidence, or that's what my therapist says. I used to be pretty, don't you think?"

She smiled bravely.

His face collapsed. "Yes, very."

Thank God for the kindness of people. "Could you please give me those directions?"

That did it. He pointed and talked. She collected her passport and driver's license and thanked him. Simon was sitting on a nearby bench, pretending to read the Times. He lifted his chin in an inconspicuous nod, his gaze wary. She hurried toward the trains. He stood up, folded the newspaper under his arm, and followed.

Eighteen

Paris, France

On the long trip from London, Liz and Simon arranged to sit within sight of each other so they could take turns sleeping and keeping watch. When they reached Paris, he rented a car, while she caught a taxi.

As soon as she settled into the backseat, she dialed Mac, but there was no answer. She left a message asking him to call, then turned her thoughts to Asher, hoping he felt better and had good news about Sarah. She wanted to tell him about London, about Tish's murder, and about Simon and MI6 and that they had learned that Melanie and Mark had been killed and the files eventually sold. Of course, she could tell none of this to Mac. To do that was to risk that whatever information she gave him would go straight to the killers who were pursuing her.

By the time she hurried into the hospital, it was early afternoon. Nurses were readying midday meds, and techs were wheeling patients to physical therapy. The hall smelled of tiredness and Lysol. As she hurried toward Asher's door, she frowned. The chair outside was gone. No sentry — CIA or otherwise — was in sight. The door was open, and she looked inside immediately.

The man asleep in the bed was balding, nearly seventy, with rolls of fat under his chin. Definitely not Asher.

She hurried back to the nurses' station. "Where has Asher Flores been moved?"

"Ah, yes, Madame Flores." It was the same nurse as yesterday. "You were not informed?"

"Informed of what? What's happened to Asher?"

The nurse's eyes grew large. "He has been checked out. You did not know?"

"I had to go out of town."

Why would Langley move Asher from where he was safe and getting the treatment he needed? Maybe it meant good news. Maybe Langley had found Sarah, reunited her with Asher, and they were flying home safely, under medical supervision.

But if that were true, Mac would have called. "Where did they take him?"

"We were not told, madame. It is, after all, none of our business. Once monsieur was beyond our portals, the American doctor was in complete charge."

"An American doctor was with him? Who?"

"The one the guard brought. I am sorry. I should have said that first thing. I am sure monsieur will be excellent."

Liz strode away, thinking hard. Even if Sarah were safe, Liz would still have to search for the

236

blackmailer and the files, but the pressure would be off. The best way to find out what all this meant was to call Mac. Traffic droned as she listened to Mac's line ring and ring. They were supposed to stay in touch. Where was he?

At last, she hailed a taxi and climbed inside. "Hôtel Valhalla. The fastest route, *s'il vous plaît*." She stared into the rearview mirror, catching part of the driver's face. "Did you pick me up at the Gare du Nord today?"

He wore sunglasses and a cap. His narrow face showed surprise. "*Oui, mademoiselle.* Lucky for me you left the hospital when you did. I needed another fare."

On the trip here, he had driven with the flair and special knowledge of the best Paris drivers. "Good," she decided. "I need to get to my hotel quickly."

"Afternoon traffic is difficult, as you know."

"Twenty euros if you can do it in under a half hour."

"Ah, inspiration!"

He pumped the accelerator and sped around one of the city's ubiquitous Renault Twingos, careening inches from its front fender. She sat back as he rushed the taxi onward, weaving and dodging, pounding his horn for emphasis. Taxis dominated the city's boulevards and streets. Everywhere she looked, they cruised and rushed and wove, their rectangular signal lights rising like baguettes above the rooflines of other cars.

Again she tried Mac. Again there was no answer. Time seemed to suspend as she gazed unseeing out the window. Finally, the taxi skidded to a violent stop at her hotel. She gave the driver his promised tip and strode to the front desk. There was no message waiting there either.

She took the elevator upstairs, silently cursing its slowness, and ran to Sarah's room, unlocked the door, and entered carefully, her gaze taking it all in. Nothing was out of place. The room and bath were empty.

She bolted the door, flattened against the wall beside the bay window that overlooked the cross street, and peered down. There she was — Mac's spotter — the muscled woman with the chiseled haircut and the red-brown lipstick who had exchanged a glance with Mac outside the hospital yesterday. She was sitting on the bench at the bus stop again, but now she wore sunglasses and seemed to be gazing directly up at Liz's window. There was something different about her today, something that made Liz uneasy. Something had happened. But what?

There was no sign of Mac. Liz sighed and turned back into the room. That was when she noticed bits of plastic scattered around Sarah's notebook computer. Puzzled, she opened the machine. And froze, stunned. The interior was destroyed: the screen shattered and the keyboard in pieces. *Who* —

She scrutinized the room again but could still see nothing unusual. The suitcases were where she had left them, the bed neatly made. Unslept-in, of course. Yet someone had broken in and destroyed Sarah's computer. Vandalism? No. A warning that she was not safe here.

She must tell Mac, but again he did not answer

his cell. She shook her head, her chest tight with worry. In any case, it was time to change her appearance. She rechecked the door's dead bolt to make sure it was solid, then peeled off her clothes and ran into the shower.

As the warm water sluiced over her, the past two days returned with force. Was everything because of her father's files? After Sarah's kidnapping and the events in London, she had to believe so. Sarah's face appeared in her mind, and for a moment she was overcome with fear for her.

She toweled off, trying to imagine where Mac could be. She was not enthusiastic about dealing directly with the CIA again, even with the woman downstairs on the bus bench, but she might have to, to locate Mac. She dressed in black trousers and a charcoal knit top from the drawers that held Sarah's clothes — dark clothes were always better, less noticeable. She and Sarah favored them.

She opened the closet to find a fresh pair of shoes. There was a moment of hesitation, her eyes denying, her mind refusing . . . and then it penetrated.

She screamed. Instantly, she clamped a hand over her mouth. Bile rose into her throat. She had seen murder before, but this was somehow worse. So unexpected. Shocking. She forced herself to look again.

Mac's big body was sitting on the closet floor, leaning back against the wall, almost as if he were lounging. His clothes had been smoothed, his hair neatly combed, and his legs crossed. But a hypodermic syringe hung limply from the side of his neck, the needle buried so deeply it had disappeared. His eyes were wide open but lifeless.

She was not fully back in harness. Not yet inured to brutality. Not cool, not casual, not impersonal. For her, it was not simply part of the job, an assignment. No amount of experience or training lessened shock, but it helped control the reaction. At the Farm, you learned that everyone was vulnerable to shock. Only her scream had given her away.

She knelt beside him, closed his eyes, and listened to his chest. An empty void. She could not believe it. *Not Mac*. She sat back on her heels and told her heart to quit pounding so she could gaze at his cold marble face and remember when it had been full of both life and weary experience. He was a professional. He could take care of himself. He was so good he had been assigned to protect her.

No, she was wrong. Another thing the Farm taught was that no operative was so good that he or she was not at risk every minute. Every second.

Eyes burning, she backed up and sat on the bed. Despite her suspicion, despite his misrepresentations, she had liked Mac. A wave of anguish washed over her. Then she jumped up and ran to the window. She needed to alert the woman, warn her. But as soon as she looked down, her cell rang. Maybe it was Simon. She grabbed her purse and took out her cell and returned to the window.

"Come to me." It was a woman's voice, a French accent.

Liz was startled. "What?"

"Come to me, and we will release Sarah Walker. Take the elevator downstairs and walk out the front door of the hotel. I will meet you. A van will arrive — the same black van that picked her up. You want her to be free, don't you?"

There was a lump in Liz's throat. She made her voice hard. "Bullshit. I've got no reason to think you have her, or, if you do, that you'd ever let her go."

She focused on the intersection, on the woman who was her last living link to Mac. The woman was on her cell, standing now and still gazing up at Liz's window. The sense that Liz had felt earlier that something had happened remained, but now it was directed at her.

As Liz stared, the voice on her cell spoke, and the woman below mouthed the same words: "Tish Childs. Angus MacIntosh. It could be Sarah Walker next. What's the harm in talking? Come down. You want to see her, don't you?"

Liz paused, absorbing the blow. The glance the woman had shot Mac in front of the hospital had not been to alert him that she was there, his spotter. Liz had expected spotters and interpreted it wrongly.

"You killed him!" Liz accused.

"He did not have your welfare or your cousin's in his heart."

More bullshit! "Just because he's dead doesn't mean she's alive — or that you have her. Who are you? What do you really want?"

The voice was soothing. "To save your cousin's life. I'll give you an hour to think about it. But only an hour. I know you love her —"

Liz stabbed the OFF button and fell to the side of the window to watch. The woman was closing her cell, her face tight with anger. There was no evidence she or her people had Sarah. In any case, from everything Liz knew, the group that wanted the files were the kidnappers, and they had Sarah. This woman did not. She worked for the blackmailer.

Enraged, Liz spun from the window, slapped on her shoes, and found the Sig Sauer still hidden behind the wall heater's grille. She checked to see whether it was loaded and strode to the door. And stopped.

What was she thinking? She glared at the gun in her hand. And then she knew. She understood. This was what the woman wanted. The woman was provoking her. If Liz would not walk willingly into her clutches, then causing her to launch an enraged, unthinking attack was almost as good.

The woman had given her an hour. That was all.

Liz's first concerns were Sarah and the Carnivore's files. She was part of a CIA team trying to rescue her, find the files, and stop the blackmailer. Mac was her link to that team, and he was dead. She needed to reestablish the link. The fastest way was to bypass the local station chief and call Langley directly.

She set the gun on the bureau and used the scrambled cell Mac had given her to punch in a number she had memorized years ago but had never expected to use. It was a direct line for outcasts like herself.

"This is Red Jade," she told the voice that answered. She recited her code number, and there was silence.

She dug the cell into her ear as she walked to the closet door, gazed once more at poor Mac, and closed it. She sat on the desk chair and stared down at her crooked finger. She had a vague memory of the terrible pain at the moment she fell and broke it and then of the lingering ache of healing. For some reason, she thought about Simon and gave a small smile. She vaguely recalled him as an adorable little boy. His childhood seemed a century ago. Hers even longer.

At last there was a crackle on the line, and her old Company door, to whom she had not spoken in years, said, "Red Jade?"

"Yes."

"Your real name?"

"Liz Sansborough, Frank. For God's sakes, don't give me a hard time." After her debriefing, Frank Edmunds had been assigned to her. Doors were special contacts for retired, semi-retired, and otherwise less-than-active agents.

"Hell, Sansborough. It's been years. What did you expect?"

"I'm not going there with you, Frank. I called with bad news. Mac — Angus MacIntosh — has been killed."

"Angus who?"

She repeated the name.

"He's one of ours?

243

"Of course he's one of yours, dammit! Why the hell else would I call!"

"Okay, okay. He's not one of my bodies, so let me check."

He put her on hold. The silence was deafening, and she wanted to scream again. At him. At Langley. At the world.

When he returned, his tone was cautious. "You're sure? MacIntosh, Angus?"

"Of course I'm sure. Why? What's going on?"

"What's going on is the last time we had someone on our roster by that name was 1963. He'd be ninety years old now. Is that your man?"

She was stunned. "You're just checking me out, right? Tell me . . . is Mac's operation coded top-secret, need-to-know? Because if it is, I'm part of it, too, and if anyone needs to know, it's me."

"There's no operation. There's no one named Angus MacIntosh who's worked for us in any capacity for forty years. It's not a cover either, at least not according to the data bank. What's going on, Sansborough?"

What *was* going on? She was standing in a Paris hotel room with Mac's corpse in the closet and an unidentified female killer waiting on the street below as she tried to think of something sensible to say into a cell she did not own to a man she had not spoken to in years and whom she had never met in person.

"Sansborough?" he asked. "What are you doing? Are you freelancing?"

"No," she said slowly, "I'm not freelancing."

There was a brief silence. "Okay, Liz, then you need help. You must be having a flashback episode. They happen. I want you to come in and —"

She interrupted, "I need you to check two things, Frank. First, I was debriefed a second time in February 1998 in a safe house in Virginia. Grey Mellencamp himself interrogated me. Do you have access to those records, because I'd like a copy or at least to talk to someone about a transcript of the interview. Second, who at Langley arranged for me to win the Aylesworth Foundation chair?"

"I can answer the last myself. I worked on your debriefing, the first one anyway, and I never heard of that foundation until you got that award. When we cut you loose, we cut you loose."

She felt stiff and cold, as if someone had drenched her in ice water. "You considered me totally compromised as an operative and of no more use?"

"We prefer to think of it as being returned whole to civilian life. You have no idea how many ex-field operatives we can't do that with. Of course, I checked on you occasionally, so I knew you won that appointment out in California. If there was anything hinky about it inside the Company, like a payoff, I would've found out. No, you were doing fine. We were glad for you, Sansborough."

"Doing fine" was code for not doing anything to cause Langley trouble. But she knew different. The foundation had to have been working with Langley, even if Frank was out of the loop. The foundation people were damn good at hiding their tracks.

"Thanks for the information, Frank. Now will you check about the debriefing with Mellencamp?"

He put her on hold again. When he returned this time, there was more than caution in his voice; there was suspicion. "Liz, there's no record of a second debriefing, certainly not with Grey Mellencamp. Hell, he was secretary of state back then, and I can't see him bothering to debrief anyone, or us allowing him to, for that matter."

"No *record?*" What was he talking about? "They took me to a safe house in Virginia. A big piece of real estate, surrounded by woods . . ."

Frank interrupted: "Never happened. That part of your file was closed after you came in and were interrogated. If we'd taken a second go at you, there would've been a notation, even if the documentation was eyes only."

She shivered involuntarily. Then: "Who's Themis?"

"Themis? What are you talking about? I've never heard the name." His voice deepened with distrust. "You *are* having flashbacks. You're hallucinating. I'd better send help. Where are you?"

"Where's Asher Flores? Sarah Walker?"

"Give me a sec." Now he was humoring her. "Here we go: Flores is on leave in Paris with his wife. They're on *vacation,* for God's sake. Listen, stay where you are, Liz. This sounds bad. We're going to locate you and get you help. Now —"

He did not know about Sarah's kidnapping or Asher's being shot. *He really did not know.*

If he did not even know she was in Paris . . .

Did not know about Mellencamp . . .

Did not know about Mac or Themis . . . or Asher lying injured in a hospital, guarded by a CIA man, and taken away God knows where . . .

Then he knew none of it . . . and neither did Langley.

Shaken, she broke the connection. From as far back as her meeting with Grey Mellencamp years ago, nothing had been CIA. The CIA had *not* been manipulating her. Neither the CIA nor the Sûreté was searching for Sarah. The CIA was *not* taking care of Asher or her.

Asher had been fooled, too. Was Sarah's kidnapping even real? Yes, it must be. Asher's wounds were. The danger was as bad. No, worse.

She no longer knew whom she could trust, where she could go. She cut the connection. Cold sweat bathed her. She was still living in a controlled, manipulated world. But controlled and manipulated by some anonymous person or group with staggering power.

PART II

Money has no smell.

— ROMAN PROVERB

Nineteen

Conference call from Paris, France

"What do you mean you've heard nothing, Cronus?"

"Be patient, Themis. I meant simply that there's nothing new of momentous import. Is everyone on?"

"Atlas here. I've been waiting for a report, too."

"Why is this taking so long? This is Prometheus."

"Ocean here. Do we have the files yet?"

"Gentlemen, please. Is Hyperion on the line?"

"Yes, of course."

"Very good. Sansborough is back in Paris. She's discovered that Flores is missing from the hospital and is obviously disturbed by that. The last time Duchesne and I spoke, she was taxiing to her hotel. As soon as he has something for us, I'll let you know. What's important is that the pressure on her and on the blackmailer is increasing. Keep that in mind. Also that we've never had a failed operation. Considering our united desire to have the files and our willingness to do what's necessary, I have full confidence this one will end in complete success, too. It is only a matter of time."

Angry and determined, Sarah Walker threw

herself onto her cot and stretched onto her back, ankles crossed. She held up her hands, frozen in a curled position, and willed them to open. With a jolt of pain, her circulation returned, and she stretched her fingers. She sighed and dropped her throbbing hands to her sides.

The room was dry and dusty and full of cobwebs, as if it had been closed for years and forgotten. Sarah stared up at the ceiling. A long crack in the plaster curled across it like the River Seine. When it reached the far wall, the crack shattered into a delta of thick streams, cockroaches slipping in and out like pelicans dive-bombing. She watched with a strange curiosity, admiring their glossy shells while wondering what diseases they carried. That was such a weird reaction. Just one more reason she had to get out of here.

Sarah jumped up and stalked across the linoleum, shaking her hands, willing them to recover so she could get back to work. She had been here two days, which she knew because she still had her watch. But she had no idea where "here" was. Not only were the two windows covered by plywood, her kidnappers always wore nylon stockings over their heads and never spoke. From the time they shot Asher, threw her into the van, and hooded her, they had been the silent enemy — unseeable, unknowable, and disorienting. They had brought her up to this room in an elevator. But blindfolded, she had not even been able to count the floors.

When she reached the wall, she whirled and resumed her anxious trek. She was afraid for Asher.

He might be dead. She wanted to scream. The last time she had seen him flashed into her mind — lying like a broken doll as the rain pounded down. So much blood. Too much!

She ached to see him. To hold him. To know he was alive. That was the most important reason she must get out of here. To find him.

With an act of will, Sarah forced him from her mind. She must think clearly. At the Ranch, she had learned the fundamentals of surviving capture:

From the moment you're taken, look for a way to escape.

Grab and hide any objects that come your way. Successful evasion and escape are often based upon the ordinary.

Never show weakness.

Remember, there is always hope.

Keep your mind busy so that fear, isolation, and despair don't paralyze you.

The first job she assigned herself was to search for hidden bugs and cameras. When she found none, she inspected the only piece of furniture — her cot, which, given the trail through the dust on the linoleum, had been dragged in recently. Nothing about it struck her as useful. The same had been true of the sink and toilet.

As she flexed her fingers, she paced past a pile of bicycle tires, an empty oil can, a footlocker of used clothes, empty crates labeled CHINA, matchbook covers and cigarette packs someone had collected into tidy bundles, and a mountain of green plastic gardening flats and pots. She could particularize them all, because she had investigated thoroughly. According to the disarray and the moved piles of dust, her captors had checked everything before deciding to lock her in here. But they had missed a prize.

Back at her cot, she picked up a man's work shirt and slipped her hands into the sleeves for protection. Gingerly, she took her treasure from where she had dropped it on the floor — thorn cutters. They were thin and small. She had found them and some forgotten packets of rose food between two gardening flats that were stuck together.

She looked up at the window. A sheet of plywood was nailed into the frame, sealing off light and darkness and escape. She had hacked around three of the nails on the right side, starting at the top, where the guards would be least likely to notice. She had stood on the cot to do it. Now she was working on the bottom corner, at shoulder height.

Sarah listened. Whenever she heard noise, she ran to the door to meet her kidnappers. The routine was they would step inside, give a cursory inspection to the room through their stocking masks, and leave a tray of food . . . or take it away. So far, none had bothered to come far enough inside to notice the gashes she had made in the wood. After all, she was hardly dangerous, just an ordinary female journalist.

When she heard no one approach, she gripped the clipper in one hand, wrapped the other hand around it for support, and jammed the point into the plywood. Again and again, grimacing, she hacked, the point sinking in, the point pulling out. Chips and splinters flew. Every few minutes, she stopped to sweep the debris close to the wall.

Chantilly, France

The Château de Darmond spread over rolling green hills near the picturesque village of Chantilly, some twenty-five miles north of Paris. In his rented Peugeot, Simon cruised toward it. The turrets and arched arcades of the impressive château rose above a high stone wall on which wire was strung almost invisibly, probably electrified or equipped with motion sensors.

As he approached the front, carved wooden gates swung open, and a chauffeur-driven Rolls-Royce glided out — a beautiful old Silver Cloud. In the back sat the baroness. She looked just like the photo he had pulled off the Internet — gray-haired and steely faced. The gatekeeper whisked off his cap. The baroness nodded. Noblesse oblige.

Simon continued around the estate, soon passing a kiosk at a second gate, this one for merchants and servants, according to the sign. He spotted sentries patrolling the perimeter. The place was well protected, difficult to breach in daylight. He would have to find another way in.

He accelerated back to the main road and continued on into Chantilly, where the baroness's Rolls was parked beside a row of picturesque shops. He hung a camera around his neck and strolled, looking in every window and taking

255

photos of the flowers that fronted each. When at last he spotted the baroness in the patisserie, he sauntered in and admired the assortment of pastel meringues in the glass display case.

"You will deliver them to the château now," the baroness said in French to the woman behind the counter.

"Of course, madame." The woman had glistening pink cheeks. "With pleasure."

This was more like it. Back on the street, Simon checked his cell. No messages. He turned it off and took a few items from his gym bag, looking alertly around as he worked. He locked the bag in his trunk. Pulse throbbing into his ears, he kept his steps to an amble as he entered the bakery's drive. When he saw no one, he bolted down the drive and slid behind a Dumpster just as the driver stepped out of the back door, carrying a stack of pastry boxes. A slight, pretty woman of about eighteen, she slid the boxes onto shelves inside the van's rear doors and anchored them with bungee cords.

When she closed the doors and returned to the kitchen, Simon burst out, cracked a rear door open, and jumped inside. He closed it quietly and crouched beside the boxes, his muscles tense. With luck, the van would get him onto the estate. How he left was something he would have to deal with when the time came. Resourcefulness was key to any operative's survival.

At last, her footsteps returned. Since she had closed the van's doors, he expected her to get behind the wheel and drive off. Instead, she headed toward the back again. If she opened the doors, they would be almost nose-to-nose. Her footsteps were light but discernible on the asphalt. She stopped at the rear doors.

Swearing to himself, he scrambled into the front passenger seat, banging his shoulder on the dashboard, just as the girl yanked open the rear door. Cardboard slid. Bungee cord snapped. The door closed again, and he sighed and clambered back.

Before he had completely settled down, rubbing his shoulder, she jumped into the driver's seat, ground the engine to life, and shot off. She smoked Gauloises cigarettes and accelerated before every curve, making the van careen dangerously. As the bilious smoke mushroomed into the back, she gunned the engine and hurtled over a series of bumps, causing Simon to worry about not only his oxygen intake but his dental work. He held on to a door grip with both hands and braced his feet against the side of the van. No wonder she tied down the pastry boxes.

At last, she slammed to a stop at the Château de Darmond's service entrance, conversed with the guard, and drove sedately, innocently, onto the estate. Gravel crunched beneath the tires just before she parked. As soon as she jumped out, he slithered into the front.

"Monique! Good to see you!" A man's voice radiated appreciation in French.

As she answered, Simon rose up, peered out the windshield, and saw the man wore a chef's hat. It was only a matter of time until she unloaded, and Simon needed to be out of sight. He slid to the other side of the front, quietly opened the door, dropped to the ground, and pressed the door closed. Crouching, he watched their feet, which were now facing his way. At last, they turned toward the kitchen again, and he ran for it, diving behind bushes that lined the long kitchen wall.

Quickly, he took in the situation: The white van was parked at the kitchen door. The aromas of roasting meats wafted out an open window. Inside, a woman in a chef's hat worked. The area outside the kitchen was a partial courtyard that extended into a gravel parking lot hidden from the front and back of the château by the curve of the kitchen wing and a chest-high wall. Judging by the old cars that vastly outnumbered the new, this was an employee area.

He surveyed one more time and ducked low behind the bushes, working his way along the wall toward the front of the château. When three gardeners carrying clippers suddenly appeared from a woodsy path, he darted behind a buttress. For a moment, he thought he saw someone else inside the trees. Perhaps a sentry.

Finally, the gardeners disappeared, and he sped ahead, hugging the château until he could peer around another buttress. That's when he struck gold, and his smoke-clogged lungs and aching shoulder became meaningless: Not twenty feet away, two men in suits sat in a secluded patio, lunching like Eastern potentates at a linen-covered table beneath a striped umbrella, which protected them and the silver and the crystal as if from a relentless desert sun.

Simon recognized the long, wrinkled face of

Baron Claude de Darmond, whose chair faced in his direction. Excellent. Having the baron occupied was an opportunity not to be missed. Somewhere inside the château, the baron would have an office, and Simon wanted to search it. He waited a few minutes longer, hoping the other man would turn. Perhaps he would recognize him, too. But the pair talked on, involved in some kind of intense discussion.

Simon gave up and backtracked. Cautiously, he opened a side door and stepped into a hall lined with antique tapestries, portraits, and miniature paintings. The air was hushed. He was sweating, pumped with adrenaline, as he hurried in the direction of the kitchen, passing a washroom and a cannery. He quickly located the male employees' staff room, where he found just what he needed — a footman's uniform that looked about his size.

It fit well enough to pass. He grabbed a silver tray from a stack beside the door, propped it onto his fingertips, wiped the sweat from his brow, and left to reconnoiter.

The formal sitting rooms were filled with antiques that glowed with the deep luster of centuries of polish. Lions' skins, stags' horns, and paintings glorifying the hunt decorated the dining room. As he padded onward, checking behind every door and looking into every archway, soft footsteps approached. He ducked inside a closet that smelled of bleach and lemon wax.

When the footsteps passed, he resumed his search, eventually heading upstairs.

That was where he found the baron's office,

big enough for the *Queen Mary* and overlooking the front grounds. A Louis XIV desk and credenza stood at the far end, positioned in front of French doors. To the left was a walk-in fireplace, with large chairs arranged decoratively around. What identified this as the banker's personal haven was a wall dedicated to photos of him with various luminaries over the decades — everyone from Henry Kissinger to Maria Callas, from Arnold Schwarzenegger to former Prime Minister John Major, from both George Bushes to secretive multinational moguls.

In intelligence gathering, small was usually best. Simon had brought a miniature digital camera that looked like an English shilling. It could snap several images at a time. With it, he quickly recorded the wall of baronial photo ops. Then he hurried to the Louis XIV desk, where manila folders were stacked, waiting for the baron's attention.

There was no time to read. So Simon opened the first and went to work, photographing each page. He had reached the final file folder when voices approached out in the corridor. Quickly, he photographed the last three sheets of paper, dropped the "shilling" into his pocket with his left hand, restacked the folders with his right, while his feet backed toward the French doors.

As the doorknob turned, he ducked out onto the balcony, pressed the door shut, and flattened to the side. He strained to listen.

"This has gone on too long!" It was the banker-baron, complaining angrily in French.

"You're overreacting, Hyperion." The second

voice was calm, almost disinterested.

Simon did not recognize it. The French was good, but not a native's. And what was "Hyperion" all about? A code name? The baron was not old enough to have been *maqui*. A former Deuxième Bureau operative? Perhaps SDECE?

"Using the gray areas of the law to make money is one thing," the baron declared, his tone rising. "Killing's entirely different. The woman in London and now the man here in Paris — much too close! That bastard Terrill Leaming was different, of course. But now I see I was a fool to let you talk me into any of it. How many have to die? *It's got to stop.* I'll give you the money, but only for the Carnivore's files. That's my price. The files, all of them, or you'll get no support from my bank, and I'll fight you at Dreftbury. If it comes to it, I'll even tell the Coil that you're the one."

A wave of cold anger engulfed Simon as he listened. The other man was the one he had been looking for. He was the blackmailer, the ghoul who had driven Sir Robert to kill himself.

The baron's voice rose, resonating with horror. "*Mon Dieu!* What —"

Excited, furious, Simon edged toward the French door's glass panes. He had to see the bastard's face. *Who was he?*

There was a gunshot, silenced. *Pop.*

Adrenaline jolted Simon. He yanked out his Beretta, lowered his shoulder, and crashed through the French door just as the hallway door closed. There was a sliding sound behind him. He whirled as the baron toppled to the floor, limp as a dead rat. Blood and brains splattered the back of his tall desk chair. Simon tore across the room and out the door, chasing the killer.

Twenty

Paris, France

With the thorn cutters, Sarah jabbed again into the plywood. She had separated three more nails from the wood, loosening it so that it bounced with each hit. Who would think that such a small thing as a bouncing sheet of wood could give such satisfaction? She started to smile at herself when she heard a noise in the hallway. Her chest contracted and she paused, the cutters raised above her right shoulder, ready to make the next blow.

It sounded like rolling wheels. That was new. Instantly, she dropped the tool onto the plastic flat where she had found it, pressed a stack of flats down on top, threw the shirt into the footlocker, and pulled her cot beneath the window to hide the plywood chips and splinters and dust.

She rushed to the door, brushing her clothes and face with cramped hands. It swung open, and a man, wearing the usual stocking mask, hurried in and stepped to the side, aiming his Uzi at her. Behind him, two more guards pushed a gurney toward her, accompanied by a rolling pole from which an IV bottle swung. Her pulse pounded. She stared, unsure . . . hope growing. . . .

Trying to control her excitement, she advanced as one of the men pulled off the patient's hood. Her heart swelled with joy, and she ran. Asher! His eyes were closed, and his face slack, but it was Asher. Alive! His black brows and wiry black hair were stark against the white hospital pillowcase. The few strands of gray that threaded up from his temples made him seem terribly vulnerable.

"What have you done to him?" she raged. "Why isn't he in a hospital? Why —"

But they were already leaving. One dropped a paper sack onto the gurney. The door closed. The lock clicked.

"Asher, darling." She kissed his forehead. "Asher?"

He did not respond. A tear spilled down her cheek. She brushed it away angrily. He was alive; that was all that mattered.

She checked the IV bottle and was encouraged — only a saline solution, which would keep him hydrated. His skin temperature felt normal. The paper sack held two bottles of pills, the labels typed in French, no doctor or pharmacy listed. One was an antibiotic, the other a painkiller. Also inside were first-aid supplies to take care of his wound — bulk hospital brands not found in retail pharmacies. She lifted the blankets and his hospital gown and checked the bandage on his chest. Clean, no visible bloodstain or seepage, no angry red flesh indicating infection.

Relieved, she rolled his gurney to her cot and sat. As she stroked his cheek, he stirred. "Asher, darling, can you hear me?" She brushed wiry curls from his forehead. When his eyelids fluttered, she kissed his ear and whispered into it, "It's Sarah. You're with me now. It's terrible that they got you, but I'm so glad to know you're alive."

His voice was light, almost dreamy. "Hi, sweetheart."

She pulled back. "Asher! Have you been awake all along?"

"Nope, just recently." He looked deep into her eyes. "Had to wait long enough to be sure they weren't coming back. The dog-breaths drugged me at the hospital. That's how they sneaked me out of there."

A lump filled her throat. "Asher —"

He said huskily, "Come here. I can't believe it's really you. I missed you, you know. It scared the bejesus out of me when they snatched you."

She leaned forward to kiss his cheek, but he turned and caught her lips with his. What she intended to be sweet and reassuring exploded with intensity. With survival and defiance and a hunger to live. His mouth was firm and irresistible. Heat spread through her. He wrapped an arm around her and pulled her close. She fused into him.

When he released her, she was unsteady. Love glowed on his swarthy face.

"You never stop surprising me." She smiled at him. The hollow ache that had grown around her heart over the last two days vanished. "Tell me about your wound. A chest injury is nothing to take lightly."

"Bullet went clean through. Well, it did nick a rib and a few other things. But they tidied up the splinters and sewed me up. I saw the stitches. Nice job." He looked around the room. "The doctors said I could check out in a couple of days, but I doubt this was where they had in mind. Let's talk about what's really important — you." His brow furrowed as he scrutinized her. "Are you okay?"

"Other than going stir-crazy, I'm fine. Don't look at me like that, Asher. I'm not lying. I really am fine, especially now that I know you're getting that way, too."

"Everything's going to be copacetic now," he decided. "We're together."

"They don't have a chance, whoever they are."

"You don't know?" he asked.

"The only thing I know is they've been careful to make sure I couldn't identify them, which leads me to think they intend to release me while I'm still breathing. However, I'm not relying on their goodwill. How about you?"

"I can identify by sight the three guys who took turns guarding me at the hospital, but you're right . . . no one else. Now for the bad news . . ." He described the ruse that had fooled both Liz and him. "CIA, my big toe! Liz and I were manipulated like puppets. The guys at the hospital were so knowledgeable about tradecraft, jargon, methods, I never questioned they weren't Langley. And, of course, I never called in to check on them."

"What about the files? Did Uncle Hal actually keep a record?"

"With all this fuss, I've got to believe so. Liz says there were two attempts on her life in Santa Barbara, probably by whoever's got them. The problem is, I talked to her only once, so I don't know what she's found out since. What's worrying me is she could still think she's working with Langley."

"Oh, dear God."

They stared at each other, their future and Liz's future tenuous between them.

"We've got to get out of here."

"I've been working on that," she told him.

"Ah? Talk to me."

Chantilly, France

In the Château de Darmond, Simon paused in the corridor outside the baron's office. He listened, ears straining, as a door closed somewhere around the corner, echoing in the emptiness. Where had the bastard gone? Propelled by fury, he raced along the corridor, opening doors. He had checked only four rooms when he heard the voices of a man and a woman as they headed upstairs. Servants, going about their duties, the silenced shot unheard in the vast château. There were three more doors in this wing.

He sped onward, opening the next two doors, glancing inside, finding only unoccupied rooms. The last room was empty, too, some kind of secretarial office. But across the office, through the French doors, he caught a glimpse of a man running from the woods, where Simon thought he had seen movement earlier.

Simon sprinted to the glassy doors and looked down. Instantly, he recognized him: Dressed as before in an expensive business suit, he was the same janitor with the cane who had killed Terrill Leaming, but there was no cane today. Still, something metallic glinted in his hand. A knife?

Simon wanted to watch longer, to see why he was running toward this side of the château, but the voices of the two people ascending the stairs were closer. He bolted out of the room and around another corner, heading toward a second flight of stairs. He must get off the estate without being noticed.

As soon as he reached the first floor, he heard someone walking toward him. Heart pounding, he smoothed his hair, straightened his footman's uniform, lowered his gaze, and advanced. The other person's shoes came into view first — men's, cheap, with a high gloss. A well-trained, well-turned-out servant. Simon looked up, gave a relieved nod to another footman, and continued on just as distraught shouts sounded from the floor above. Help for the baron. The voices rose, full of panic. *Le baron* was shot.

Soon the narrow back hall filled with alarmed servants, wondering aloud what had happened as they converged on the staircase Simon had avoided. He tried to weave through them, but for a full minute they packed its width, all moving in the opposite direction from the one he needed to go. He pushed and shouldered, but the flow dragged him back toward the stairs. Finally, he forced himself to quit fighting. He eased sideways until he reached a wall and pressed into it, pinned against the wainscoting as the stream rushed up the stairs. Fear was in their faces . . . fear of change, fear for their livelihoods.

In seconds, the worst of the crush was over. Head down again, he hurried off, thinking about the employee parking area. As a plan formed in his mind, he paused outside the men's staff room, listening. He suspected that everyone with two functioning legs would be upstairs by now, wanting news about the baron. The staff room should be empty. When he pulled open the door, he saw he was right. He searched through the lockers, checking all trouser pockets, until he found a car key with an electronic remote control.

He retrieved his own clothes from another locker, tucked them into a tight bundle under his arm, and ran back to the corridor through which he had entered the château. Panting, he gazed outside. No sentries in sight. With luck, they, too, had rushed into the house. The baron's murder had become the advantage he needed.

He straightened his uniform and, as if on a crucial errand, followed the walkway around to the gravel lot outside the kitchen where employees parked their cars. This was his chance. Probably his only one. As he closed in, he pressed the unlock button on the remote device he had filched.

Lights flashed on a beige Renault. With relief,

he checked all around. Satisfied, he ran to it, jumped in, and revved the engine. As he sped the car toward the service entrance, he concentrated on psyching himself for the next scene he must play. This was one of those times when absolute conviction counted: He was a footman with double emergencies to address. As he focused, a distressed expression spread across his face. His chin rose; his eyes widened. He loosened his collar, rolled down his window, and slowed as he neared the service gate.

Frowning, the guard stepped from his kiosk. "What are you doing in Monsieur Pietro's car?" he demanded in French.

Dazed, Simon looked up from his window and answered, naturally, in French, "It's a tragedy. A *terrible* tragedy. Someone has shot the baron! And now my wife is about to deliver our son. What do I *do?* My God, I am overcome. Then Monsieur Pietro kindly throws me his car keys and says, '*Go.*' Did you not know about the baron?"

The man's complexion turned gray. "*Merde alors, non!*" The phone in the kiosk rang, and he leaped to answer. "Dead? He's dead? *Murdered?* You're sure?" He clasped the top of his cap in alarm.

Simon rose out of the Renault, tapped the horn, and gestured anxiously at the gate. The sentry had just had confirmation that half of Simon's story was true; with luck, it would make the part that was a lie believable, too.

The guard gave a startled look, as if he had forgotten Simon. He nodded, pressed a switch on his console, and returned to his conversation.

The big gate swung smoothly inward. Simon hit the accelerator and shot out to the road. The local gendarmes were probably already on their way. He needed to put distance between himself and the château before Monsieur Pietro — whoever he was — missed his car, or before the gate-keeper began to think more critically about the stranger who claimed he was about to become a father.

But he drove no faster than the speed limit; attracting the wrong kind of attention was the last thing he needed. As the car sped onward, he allowed himself finally to appreciate how close he had been to discovering the monster who had provoked his father's death. Hot rage swept through him. His chest tightened, and his hands knotted on the steering wheel. That bastard . . . that blackmailer . . . had as much as murdered his father.

Trees rushed past, a blur, and the road stretched ahead like a gray snake. He fought to control his fury, reminding himself that since he had managed to get this close once, he could and would do it again.

As the minutes ticked past, he found himself calming, becoming more rational. He had learned a great deal. He did not know what all of it meant yet, but with the passage of time and the collection of enough information, he would put together the puzzle of the killer's identity.

He took a deep breath. Listened to the hammering of his heart. And moved his mind to what he must do next — get the film developed and printed quickly. The blackmailer had some kind of deal going with the baron, and the file folders on the desk were probably what the baron had been working on. Information about the deal was likely in them. Simon knew a woman in Paris he could trust to handle the miniature film and say nothing.

Tense as a steel spring, he hardly noticed a sleek black Citroën sedan pass, its windows darkened. It was also heading in the direction of Chantilly. He blinked to return himself to the present. A police car raced past in the opposite direction — toward the château — its siren shrieking.

As soon as it was out of sight, Simon floored the gas pedal, whipping past trees and farms, slowing only when he reached the outskirts of the village. Everything appeared normal there. Tourists and locals shopped. Cars cruised.

He parked behind his rented Peugeot, got out, and strolled around it, checking the locks and tires as he also covertly scanned for surveillance. He saw no one, and nothing looked suspicious. Through the fabric of his trousers, he felt for the miniature MI6 camera. Yes, it was still there. Reassured, he left the keys to the borrowed Renault on the car's floor and returned to his sports car.

But just as he swung open the door, a bicyclist hurtled past. His handlebars nicked Simon's door, and everything happened in seconds: The bike skidded in an arc and slid out from underneath the rider, who grunted and swore as the force of the fall propelled his shoulder under Simon's front fender. He lay almost motionless, only his arm rising under the car, as if to ward off a blow.

Simon closed the door and hurried to him. *"Est-ce-que je vous ai sait mal?"* Are you all right?

The youth crawled out, shaking his head, dazed. *"Imbécile!"* He wore a bike helmet, and his blond hair straggled out from under it, stringy with sweat. He glared indignantly, continuing in French. "This is all your fault! You should look around sometimes. You're not the only person on the street!" His shirt was ripped by the cobblestones. Drops of blood beaded on fresh scrapes.

"Sorry." Simon tried to help him up. "But you were riding on the sidewalk."

The young man shook Simon off, stumbled to his feet, and lurched toward his bike. With each step, he regained his balance and his indignation increased.

He yanked the bike up onto its wheels. "Look at that paint!"

Simon studied the scratches, which were minor. The bike was a simple five-speed Schwinn, but the fellow was either inordinately fond of it or was trying to shake him down. People were gathering, and Simon could risk no more delay. He must put distance between himself and the stolen car before anyone, especially the police, came looking. Besides, he had to get back to Paris to get his film developed.

He took out his wallet and made his voice conciliatory. "Look, I know this is beyond mere money. You have a fine bike there. Let me give you enough to make sure you can get it repaired and maybe a complete new paint job as well."

"Not so fast . . ." The outrage in the youth's voice faded as he watched Simon count out euros.

At 150, Simon stopped. He gauged the fellow's eyes, which were focused on the currency. There was greed in those eyes, which was usually enough to clinch any deal.

Simon withdrew the cash. "I shouldn't offer you money," he said smoothly. "I've insulted you." He started to put it back in his wallet.

"*Non, non.* Perhaps it was partly my fault. I shouldn't have been on the sidewalk. . . ." The bicyclist grabbed the euros.

Simon smiled. "That's very generous of you."

The bicyclist tucked the money into a pocket and pushed off. As the little crowd broke up, muttering and shaking their heads, Simon climbed into the Peugeot and drove away. Soon he was on the highway, rushing back to Paris, to the answers he felt certain awaited.

The bicyclist, whose name was Étienne, pedaled off into the street, then doubled back to the alley where the man in the tailored business suit waited beside his expensive black Citroën. The motor was idling, exhaust fumes making the old passageway stink.

Etienne hopped off his bike. "You saw?" he asked with his usual bravado. He imagined himself a fine actor. He had played in two small theaters outside Paris. Someday he would be bigger than Jean-Paul Belmondo or Gérard Depardieu or even Tom Cruise. Today's job would be the most money he had earned for his talent — yet. He was also a petty thief and gangster, but that part would soon be past.

"I saw," Gino Malko confirmed, wondering who the Peugeot's driver was.

Malko had run into the man first — literally — in Zurich with Terrill Leaming. Little more than an hour ago, he spotted him again on a balcony at the baron's château and then saw him take the Renault from the employees' lot. All of this was too much coincidence for Gino Malko, but he had not been able to deal with the man there. Malko had the underbutler to eliminate, and then he must get his boss off the estate quickly, which required an enormous bribe. So as they left, following the stolen Renault toward the village, he'd made a cell call, which led to employing the bicyclist. After that, he had sped his Citroën past the Renault, so he could be in the village to point out the target.

Malko walked past Étienne to the mouth of the alley and looked out carefully at the busy street and the scattered pedestrians on the sidewalk.

Étienne asked curiously, "Why did you want me to put a magnet under his car? It won't explode, will it?"

Malko did not answer. Satisfied no one had followed the youth, he spun on his heel, walked straight to him, and with violent force slammed the heel of his palm up under the chin of the unsuspecting teenager.

The head snapped. The spine cracked. The boy crashed back into his bicycle. Before either hit the cobblestones, Malko's stiletto was in his hand. It was the same one he had used less than an hour before to kill the underbutler, who had been the only one the baron allowed to serve — and witness — the lunch with Malko's boss.

Malko traced the tip of the stiletto down the Lycra shirt of the unconscious youth until he found just the right spot beneath his rib cage. Then with smooth, practiced force, he thrust the blade straight up and into the heart. There was little blood until he withdrew the stiletto, when it gushed. But Malko's hand was already gone. Not a drop touched him.

He cleaned the knife on the boy's shirt, returned it to the sheath on his forearm, and dragged the light corpse and then the bicycle over to the side. He took the euros the stranger had paid the boy. The crowd would remember the transaction, and the murder would be blamed on robbery.

He took one final look around. Satisfied, he climbed into the idling Citroën. The car glided onward to the alley's opposite end, its darkened windows black voids in the sunlight. No one could see his boss. No one could see him.

Twenty-One

Paris, France

Liz stood in the center of her hotel room, gripping the cell Mac had given her. Her chest was tight with fury, but her mind had a new, diamondlike clarity. She checked her watch. She must move quickly. The woman had given her an hour, and there were only forty minutes left. She replayed everything she had learned.

Her whole life from the day she had left the "second debriefing" had been so believable that it had seemed only the CIA could have created it. As her troubled gaze settled on the closet door, she felt angry about how easily she had fallen for Mac's act — except for his slip about when the decision was made to postpone her series.

The truth was, her producer had no reason to lie. The network must have settled it the night before, just as Shay said. But to make his movie more plausible, Mac lied, giving Langley credit. *We want nothing to compromise our search for Sarah.* His bosses were afraid she would turn up the files somewhere beyond their control. It was a tiny chink in the illusion. A larger chink was their

277

mole, or a traitor — someone within their group was feeding information to the blackmailer.

Illusion. She stared down at the cell in her hand. The illusion, the movie, the facade depended on their ability to control her world. Would they then have relied solely on Mac to shadow her here? Not likely. She flipped the phone over, popped open the battery compartment, and inhaled sharply.

She had guessed it, but still she was shocked — two tiny bugs, the size of shirt buttons. One was a GPS tracking device, the other a microphone.

She stared. The enormity of what their presence meant appalled her. The kidnappers had followed her every move, and they had heard all of her conversations — with Mac, with the hotel desk clerks, with Tish and Simon and Jimmy Unak and the Waterloo ticket agent and the taxi drivers and . . .

They knew everything she had said. *Everything.* What everyone had told her. If it was auditory, someone had heard it or recorded it or both. The slightest cough, a clearing of the throat, the scraping of a chair, Simon's light snore, a toilet's flush. . . . It took her breath away, and she felt violated.

Yet why was she surprised? After years of studying her, they had known she would search for the files to save Sarah's life. So they arranged not only the kidnapping but the tracker and the listening device to leave nothing to chance. That explained Tish's murder: Liz had given Tish's address to her London taxi driver. Whoever was monitoring the listening bug heard it and passed it on to the mole directly or to a group that included the mole.

She paused, considering. After that, information must have dried up. Otherwise, the janitor would have simply followed her to the lockup. And if he missed her there, he would have found her at Jimmy Unak's nightclub.

She paced across the room, thinking what the lack of further pursuit meant. And then she knew: The kidnappers must have figured out they had a mole. The mole was dead or sidelined, or they had cut off information to him.

She turned and paced back. Her most immediate concern was whether what the kidnappers knew could harm anyone. . . .

There was nothing more they could do to poor Tish Childs, and Jimmy Unak was irrelevant now. But there was still Simon. The bug's monitor knew Simon was planning to visit Baron de Darmond, and that the baron was connected to the Carnivore and the files. That could be very bad for Simon.

She rushed into the bathroom, turned on the shower, and left the cell on the sink. In the bedroom, she used the regular hotel phone to call.

"Answer, Simon. Answer!" But he did not. As soon as a beep sounded, she spoke urgently, "Simon, this is Sarah. Be careful. The people who hired that janitor in London may know you planned to go to the baron's today. I don't have to tell you they're dangerous. I wish I knew more, but I don't. I'll be in touch when I can."

She severed the connection, stalked into the bathroom, and snatched up the cell. Enraged, she started to hurl it against the wall, then stopped. And smiled. It was a cold, thin smile. She crossed to the window and peered around the edge. The female janitor was still on the bench, her handbag neatly on her lap, convincingly ordinary, waiting for Liz to show up or for the hour to expire.

The woman was the key: She worked for the blackmailer.

As a plan formed in her mind, Liz opened the closet. She gazed down at Mac and said a silent, angry good-bye. She grabbed a black zippered jacket from a hanger. Once Mac's corpse was discovered, there would be no way she could return.

She found her own purse, removed all of the cash and credit cards, and then grabbed Asher's beret and Sarah's glasses. Where had she put Sarah's shoulder bag? It was sitting on the bureau — next to the Sig Sauer. As she tucked everything into it, her gaze kept returning to the gun, a 9-mm pistol in pristine condition. She remembered the heft of it in her hand. From where it lay, it seemed to call like a long-forgotten love.

Tormented, she did not touch it. She closed her eyes, recalling a study about soldiers in battle. The firing rate among American troops in World War II was only 15 percent. Most had been too scared to pull the trigger, because humans have an automatic safety catch to not kill their own kind.

For the army, the desire *not* to kill people was a problem. So their psychologists — people like herself — created a training program, which was really just behavioral conditioning, to produce warriors who could shoot and kill without thinking too much about it. By Vietnam, the firing rate rose an astounding six times to 90 percent.

She remembered Vienna. It was 1991, twilight, an area of small shops and quaint street lamps. Although a retiring man, faintly afraid of everything, the watchmaker she was on her way to meet was a valuable CIA asset. Andreas Bittermann's shop was known for fixing the poorly made timepieces that came out of the Soviet Union. Of course, Communist officials stationed in Vienna promptly bought Western watches and clocks, but since they would have to return home eventually, where an ambitious apparatchik's career — not to mention his life — could be endangered by too much Westernization, they also sent their Eastern timepieces to Andreas to be refurbished.

Secretly fluent in Russian, Andreas listened to the gossip among the wives, girlfriends, and children and passed on to his handler the promotions and demotions, comings and goings, and ambitions and weaknesses of Soviet authorities. With that, Langley uncovered gems of intelligence. Liz had met him twice and had been charmed by his French-accented German and his old-fashioned muttonchops.

By 1991, the Berlin Wall had crumbled, and Soviet states were spinning off into independence. Still, the Politburo remained nominally in charge. It was desperate to hold on to its few remaining reins of power and was often grandstanding — showing strength by eliminating "problems." Andreas was frightened; he sent word his anti-Communist activities had come to the Politburo's attention.

As she approached his shop, she slipped her hand inside the roomy pocket of her raincoat, where her Walther was hidden, just in case. The sound suppressor was not screwed on, since that would make the weapon too long for her pocket. She was wearing a scarf over her hair and low-heeled pumps, just another hausfrau out running last-minute errands before dinner.

But when she reached the glass door, her hand on the knob, she saw Andreas was already dead, and it was a wet job. Her throat tight, she felt an odd tremor in her chest — half fear, half excitement. His body was sprawled forward over the counter like a broken bird. The back of his neck was shattered from a bloody exit wound.

As she stared, his assassin backed toward her, shoving his pistol with its attached sound suppressor inside one of those dingy overcoats all Communist janitors seemed to wear in those days.

Looking at the mirror across from him, the killer saw her reflection. She saw him see her. They locked gazes. Of course, by then she had her gun in her hand.

He whipped his weapon back out and spun, his first bullet fracturing the glass door and whining over her left shoulder. She had just enough time to duck. The glass shards cut into her raincoat but missed her face.

She looked up. His finger was squeezing a second time, his muzzle steady on her, confident because she appeared ineffectual.

She fired. Her bullet slammed into his chest. The noise of her unsilenced shot was volcanic in the quiet, shop-lined lane. His certainty had cost him: His muffled bullet went wild. Pedestrians screamed and ran for cover. He tottered back, hit the big mirror, and slid down the wall, an expression of astonishment on his dying face.

She returned her pistol to her coat pocket and hurried off, full of confusion. It was her first killing. As soon as she saw Andreas was dead, she could have run. That way, his murderer would never have seen her, and she could have reported the incident to her station chief and asked for instructions. But she had stayed. Was it because she felt responsible for Andreas, a kind, brave man?

He was dead, and his assassin was dead. For those who kept score, it would seem a fair outcome. For her, that was not the question. The problem was, she had enjoyed the contest, had liked that the killer had underestimated her, had been amazed that she had throbbed with the thrill. She already knew she liked to win, but this was different. She had an odd feeling that something inside her had just taken on new life.

Of course, in the nature of assignments and the brutishness of those times, she had killed again. Only later, when she learned the true nature of her parents' work, had she begun to wonder how much she was like them.

For a long time, she had looked for a reason for what she had done. Somehow patriotism was no explanation, because, as with the watchmaker's death, she could have turned the crime over to higher-ups. Killing for fun did not work either, because it had not been "fun," more like a blind drive to get on with it, correct, accomplish.

Later, she would feel waves of queasiness. She had not understood herself, not really recognized herself, but perhaps that was because she had been like the soldiers in Vietnam — psychologically primed to squeeze the trigger without much thought about right or wrong or the humanity of the person who was going to take the bullet.

Maybe that was her parents' legacy. Maybe it was society's. Maybe it was Langley's. It had left her reeling with guilt.

Now violence was spreading everywhere. Juvenile crime was soaring in Britain and across the Continent — France, Germany, Russia, even staid Sweden, where the average age of male criminals had dropped from twenty to fifteen. In the United States, so-called school murders were almost commonplace. Guerrilla wars killed people around the planet, while terrorists were alternately called patriots or murderers, depending on one's politics. There was 9/11, Afghanistan, Iraq. Her academic mind was packed with those sorts of statistics, anecdotes, observations, and theories.

In the hotel room, she took a long, slow breath and gazed at the Sig Sauer lying so invitingly on the chest of drawers. If humanity did not adhere to certain basic moral principles, there would be chaos. A world without ethical norms was not a place worth living in. Peace was born in the mind. Nothing could be achieved without the upliftment of the individual, and a violent mind was not a place where peace could prosper.

For her, these thoughts were almost a religion. She returned the gun to its hiding place, put the cell in her shoulder bag, and hurried out of the room resolutely unarmed. She must find a way to slip out and return to the hotel so she could observe the woman. She checked her watch. Only twenty minutes left, and she had no disguise.

In the elevator, she punched the button to the basement. When the doors opened, she stepped into a shadowy parking garage touched with the briny scent of the sea. Against the far wall, a small refrigerated truck was parked by the service elevator, the deliveryman unloading fresh fish into an ice cooler. He closed the truck's door and carried the cooler into the elevator, probably heading up to the hotel kitchen.

She remembered something her father once told her: *Use what you have. Fools throw up their hands. Geniuses steal.* As the elevator closed, she studied the truck. An idea struck her. Had the man bothered to lock it? After all, this was a guarded garage, and he probably expected to be right back. She looked around. No one was in sight. She strode to it, opened the side panel, and peered into the chilly interior.

Crates of fish were stacked one upon another. Smiling grimly, she jammed the cell down into a bin, the fish clammy and sandpaper-rough on her skin. *Let the bastards track her now.* She grabbed a rag from a hook, cleaned up, and closed the door. By the time the fish man returned, she was

285

leaning against the hood, holding her ankle.

"Oh, pardon!" She hobbled off, hoping she could talk him into what she needed.

He was small and round, his white apron stained red, his cheery face weathered brown. He said in French, "Are you all right, mademoiselle? Are you injured?"

"It's nothing. Well, maybe it's something. My boyfriend, you see. We had a fight . . . and . . . and . . ." She shrugged helplessly and gestured. "He left me here. When I ran after him, I twisted my ankle. I'm sure it'll be fine in a few minutes. I was just resting against your truck. Please don't concern yourself."

He nodded, understanding. "Ah, yes. Love. One never knows when the breeze will turn. Even now at my age . . . well, you don't need to know about that. Too bad there is nothing I can do." He shrugged. "Love!"

"Well, there *is* something, if it would not be too much trouble. My uncle has a shoe store nearby. Would you mind driving me? An important man like you has precious little time, I know, but perhaps it would not be too much trouble?" She hobbled again, caught her balance, smiled prettily up.

"Well, you say it is close? Of course, it is a small thing. I would be happy to."

"How kind of you. How incredibly kind. Thank you very much."

When he turned on his engine, Edith Piaf sang from his CD player, and they listened to a wise but sad melody of *amour* as he drove her up toward the street. This was where the danger of

286

discovery was sharpest: She must not be seen leaving.

She sighed and groaned, reaching down to massage her ankle.

"Is it hurting, mademoiselle?" he asked with concern.

"Just a twinge." She massaged enthusiastically, staying out of sight.

As he spun the steering wheel to the right, she counted to ten. When she finally sat up, they were safely beyond the hotel. She directed him two more blocks, and he left her in front of a shoe store she had done business with the last time she was in Paris.

She limped inside. When his truck disappeared, she ran out and used a public phone to call the hotel with an anonymous tip about a dead man in room 405. She stopped to buy a few items to disguise herself and hurried back toward the hotel, thinking about the woman killer.

Twenty-Two

The Paris police hustled in and out of the Hôtel Valhalla and assembled a barricade as the press pursued with cameras and microphones and note pads. Pedestrians stopped in the hot sunlight to stare. Wearing sunglasses and a black straw hat to accompany her dark slacks and jacket, Liz hid in a doorway beside another poster for the Cirque des Astres. The poster was a good-luck beacon, she decided. From here, she could observe not only the hotel and street but the female killer, too.

With grim satisfaction, Liz saw the woman's neutral mask had shattered. She radiated rage, from the knife-thin line of her lips to her slashing gestures, as she made a slew of cell calls, apparently issuing orders. Her sunglasses were locked on the commotion at the hotel at all times. Finally, she paused. Seemed to rally. She dialed again. This was a longer, more thoughtful call, and when she ended it, she appeared calmer, as if a decision that she liked had been reached.

Then what Liz had hoped to trigger happened:

288

Still carrying her shopping bag, the woman marched off. Liz skirted around and followed, while a man who had been hovering at the barricade slid into the woman's place, continuing to surveil the hotel. As Liz trailed through the winding, confusing streets, the woman backtracked. She stepped into shops and exited through side doors. She rushed and slowed, trying to flush out a tail. The woman was very good.

Liz hung back, then she accelerated without appearing to rush. She took off the straw hat and put on Asher's beret. Took off her jacket and the beret. Put on the straw hat again. Automatic, instinctive, the past reached out and propelled her on.

For the most part, it was an invisible dance to the local crowds, and no one seemed to notice except a taxi driver, who paced Liz, his roof light on, looking for a fare. She studied his face, suspicious because one driver had picked her up twice. She did not recognize him. Still, she waved him on and watched until he stopped on the next block and picked up an older couple. Just then, the woman turned down another street, and Liz followed, the taxi driver slipping from her mind.

Under glowing street lamps, César Duchesne limped toward his safe house north of the Eiffel Tower. He still wore his flat taxi cap, and beneath that his miniature earphones. From his belt hung his CD player. The long, moist shadows of late afternoon drenched the sidewalk. His alert gaze moved constantly, sweeping traffic and people, alleys and parked cars. He did not expect to be stopped, certainly not identified, but one never knew. In a long life of clandestine activity, one learned to trust neither humanity nor one's luck.

He found the place on the CD that he wanted to rehear. As the Coil's chief of security, Duchesne was not only in charge of the operation, but also the sole monitor of the listening device in Liz Sansborough's cell. He was still trying to identify the woman's voice. She spoke English, but with a French accent.

"Come to me."

"What?" That was definitely Liz.

"Come to me, and we will release Sarah Walker. Take the elevator downstairs and walk out the front door of the hotel. I will meet you. A van will arrive — the same black van that picked her up. You want her to be free, don't you?"

He swore with disgust. He did not recognize the voice, and none of his people knew what she looked like. He listened again.

"Tish Childs. Angus MacIntosh. It could be Sarah Walker next. What's the harm in talking? Come down. You want to see her, don't you?"

"You killed him!"

Duchesne stopped the CD. He did not like this at all. For a moment, he felt his past so close it was inside his skin. It was the metallic scent of blood, the whiff of expensive perfume. It was also a sense of loss more profound than the memory of love. The blackmailing bastard's greed had killed Duchesne's wife and left Duchesne at first quivering, then yanked back into the underbelly. Now he lived with rage and resurrected skills he had been forced to hone again.

To live as he had lived for more than four decades produced a sixth sense about the future. Although the operation appeared to be spinning out of control, it was necessary. How else to force the hand of the beast with the files? But the risks were high and growing higher, and he found himself doing something that surprised him: He worried. Until his wife was killed, he thought he had forgotten how.

He climbed the stairs of the old apartment building, dragging his right leg. He paused on the first landing, listening for the sounds of children above. One, a boy of about six, was fascinated by his limp. Jean-Luc wanted to be friends. But Duchesne had no friends, especially not vulnerable children. So now he paused to make certain Jean-Luc was not waiting.

When the only noise was of televisions behind the two doors on the landing, he continued up to the next floor, where he checked the filament above his door. It was still there, invisible to sight but not to touch. No one had broken in. He unlocked the door, stepped inside, and waited until his eyes adjusted to the shadowy gloom. He sniffed, could smell no one. Satisfied, he locked and bolted the door.

He took a can of tomato juice from the refrigerator. As he drank, he tapped Cronus's number into his special cell. When Cronus answered, Duchesne sat down wearily.

Call to Brussels, Belgium

"I have information, Cronus. My people checked Atlas, Ocean, Prometheus, and Themis. All were in Paris this afternoon when Baron de Darmond was killed."

"In Paris? But it happened in Chantilly. So none could —"

"It's not that simple. We could find no one who'd admit seeing them leave central Paris, but that doesn't mean one or more didn't. Each could've taken a car, a bus, or the Métro. Remember, the police report says the meeting between the baron and his killer was a secret even from the baron's staff."

"So you're saying anyone in the Coil could have killed him?"

"Any and all. Including you. You were in Paris, too. But then, so was I."

Paris, France

Liz's quarry entered the Saint-Michel Métro station, where she boarded a train going north. At Réaumur-Sébastopol, the woman got out and ate an early dinner at an outdoor café. She appeared unhurried and unconcerned, but her gaze was never at rest, watching everything, studying faces.

Liz made herself eat, too, and followed again, this time onto line three, heading east, where the woman exited at the Gambetta station in the working-class twentieth arrondissement. When Liz emerged into the twilight, still following the woman, there were a dozen people between them, good protection. As a wind whipped the poplars and dusk deepened and a directory of African languages salted the air, Liz tracked the woman into Belleville's farthest outskirts, wondering what pulled her there.

With a violent thrust, Sarah hacked one final blow with the cutters. Her hands were numb claws, and her arms and shoulders ached, but she felt better than she had in two days. She peered up at the plywood. She had managed to cut away the wood from the nails on three sides — left, right, and bottom. As soon as her circulation returned, she would raise the plywood and see what the window opened onto. She was hoping for a fire escape, or a roof at a convenient distance below, or even a good strong tree.

She heard a noise and turned. "Asher! No —"

He was sitting upright on the gurney. "Told you I'm good. I was walking around my room at the hospital before those skunks decided to steal me. I'm slow, though. Dignified. You always wanted me to be dignified."

"I did not. You're trembling."

"Only because I have you in my sights. Never could resist you."

"Asher," she warned.

He grinned.

She sighed. "Oh, all right. You can help."

As promised, he moved at a sedate pace. He stopped beside her, panting lightly, his expression hopeful. "I'm wishing for an elevator out there."

"Wish away. I feel as if we're christening the *Queen Elizabeth*."

"Better that than the *Titanic*. Although I'm sure the champagne was excellent."

They exchanged an optimistic look and together lifted the plywood a few inches toward them, where it stopped, caught by the nails still embedded at the top.

"Here we go," she said, lowering her back under the plywood. "I can do this myself. You be lookout. Tell me what you see out the window."

Pain showed in his tight mouth. He nodded silently, backed up, and sank to her cot. "Good view from here. Front-row seat."

She nodded, planted her feet wide apart, and used her whole body to lift. The plywood rose. Nails shrieked in protest. The wood bit into her back. Splinters and dust rained down.

"What's there?" she asked.

"Stars. It's night. The stars are out."

She did not like the sound of that. With the nails loosened, she pushed the plywood farther up until she could slide under it. She looked down and repressed a gasp. They were six stories up, the street a rush of car roofs and streaking lights. The sidewalk seemed to be at the bottom of a dark well. There was no elevator, no fire escape, no rooftop, no tall tree, not even a rope. They were six stories above a sure plunge to death.

Twenty-Three

Simon's steps were long and angry as he returned to his car. Too many deaths, too many unexplained events, and now he was worried about Sarah. This was the chronic tension of the endless, pitiless wait that was the lot of real spies. Waiting alone on some dark bridge or godforsaken street corner for an asset. Waiting in an empty room for a courier to deliver instructions or new credentials or an escape route from an alien city.

As soon as he had returned to Paris, Simon drove straight to the photo shop of a colleague — Jacqueline Pahnke, formerly of French intelligence — and dropped off his MI6 miniature camera. As he hurried back to his car, he checked his cell and found a single message, a disturbing one, from Sarah: *The people who hired that janitor in London may know you planned to go to the baron's today. I don't have to tell you they're dangerous. . . .* But he had seen nothing at the château to indicate anyone there had been warned to watch for him or that the baron's murder was related in any way to his being there.

Then came the next unsettling event: He dialed Sarah's cell, and a man answered.

"Yeah?" The man had an American accent.

Simon's brows rose. "Who are you?"

"A friend. Who's this?"

"Tell Sarah it's Simon."

"Hold on." A noisy clatter as the phone was set down. The voice returned. "She's busy. She says she'll phone you back. Give me your number."

That did it. Simon swore and hit the off button. Sarah already knew his number, which meant some stranger had her cell. He jumped into his car, and sped to her hotel, where an army of gendarmes had cordoned it off. He had to show his MI6 ID to persuade them to reveal a tourist had been found murdered in a room registered to an American couple — Asher Flores and Sarah Walker.

But Sarah had said Asher was not in town. What in bloody hell was going on?

Now Simon fought heavy traffic north. Horns blasted, drivers shouted, but he ignored all of them. He found the phone booth Sarah had described at the intersection of the rue de Bassano and the Champs-Elysées. As she had predicted, there were a dozen notes. The problem was, none was from her.

Perhaps Sarah was held up somewhere. Perhaps . . . He shook his head. *What crap.* Her cell was in the hands of a stranger. There was a dead tourist in her hotel room. And Asher was in Paris, or at least he had been.

Something had happened all right, and it was all bad.

He bought an *International Herald Tribune* and

chose an outdoor table at Chez Paul, where he could watch the glass booth. He forced himself to eat dinner as he scrutinized every face and body type that passed. When he finished the meal, he opened the paper. The G8 meeting on Monday dominated the news. Hideously boring. He turned pages, glancing up every few minutes, reading everything and remembering nothing, until finally, buried in the back, a two-paragraph story about Viera Jozef's death jumped out.

A wave of sorrow washed through him. No photo this time, and it was little more than a re-hash of yesterday's news, with finger-pointing by local police and a few heartrending quotes from her brother. The whole thing made his chest knot. Life was not only impossible to understand but far too fleeting.

He paused as an image of himself as a child flashed into his mind. His mother tucked his hand protectively into hers while Sir Robert stood next to them in his three-piece suit, sheltering them with an umbrella as rain pelted down like artillery. He had felt safe then. Perhaps such a sense of safety was, in the end, possible only for a child.

He continued flipping through the paper. With a lurch, he saw Sarah's mug shot, with a short piece about the murder of Tish Childs in London. But the photo was labeled *Elizabeth Sansborough*, and the story quoted police sources that a pistol discovered in a nearby alley was registered to Elizabeth Sansborough, Santa Barbara, California.

Simon frowned. Liz's photo. Liz's gun. Still, he

could not believe Liz would have had anything to do with Tish's murder, so there was only one logical answer: Tish's real killer must have planted the pistol. But if Sarah were telling the truth about pursuing the Carnivore's files on her own, for her own reasons, why would the killer frame Liz?

He sat back, thinking, not liking at all the conclusion he was reaching: If the French or English coppers made her, it would not matter what her name was, at least not at first. That mug shot looked exactly like her. She had been in London at the time of the murder. And with the blackmailer's impressive resources, she would be a doable target if she were taken into custody.

Simon's chest contracted and his mouth went dry. Sarah had been expertly set up to be eliminated.

When his cell rang, his relief was profound. He snapped it open. "Sarah?"

Instead, it was Jacqueline Pahnke, announcing his prints were ready. "You are being unfaithful to me," she accused. "Who is this Sarah? I will hurl her into the Seine."

Quickly, Simon adjusted, assuming his devil-may-care attitude. "How could you doubt me, Jackie? Sarah's merely a code name for a very middle-aged accountant with no hair. Did the prints turn out well?"

"*Mais oui*. But they look so boring, *chéri*. Whatever do you want them for?"

"Don't worry your pretty head about it." Simon waited for the explosion. He had known her to slice a man's ear off for less.

Instead, there was a chuckle. "You are such a clown, Simon."

He made his tone sad, despairing. "Exposed, *je suis desolé.*" And smiled into the phone, transmitting it into his voice. "I'll be right there." He closed his cell. Instantly, his expression turned grim.

He inspected the phone booth once more and hurried off. His Peugeot was three blocks away. As always, he approached alertly, scanning for surveillance. Satisfied, he inspected the car's locks and tires. At last, he climbed behind the wheel, started the engine, and pulled out into the street. He did not want to leave, but the photos might give him the answer to who had killed the baron, which could lead to the killer who possessed the Carnivore's files. If Sarah really were in trouble, perhaps it would lead him to her. With luck, he would have the blackmailer's identity within the hour.

As he drove off into Paris's glossy night, he puzzled again at the name Hyperion. That was what the killer had called the baron. He must not forget. The name sounded significant, a clue somehow to the blackmailer's identity.

In his black Citroën, Gino Malko followed the Peugeot through Paris's nighttime streets, hanging back a good quarter of a mile, where he was certain he would not be spotted. The bicyclist in Chantilly had planted not a magnet but a miniature GPS tracking device under the Peugeot, and Malko himself had just added a second GPS tracker for backup, concealed inside the rear fender.

He glanced down occasionally at the screen of his GoBook MAX laptop, which showed not only the sports car's current route but a history of everywhere it had been since Chantilly. Accurate to within two feet, using a signal bounced off GPS satellites that regularly circled the earth, the electronic map also listed street addresses and the length of time the car stopped at each location.

Gino Malko liked this. He approved of technology and science and the advantages it gave a man of his profession. As he drove, he saw this as his pattern — always reaching forward, very different from how he was raised in steamy Jacksonville, Florida, where his Russian grandfather worked in the shipyards from sunrise to sundown, when he was lucky enough to have a job. He was the one who had shortened the family name, Malkovich, to Malko.

Gino had been fond of the old man, whose optimism was too large for his purse or his family's patience. Each January, his grandfather bought a new Cadillac, funded by loan sharks, who inevitably repossessed it by March. When they tired of his charm and vows, they killed him. That was when Gino learned that optimism could kill.

By then, his Italian mother had broken a beer bottle over the head of her drunken husband — Gino's father — and taken him and his two sisters to Miami, where she worked as a "hostess" in one of the clubs in Little Havana. From her, he learned that hard, humiliating work did not provide a living. By the time he was twelve, he was on the streets, running with the drugheads and the hookers and the immigrants. He hated the filth and hunger, but whenever he slipped over to Miami Beach, where the rich played and the rest of the world served them, his problems evaporated. His pulse raced with excitement, because there he saw affluence in fascinating, showstopping display.

Because he was not optimistic, Malko could not be daring. Still, he wanted the world of the extremely wealthy. In fact, he felt protective of it. The rich had qualities he would never have. So he went to work as simple muscle for a gangster who bought beautiful women and mansions, lawyers and politicians. But the first time Malko was sent out to "talk," he got too excited and whacked the guy. It was a mistake, but it paid off in a promotion. After that, he was officially an enforcer.

When the gangster was sent to prison, Malko moved on to Memphis, then to Atlanta, and eventually to Chicago. Along the way, he picked up manners and how to dress and learned some French — he already spoke Spanish and Russian. In Chicago, he went independent, easily sliding into the underworld, where word of mouth was the only advertisement. He had impressive word of mouth. Jobs sent him across America, coast to coast, and he made more money than he had ever imagined back in Jacksonville. Sometimes he thought about his grandfather and what the loan sharks had done to him. He pitied the old man, but now he understood why he'd had to die.

As Malko stopped at a red light, he checked

the electronic map. Following the Peugeot was child's play. But the driver was another matter. Each time the man parked, he walked. By the time Malko got there, he was gone. The man was well trained — that was obvious from the first time Malko saw him, when he had chased Malko all the way to the top of the Lindenhof.

Malko needed to know who he was. He had snapped a digital photo of him outside the Hôtel Valhalla and sent it by e-mail to private and government data banks, to which his employment secured unlimited access. There had been no match. He had lifted fingerprints from the Peugeot's door frame, but again nothing. He asked for and received via e-mail a copy of the Peugeot's rental agreement, but the renter paid in cash, and the driver's license turned out to be fake.

Ordinarily, Malko liked a challenge. But not today. He had no identity for his prey; worse, he had no idea what he wanted.

Jacqueline Pahnke's business was in Paris's popular Marais district, near the elegant Place des Vosges, where brick and stone buildings from the seventeenth century towered elegantly around the leafy plaza. The night was close and muggy. As Simon passed a barbershop, one of the barbers stepped outside with a bowl of sudsy water and a cloth. Dressed in the traditional full white apron, he nodded a greeting and went to work cleaning the glass on his front door, readying the shop for morning.

Simon nodded back, his steps quickening as he

closed in on Jackie's shop, two doors away. The lighted interior showed through the plate-glass window, displaying the usual accoutrements of a photo studio — cameras, flashes, tripods. When Simon opened the door to the narrow old shop, a bell tinkled, announcing his arrival.

Jackie came from the back, rushing as if he were the most important customer in the world. Bristling with vitality, she was nearing fifty. Her pale hair was short and framed her oval face. She had pushed her reading glasses up into her hair.

"What I have for you!" she exclaimed in English as Simon shook her hand.

"Qu'est-ce que c'est?"

"Talk the English. It's better for my language skills. Someday I will learn your barbaric tongue very well. Come." She beckoned, leading him back through the clutter of a business run by an artist. She offered photographic printing services as well as selling the usual stock of camera items, but her heart was in her own photographs. That was evident from the dramatic black-and-white landscapes and character studies that hung high on the walls — her private showroom.

Through a door at the back was her workroom. It was simple, with cabinets, counters lined with supplies, and wires strung across one corner, from which film and prints hung, drying. An odor of chemicals tinged the air.

"This is the stack." She pulled a pile of prints toward the center of a worktable. Most were eight-by-tens, while three were sixteen-by-twenties. "Sit, sit. All those numbers. These are the only ones that interest." She picked up the

303

oversized prints, each showing a different part of the photo wall in de Darmond's office. He was in every picture. "I made them very big so you could see the faces well. Who is this man? He thinks much of himself, does he not? Perhaps I know him?"

"You've probably seen him in the papers or on television. Claude de Darmond."

She considered. "Ah, yes. Indeed. I notice it now. He's that famous banker. The one who plays polo and goes to all the important horse races. Baron de Darmond, *oui?*" At one time, she had worked for French intelligence. On her last job, and his first, they had met. She cocked her head. "So you're after the grand baron?" She frowned. "Oh, no. He is dead today. Murdered! I saw it on the television!"

"Yes, I heard." Simon sat at the desk, eager to work. "Photographing his wall was a lark. Doubt there's anything useful in that hodgepodge of glitterati. Probably nothing here either." He tapped the remaining papers, sincerely hoping he was wrong.

She cocked her head. "Not for an instant do I believe you, Simon. You wouldn't go to the effort otherwise. I will not ask when you took the photos."

He grinned. "I'm erratic, remember? I don't always have a good reason for what I do. Just ask my boss."

"I think you have been a bad boy again. Business papers and applications. Ugh!"

"*Merci*, Jackie."

In the front of the shop, the bell chimed again.

"Numbers," she sniffed, turning toward the sound. "I abandon you to your misery. *Ciao.*"

As the door closed behind her, Simon set aside the photos of the wall and thumbed through the other prints. They showed summaries of contracts, due-diligence reports, proofs of insurance, tallies of profits and losses, histories of loans and investments, on and on with mind-numbing repetition that would surely make only an accountant's heart sing.

Simon kept at it, remembering the baron's words — that he would loan his killer no more money for his "deal" unless he received the Carnivore's files. As soon as Simon formed an overview, he found a pad on the desktop, took out his pen, and made notes.

Twenty-Four

As the night closed around them, Liz followed the woman into an urban wilderness where every square inch of habitable space was crammed with buildings, all crowded together like victims awaiting execution. Violent graffiti and posters smothered surfaces up to fourteen feet above the noisy streets — the height someone standing on a ladder or a friend's shoulders could reach. There were few pedestrians.

At an age-ravaged building of dirty brick, Liz saw the woman slow. The glass entry door had been boarded over. Above it hung a battered sign: EISNER-MOULTON. The place looked abandoned. Liz recalled reading that the company was having financial problems. Despite being one of the world's largest multinationals, Eisner-Moulton was closing and selling off properties throughout its many divisions.

As the woman stopped beneath the sign, an unmarked panel truck coasted in beside her, its engine dying before its wheels stopped. It was an aging Volvo, like hundreds of thousands — millions — on Europe's highways. The rear doors swung open, and eight men jumped out. Dressed in jeans and shirts, they were striking only because of the powerful rifles they carried. They encircled the woman as she gave orders.

One carried a tire iron. He ripped the boards off the entry door, smashed the glass, reached through, and unlocked the door. All but the driver swarmed inside. No one on the sidewalk or in the cars rushing past paid attention. Crime was just another way to make a living in this run-down part of Belleville.

When muffled gunfire erupted somewhere inside, the metal garage door rolled up, and the driver skidded the truck inside. As the door dropped shut, Liz recalled a proverb: "The enemy of my enemy is my friend." Maybe not always a friend, but certainly worth looking into. Her senses afire, Liz checked left and right, slung her shoulder bag across her back, and darted through traffic to the building's broken door.

Sarah described the problem. "The good news is the glass in the window directly below ours is broken. So if we can figure out how to make a rope, we can lower ourselves and go in there. The guards won't be expecting that. Then we'll have a chance to slip away." She considered Asher. "But are you well enough? Strong enough? Because if you're not, then we'll both stay here and —"

Asher interrupted. "Pain is just pain. It's a nonissue, considering the alternative." He looked around. "There's no rope?"

"None. I've searched everything."

"Damn. Okay, then we'll have to find something else. Improvise." He focused on the mounds of castoffs. "Any bedsheets or rolls of canvas? A hose? I see a lot of garden stuff. How about plastic tarps? Or maybe a long chain, like an anchor chain?"

As she shook her head, he paused, staring at the stack of bicycle tires. Sarah followed his gaze. The tires were thin, highly flexible, the kind used for racing.

"A chain of tires!" Sarah said. "We can link them together using slipknots." But as she headed for the pile, she stopped. "Listen!"

Asher scowled. "Gunfire!"

"Someone's coming. Lie down. Quick!"

She pressed the sheet of plywood back against the window and rushed the gurney toward him. As he lay down, the door slammed open. Two armed men in stocking masks burst in, while a third remained in the hall, his Uzi moving smoothly back and forth, alert for trouble. She had never seen them act defensively. They had always been in control.

One grabbed her arm and put a gun to her head. A second pushed Asher's gurney toward the door. She could almost smell the tension. She stomped her guard's shoe, wrenched away her arm, and ran to catch up with Asher. She took his hand. His mouth was working with frustration, a flush of rage rising up his throat.

"Behave yourself," she whispered. "Maybe we're being rescued."

She glared into his eyes, and he grimaced acknowledgment. This was not the time or place to fight, not in his condition and with their lack of resources. The guards hurried them along the hall. It was lined with closed doors. Paint peeled from the walls. Ahead waited a freight elevator, its doors opening up and down, like a shark's jaws. The men pushed them inside and hit the DOWN button.

Sweat poured off César Duchesne as he methodically raised and lowered the thirty-pound free weight, working his right pectoral muscles. He sat on a stool, gazing out across Paris's serrated skyline toward the Eiffel Tower. It stood silver and glimmering in the dark, like a surreal Christmas tree.

Air-conditioning rustled the curtains, cooling his sweat as his mind weighed the information he had and what he still needed to know. He had still not reported to Cronus that Mac had been terminated and Sansborough was on the run. But then, he had not reported everything anyway. It was clear the operation had become far more unstable than anyone expected. Before he talked to Cronus again, he wanted to add good news to balance the bad. This was not a job he intended to lose.

Still, when his cell rang, he did not rush. He finished the curl, lowered the weight, and limped to his bedside table. *"Oui?"*

It was Trevale, his nasal voice instantly recognizable as he shouted in French, "We have lost Sansborough!"

César Duchesne had raised emotionlessness to

an art form, but this was too much even for him. He swore and ran a powerful hand over his shaved head. When Sansborough returned from London, Duchesne had ordered a three-person surveillance team to wait at the Gare du Nord. The team was both diverse and natural to the cityscape — a taximan, a deliveryman, and a female student on foot. Of course, there was the GPS tracker in Sansborough's cell, too. So when the tracker alerted them to a truck emerging from the hotel's underground garage, they followed, until they realized she was not inside. Instantly, they returned to the hotel but picked her up visually only when she stepped out to tail some middle-aged woman.

Duchesne demanded, "Where did Guignot lose her?"

"Belleville."

Not Belleville! "What happened?"

"Renée was able to stay with her on the Métro, and then Guignot took over at the Gambetta stop, where Sansborough got off." Trevale sighed. "He had a flat tire."

"A flat tire? How is that possible?"

"Not all things can be controlled. He ran over a nail and the tire expired."

"What about this woman she's been following? Who is she?"

"We think . . . she may have been there . . . outside the hotel yesterday, too. Sitting." Then, in a rush of guilt: "You know how busy that intersection is."

"She was staking out the hotel? And you missed her!" Worse and worse. This could be the woman Sansborough suspected of killing Mac. "Did Guignot say Sansborough was *still* following the woman?"

"Exactly. Then his tire blew."

Duchesne went into action. "Send everyone to Belleville, but tell Guignot to stay back. She'll recognize him. We must see what she finds." As he grabbed his coat and cap, he issued more orders, gave an address, and cut the connection. Running out the door, he punched in more numbers and barked in French, "You may have dangerous company."

"You're too late! They're here!"

Liz glided inside the warehouse's front door, stepped over broken glass, and slipped to her right in the gloom. The place reeked of mold and gasoline. Only two overhead fluorescent lights illuminated the vast first floor, leaving much of it in deep shadow. She crouched at the edge of what once must have been a lobby, but the walls had been torn down. Beyond it was a loading area and an elevator.

There was no one in sight, and the shooting had stopped. Somewhere above, shoe soles slapped concrete. She advanced cautiously, hugging walls. That was when she saw the black van — parked on the other side of the panel truck, not far from the elevator. The kidnap vehicle was a black van, and this deserted warehouse looked like a good place to hide a prisoner. But there was nowhere here in this open place to conceal anyone. If Sarah was here, she would be upstairs.

Behind Liz was an open door in a side wall. She moved swiftly toward it. Just as she had hoped, inside was a stairwell. Light glowed faintly far above, down through the darkness. She closed the door and rushed blindly toward the stairs. And stumbled.

She had run into something heavy, pliable. She bent to look, waiting for her eyes to adjust. And recoiled. It was a human leg. She breathed slowly. The leg was still attached to a corpse. An Uzi lay near the dead man's hand. He wore a nylon stocking over his face, and his white shirt glistened with blood, the exposed flesh raw. There were bullet wounds in his left leg, too. But unlike the shot through his chest, which had entered from the front, the leg wounds had come from the side. Either he had twisted sharply to run, or more than one shooter had gotten him.

She pressed his carotid artery. No pulse. She peeled up his stocking mask and stopped, surprised. It was the man who called himself Chuck Draper, Asher's hospital sentry. She swore under her breath. Since Draper was here, maybe both Sarah and Asher were, too. She must hurry. But as she raced upstairs, gunfire detonated again. Bullets ricocheted down, exploding brick chips from the walls. The battle had reignited, and now she knew how Chuck Draper had died — from wild fire here.

Heart racing, she turned, plunged down the steps and out of the stairwell.

Near the loading area, she crouched, watching two men bolt down the ramp near the elevator. They had M-16s. The woman and a third man followed, both with French 5.56-mm FAMAS assault rifles. As the quartet converged on the elevator, two masked figures slipped across the back of the open area and disappeared into shadows.

As the gun battle raged, the oversize elevator carrying Sarah and Asher descended. At each floor, the three guards peered warily through the metal latticework, assault rifles ready. Bullets blazed past. Shadows darted. Tension grew electric.

"Police, maybe?" Sarah asked.

No one answered. Abruptly, the cab stopped. The unexpected jolt threw them to the floor. The man nearest the controls rebounded and smacked the START button, while Asher heaved one leg back onto the gurney. The two other men dragged Sarah up. When the elevator did not move, the man punched the UP button. Again nothing. He jammed it with his thumb, holding it in. Nothing. They were stuck between the second and third floors, helpless. Desperation in their motions, the men paced and peered up and down, searching for the enemy or perhaps a way to escape.

"Either the elevator's broken, or they've trapped us," Sarah told them.

"Climb out of this coffin," Asher urged. "Save yourselves."

But the one at the elevator's controls said, "We've got to tell the poor sods."

"Dammit, shut up!" said the middle man.

The first one ignored him. He turned his

masked face to Sarah. "This wasn't supposed to happen. The blokes that hired us said to keep you incommunicado but safe. We don't know who the bloody hell's out there, but odds on it's not the bobbies. You'll want to stick with us. We're your only hope. It's got to be you they're after."

Sarah's mind reeled. *Incommunicado but safe? What kind of kidnapping* — The elevator gave a sickening lurch and descended once more. If the attackers were not the police, who were they? Why would they want Asher and her?

"Stay with us," the man whispered. "You'll live longer."

Hunched close to the floor, both curious and wary, Liz held her breath as the elevator cage lowered into view. Her first sight was of three men in stocking masks, who dropped to crouches, aimed their Uzis through the steel mesh door, and fired.

Almost simultaneously, the quartet that had been waiting opened fire, too.

As the air thundered, Liz's stomach knotted with fear. In the back of the elevator was what looked like a gurney, capsized to create a metal wall. White sheets and blankets were a chaotic tumble in front, while behind it wiry black hair rose up. *Asher.* With a surge of joy, she drank in his hawklike face, the piercing black eyes, the furious scowl. And then he dived back down as if yanked. Sarah? Sarah must be there, too!

Just then, one man in the elevator fell onto his side, yelling and holding his bleeding thigh. Before he hit the floor, another bullet slammed into his head, exploding it. At the same time, one of his comrades pitched forward, a bullet sundering his throat. The last man had little chance, out-gunned four to one. Still, he dropped flat behind one of his dead friends, propped up his rifle, and fired.

Desperate, Liz leaped up and ran toward the truck, planning to steal it. There must be some way to disarm the driver. She would ram the damn attackers.

Behind her, feet hammered down the stairwell. She glanced back, saw two men, saw one fire. Never saw the bullet. It ripped through her arm. The force spun her around. She fell as the gunmen raced past.

Sarah screamed, "Liz! Liz! I see her, Asher! Liz!"

Reeling with pain, Liz tried to get up. To reach Sarah. She saw Asher on the gurney, being pushed into the panel truck. He was strapped down and shouting. Two men carried Sarah by her arms. She yelled and swore and tried to kick them.

Frantic, Liz dragged herself back to where Chuck Draper lay. As she groped his corpse and the floor, she heard the truck's engine roar into life. The Uzi was gone. It must have been swept up by the men who shot her. Arm pulsing blood, she pushed herself to her feet and lurched back to the loading area.

They had shot out the overhead lights, making it almost impossible to see. Tires squealed, and the panel truck bolted out through the open door, lights streaking. She yelled, forcing her feet to move faster, following the red taillights. She stumbled along the sidewalk. Dirt smudged the truck's license plate, making it unreadable.

She tried to accelerate again . . . to catch it . . . to believe she could still save them. Fury shook her, blinded her, settled into her chest, and mingled with a bone-deep fear for them that wiped away her pain. If she'd had a gun when she arrived, she and the doomed men on the elevator could have caught the four attackers in a cross fire. After that, she would have had to figure out how to deal with them, but she knew she would have. In her gut, she knew she could have rescued Sarah and Asher.

They were the only people left whom she loved, and now they were gone. What did it matter what she thought of herself? Theories were worthless when lives hung on a razor's edge. She had been full of hubris, filled not with utopian ideals but with self-indulgence. When all seemed lost — knowing there was no other way to help them — she had turned into an animal, groping the body of a dead man in search of his weapon.

Grim, her eyes hot and dry, she turned and hurried back toward the warehouse. There were other corpses there. Other weapons.

Twenty-Five

Abandoned, full of violent death, the Eisner-Moulton warehouse emanated an almost unearthly chill as Liz slipped in through the open door. Behind her, the sidewalk was deserted. Few considered flying bullets a spectator sport. She stopped to dig through her bag until she found her flashlight. The high-powered beam revealed three bodies in the elevator and a fourth on the ramp. She quickly checked all, but there were no weapons.

Holding her throbbing arm, she returned to the loading area. The van's tires were shot out, but inside was a medical kit. She collapsed in the van's doorway and swallowed aspirin. A fit of violent trembling overcame her, and her teeth chattered — a delayed reaction to being shot. At last, with a final shudder, it passed, and she was able to ease out of her jacket and knit top.

She inspected the wound. The bullet had plowed across the fleshy part of her left arm, creating a lot of blood but no lasting harm. She cleaned and bandaged it and pocketed the pack of aspirin. She paused until nausea passed. Using the med kit's scissors, she cut off the sleeves of her top and put it back on. There was a man's lightweight blue jacket on the front passenger seat. Good. Hers had a bullet hole burned through the sleeve. She did not need that advertisement.

She put on the jacket and surveyed the shadowy warehouse and the corpses lying like junked toys. Her father had once told her, *Your enemies are often as afraid of you as you are of them, but most of the time they secretly think they're better and smarter. It's a weakness.* He had understood human nature and used it to his advantage. But why keep records? He had been many things, but stupid was not among them. Was it hubris? A sick desire to revisit his wet jobs? She had never seen that in him.

Maybe it was his sense of orderliness, of completion, of proper procedure; he had been meticulous, planning to the smallest detail. Perhaps it was a willingness to stand up and be judged, to face history, trying to prove those he executed had committed at least moral crimes. Or was that only what she, his daughter, would like to believe? In the end, the reason made no difference. The result was the same: He had created misery and death while alive, and now from the grave, he had triggered a new onslaught.

She shivered, thinking. The gendarmes would eventually hear about tonight's gun battle. They always did, and she could not be here when they arrived. Coated in sweat, she quickly searched the rest of the van, checking for weapons or cells or clues to the identity of the blackmailer. She found the usual junk food, cigarettes, and

M&M's, but no registration, no hint of who owned or had hired the van.

The aspirin was working. She still felt like hell, but the pain was more tolerable.

She jumped out of the van and patted down the corpses. Each carried ID, but all were clearly new, which meant they were probably phony. No weapons or cash. No cells. She hurried to the ramp, hoping for better luck upstairs.

As she left the first floor, she spotted movement again against the far wall, where the two dark figures had vanished earlier. Instantly, she turned off her flashlight, but shadowy light from someplace outside illuminated enough area that she could see someone limp swiftly out through a door, slightly dragging his right foot. She remembered passing an alley on the way here. The door might open onto it. The figure wore some kind of cap. She saw no weapon. Heard no door close.

Liz shook off a chill and continued up, turning the flashlight back on. She explored each story. At the top, two more bodies lay in the hall. Again, no weapons or cells. So six men had held Sarah and Asher, while nine attacked.

She lifted her head, listening. A siren wailed in the distance, and she rushed back down, supporting her arm. She was in luck; the police had taken longer than she expected. On the other hand, this was a rough part of Paris, and either the word had been slow to reach the gendarmes or they were underenthused about responding.

As she descended to the inky loading area, she saw more movement and turned off her flashlight. A figure was gliding in through the garage door. Police? A gunman returning? Perhaps it was the man who had limped away.

Pulse pounding. Liz sank to her heels, making herself small as the figure — a man in his twenties — slid against the wall and paused. He needed time for his eyes to adjust, but she did not. He was white. A cruel raised scar ran from his ear to his throat.

She worked to stay calm. The police siren was closing in, and she was still not thinking as clearly as she would like. Feeling stupid scared the hell out of her, too.

The intruder lifted his head, listening. As a knife glinted between his fingers, he whistled. Three more men scuttled in and spread out as if they had done this many times. They had come to rob bodies, find weapons, scavenge. They had not come for her, but that would not stop them from ripping her to bits out of fear and greed.

Using their footsteps for cover, she slid through the shadows, moving toward the alley door. She was halfway there when her shoe struck something in the murk. It clattered away. She froze. Her pulse hammered in her ears.

The youths were hunched over corpses. They jerked up and peered into the dark.

The hairs on her neck seemed to stand on end. She sprinted.

Like a wolf pack, they rose and loped after. Stumbling over more trash, she reached the door. It was ajar, which explained why she had not heard it shut.

She slipped through and glanced left and right

at garbage cans and litter. A dark green jacket lay on the cobblestones about ten feet distant, on the way to the closest cross street. Someone must have dropped it. Maybe there was a weapon or a cell inside.

She ran as if the dogs of hell were on her heels, paused just long enough to sweep it up, and hurtled off again as cursing and raging in gutter French followed. She crushed the jacket against her. There was a small rectangular lump. She reached into the pocket. A cell! And something else — a piece of crumpled notepaper. She jammed it back in the pocket.

Humidity hung thick, and sweat poured off her as Liz tore between a parked taxi and an old Audi and across the street and past open bar doors and clumps of people standing outside, drinking and smoking and staring. She hugged the jacket as if her life depended on it and gripped the cell like a weapon. The door to a club swung open, and heavy-metal rock blasted out. Never slacking, she ran from the jackals in the warehouse and from the sirens that screamed closer. The sky was black and far away, unreachable.

Liz Sansborough was far off by the time César Duchesne ran out of the alley, too, limping badly. The police had arrived, and Duchesne was moments from discovery. He had no time to unscrew the sound suppressor from his Walther, no time to look for Sansborough. He dove into his taxi and peeled away. Now he had no choice. He would have to report to Cronus.

Brussels, Belgium

Cronus left the Old Hack, a watering hole favored by English-speaking newshounds, and turned up the well-lit boulevard Charlemagne. He was returning to his office, despite the late hour. His chin was thrust forward, and his hands were cupped behind his back, the top one patting the palm of the lower, as he grappled once more with Hyperion's murder. He shook his large head, disturbed and angry. Too much had happened over the past few days. It was mystifying. Outrageous.

Without looking to either side, he passed pubs, shops, and cafés where civil servants, politicians, diplomats, and lobbyists gathered during breaks from working with the European Commission, the Council of the European Union, NATO, and the other national and international agencies that had settled here in the Leopold district. This was his world, and he looked the part, dressed in one of his favorite Savile Row suits and club ties. His mind returned to this afternoon, when he had heard the news about Hyperion's murder on the radio. At first, he was shocked. Almost instantly, though, he realized his reaction was ridiculous. In fact, naive.

Hyperion was being blackmailed. Now Hyperion was dead. The blackmailer had struck again. Ergo, ipso facto.

As he strode along, he willed himself to put the murder from his mind. There was nothing anyone could do until the blackmailer was found. From the beginning, it had been obvious the

Carnivore's files had given someone far more power than he knew how to use well, much less wisely.

As Cronus walked on, he listened to the clamor of languages, for which *cosmopolitan* was an inadequate description. He liked Brussels, felt vigorous here. Because of its central location and the international organizations it hosted, the old city thought of itself as the capital of the European Union. To Cronus, that was, at best, wishful thinking. Brussels was not yet London or Washington, D.C., or even Moscow, where the federal offices of great nations were entrenched. It would be years, if ever, before Brussels was allowed to consolidate so much power.

He approved. Europe's unification must proceed cautiously, evolving step by step, so it would endure. More important, Britain could maximize her position before the union was final. His bias was something he would admit to few. After all, as an EU commissioner, he had sworn to put the interests of the union before the interests of any individual nation. In most cases, he did. Still, there were occasions when he shaded a decision. It was human nature to want to bring home a little pork, as the Yanks called it.

Thinking about it all, feeling more settled within himself, Cronus turned onto the broad rue de la Loi, where starkly modern EU buildings rose above the streaming nighttime traffic. He pushed into the commission building.

"Good evening, Sir Anthony." It was Jacobus, inclining his head respectfully from the security desk. He was a man with a long memory and a tiny, ferretlike face.

Shrewd, honored, even fabled, Cronus was Sir Anthony Brookshire — Britain's foremost delegate to the European Commission. A former chancellor of the Exchequer, he had inherited his wealth and title but had earned his visibility and influence by decades of loyal service to the Crown.

Sir Anthony nodded. "A bit warm, isn't it, Jacobus." A statement, not a question.

The quiet building was cold as ice chips from a hyperactive air-conditioning system. Few people appeared to be working late tonight. But then, bureaucrats liked to go home on time. Sir Anthony took the elevator up to his office, thinking about the conversation he had just left at the Old Hack, where he had indulged a *Sunday Times* journalist with a private interview over dinner. His favorite question of the night was: *Do you think it's realistic for the EU to expect to have the world's most competitive economy by the end of the decade?*

That had made him smile. "In the 1980s, no one could beat Japan. In the 1990s, the United States set the economic standard. This decade will be Europe's," he assured her. It had been good to get his mind off Hyperion.

Shaking his head, he went into his office and walked straight to his window, which looked east toward Brussels's Grand-Place, the best-preserved medieval townscape in Europe. It was textured by city lights and deep shadows, the chiaroscuro effect reminding him of some Rembrandt painting. The regal tower of the Hôtel de Ville dominated the skyline.

He settled into his chair and put on his reading glasses. He was sixty-two years old, still married to the same woman after nearly four decades. They had two grown children. He was a man of strong convictions and the highest moral standards, or so he'd had to remind himself recently.

He sorted through his messages. He had been in Paris until midafternoon, so the pile was thick. When he heard a phone ring, he glanced at the one on the corner of his desk, but that was not it. He removed a cell from his inner pocket and answered.

"Cronus here."

"It's Duchesne," the American-sounding voice announced. "We have a situation." As always, the tone radiated confidence.

"What's happened now?" Sir Anthony demanded.

Duchesne said bluntly, "Mac's been murdered."

Sir Anthony sat back. "When? *How?*"

"He was found in Sansborough's hotel closet in Paris, a syringe in his neck."

"No! *Rauwolfia serpentina* again?"

"It would be consistent."

The lab report had come back earlier that day, reporting it to be the drug in the hypodermic that Mac had taken from the man outside the American Hospital. Related to common tranquilizers, *Rauwolfia serpentina* could be injected, inhaled, or sprayed onto the skin. Still a highly secret U.S. drug, it depressed the central nervous system, killed in seconds, and was almost un-detectable. Sir Anthony suspected it had been the cause of Grey Mellencamp's death.

"The police received an outside tip," Duchesne continued. "But this situation is different from when Flores was injured and we controlled events from the start. This is out of our hands, unless you want to pull strings."

"I can't have any association with this. You know that!"

"I thought you'd say that. Mac's true identity never needs to come out. He had a secure legend — passport, credit cards, and a driver's license from New Jersey. I'm having a wife created to claim his body, and she'll tell the police he had gambling debts. Once the Paris police think the underworld's involved, there'll be little interest in looking for some other reason for his murder, not that there's anything to connect him to the Coil anyway. And of course we'll pay off his family, such as it is."

Sir Anthony was still furious. "Who did it?"

"We believe it was a woman who'd staked out the hotel."

"Staked out Sansborough? She should've been scratched!"

"Agreed. I've reprimanded the team. I'm reluctant to fire anyone, especially right now. We need all of our bodies."

Sir Anthony said nothing, seething. How could what was intended to be so good have gone so bad? He had never met Mac, although Mac had been a loyal employee for years. But then, Dean Quentin and Professor Tedesco in Santa Barbara had also been loyal employees. Now they were gone, too, because Sansborough had learned they reported to Themis. Through them, Themis could have been traced, if someone looked hard enough. And that would have jeopardized the Coil.

Although necessary, the liquidations had shaken Sir Anthony. He had not accepted the role of Cronus to authorize murder. Yet this was an extraordinary situation. Throughout history, kings and presidents had been put in the same position and had risen to accept their duty. He could do no less.

Duchesne continued, "There's more bad news. Sansborough's dumped her cell. We dug it out of a bucket of fish at a street market. The GPS tracker and listening bug were still in it, but they'd been moved slightly. We figure she found them and is sending us a message — telling us she knows what we're doing. Or at least the part concerning the Carnivore's files."

"I bloody well hope you haven't lost her!" Sir Anthony was not interested in motivations.

"Of course not. She's in Belleville." Before his boss could shout again, Duchesne continued, "The woman Sansborough was following attacked our people at the warehouse and took Sarah Walker and Asher Flores. Sansborough was injured slightly. I found witnesses who described enough that I'm certain that's what happened. For our purposes, this isn't a disaster. After all, Sansborough survived, and she got away safely." Without apparent emotion, Duchesne recounted the details. Fortunately, his ploy had worked: Sansborough found the open rear door, escaped, and picked up the jacket. But he had not counted on the four young outlaws attacking him when he emerged from his hiding spot in the alley. In the end, he had been forced to scrub them. He repressed a sigh. Too often the poor feared life more than death.

Sir Anthony took off his glasses and massaged the bridge of his nose. His face was hot, and he could feel an attack of indigestion coming on.

He snapped, "You're there now?"

"In Belleville, yes. The police are at the warehouse, cordoning it off. I'm driving, looking for Sansborough. My people are on it, too." Duchesne regretted not having had a tracking device to plant in the cell. It was, in fact, his cell and his jacket. He had improvised at the last moment. "We'll find her."

"You'd damn well better! If she locates the files while she's out of our control, she could keep or hide them, and we'd never know. How do you propose to prevent that, Duchesne?"

There was a knowing smile in Duchesne's voice: "Simon Childs is the answer. As you recall, they worked together in London, and they exchanged cell numbers so they could stay in touch in Paris. She's in a bad part of the city, injured, and needs help. Not only is he trained, he's her cousin. She'll have to call him. There's no one else. He rented a Peugeot at the Gare du Nord. Through the Peugeot, we'll track her. I have another idea, too."

"Tell me."

"When Sansborough found Mac dead, she

phoned her door, asking for help. We can use that."

Sir Anthony listened as his chief of security made suggestions, nodding to himself, beginning to forgive Duchesne again. Duchesne had the quality of being both maddening and brilliant. There was something that was driving the man, something personal. Sir Anthony suspected Duchesne himself had had a run-in with the Carnivore. Maybe Duchesne's name was in the files or the name of someone he cared about. Sir Anthony had questioned Duchesne several times but had gotten nowhere.

"Good idea, Duchesne. Of course you're right. Once she's phoned her door, it becomes inevitable she'll do it again. And we can use MI6, too."

"We'll find her," the security chief vowed. "We'll protect her. And she'll lead us to the files. The files *must* be found. Our plan is good. Solid."

"*Your* plan, Duchesne. And you're right — there's no reason to deviate from it."

Twenty-Six

Paris, France

In the photo studio near the Place des Vosges, Simon arched his back to ease the stiffness from bending over the photos of Baron de Darmond's documents, reading and compiling, trying to make a connection between the slew of loan requests and the baron's killer. He rolled his head from side to side and stretched. As soon as his attention left the work, Sarah returned to his mind, and worry riddled him. Sternly, he reminded himself he could do nothing more. He needed to keep his focus.

Seven multinational corporations were asking for one kind of loan or another from the Darmond Bank AG. They were empires, doing business around the globe:

> Temple Eire Group
> Eisner-Moulton
> KonDra Poland
> Gilmartin Enterprises
> InterDirections Britain

FabriMaire Systems
Trochus Pharmaceuticals

Simon figured the baron's killer must be in a position to negotiate on behalf of the corporation, or he had to have a stake so great he was willing to go directly to the banking baron, hat in blackmailing hand. Temple Eire was a software developer and manufacturer. Eisner-Moulton built cars and trucks. KonDra Poland was a shipping concern. Gilmartin did engineering and defense. InterDirections was a media conglomerate. FabriMaire specialized in home and food products for the masses. And Trochus Pharmaceuticals created and manufactured drugs.

Simon had listed the names of those who had signed the loan papers, as well as those of whatever other officers and board members he could find. There were three personal letters requesting loans, too, and he added their names, too. This was another part of espionage the public never knew — the wearying, detailed sifting of data. Turning pages, cataloging names, pausing to weigh the facts.

His cell buzzed. Suspicious, he stared at it. He allowed himself no excitement. Sarah? At last?

Trying not to hope, he touched the ON button. "Yes?"

"Where have you been hiding yourself?"

It *was* her. The same melodious voice, but breathless, as if she had been running. Simon paused as a tidal wave of relief swept through him. Nearly ten hours had passed since they parted at the Gare du Nord. He opened his mouth to shout with frustration, then closed it.

"Very amusing," he grumbled. "Bloody hell, Sarah! You scared the bejesus out of me. Thank God you called. Are you all right?"

Sore and exhausted, Liz smiled. "It's good to hear your voice, too." She was surprised, in fact, at how very good it was. Constantly scanning for trouble, she was pressed against the wall of a tenement in an alley five blocks from the Eisner-Moulton warehouse. Out on the street, traffic hummed. In the distance, rock music rumbled.

"You have a lot of explaining to do," Simon was saying. "Who was the dead chap the police found in your hotel room? Who was the bloke who answered your cell? What was that warning all about that you left me? It's high time you told me what the deuce is going on!"

"You may be right. The murdered man was working with me. His name was Mac. I found him dead, which told me they were getting too close. When I couldn't figure out how they'd managed to stay with me, I checked my cell. There were tracking and listening bugs in it."

"Both tracking *and* listening?" He swore.

"Yes. Nasty, huh? So of course I dumped the cell, and after that, there was too much happening for me to call you again. I'm sorry I worried you."

He ignored the apology. "The dead guy was CIA?"

"Yes and no."

"Yes and *no?* What does *that* mean?" He was not going to let her dodge anything anymore.

"I'll have to explain later. It's complicated."

"I'll bet it is. I have the patience of Job. I'll wait, because you *will* explain. You think the blackmailer planted the bugs?"

"No, it was someone else."

"Who?"

"I told you, it's complicated. We really need to talk."

"No kidding. Who was the American who answered your cell?"

"It must've been someone from or with the guys who planted the bug. I expected them to track the cell after I junked it. I guess they did."

"They of the CIA or maybe not CIA?"

"Sorry, but yes," she said. "I'm desperately hoping you have good news about the Carnivore's files or the blackmailer. I could really use some good news."

"As a matter of fact, I had an enlightening experience in Chantilly. Productive. I'm working on what it means. We can talk about that, too. Where are you?"

"I'm hiding in an alley in Belleville. It's too narrow to drive into. How much would it cost to convince you to give me a lift?"

"Since you've already apologized, I'll let you off the hook. Tell me where you are." As she talked, he jotted directions. He did not like her location — very dangerous. "Are you armed?"

"I have my cell."

"Swell. Wait there. I'm in the Marais. Figure at least a half hour, depending on traffic. Don't leave without me."

"Not if you paid me."

Smiling for the first time in hours, Simon

broke the connection and gathered up the prints and his notes. He spotted a stack of new photo portfolios, chose a small one, and dumped his notes inside. He folded the oversize prints and added them to the eight-by-tens and put them in, too. As he scribbled a letter thanking Jackie, he heard the bell on the front door tinkle. A dozen customers had come and gone while he worked on the photos, but none in the last — he checked his watch — hour.

Jackie's voice was raised, so he would hear: "So sorry, monsieur. I am closing."

Simon stepped softly into the hallway.

A man's voice said in bad French, "He drives a Peugeot. I'd say he's about six-two or -three. Brown hair, wavy, on the long side. Blue eyes, with a nose that looks as if it's been smashed by a fist."

"Oh, my, how mysterious. Do you have his name? That might help."

"No name. My car hit his accidentally after he'd walked away. By the time I parked, he'd disappeared. I didn't want to leave a note, because I hoped he and I could work something out privately. You understand."

"Absolutely." Her tone was sympathetic, the perfect response of someone who was about to deny everything. "I do wish I could help, but I haven't seen him. You're sure he came this way?"

Simon slid along the hall until he could see. His chest tightened. It was Terrill's killer, the one who had later lurked in the trees near Baron de Darmond's château. Dressed in the same suit as earlier today, he was solid-looking, with a long face, flat gray eyes, and medium-length hair. Despite his civilized attire, there was something sinister about him, as if whatever power he had came at the expense of others.

As Jackie turned on the charm and it became evident she would get rid of him — a tribute to her years in French intelligence — Simon returned to her workshop, left euros on the table to cover the cost of the prints and supplies, and opened the back door. He glided out into the night, thinking about Belleville, eager to see Sarah.

Gino Malko was a careful man, fastidious not only in his grooming but in his habits. Because of the highly sophisticated trackers planted on the Peugeot, he knew the man had stopped here in the Marais district earlier, which in itself was interesting. And it gave Malko an advantage. Using his computerized map, he had drawn one-quarter-mile circles around the two parking spots. Statistically, it was most probable the man's destination was somewhere within the overlapping area.

It was late now, and most stores were closed. Still, he went door-to-door, telling lies to cover his questions. After he left the photo studio, he found a barber closing his shop two doors away. Malko showed him the photo, and the barber recognized the man. Malko felt a frisson of excitement. This moment of success was not due to good luck. He did not believe in luck — good or bad. He believed in complete attention to detail and a relentlessness that left his competitors choking on his dust.

"*Certainement*," the barber said as he smoothed his white apron, continuing in French, "I saw him but a few hours ago — two, no more than three. He went into Madame Pahnke's shop. You know Madame Pahnke? Ah, I see you do. A delightful woman, a pleasure as a neighbor in business. But he must be gone by now. Who stays in a photo store for hours, other than the owner or the clerks? In and out, in and out — those are the customers who keep us small businesses alive."

Malko's natural carefulness made him pause. This woman — Madame Pahnke — had lied convincingly. She was protecting the man, but why? "This is a very fine street for businesses and shops. You have been here long?"

"*Oui*. Since my father opened in 1959 on this very same spot — when he was a young man and the great de Gaulle was running France. Those were glorious days."

Malko nodded. "And Madame Pahnke? She has also been here so long?"

"*Non, non*. Just five years, a newcomer."

"She fits in well? I mean, she certainly appears to. But there's something . . ." Malko waited, hoping the barber would rise to the bait. Few people could leave a provocative sentence like that dangling.

The barber leaned forward conspiratorially. "Strange people come and go there all through the night sometimes. Intriguing, yes?"

"She's discreet, confides little about herself or her business?"

"Oh, yes. You can say that several times and

336

loudly. *Very* discreet."

Malko thanked the barber. Back on the sidewalk, funnels of light shone down from the tall lampposts. Tires hummed over the cobblestones. The barber was right: Madame Pahnke and the man's visit to her were intriguing. Her nighttime visitors made Malko think of drugs or stolen goods. Or perhaps intelligence agents. The underground or the undercover. The man in the Peugeot could fit into either world.

The front window of her store was dark now, covered by a blind. A sign announced CLOSED. He looked both ways, cupped his eyes, and peered around the blind that covered the glass door. From what he could see, there was no movement inside. Not even a shadow wavered. He padded a few doors away, allowing pedestrians to pass. He took picklocks from his pocket.

When he returned, he stood close to the door to hide what he was doing. The French had two-stage locks, which were more difficult to pick than those in other countries, but he soon found matches and opened it. Warily, he slipped inside, his crepe soles silent. But it was the somber suit that really disguised his purposes. Who would believe a man in a business suit was burgling?

He turned on the small but powerful flashlight he kept on his key chain and went to work searching the drawers behind her front counter. He found nothing particularly interesting, except a little .22-caliber pistol. That was hardly earthshaking. Small businesses kept defensive weapons on hand in case of robbery. He returned it to the drawer. His flashlight beam pointed the way through the gloom as he advanced down a narrow hall, stopping to open a storage closet, a bathroom, a developing room, and a print room. Again, he found nothing that seemed important.

In the rear room, he aimed the beam across an empty worktable and counters lined with chemicals and boxes of photo paper. Prints hung from drying lines. He examined everything closely, finally pausing at the wastebasket. It was full. He dumped it onto the table. At first, all he found was a useless mishmash of discarded photo prints, facial tissues, torn labels, an empty ballpoint pen, and junk mail. When he worked his way to the bottom, which was what had been on top, he stopped, riveted.

He picked up three prints of uneven quality — one was too dark, and the others too light. Still, they were readable. One of the light ones was a simple record of some framed photos hanging on a wall. What was important was a photograph in the upper-right-hand corner; it was his employer with Baron de Darmond. His suspicions heightened, he inspected the other two prints, which were different from any he had seen — parts of a financial statement. He recognized the name of the company. Fortunately, it was not his employer's. But it was that of a client — a valued client.

When he returned to study the other photos on the wall, he swore loudly. Baron de Darmond appeared in each.

He lifted his head, thinking. From the baron's château? If the man with the Peugeot had photographed these, what else had he recorded?

What else had he seen?

With cool efficiency, he slid the three prints inside his suit coat and returned the trash to the wastebasket, and the wastebasket to where he had found it. He gave one last look around to make certain nothing indicated he had been there. At last, he trotted back through the shop and out into the night. He had an urgent phone call to make.

Twenty-Seven

From the air, the lights of nighttime Paris dazzled from horizon to horizon. Sir Anthony Brookshire admired the panorama from his window in his private jet as it circled downward toward Charles de Gaulle Airport. The sight brought back memories of the 1950s, when he was a teenager and accompanied his mother and aunt to Paris for shopping, culture, and "life," as they enthusiastically called it. They would leave from Victoria Station, take the Newhaven–Dieppe ferry, and stay at the Ritz or the Bristol.

Often it was dinner at the Crillon, where diplomats from nearby Embassy Row bought and sold Third World countries in the elegant bar, followed by late-night drinks at any number of private homes or bistros, where affairs of state were far more important than affairs of the heart. He swam in the Piscine Deligny, learned about Kronenbourg beer at a jazz cellar in Saint-Germain from streetwise older boys who thought they could take advantage of his generous allowance, and at dawn walked to the place de Clichy alone, where Paris never slept: Already street cleaners were scrubbing the streets, while people thronged the cafés for coffee.

But by the time he was twenty, everything had changed: His mother and father divorced. His aunt was dead of alcoholism — her liver finally failing. He was about to graduate from Cambridge, and he had "A Future." There was no more time for midnight swims or to listen for the romantic call of jazz wafting across the Channel. Sir Anthony was hardly a nostalgic man, but the world pressed heavily on him tonight, just as it had then. He had not thought about Paris so sentimentally in a long time.

As the jet landed and rolled to a stop, he sat back. The business of the Carnivore's files was difficult. Still, no matter how unpleasant, he would resolve it.

"Shall I fetch you a drink, sir?" His man, Beebee, appeared at his side. Beebee's real name was Horace Bedell, but Sir Anthony's oldest child, Thomas, had been unable to say Bedell when he was a little boy.

"A brandy will do. The Cordon Bleu, I should think. Two snifters, eh?"

"Of course, sir." The voice faded. Footsteps retreated. Soon Beebee returned. A cut-glass snifter touched the back of Sir Anthony's hand. "Here we are, sir."

Sir Anthony picked up the snifter by the base. He sipped, savoring the fiery liquor as it warmed his throat. Beebee set the other snifter on the small table attached to the overstuffed seat across the aisle and returned to the bar, where he resumed polishing the already-polished glasses.

As the jet's powerful Rolls-Royce engines quieted, the door opened. Sir Anthony heard the brisk footsteps of his passenger climbing the rolling staircase. He gathered himself, banishing maudlin thoughts that might interfere with hard decisions.

He stood, ran his hands down his suit jacket, and straightened his tie.

Themis stepped into the jet, and Sir Anthony walked to him. They shook hands.

"Good to see you," Sir Anthony told him. "How was business in Paris?"

"Tolerable. How was your flight from Brussels?"

Themis — Nicholas Inglethorpe — was tall and rangy, with swept-back golden hair showing flecks of gray, a strong jaw, and an aquiline nose. Dressed in his Armani suit, the media magnate radiated charm and intelligence. Sir Anthony had known him twenty years, since he was an untidy young hotshot in jeans and sweaters, buying up radio stations in America's South and plotting to create an empire. Now he was the kingpin of InterDirections, wore designer suits, and had his nails manicured and his hair cut by "artists" in his office high above Wilshire Boulevard in Los Angeles.

Still, the sharpness in his gaze and the hunger in his face had only deepened with the years. Obsessed with success, he was worth billions, and although he had adopted the trappings of genteel society, he remained a pirate at heart and, as such, not completely reliable. Which was why Sir Anthony needed him now.

"The flight's been uneventful," Sir Anthony told him, "but the drive to the airport was a bloody nightmare."

"Always is."

"How are Mindy and the children?"

"Out of my hair, thank God. They're at our place on Majorca for a few weeks."

"Pleasant there this time of year." Sir Anthony stepped back into the cabin. "Good of you to join me. Did your assistant go on ahead?"

"She'll meet me in Belgravia." Inglethorpe maintained one of his homes in that swank London neighborhood. His assistant was one of his mistresses.

"Fine." Sir Anthony resumed his seat and gestured. Inglethorpe sat across from him and loosened his tie. Sir Anthony watched, disapproving. That was an American for you. They tried to excuse informality for any number of reasons ranging from comfort to an expression of equality, but in truth, it was bad manners and sloth.

As the noise of the jet engines increased, Inglethorpe pulled off the tie, picked up his brandy, and inhaled appreciatively. "Always thinking ahead. Cordon Bleu." He raised his glass in a toast. " 'Preciate it, Cro—"

Cronus shook his head in warning. He turned. "Thank you, Beebee."

He watched as his servant left the bar, headed down the aisle past them, and stepped into the cockpit, where he would stay until summoned. As Cronus turned back in his seat, he caught his reflection in the window on the other side of the jet — perfectly groomed silver-gray hair, baby pink cheeks, and a look of stern wisdom that he had cultivated into a personality trait. The contrast with Themis in age and demeanor was noticeable — two titans in their own right, but with twenty years' difference between them, one coolly representing the Old World, the other aggressively the New.

Inglethorpe said mildly, "After so many years, surely he knows about the Coil."

"Probably, but I expect him to be discreet, even with me. Never rub an employee's nose in a secret while at the same time telling him he must not know about it. Tends to make even the most loyal resentful."

"All these code names are a nuisance anyway."

"They're necessary."

"Oh, for God's sake. Our cells are scrambled. No one can listen in. The electronic age has arrived."

Sir Anthony bristled. "The code has been an important part of our security protocols for more than fifty years. It's crucial we keep the Coil secret, now more than ever. Possibly the code *is* outdated, but it's served us well. What's that wretched expression you Americans employ?"

"If it ain't broke, don't fix it."

Sir Anthony winced. "Yes."

Inglethorpe shrugged and raised his glass. "To the Coil."

"To the Coil," Sir Anthony agreed, "and I think we can at least dispense with the code names here, don't you, Nick?"

"Ah, hell, I don't know, Tony. I kind of like

them." Nicholas Inglethorpe laughed.

Sir Anthony smiled.

They drank and eyed each other as the jet taxied toward the runway.

Inglethorpe set down his glass. "All right, there's a reason you invited me to ride with you. Let's have it."

"You heard about Hyperion?"

"De Darmond? Yes, of course. Terrible thing. As a matter of fact, I'd just recently applied to his bank for a hefty loan for InterDirections." Inglethorpe dusted an imaginary speck from his slacks. "It would've been a good investment for Hyperion."

His voice was nonchalant, but Sir Anthony detected worry about where the money would come from now. He repressed a cutting remark about InterDirections. It was a media conglomerate stamped with its assembler's personality, because, in the end, Inglethorpe had done far more assembling than building. Building required years of patience — creating good products and convincing more people to buy. Mergers and acquisitions was simply mechanics — knowing how to move the money around and where the bodies were buried. One never ran out of bodies, but financing such paper growth required an endless flow of capital . . . or corrupt accountants. But in these days of sensitivity to corporate fraud, it was better to hire reputable accountants and borrow the cash. He had heard Inglethorpe was on a new merger spree, this time in Germany.

Sir Anthony said, "Our man Duchesne says the

French police are holding back information about the murder while they investigate."

There was a bright look in Inglethorpe's blue gaze. "It *is* high profile. Does Duchesne know what they're not saying?"

"The baron apparently had an unlogged visitor he met personally at a side entrance, lunched with on his private terrace, and escorted unseen up to his office. According to the servants, he was secretive about his most powerful clients."

"One of the reasons the baron is — or was — in trouble with the authorities, no doubt. Did anyone see this 'visitor'?"

"One servant — the underbutler, who served lunch. He was also killed. Nasty bit of work, that. Found stabbed to death."

Inglethorpe stared into his glass. "Not surprising, I suppose. He would've been able to identify the killer." He looked up. "Do the police have any evidence?"

"One small oddity. A footman stole a car at about the same time. The problem is, all of the servants were accounted for. Still, the guard at the gate house swears he saw a man in a footman's uniform drive away in the stolen car. It was found later in Chantilly."

Inglethorpe sipped brandy. "The car hardly levitated there. What do you make of it? Was the thief the killer?"

Sir Anthony was about to give an incomplete answer, when the intercom announced they would take off now. He drank deeply as the engines roared and the jet sped down the runway. The wheels lifted smoothly, and the craft climbed, banking north. He gazed down again at the vast sea of glinting lights, but instead of romance, he now saw a hardworking city winding down toward exhausted sleep, a place where a lot could go wrong and did. Where the leading member of a legendary banking dynasty could be killed on his highly secure estate, while the police had few clues.

Nick Inglethorpe said, "Is there anything more about the baron's murder?"

Again Sir Anthony noted Themis's interest. Still, he must not read too much into it. After all, the baron's death also might mean the end of his best chance to secure a loan at the sort of favorable conditions one member of the Coil was inclined to give another.

"That's the only information I have," Sir Anthony said, "except, of course, that the baroness is distraught."

"To be expected."

"There'll be a large funeral. A cortege the length of the Champs-Elysées, or at least that's what she hopes for. From her viewpoint, not unrealistic, considering his prominence and their two families."

The men nodded to each other.

"We'll have to elect a replacement," Inglethorpe said carefully. He was junior — at only five years, the most recent addition to the Coil — and had not yet participated in choosing a new member. "Have anyone in mind? Someone from Europe, of course, to keep the balance with the United States equal."

"I have ideas. I'm certain you must, too."

347

"The baron's brother comes to mind," Inglethorpe said immediately. "He'll take over running the bank now, no doubt."

"No doubt." And if he were the new Hyperion, InterDirection's loan would likely be advantageously funded. Sir Anthony asked the question that had been burning in his mind: "Any thoughts about who would've wanted to kill the baron?"

Inglethorpe's blond eyebrows rose, and he looked away. "As I said, he was in trouble with the authorities. Perhaps one of his clients ordered it. It'd be smart to kill him in France, away from Zurich." He moved his pale gaze back to study Sir Anthony. "Tell me the rest. What about the Carnivore's files? Have we found anything?"

"About the files, still nothing. But Mac's been murdered, and Liz Sansborough has discovered her cell was bugged. She's on the run, but since she met her cousin Simon Childs in London, it's likely she'll contact him." He paused. He knew the Childs family well. "Simon Childs is MI6."

Inglethorpe swore a long string of barbaric American oaths.

"Childs learned his father was being blackmailed," Sir Anthony went on, "and now he's on a private crusade to find who has the files, too. This could be beneficial, if we can keep him quiet as well as track him."

"And if he's not doing it for MI6," Inglethorpe snapped.

"Apparently, he's not. But then there's still the CIA. Sansborough contacted her old door, because of course she thought she'd been working with the CIA."

Inglethorpe exploded. "How could you let this get so out of hand! Sansborough's vanished, MI6 and Langley could be burning our heels any moment, and we *still* don't know where the damn files are or who has them! You're the leader of the Coil, dammit! This falls on *your* shoulders!"

Sir Anthony repressed a sharp retort. "I'm not the leader in the way you mean, Nick, and you bloody well know it. I'm simply first among equals. Remember, I have only one vote. We — all of us — decided on this plan. Once we saw the vast amount of publicity her TV series was receiving, and that she was planning a show on assassins, what else could we do? There was no way the blackmailer would risk millions of viewers knowing about the files. You concurred, or you wouldn't have canceled her show. As it turns out, we were right. Sansborough was almost killed in Santa Barbara."

"It was a decision born of desperation," Inglethorpe said stubbornly.

"It's a desperate situation. We must find those files!"

"Does the rest of the Coil know what's happened?"

"I'll be bringing them up-to-date. Of course, we'll have to meet tonight now."

Inglethorpe fixed his hard gaze on Cronus. "You want something. What is it?"

It was time to make the brash American wait. Sir Anthony finished his brandy, enjoying its polish and richness and then the smooth rhythm of his jet in flight. There was no substitute for money and the quality it could buy. He set the snifter onto his table, and his cool, implacable gaze settled on young Inglethorpe. Inglethorpe was glaring, but there was nervousness around his eyes. *Good.*

Sir Anthony said, "Sansborough's door believes she may be suffering flashbacks. I'm concerned he may send out agents to find her. Or he might get curious about whether Asher Flores really was shot and look into that. The last thing we need is the CIA sniffing around. There's too much to find. Agreed?"

Inglethorpe said suspiciously, "They could ruin our plan, what little remains."

"Precisely. At the same time, there's MI6. Simon Childs may have incited their interest. We don't want them in the fray either. I'm sure you see my point."

"Not really."

Sir Anthony knew otherwise. "I can handle MI6 myself. You're the logical one to take care of Langley. No, Nick, listen. You've done favors for the director of operations for years. When they needed the cover of a journalist, you provided it, no questions asked. You got their people into Iraq, Iran, Afghanistan, Pakistan, Bosnia. . . . We need to stop a probe into Sansborough. Stop it cold. The intelligence community can be manipulated, but it has to be done quickly, before their machinery starts rolling. That means now. We need the CIA to back off, to stonewall her if she phones again. She must remain an independent, not interfered with. Will you take care of it?"

At first, Themis shook his head. When he looked up, Cronus saw uncertainty. Most unusual. Cronus frowned, and Themis gazed away. But then Themis sat up straight, and Sir Anthony knew he had figured out a solution.

Themis smiled. "Is that all you want? Jesus, Cronus, that's chicken feed to a boy from Texas. I know the right person for the job. His identity will have to be my secret, of course. Just between him and me, but consider it handled."

Gatwick Airport, England

Twenty minutes after the luxury jet touched down at Gatwick, Nick Inglethorpe was in a men's room stall, talking on his cell. "You're certain there'll be no blowback?"

"Not when I take anything on, Nick. You know that."

"I knew you were the one. And no need to mention this to Cronus, right?"

"If that's how you want to play it. Did the old man mention any progress on the Carnivore's files?"

"No. He just keeps botching it." Inglethorpe had sensed for some time that since his latest acquisition had raised eyebrows in some quarters, his stock was falling with the Coil and with Cronus in particular. Therefore, letting Cronus believe media magnate Nicholas Inglethorpe still had the clout to manipulate the CIA was a smart idea. "But thanks on this one. I owe you."

"Yes, Nick, you do." The line went dead.

Twenty-Eight

MI6 Headquarters
London, England

With its commanding position above the Thames River, MI6's headquarters in Vauxhall Cross, South London, looked to Shelby Potter like a bloody birthday cake, not a place for the raw business of foreign intelligence. Potter not only disliked the angles and setbacks, he found the honey-colored concrete and green glass damned offensive.

The only thing good was its location — isolated at the south-bank end of Vauxhall Bridge. Potter had indelible memories of the unmarked London high-rise that had been HQ for decades, where so much was sacrificed and accomplished. In those days, security identified it to the nosy public only as the Ministry of Defence. But then, until just seven years ago, the government had denied MI6's very existence. All of that had changed by 2001, when MI6's chief, Sir David Spedding, died. It was announced in the gossip rags. He might as well have been some bloody airhead socialite.

Scowling and grumbling to himself, Potter parked and marched inside. Word had come down that the queen would soon make him a commander of the Royal Victorian Order. A knighthood for an old spy who had spent his career paying fools to betray their country and then murdering the patriots who tried to stop them. This, after years of being passed over because of his bad mouth, bad team manners, and Janice.

He had a half mind to turn it down. Except he knew it would make Janice proud. A soldier's woman had an easy life compared to a bloody spook's. If he took the thing, he would dine her at the Connaught, where they would drink to their thirty years of out-of-wedlock bliss and reminisce about better times, when the Foreign Office did not have to advertise for spies as if they were looking for baker's assistants.

The one good tradition that endured was the late hours analysts and planners devoted to protecting Britain. He passed lighted offices and cubicles, his hands clasped behind his back, nodding soberly at those who hurried along carrying colored folders, each color indicating a level of security. They were good young people, even if they did look at him as if he were some statue in Hyde Park, not the still very alive and barking operations director in charge of all MI6 covert missions.

In his office, he flicked on the lights, sat at his desk, and leaned back, waiting. The clock read 10:44. One minute later, right on schedule, his phone rang.

He picked it up. "Tony?"

"Hello, old man. Thanks for making time for a chat." Sir Anthony Brookshire's voice had the same measured, resonant pomposity Potter associated with long nights of drinking and political discussions back when they were both students at Cambridge.

"What do you want, Tony?"

Brookshire managed a chuckle. "Always the cynic. I hear congratulations are in order. A knighthood. Very well deserved."

"I'll most likely turn it down."

"I wouldn't do that, old man," Sir Anthony said. "Janice deserves it, if nothing else. You might even marry the lass after all these decades, eh? Lady Potter. Has a ring, don't you think? So does Sir Shelby."

Potter swore, suddenly understanding Tony's underhanded role. "Dammit all to bloody hell, Tony, this was your idea. You put on the screws."

"You're overdue, Shelby. It's common knowledge among those of us with our fingers on the pulse. Unfortunate that the, ah, clandestine nature of your work has held it up. This should've happened a decade ago."

"Clandestine nature of my work, my maiden aunt." Potter snorted. "My lifestyle and outlaw personality, *that's* why C and Her holy Majesty would never do the honors." "C" was code for chief of MI6 — the director-general. Potter felt an unusual moment of respect. "Damnation, Tony, you've impressed me. How in hell did you manage it?"

A slight irritation entered Brookshire's tone. "I merely detailed a few of your many contributions over the years."

Potter smiled to himself. Translation: Tony had made C understand that Potter knew where too many ripe bodies were buried to be ignored again. But then, Tony Brookshire was a consummate politician. No one could remain in service to the queen a lifetime and rise to the rarefied levels he had without being one. The world of British national politics was fangs and claws, blood and bone, but usually covered with such a civil veneer that the rest of the planet considered the British stuffy.

"All right, Tony," Potter grumbled, "you've softened me up. Now what is it?"

"Simon Childs. Penetration agent. The former MP's second son."

"Bright young man. Bit of a maverick, which I consider an asset under the right circumstances. Sporadically in trouble. Gives his chief fits. Real potential there," Potter enumerated. "But you know that, right? Friend of the family?"

Brookshire brushed it off. "Childs has left his assignment and is running rogue with a former CIA agent, Elizabeth Sansborough."

Potter frowned. "Why haven't I heard?" He made a mental note to talk to Childs's immediate supervisor.

"The boy's been hiding his tracks damn well. We happened to stumble over him on a different matter. At the best, it shows poor judgment. At the worst . . ."

Potter pondered. "Sansborough? Ah, yes. The

355

Carnivore's daughter. I heard she was put out to pasture years ago."

"Clearly back in harness, apparently on her own initiative."

"She's turned professional, like her father?"

"Could be." Brookshire sighed. "As you may recall, Childs is her cousin. We'd like you to cut him loose and declare him an isolate. We hope he's going to come through this. But if not, we want no reflection back on the government."

Potter said nothing. It was the "we" that held his attention . . . *we'd* like . . . *we* hope . . . *we want*. Was Brookshire referring to the inner circle of government, or was he talking about Nautilus, the preeminent secret club of world movers and shakers to which Potter knew Brookshire belonged? The Nautilus Group had been behind many of the seismic global political shifts since World War II. Potter knew about such things, of course, although he would never — could never — be part of the group. He had neither the power nor the "team" mentality.

Potter asked bluntly, "How do I know any of this is true?"

"Because I never ask frivolously. Because we've known each other too long, through too much, to be less than honest with each other, especially now that we're in the twilight of our careers. This is for the good of the country, Shelby my friend. I've never asked for anything personal, and I'm not about to start now. Liz Sansborough has nose-dived off the top of Big Ben, and it's looking more certain she's taking our boy with her. We don't want to kill Childs, but we've got to make sure he doesn't hurt us. If it comes to sanctions later, so be it. For now, let's declare him taboo. He's to receive no help. To interfere will endanger his life and, vastly more important, the service."

"This is the truth?" Which Potter knew was essentially irrelevant. Somewhere far higher up than he, someone in Whitehall needed Simon Childs on the shelf for a time-out. That was, in the end, all that mattered.

"You can verify it yourself now that you know the situation."

"Oh, I will, Tony," Potter said. "But I'm sure it will check right enough, and I'll take care of it."

"Never doubted it, old man."

"And Tony? I expect I'll take the honor, despite my grumbling. Even marry Janice, if she'll have me at this late date. Come in from the windy cold, as it were, eh?"

"Glad to hear it, Shelby. Glad to hear it. We must all have dinner after the ceremony. The four of us. Be in touch."

Alone in his office, Potter almost laughed aloud. Tony wasted no time. But on the other hand, Tony would also make sure they had that intimate dinner, and he would be genuinely pleased when Potter took the knighthood. Tony would also weigh in with Janice, promoting marriage. People like Tony always wanted everyone to play the same game, play it the same way — his way.

Potter sighed. Whatever the real reason, Simon Childs would be cut off. The boy would survive, probably be the better for it. Stiffen his backbone and his skills. God knew, it had happened to Potter more than once in the old days. He dialed and leaned into the phone.

CIA Headquarters
Langley, Virginia

Boring to the outside world, the Office of Personnel had become Walter Jaffa's new fiefdom. For five years, he'd headed the Directorate of Administration, once the nervous system of the CIA, until it was eliminated in 1998 and its vast responsibilities carved up and handed out like rare chocolates. At first, Jaffa had fought the reorganization. But he had been allowed to keep his grade and salary, and as one of the Agency's most senior officials, he'd had his choice among Chief Financial Officer, Chief of Security, head of CIA University, and others.

In the end, he had chosen the Office of Personnel; it was not only visible at every level of the CIA, it was critical, from employee recruitment and screening to retirement. It gave lie-detector tests to find sleepers, moles, and those with the potential to be turned, and it oversaw the NOCs — those brave officers in nonofficial cover, whose lives in the field were on the line every day.

Jaffa took his duties seriously. Every time he walked past the windowless white cubicles of his various special groups, he felt a surge of pride. He liked his religion, and he liked his wife and children. He enjoyed his success, his work, and the Agency.

He entered his office and sat in the comfortable chair behind his paper-laden desk. It was nearly six o'clock, a time when he occasionally had these thoughts. In this frantic age, to end most days with a sense of spiritual fulfillment was unusual. Raised on the windswept prairie of South Dakota, with a hard-drinking father and a work-worn mother, he had put himself through the University of South Dakota, waiting tables in Vermilion and Sioux City and working through the blistering summers on the wheat combines. Physical survival was what mattered in those days, and that meant getting ahead. Now spirituality was the core of his life. His friends were only the most serious Roman Catholics, the most traditional and High Church — fellow members of Opus Dei, "God's Work."

His phone rang. One of his phones. But not the one that normally rang. Jaffa stared at it — his direct line, used by only the most important people, from the DCI on up. He straightened his back, lifted the receiver, and made his voice firm, authoritative.

"Jaffa," he said.

"Do you enjoy your job, Walter?"

Jaffa did not recognize the voice — tinny, distant, as if mechanically disguised. The Chief of Personnel did not receive such camouflaged calls. He groped beneath his desk for the button to alert security to activate call-trace electronics.

"Berlin, 1989," the disguised voice went on. "West Berlin in those years, to be exact. There was a girl —"

Jaffa's finger did not press the button. His hand

moved slowly back up to the top of his desk. His forehead broke out in a sweat.

"Her name was Elsa Klugmann," the tinny voice continued. "Sixteen years old. Pregnant with your child. Her father was high up in the BND — a hard man, not one anybody would want to cross —"

Her father. Walter could still see the bulldog face, its icy implacability. In those days, West Germany's BND — the Bundesnachrichtendienst, or Federal Intelligence Agency — was finally emerging from political scandal, years after Chancellor Willy Brandt's government was brought down when a Stasi mole was uncovered at his right hand. After that, the BND tightened up, became as merciless as the Stasi itself, although they never stooped to the wholesale bugging, brainwashing, and blackmail to which the Stasi subjected their own citizens in East Germany.

Not, he thought bitterly, that he could attest to it from personal experience.

He had loved Elsa, but it had been a sin to have sex before marriage. When Herr Klugmann learned what Walter Jaffa had "done" to his girl, he ordered her to have an abortion, although Jaffa begged Klugmann to let him marry her.

Herr Klugmann was an atheist. His own father had been not only an atheist but a member of the SS. He was damned if he would let that *verdammter Schweinehund* marry his Elsa. He wanted Jaffa gone. Permanently. So he arrested a Stasi spy and planted papers on him that incriminated Jaffa as a Communist asset. He promised the panicked Stasi operative that he would go free, if he helped destroy Jaffa.

Elsa sent a message, telling Jaffa about it and begging him to rescue her. Jaffa was desperate. At that point, the CIA knew nothing about any of it. Once they did, his career would be over, and he would still not be able to save the child.

Jaffa prayed for hours, using the *cilice* — the spiked thigh band — for self-mortification, until God at last gave him an idea: He had an inheritance — nearly $100,000. Using a connection provided by the legendary spymaster Red Jack O'Keefe, he contacted the best contract assassin — the Carnivore. When he accepted you as a client, you were guaranteed the wet work would be perfectly executed and never traced.

Five days later, Herr Klugmann and his Stasi collaborator died in a tragic car crash on the way to federal court. A freak accident, German police said, caused by mechanical malfunction on a steep hill. The Klugmann family was desolated, although Frau Klugmann recovered enough to remarry within three months. By then, Walter and Elsa were also married, and he had secured a transfer back to the States.

The whispery voice on the phone said, "I doubt Langley will view this as a small matter, not to mention the reactions of the attorney general and the German police. In or out of prison, your survival will be brief. The BND has a long memory — and an even longer arm — when one of its own is assassinated."

No one succeeded in the CIA, certainly did not rise high, without iron control. None of his fear showed in Jaffa's voice. "Who is this?" he demanded. "I don't know where you got this fantasy, but I guarantee —"

"Threats are a waste of time. I have a solution for you. You have a retired agent named Elizabeth Sansborough. I expect you recognize the name."

Jaffa felt as if he were standing at the edge of a bottomless void. The man *did* know, because the Carnivore's only child was Liz Sansborough. Jaffa's life of service was over. His work, his wife, his children — gone. He had expected this day to come, despite the Carnivore's near-mythical secrecy. Someday, someone would find out he had hired an assassin to terminate his children's grandfather.

The man said, "Am I correct, Walter, that she came to your attention recently?"

He recalled a minor report that she might have activated herself. But that was for operations. Still, as the question lingered in his ears, he began to hope. This bastard wanted to make a deal.

"Yes," Jaffa said cautiously.

"Her father left files. A complete record. You're in there, Walter. In detail."

"No!"

"If you do exactly as I say, your file will be destroyed."

Twenty-Nine

Paris, France

Simon parked two blocks away, closer than he considered prudent, but he was in a hurry and worried about Sarah. As he got out, shapeless forms with the parched voices of addicts whispered pleas from the night's shadows. A bar door opened, and laughter and cigarette smoke billowed out. The muggy air was clogged with the odors of dust and cooling asphalt.

He wanted no problems to slow him, but the night had a ragged feel to it, as if anything desperate could happen. He pulled a bouquet of wilted flowers from a trash bin, snapped on his sunglasses, and headed off into the night with a vacant smile, as if he were mentally unbalanced. He carried the flowers in front in both hands, like an upright corpse. With luck, he would look deranged enough, or dangerous enough, that the locals would figure he was not worth their trouble.

A pack of young men covered with tattoos and body piercings advanced as if they owned the sidewalk, their expressions dark and angry. The hair on Simon's arms rose, and he studied them for weapons, but they moved past as if he were invisible.

Two blocks later, he turned into an alley that was a narrow canyon between towering tenements. A ribbon of moonlight ran the length of the cobblestones to the other end, while the shadows on either side were black and forbidding.

He lobbed the flowers into a garbage can and advanced, his nerves afire. When Sarah emerged from a shadow, smiling that million-watt grin of hers, his heart beat faster. There was just enough light that her short hair glowed like a halo around her face. As she hurried toward him, paralleling the stream of moonlight, he imagined he could see that sexy mole that was so tempting at the corner of her mouth.

Suddenly, she was running.

Surprised, he felt himself open his arms with a guilty thrill. His steps quickened, eager. He wanted to pull her to him, inhale her scent, hold her — and saw she was no longer smiling. Her eyes had narrowed, and her right hand hung low at her side, urgently signaling: *Keep coming forward. Keep doing what you're doing.*

Her gaze was locked on something beyond his shoulder. He started to look, but she swung her finger left and right — *no.* A chill shot up his spine. The skin on the back of his neck puckered. He listened but heard nothing unusual.

He kept up his pose, his arms still wide. "Darling!"

Sarah lunged past.

Simon heard her shoulder bag hit the pavement. He whirled as her foot lashed up and knocked the arm of a man who had been just six feet behind. Something shiny — a stiletto — dropped with a metallic clatter and skittered into the moonshine.

Simon started to rush to help, but she deflected a punch and chopped left and right with paralyzing sword-hand strikes into either side of the man's neck. Simon was amazed at her skill and speed. She had the advantage of surprise, but that did not explain the professional level of her execution. There was no pause, no motion wasted. If she had hesitated or made the tiniest mistake, she could be dead — and so might he.

As the man toppled backward, the moonlight caught his face. Christ. It was that bastard from Jackie Pahnke's photo store again. Simon ran to him.

Panting, Sarah stared down. "Who is he?"

As he told her, Simon snapped up the stiletto, stepped on the blade, and broke it from the handle. He kicked the halves into a trash pile. "I saw him again in a photo shop right before I drove here." He stared at her sleeve. The cloth was wet and dark — blood? Now her face revealed fatigue and tension, hidden earlier by her big smile. She had put on a great show. "You're hurt." He gestured at her arm, concerned.

"It's nothing." Liz pushed her throbbing wound from her mind. *If it's not life-threatening, don't think about it.* What was important was that Simon was here. She looked him up and down, savoring his rangy body and handsome face, his smashed nose and intelligent eyes. She was growing fond of him.

He nodded, scanned the alley once, and crouched to search the man's pockets. He would argue with her about her arm later.

She knelt beside him. "So he followed you."

"Looks like it," Simon admitted. "I never spotted a thing."

"He's good."

Simon found no identification or clue to as who the killer was or why he was in pursuit. He pulled a Glock from the fellow's shoulder rig and checked the ammo clip. It fired 9-mm Parabellum cartridges. The clip was full. He set the Glock beside him and inspected the man's shoes. They had crepe soles, which explained why his tread had been so quiet. When Simon looked across at her, she was staring at the weapon.

The gun was a Glock 19, a self-cocking automatic that was reliable, compact, and relatively lightweight, because some 40 percent of it was molded from plastics. Police and military forces around the world, including in the United States, favored it or the Glock 17L, essentially the same weapon but with a longer barrel.

As she stared, Liz felt a wrenching moment of indecision, the final few seconds in which one could still rethink one's position. In the end, it was simple: All violence was wrong. She knew the future — if there were to be a future — would be without violence, no matter how distant that future might be. But the future was also now. What she — what any of us did *now* created the future.

Torn, she felt again the pain of her guilt about

Sarah. Tish Childs. Mac. The dead men in the Eisner-Moulton warehouse. The dean and his wife. Kirk.

"What is it?" he frowned, puzzled.

"Give me the gun."

Simon raised an eyebrow. "Changed your mind?"

"Seems so." Her tone was emotionless. She took it, hefted it in one hand, and turned it from side to side, getting the feel. "It'll do."

As Simon watched, she rose to her feet, and her gaze and the pistol moved effortlessly together, as if they were connected. She was standing sentry without being asked. He noted this as the memory of her karate attack lingered in his mind. For a journalist, even one who had received special training at the CIA's ultrasecret, highly regarded Ranch, she was remarkably capable.

On the dark alley floor, the man moaned. "He's coming around," she said.

"Time to have a chat with the bugger," Simon agreed.

A second, less insistent moan followed. Keeping his voice low, Simon demanded, "Who are you? Who do you work for?"

The man had a face that seemed untouched by emotion, almost unused. Simon bent to shake him, when suddenly Sarah's palm rammed Simon's back, catching him by surprise. He sprawled onto his face, lying on top of the attacker.

Sarah dropped flat beside him and whispered, "Stay down!"

He turned to look at her. She was staring back toward the alley's mouth, where he had entered. The Glock followed her line of sight to a stout woman who slipped along a shadowy tenement wall as she pulled an Uzi from a shopping bag.

Without a word, Simon carefully rolled off the semiconscious man and aimed his Sig Sauer. Behind the woman, street traffic continued to hum past.

He whispered, "She doesn't look dangerous."

"She's a professional killer," she whispered back. "She makes herself look soft and overweight, but that's muscle. She carries a shopping bag and acts like an ordinary housewife so she can lull people, make them careless."

The woman had not bothered to change her appearance — the same cropped brown hair, the same red-brown lipstick, the same serviceable trousers, blouse, and jacket. She advanced carefully, searching for something . . . or someone.

"How do you know?" he asked.

"She's been surveilling me off and on, and I'm pretty sure she killed Mac. She's working for the people who have the files." And she had led the team that had kidnapped Sarah and Asher a second time.

On the cobblestones, the man twitched. Definitely returning to consciousness.

"So . . . if by chance she's with our friend here —" Simon began.

"They know you're looking for the files. Remember, my cell was bugged. Whoever has the files has decided he needs to wipe you, too."

"Just what I wanted to hear."

The man's eyes fluttered. As soon as Simon pressed the muzzle of his Sig Sauer against the man's temple, one hand shot up to grab it.

Simon cocked the trigger. "Hear that, bloke?" he asked softly. "That's your last memory before your brain blows."

The eyes flew open. Saw Simon. Checked out the gun. His expression did not change. He lowered his hand. "We need to talk."

"Don't talk. Whisper," Simon ordered. "Who sent you?"

Liz rose to a crouch and focused on the woman as she continued to prowl toward them. She was hugging the tenements now, where the shadows were densest. The only reason she was visible was because she was erect and moving, reflecting just enough moonlight to be seen by anyone who knew where to look. The traffic and distant music were loud enough to cover their whispers, and she apparently had not yet heard or seen them where they hunched in dark shadow.

"It's just what she said," the man told Simon, lowering his voice again as Simon pushed the gun deeper into his temple. "We know you're working together."

"You didn't answer the question. Who are you? Who's paying you?"

With no change in expression, without a tic of muscle to warn them, the man's mouth snapped open, and he bellowed, "Beatrice!" He rolled away from Simon's gun, kicked Simon, grabbed his ankles, and threw him. Not only solidly built, he was strong, and this time *he* had the advantage of surprise.

As Simon lunged back, the man ducked and yanked the knife from the ankle sleeve under Simon's trousers. Now he was armed. At the same time, the woman yelled, "Malko!" She opened fire and ran toward the sound of his shout. Her bullets exploded into the cobblestones, searching for them, sending chips flying like razors.

All of this happened in seconds. As Simon kicked and searched for an angle to fire his Sig Sauer, he roared, "Sarah!"

Liz felt paralyzed where she crouched, one knee up, both hands aiming the Glock. Then a voice inside her mind spoke calmly, *You made a decision. You don't have time to agonize.* She squeezed the trigger.

The Glock's kick sent a battery shock up her arms, and something inside her shattered. A piece of her that she valued vanished, but her bullet hit Beatrice dead-on. Beatrice continued two more steps, then slumped as if her spine were dust.

As she pitched forward, the man punched a fist straight into Simon's belly and slammed the other up into his jaw. Simon collapsed, and Liz whirled the Glock to shoot again. The man kicked it out of her hand and ran.

Swearing, Liz scooped up the Glock and gave chase, but the man named Malko was next to the tenements, in the deepest shadows. Before she could close in, he disappeared into the darkness, a phantom swallowed by the night. She spun on her heel, raced to the woman, and rolled her over. The chest was bloody. No pulse. For a moment, Liz looked at the dead face and wondered who she really was. Whether this woman, Beatrice, had a husband, children, a life.

Then she shook the thought off. She would mourn later. Now there was a job to finish, a blackmailer to stop, and Sarah and Asher to find. Liz searched the woman but found nothing useful. She grabbed the woman's Uzi, ran back, snatched up the Sig Sauer, and bent over Simon.

"Simon?"

His eyes were closed. His right foot was tucked up under his left thigh in an unnatural position, and his head was twisted to the side. Blood glistened on the cobblestones.

Thirty

Terrified, Liz pressed her ear against Simon's chest. When she heard his strong heartbeat, she sat up and wiped moistness from her eyes. *Thank God.* She glanced around. No sign where their attacker had gone.

Simon groaned. Liz studied him. His wavy hair was a disaster, his big features splotched and dirty, and his sports jacket and trousers rumpled. She smiled. "Look at you," she murmured. "Still the family bad boy." She straightened his leg and adjusted his head gently. Then she shook his shoulder roughly. "Simon, wake up! Wake up, dammit. We've got to get out of here!"

He opened his eyes and groaned again. "Bloody hell. I screwed up proper."

"You did fine. We were both distracted, and he knew what he was doing. He beat me, too. Ran off before I could stop him. Can you walk?" As he swayed up to his feet, she watched the alley, wondering again how Malko had found Simon here.

"I hope so. I'm too banged up to drive." He holstered his Sig Sauer and knife, then limped off, heading for the other end of the alley. "Better we go out this way, in case we get any more visitors," he explained.

She joined him. "Your mind appears to be working fine, but your wobbling feet indicate drunkenness."

"I wish. Do something useful, will you? Shoot out that blasted streetlight."

"When we're closer. My aim's not reliable. It's been too long."

"Looked bloody reliable to me. Dropped Beatrice with one shot."

"Trust me. It was pure luck."

Above them, the tenements towered seamlessly one after another, not a breath of air between. On high alert, Liz kept the Glock in her hand and tucked the Uzi into her purse. The grip still stuck out, but at least the weapon was less noticeable.

At the mouth of the alley, they peered out. The street was mixed residential-commercial. The bars exploded with noise every time a door opened. Rusty heaps jammed the curbs, sandwiched together as if by a Goliath's putty knife. Traffic rolled past. Pedestrians walked, strolled, and staggered.

Simon was quiet, still collecting himself. When there was a break in pedestrians, Liz shot out the streetlight, and they hurried off. It was only a matter of time until he bombarded her with questions. Right now, she had a large one for him.

"I've been thinking about the guy with the stiletto," she said, keeping her voice low as she scanned the neighborhood. "Beatrice called him

Malko. If Malko had a team to back him up, they should've been around to help when I jumped him. But there was only her. Since he called to her, I assume he was expecting her."

She glanced at Simon, saw he was staring at her.

He looked away quickly. "You have a theory?"

"As a matter of fact, I do," she continued. "Maybe the reason you didn't see him surveilling you was because he really *was* out of sight. And maybe he didn't need a full team, because he could surveil you alone . . . because he or someone else planted a tracking device on your car, the way the kidnappers did with my cell."

Simon shook his head. "No way. No one went near the car before he found me. No . . ." Then he remembered. "Damn and damn again. The bicyclist." He described the "accident" in Chantilly. "The kid fooled me, but it was that guy — Malko — who must've set it up. He could've tailed me to the village from the baron's château."

"These people are damn good, and they have one hell of a lot more people power than we do." She sensed he was staring at her again. She turned quickly, caught him in the act, and had an uneasy feeling she knew what was on his mind.

"What?" she demanded.

He hesitated, then said slowly, "You look damned comfortable with a weapon in your hand. You took out Beatrice with one shot, even though she was running. You know far more than the rudiments of karate. You're good at tactics and execution, too. You play a role believably —

you didn't miss a beat when we interviewed Jimmy Unak. And now you went straight for a tracking device to explain how the killer found me. Not to mention, of course, that you're injured and trying to ignore it."

Inwardly, she sighed. "I'm sure there's a point somewhere in your rambling."

"As if you didn't know." He gave a short smile. "Let's think. If I'd wanted to send someone after the Carnivore's files, it would've been his daughter, not the niece who barely knew him. Obviously, Liz is the better-informed, far more experienced hunter, not Sarah. At the same time, why are you so very good at what Liz was trained for? True, you've had some tradecraft, but not enough to explain your expertise."

He watched her face for a reaction. Her eyes were dark pools, unreadable.

Finally, she murmured, "All right. Say it, Simon."

"You're Liz."

She heaved a sigh. "You always were a little rat." She smiled. When she saw his expression, she chuckled. "I was going to tell you now anyway."

He felt himself flush. "Bloody hell, you *are* Liz. You could've let me in on this before. Damn irritating of you." He scowled. "And I told you about my crush. Of all the underhanded tricks. You should've trusted me!"

"I couldn't trust anyone. But now you're beginning to impress me."

"Thanks. I think."

Paris's two-tone police sirens wailed in the distance. They traded glances and broke into a lope. Someone had reported the gunshots in the alley.

She studied him as they rounded a corner onto a wide, busy boulevard. "Level with me, Simon. Is MI6 after the files, too?"

"You believe I'm lying?"

"I know how agencies work. The service and the mission first. *Always* first."

He pulled her into the shadow of a plane tree and poked a finger at her. "We've got to get this straight. I could jolly you with another smart remark, or we could make an agreement right here, right now, that we're operating on a level field. I respect you . . . and you respect me. We work together as equals. Never mind my age, my attitude, or your being out of the game for five years. And no more lies."

"Well, I can hold up my end. But eight years is a big difference. Remember, I changed your diapers. Think a kid like you can hold up your end?"

He threw back his head and laughed. "You haven't changed a whit. It's been a long time since anyone could irritate me and make me laugh at the same time."

"Know what you mean. Let's move. I want to tell you about Sarah and Asher." They walked quickly on.

Yes, he made mistakes, like worrying about Beatrice and her when he should have been focused on Malko. And he was flippant, occasionally inappropriate, and much too interested in his own sex appeal. On the other hand, he was fearless when necessary, smart as hell, and a decent sort.

With cool, detached tones, she related the highlights of the attack on her in Santa Barbara, Sarah's kidnapping, and her flight to Paris with Mac. She did not bother to tell him about the movie in Santa Barbara yet, and she glossed over London, since he knew most of that anyway.

"Jesus," he breathed, stunned. "So that's why you've been chasing the Carnivore's files. You needed them to ransom Sarah. They're damn bloody fiends to have shot Asher just to make the movie believable!"

"Yes." She heard the bitterness in her voice and did not care. "I can see why they took him from the hospital later — it upped the ante, keeping me on track. Except, of course, it didn't work, because I figured out what was really going on when I found Mac and the bugs in my cell. That's when I decided to follow Beatrice." She described the team assault on the Eisner-Moulton warehouse. "I actually saw Sarah and Asher for a few seconds. Oh, Simon, it was horrible. They could've been killed so easily, and God knows whether they're still alive."

He inhaled and shook his head. There was a distant look on her face that he could not quite read at first. Then he understood: She was not only furious with the kidnappers but with herself, and feeling terribly guilty.

"We'll find Sarah and Asher again," he said confidently, although he could not see how. "Have you told anyone else about this?"

"Who could I possibly tell?" She scanned the street. "And I haven't given you all the details yet. How much farther? We need to get away from here." Her wound was on fire, and she felt drained. Still, she had survived, but had Sarah and Asher?

He watched as she clasped her arm to her chest. "My thought exactly." She was definitely no whiner. In fact, she was rather admirable. "The car's in the next block."

The Peugeot waited in the glow of a street lamp, squeezed between other parked cars. They stepped into a doorway to observe the street. A sharp stench of urine arose from the corners beside their feet. They studied the sidewalks for anyone who looked out of place, who showed too much interest in the car, or who was hanging around alone, busying himself or herself with the customary cigarettes, chain-smoking to cover the fact that a stakeout was in progress.

Simon found himself glancing at Liz. Now that he knew who she was, whatever feelings he'd had about her seemed an eternity ago. Still, there was something about their standing shoulder-to-shoulder in the dark, silently surveilling in unison, that seemed especially familiar, as if they had done this many times. He liked that, then instantly dismissed the thought.

"I've been wondering why the blackmailer went to the trouble of taking Sarah and Asher," she said. "The only reason I can see is leverage. He made no attempt to kill them."

"Maybe it's not about them or you at all. Maybe he has a reason we can't see." He pressed the side of his wristwatch. A light flicked on. Although it was faint, it was enough to illuminate the dial.

"How long have we been here?" Liz asked.

"Fifteen minutes. If you're right about the tracking device, that'd explain why no one's watching. Malko figures he can pick me up again whenever he wants."

A police car rolled past. They tensed until it disappeared down the street.

He memorized the plate. "Might as well give it a go. Cover me." Simon slipped out, dashed through traffic, and circled the Peugeot, inspecting. Everything looked normal.

He nodded at her, jumped in, and turned on the engine. She ran, dodged, and slid in next to him. He gunned the sports car out into traffic. Seven blocks later, they were in a new neighborhood. While he parked, another police car with a different license plate cruised past — and pulled to the curb four cars ahead.

Edgy, they watched as it parked. But the two gendarmes were on a mission of their own. They hurried toward a brightly lit bistro on the corner, hiking up their trousers with anticipation, and vanished inside. This bistro was off the beaten track, a good spot for a quiet *bock*, where no one would trouble them or report them.

"They'll be there awhile," Liz decided. Relieved, she rolled down her window.

Without a word, Simon got out, removed his flashlight from the bag in the trunk, crawled under the right front fender, and found a miniature GPS tracking device where the bicyclist had skidded.

He slid back out and showed it to her. "Good guess." His face was irritated.

She nodded. "Let's get out of here."

"Not quite yet."

"Simon," she warned.

But he was already trotting away through the shadows. He slowed, waiting for two women who were holding hands to pass. At last, he bent to adjust his trousers. He glanced up, saw no one was looking, and stuck the tracking device onto the undercarriage of the police car.

Grinning, he jogged back and jumped in behind the steering wheel.

Liz was laughing. "I wish I'd thought of that!"

"Thank you." He let out a hoot of laughter, started the car, and threw it into a U-turn, heading back into the center of Paris.

As their laughter subsided, she curled up, her cheek resting against the seat's back cushion, studying him as he drove. Behind the facade of carelessness and youth, he was turning out to be a skilled, imaginative agent.

He said, "Talk to me about the attack on you in Santa Barbara and Sarah's kidnapping. I'm still trying to understand. It sounds as if they were simultaneous. Both groups went into action at once, apparently without communicating."

"Exactly. But they did communicate. The trigger seems to have been the advance publicity for my show on assassins, especially since a lot of the media reported that one would be the Carnivore. Of course, neither the blackmailer nor the kidnappers wanted me to reveal the Carnivore might've kept a record. At the same time, anyone chasing the files might think I had them or that I'd uncover them."

"Which set Sarah's kidnapping and ransom into motion, I should think." He frowned at her, then resumed his careful watch of traffic. "That warehouse where the kidnappers were holding Sarah and Asher would've been top secret. So how did the blackmailer find out about it? How did he know to send his people there?"

"You've just hit on a major problem for both groups. The ones that want the files — the kidnappers — have a traitor."

His brows rose. "You have my full attention."

"It's the only explanation for how the blackmailer has been able to stay one jump ahead of me a lot of the time. For how he could send janitors to kill me in Santa Barbara in order to stop the kidnappers' plan in Paris before it really got off the ground. For why the janitor in London had to beat up Tish to find out where I was going next."

"So that's it. Some insider is feeding the blackmailer information, but not complete information. That explains why janitors weren't waiting for us at the Gare du Nord, and why Malko wasn't at the baron's château to kill me. If he were, he would've stepped in. Instead, he was there to protect the baron's murderer — Malko's boss, the blackmailer. So the people who want the files are holding back information in an effort to smoke out their Judas while keeping us on task."

She stared at him, thinking, seeing another possibility. "Maybe we haven't taken this far enough. What if we're wrong? What if there's no mole among the kidnappers?"

"What do you mean?"

She sat up straight. "The blackmailer himself could be the mole — the traitor — as well as one of the kidnappers. They could be looking for one of themselves!"

Simon's face was hard granite. Car lights flashed across it as he said, "I'd be amused, if Sarah and Asher's lives weren't at stake. And if the blackmailer hadn't driven my father to suicide. The only good thing is that now, with luck, all of them have lost track of both of us."

Thinking about the power of the two groups infuriated and frightened her. She could still hear Sarah's voice in the warehouse, calling excitedly to her. She closed her eyes, about to relive again the pain of losing Sarah and Asher, then snapped them open. Thinking about the past and allowing herself to feel outmatched would not help. She must focus on the future. That was where the solution lay.

"What about you?" she asked. "Did you learn anything from the baron?"

He peered at her, surprised. "You haven't heard?"

"Heard what? Remember, I've been a little busy. Haven't had time for newspapers or telly."

"De Darmond's dead. Murdered today at his château. I was outside on the balcony — no, I'll explain that later. Just listen. This is what's interesting right now: The baron threatened to hold up some business deal the killer wanted, unless the killer turned over the Carnivore's records."

She sat up fast. "The baron's murderer has the records?"

"I think we can assume so, considering everything that's happened. I'm hoping his name is somewhere in the documents and pictures I photographed. The problem is, I have no way to figure out which name is his — yet." He described the files on Baron de Darmond's desk and the photo wall in his office.

"That's my cousin. Clever fellow. I want those documents. Maybe I can see the answer."

He glanced at her and then away. His mouth was set in a thin line. "We're not really cousins, you know. At least not blood cousins."

There it was again, that feeling deep inside her. "Maybe, but we've known each other so long, we might as well be. Where are the photos?"

"In the portfolio on the backseat."

She reached back. He caught himself eyeing her long waist. Her arm brushed against his shoulder as she returned to her seat, placing the portfolio onto her lap and opening it. She thumbed through the thick stack of photos and focused on the oversize three that showed the photo wall.

"Good Lord," she said in awe, "this is a who's who of celebrities, politicians, military leaders, and corporate legends. We need good light and a place to work. Someplace private."

"Everything's closed now. We could get a hotel room, but you'd have to show a passport." Which would make locating them easy for anyone with the right connections. Every Paris hotel, motel, rooming house, or guest residence was required by law to report guests' names.

She frowned. "Considering how thorough

these people are, and the amount of muscle they're able to muster, they've probably got my friends and everyone I've worked with in Paris under surveillance."

"True. There's another problem, too. I studied those photos for quite a while, and I made endless lists. I tried to correlate and cross-reference but got nowhere. The data's worthless without someone who can interpret it or see a pattern, or who simply knows a lot more about the multinational world than I do. What about you? Are you an expert in any of those fields?"

"No. You're right — we could use some help. But because of Sarah and Asher, time's of the essence. What's your suggestion?"

"I'm going to phone MI6 and report on the level. After Barry hands me back my head, I should think he'd send us to a safe house."

She considered. The power and resources of MI6 were just what they needed, especially now that they knew firsthand how large, brutal, and relentless the organizations were that they were challenging.

"I like the idea," she told him. "Actually, it's comforting."

"Know what you mean." Simon jerked the steering wheel, shot across traffic, and pulled into an alley. He parked and picked up his cell to phone London.

Thirty-One

Even at MI6 London, the hour was late, long past the regular working day. Simon knew that unless Barry was on a big project, he was probably home. If so, Simon's call would be forwarded to the suburb where he lived. Few people had private lives more ordinary than HQ bodies.

As it turned out, he was right about Barry's being gone. The call was forwarded, and soon a slurred, drunken voice answered. When he heard it was Simon, Barry snapped, "I don' know you. Don' call again!"

Simon frowned. "What do you mean? What the devil's going on?"

"Goddammit, Simon! *You're detached without recourse.* I don' know what the hell you're up to. *Don'* tell me! Don' explain! Stay away from me, from Ada Jackson, and for God's sakes stay away from MI6. I hope like hell you *are* Simon Childs, because this is the only warning you're getting!" The line went dead.

Simon sat motionless, stunned. He lowered the phone, looked at Liz, and repeated what Barry had said. "I've worked with him for years," he concluded, his voice tight. "This is no joke."

"You said he sounded drunk. Maybe he's confused or hallucinating."

Simon's blue eyes were dark and stormy. "There's a way I can check."

He redialed MI6 headquarters. This time, a machine answered: "The number from which you're dialing is no longer accepted by this agency. Do not try to call again."

Simon's chest tightened. His breathing grew shallow. As he hit the OFF button, he replayed the two calls in his mind, working to absorb that MI6 had been conned, bribed, or used. MI6 suffered from the usual office politics, occasional jealousies, and scattering of incompetents, as did any large organization. Which meant it could be damned annoying. But at the same time, it was vital to Britain's security, and it was the one stable element in his life. He did not like to think what it meant that even MI6 could be penetrated. He liked even less parsing what it meant to his and Liz's safety.

She was growing alarmed. "What's happened?"

"The blackmailer's compromised MI6. It's the only answer. My God! How could he? *MI6.* Christ!" He gripped the steering wheel so hard his knuckles turned white. "They let me talk to Barry once, so he could warn me. They won't let me in again, not if I use this cell or my real name. If I try to trick them or go around the rules, they'll declare me unsalvageable."

"A death sentence! Why? You haven't done anything to make them sanction you without recourse!"

"Who *is* this blackmailer? Who has so much power!"

Liz hugged herself, chilled. It was time to tell him about the movie: "The people who manipulated me for five years and kidnapped Sarah and Asher have that power."

"Manipulated?" He frowned.

"Tricked. Controlled. Handled. A beautifully constructed, impeccably orchestrated movie on me." Angrily, she described the half-decade marionette show in which she had lived, right up to the death of her fake CIA handler, Mac, and her cell call to her door at Langley.

"Christ," Simon breathed. "You're telling me the CIA *didn't* run your show?"

"That's exactly what I'm telling you. These people have the influence to make a prominent foundation award me an academic chair, one that probably several dozen scholars were more qualified to win. They forced my TV series to be canceled on the instant. And then they had the resources and knowledge to mimic Langley tradecraft and customs so perfectly that they fooled not only me but Asher."

The vastness of the power of the two groups took his breath away. No wonder she had been reluctant to reveal any of it. With his MI6 background, he could easily have been part of her nightmare.

He said, "Sarah, Asher, you, me . . . they're trying to trap us like flies in a spiderweb."

In the alley, they sat quietly in the dark car as the engine idled. She tried to shake off the sense of being hunted, the fear that in seconds someone would jump out with an Uzi and rake bullets across the Peugeot. She looked across at him. He was sitting upright, his hands knotted on his knees, his eyes staring straight ahead at garbage cans and brick walls, his expression grave.

He turned, and they exchanged a long look of understanding. For a few seconds, the car became a cocoon against the noises of the city and the ceaseless threat of their pursuers.

"What about Langley?" he asked.

Liz was already considering it. After all, it had not been Langley that debriefed her the second time. It had not been Langley that created the obscene movie in Santa Barbara. At worst, Langley was guilty of active disinterest; at best, benign neglect. And Langley's experts were among the best in the world. She and Simon could get all the analytical help they needed for the photos and documents.

"All right, then," she said briskly. "Langley it is. They maintain several safe houses in Paris."

"You're sure? When you talked to your door earlier, he acted as if you were unbalanced."

"That was before I told him the CIA had a pointed interest in all this — Asher. One of their own, and he's missing. You drive. I'll call. We don't want to stay anywhere too long."

He threw the car into reverse, zoomed out of the alley, shifted again, and darted the sports car into traffic, the flow pulling and pushing with them. At the same time she dug in her purse until she located the cell she had found in the jacket. Next to it was the light jacket from the alley and a crumpled piece of paper that had also been in the jacket. Someone's note. She would have to tell Simon about that later, too.

She dialed. Frank Edmunds was in his office. "It's me again, Frank," she told him, resigned.

"Yeah? I'll be damned. You finally gonna let me help you?"

CIA Headquarters
Langley, Virginia

Frank Edmunds was disturbed. As soon as the conversation with Sansborough ended, he severed the connection and sat motionless in his gray office. Mr. Jaffa had ordered him to have a safe house ready in case she called, and now she had. Obviously, Jaffa knew more than he did and had anticipated what she would do. Yet Sansborough had sounded so damned normal this time, so convincing.

Outside his window, the tree-studded green hills of Virginia spread into the distance. Inside his office, stacks of files and papers testified to his never-ending work. On his computer screen, three windows were open, showing personnel inventories he was tidying, readying for changes in assignment.

He had never liked Sansborough. How could you trust someone raised by assassins, especially when they crossed over to them? And then when they strong-armed their way back in from the cold, pledging intel that was never delivered? At the same time, he was a professional. He treated all his bodies, even her, with respect. In the covert world, one never knew whom Langley would need, if only to deceive.

He paused to mull what the director had told him she would say, and yet she had not said the worst of it — the ridiculous lie that the Carnivore kept files. He had been thinking about it off and on since the director warned him. If it were true, what a bombshell. But, of course, that would be just another of her fantasies.

Still . . . Asher Flores was a different matter. If he really had been kidnapped —

He dialed Walter Jaffa.

"Yes, Frank," Jaffa's secretary said immediately. "He hoped to hear from you."

Two clicks later, he was again talking to the chief. He told Walter Jaffa what Sansborough had said.

"Those two professors in Santa Barbara that she's talking about are the ones *she* arranged to have killed," Jaffa reminded him. "And don't forget the woman in London she personally eliminated. As for Flores being snatched, that's another of her creations. He's undercover, so deep I can't tell you where. She must know that, don't you see? *Damn.* She's even penetrated us! She has to be stopped, Frank. *Right now.*"

"I . . ." Frank Edmunds let out a long stream of air. "She sounded so sure."

"You *believed her?*" Jaffa sounded exasperated. "That should tell you how good she is. She obviously needs a place to hide, so she's come up with a fairy tale to appeal to your sympathy. She knows you can get her a safe house on your own initiative. She figures by the time you check out everything she's said, she'll have thrown off whoever's after her, and then she can be on her way, clean as soap."

Frank silently cursed himself. He was just another of her marks. Was he going soft? Missing all the signs? He said firmly, "We'll make it look like an accident, just like you said."

Paris, France

Gino Malko slowed his Citroën as two gendarmes left a corner bistro and headed toward their squad car, smiling. He swore and pressed his gas pedal. Looking in his rearview mirror, he watched them climb inside, completely ignorant of the GPS device planted on their vehicle, no doubt by that bastard Simon Childs.

Malko raced the Citroën around the corner, studying his GPS screen. Simon Childs thought he was clever, but Gino Malko knew how to hunt both a Florida fox and a man on the run. No good tracker ever went out without backup. Which was why Malko had slipped a second device inside the Peugeot's rear bumper, where it was less likely to be spotted. It had been easy enough, when Childs parked for a long time a few blocks from the Champs-Elysées. Simon Childs was good, but not good enough, or he would have examined his car more closely.

Allowing himself a moment of optimism, Malko checked his electronic map. The police car was the stationary signal. Therefore, he would follow the moving one. That was the Peugeot. Simon Childs was going down.

Ten minutes after she said good-bye to Frank Edmunds, Liz dialed again. He was waiting with the address of a CIA safe house in the sixth arrondissement.

"It's a good one," he assured her. "I'll call you there to make sure you're okay. Where are you now, so I can give them an idea of when to expect you?"

They were passing through an intersection in Montmartre, and she read the street names to him.

"Be careful," Frank continued, his voice concerned. "I hope you're armed."

"Of course."

"Good. The MI6 guy, too?"

"You know he is."

"Okay, what are you driving, and what's the plate number? I'll need to alert our people so they can scope you fast if anyone's pursuing."

Frowning, she said, "I can lose a tail, Frank, and it's a Peugeot." She asked Simon for the license number and repeated it into the cell. "Why do you need all this?"

"The safe house has a courtyard. The gates are huge — solid wood. They'll need to be open for you to drive in, so the faster they recognize you, the better. Anything special I should have waiting for you?"

"Nothing, thanks."

Edmunds laughed. "That's what my wife always says — 'nothing.' Then she remembers when I'm in bed. It's 'Frank, will you go down and check the doors?' 'Frank, will you let the dog in?' Frank this and Frank that. And if I don't want to go, she reminds me of when I didn't and the 'terrible consequences.' You'd think she was keeping files on me of all my mistakes. Maybe she plans to blackmail me. But after you've been married twenty years, I guess it's not so unusual. . . .'"

Liz's breath froze in her chest. She instantly cut the connection and stared at Simon, shocked. *"He knows about the Carnivore's files."* Fear turned her throat dry as tinder. "I can't believe it. He *knows.* He was keeping me on the line with all those stupid questions. Langley's been compromised. Now *they're* after us, too. Worst of all, I gave them the ammo to find us!"

There are times when betrayal made sense, when it arose from human emotions like jealousy or lust. Sometimes it came from weaknesses like greed or malevolence. Institutional betrayal was something else — so large as to be beyond one's grasp, and far more offensive when the institution represented something bigger than the individual. Something that was supposed to be greater, better, wiser than its parts.

Somewhere deep inside, Liz's anger at Langley had seethed for years. Now it exploded in a tidal wave of fiery outrage. She trembled with the force of it. In her mind, she saw clearly the first time she walked through Langley's doors. She had stood there in the lobby and stared at the high walls, the carved stars, the expansiveness of light and space that seemed to promise nothing was impossible to achieve for the good of humanity. She had been awed and full of hope.

Simon's jaw was set hard as he drove. "You're certain he knows?"

"I didn't tell Frank the Carnivore kept records. Someone else did. It's a trap. He — Langley — they've set a trap for us at that safe house. And the bastard has this cell number now, too." She shook the phone. "They'll be looking for us within minutes."

"Damn! We've got to get rid of the car. What exactly did he say?"

She repeated the conversation. "The final clue was his bad joke about his wife's keeping a file and using it against him. The unconscious is like an underground cauldron, full of the unspoken. Percolating with Freudian slips. Plus, there was the inanity of the rest of his talk. It made no sense, unless he was keeping me on the line to trace the call. He was free-associating, thinking about files that could be used for blackmail, and it slipped out. Now Langley can zero in on us."

Simon whistled. "You've got another problem — the Paris gendarmes. The *Herald Tribune* published your photo today in connection with Tish's murder."

"Oh, no! If they have, other French papers probably have, too. Any more bad news?"

"What we have is quite enough, I should say."

More than enough. All cell phones were registered in the databases of the wireless companies that serviced them. The companies had the authority to use satellite and ground mobile positioning to figure out the exact latitudes and longitudes of where a call originated and where it was received, so they could bill for minutes and roaming charges. At the same time, Langley could either access that information or calculate themselves where mobile-phone users were, based on their position relative to a service's base station. Even if she turned off her cell, it might still emit a homing signal, and there was no way she could find that out without proper equipment.

One way or another, it was possible Langley had already discovered where Simon and she were. Heart thumping, she rolled down her window and hurled the damn cell onto the street. With brittle satisfaction, she watched the side-view mirror as the tires of the car behind crushed it.

CIA Headquarters
Langley, Virginia

Frank Edmunds was stunned. He stared at the phone in his hand. The bitch had hung up on him. He punched numbers. "Did you trace Sansborough?"

"Yessir." The technician repeated the street and address.

He hung up and dialed Paris. "Sansborough's tumbled. She's armed and still with that rogue MI6 body. Pull the team off the safe house and find them. You know what to do." He repeated the license plate number and the results of the trace. "And keep the Paris cops out of it. They're not going to like us mucking around in their territory."

He took a deep breath, trying to quiet his hammering pulse. Then he made the most difficult call of all. "Mr. Jaffa, I've got some news you're not gonna want to hear. . . ."

Thirty-Two

Paris, France

Simon guided the Peugeot around the curving back streets of Montmartre and down into Pigalle, Paris's red-light district, once the haunt of Toulouse-Lautrec, Gauguin, Van Gogh, and hundreds of titled Victorians. Most of the great cabarets were gone, but at night the old *quartier* was still madly alive, pulsing with sleazy bars and peep shows, *tabacs* and saloons.

Liz and Simon watched for pursuers and for a place to get rid of the car, but not on the street, where Langley and MI6 or Malko could spot it quickly. The traffic was bumper-to-bumper with the usual cars, trucks, and — as always on Paris's thoroughfares — taxis, which were the city's transportation curse as well as lifeblood.

"Something had better turn up soon," Liz muttered.

Simon glanced at her tense face, her eyes large, bright, and hyperalert. Nothing got past those eyes. At the same time, her expression was composed, calm.

Liz gestured at three taxis, one right after the other, a caravan. "I've been thinking about all of the cabs. One never really notices, does one? Not in any big city. Like the mailman or the street cleaner, they're just *there*." She told him about the driver who had picked her up twice. "Statistically, that's one hell of a coincidence in a city overrun with them. Every time I look, I wonder. Any could be watching me — us."

Suddenly, Simon swore and slammed the brake. Liz gripped the dashboard. Her seat belt cut into her chest. A small Fiat had darted in front, barely missing their fender.

"Did you see their faces?" Simon asked, clenching the steering wheel.

"No." Liz peered ahead, straining to see in the garish light of the crowded street.

The Fiat slowed, forcing Simon to slow, too. To their left, cars throttled past. They were nearing an intersection.

"I'm going to turn." His voice was tight.

"I'll watch the Fiat."

Sporty small cars like the Fiat were seldom used in surveillance or pursuit. They were too noticeable. Much better to have an ordinary car, but one with a tricked-out engine. Still, there were exceptions, and as Simon turned the corner, the Peugeot's tires squealing, she focused on the Fiat. It stopped sedately at the curb, and a young man in a tuxedo jumped out. He ran around to the passenger door, opened it, and a young woman in a short skirt snaked out and grinned up through her lashes.

Liz turned back in her seat, smiling a little.

"We don't have to worry. They have other things on their minds."

"Speaking of worry . . ." He nodded at her arm.

"A scratch. A bullet creased my arm, that's all."

"Finally you tell me."

"It didn't seem important, not with what was happening. I bandaged it."

"It's still a wound, and —"

She swiveled in her seat. "You just passed a parking garage. We could leave the car out of sight there, if we can talk our way in."

"It's worth a try."

In traffic-dense Paris, private parking garages were usually fully rented. Car owners waited months, sometimes years, for a slot to become available. With such high demand, most garages did not bother to post a display sign, much less advertise. She had noticed the narrow opening only when they were halfway past.

"Okay if I put the Uzi in your gym bag?" she asked. "It'll be out of sight there."

"Stick the portfolio inside, too, will you?"

He circled around the block, approaching the garage's dark entrance again. A gang of partygoers darted through traffic. Horns bleated in protest, and Simon took advantage of the pause to pull into the garage.

An attendant hurried toward them, scowling, shaking his head, and waving them off. *"Non, non."* He had a grizzled chin but a clean, neatly pressed uniform. His gait was easy, although his expression was determined, official.

"Do you want me —" she began.

"I'll handle it." Simon rolled down his window. *"Bonsoir, monsieur."* An air of confidence, a certain glibness, and a common French name were the tools for this short movie.

The attendant was indignant. "Private parking *only,*" he announced in French, moving his hands as if to push the Peugeot back out to the street.

Simon gave him a brisk, casual smile. "I'm using my friend's space," he explained in French. "He's in Nice for a few days. Surely he told you?"

The frown deepened. "I have no memory of you, monsieur."

Simon grimaced. "That bastard Jean-Michel. I'll bet he forgot. Not your fault. But that's Jean-Michel for you. Much too nonchalant, don't you agree, darling?" He looked at Liz.

She forced a smile. "I would say lazy, *mon chéri.* Jean-Michel is seldom reliable, except when it comes to the girls. Then, of course, he is a satyr." She peered at her watch. "May we park now? Mustn't disappoint Marie."

"Right you are." He gazed up at the guard. "We've bothered you enough. I can see you have many responsibilities around here. Jean-Michel gave us the slot number. We'll find it ourselves."

The guard glanced across to a small glassed-in office, where a thermos and a croissant waited on a table. He was a man with priorities.

"Merci beaucoup," Simon said cheerily. And then drove inside.

"What's he doing?" she asked immediately. "Is he following? Making a phone call to report us?"

She did not want to increase suspicion by looking back.

Simon eyed the rearview mirror. "He's still standing there, watching, frowning." He drove the Peugeot up the narrow ramp slowly, past cars that were parked so tightly no door could be fully opened.

"Anything now?" she asked.

Simon felt his gut relax. "He's heading back to his thermos and croissant."

As the Peugeot continued up and around, they watched for a free space. Finally at the top, Liz spotted one. Simon drove in and cut the engine. Abruptly, the car and garage were quiet. With its low ceiling and crammed-together vehicles, the dark place had all the charm of a mausoleum, but it was as safe as anything could be right now, and they simultaneously sighed with relief.

"We've got to keep exchanging information," Liz said, looking back over her shoulder. "If something were to happen to one of us —"

"Okay, you're right. Let's take a few minutes. You keep going."

"Nice try. It's your turn. Tell me about the baron's murder. You said you were hiding on his balcony?"

He released the steering wheel. He had cleaned the blood off his knuckles, but the scrapes showed, small red wounds, almost black in the garage's dim light. He turned in his seat to face her, leaning back against the car door, but his body was not relaxed. It seemed coiled, as if ready to leap into battle.

He began without preamble. "The baron was

indignant, outraged. He was railing against the other man. He said, 'Using the gray areas of the law to make money is one thing. Killing's entirely different.' Then he named people he claimed the other fellow had ordered murdered — Terrill Leaming in Zurich, a woman in London, and a man in Paris. The blackmailer's death list, of course."

"Yes." Poor Tish. For a moment, Liz saw her sweet face, the heating pad on the back of her chair.

"Then he said something about being a fool . . . that he shouldn't have let himself be talked into it. He asked how many had to die, and he mentioned a place called Dreftbury. Then he said, 'I'll give you the money, but only for the Carnivore's files.' If not, the man would get no help from his bank. He threatened to tell the Coil, whoever or whatever that is, and then I heard the gunshot. It was silenced, which meant the killer had come prepared. This isn't about only the Carnivore's files — there's a great deal of money involved. No one gets a private audience with an international banking tycoon like de Darmond unless it involves a fortune . . . or serious blackmail. Although it certainly seemed they already had a banker-client relationship."

"Until the baron had second thoughts, and they came to a parting of the ways. A fatal parting."

Simon nodded. "The killer said one thing that could indicate a more personal relationship. He called the baron Hyperion. Of course, the baron has many names, the way all French and British aristocrats do, but Hyperion isn't one. I checked."

Liz sat up straight. "Hyperion? In Santa Barbara, Kirk and the dean reported on me to someone named Themis."

Simon looked mystified. "So, what does —"

"Hyperion and Themis were two of the Titans."

"The Titans?"

"What happened to the British classical education? The ancient Greeks believed heaven and earth were the first parents, and the Titans were their children. The gods came later. They were the Titans' children." Her heart rate sped, and she pulled the crumpled paper from her shoulder bag. "There's something I intended to show you. . . . When I grabbed that jacket in the alley, I found not only a cell but a note in it."

He turned on the map light, and she smoothed the paper. They read it together:

Call Cronus at 4:00 p.m.

"Cronus is also a Titan name," she told him. "That makes three. Too many for a coincidence."

"How many Titans were there?"

"Seven primary ones, and Cronus was the most important of all. He was in charge, until his son Zeus dethroned him."

"Damn, just the sound of *Titans* makes me uneasy. That implies power. Huge power. The kind Baron de Darmond certainly had."

"The one who manipulated me — Themis — obviously had plenty. But what do the names mean? Some kind of group?"

"A club?" he said, rattling off possibilities. "A fraternity? A drinking society?"

"Could be any of those. And now we have a link not only between the baron and Themis but between Cronus and someone who was in the warehouse with Sarah and Asher."

"Someone employed by either the kidnappers or the blackmailer."

She nodded, her mind moving quickly on. "What do you think the baron meant when he mentioned Dreftbury? There's a famous golf resort in Scotland by that name. When I was a schoolgirl, we stayed at the hotel and visited one of my mother's old friends nearby. Perhaps the baron and the blackmailer planned to meet at Dreftbury. But when? Maybe the Titans are some kind of high-end golf club, and we can figure out through that when the blackmailer's planning to be there."

"Dammit!" His voice rose, excited. "I should've seen it. The baron meant the Nautilus meeting!"

"Nautilus?"

"Yes, it's meeting at Dreftbury this year. The Nautilus Group is a low-profile but very powerful organization of global movers and shakers. Considering the baron's wealth and influence, it's logical he was a member. As much press as the next G8 meeting is getting, you'd think I would've put the two together. You see, Nautilus always sets its annual get-together for the weekend before the G8, since so many in Nautilus go on to it. The G8 opens Monday in

Glasgow, very convenient to Dreftbury. That means Nautilus starts tomorrow afternoon." The G8 was an informal summit of the leaders of the world's seven wealthiest nations — Britain, Canada, France, Germany, Italy, Japan, and the United States — plus Russia. Senior officers from the IMF, the UN, the World Bank, and the WTO also attended.

She grabbed her shoulder bag and reached for her door. "And we have to be there! We —"

She froze, listening.

He wheeled around in his seat. "I hear it, too."

They drew their guns, and she saw the flash-light beam. "It's the attendant."

The shaft of light swept the cars below them on the slope, finally settling on their Peugeot, flooding it with blinding light.

A voice demanded loudly in French, "*Sacré bleu!* What do you do in there?"

"He's better than I thought. He remembered the car." Simon opened his door and crawled out, his Sig Sauer behind his back. He hunched beneath the low ceiling as the flashlight scoped him up and down.

"Anything I can help you with, monsieur?" Simon asked genially in French.

Glowering, the man stood his ground but let the light drift to Simon's feet. Now Simon could see that in his other hand, the man gripped a billy club.

"I waited for you to come out," the attendant grumbled, "but nothing. You must know Pigalle is sometimes rough. Perhaps something has hap-pened to you, *non?*"

"My wife and I needed to talk. Don't worry about us."

"*Non, non*. What if one of my patrons reports a loss? You don't look like thieves, but how am I to know? Drive out, or walk out." He gestured at a central stairwell. "It does not matter. But one way or the other, you must leave. Or I call the gendarmes."

Liz climbed out of the car, carrying her purse and Simon's gym bag. She looked across the car roof at Simon and smiled sweetly. "It's fine, Homer. I'm hungry anyway. We're late for Marie's. Really late now."

He blinked at her and turned back to the guard. "She's the boss."

They walked away, and she handed him the gym bag. As soon as they stepped into the stairwell, they heard the man plod toward the car ramp.

Simon set his gun inside the bag but left it unzipped. He gave her a short smile. "I never thought of myself as a Homer."

She smiled back. "You got even by calling me the boss."

Chuckling, she preceded him down the steps, her apparent good humor hiding her desperation for someplace safe to work and an expert to help them understand Simon's documents. She had a feeling they were close to learning who and what was behind all of these murders and where the files and Sarah and Asher might be, assuming they were still alive. She repressed a shudder and quickened her pace.

They had gone only a half flight when she

stopped abruptly. Her smile evaporated. Light footsteps headed up the staircase beneath them.

"More than one person this time," Simon whispered. "Trying to be quiet."

"It could be nothing."

"Or something."

With memories of the bloodbath at the Eisner-Moulton warehouse fresh in her mind, she broke into a run down to the third floor. Simon was right behind. They ducked off the staircase and out of sight, waiting.

Thirty-Three

Sixty years old, in excellent health, Prometheus jogged along the dark embankment above the River Seine. Sweat drenched him, but he hardly noticed. Of medium height and build, he had always been an athlete — tennis, golf, and jogging. His darkly tanned face was scored with lines from years of exposure to the sun.

In public, he was known for his wealth, compassion, and platinum Rolodex. But the truth was, Prometheus lived a secret life of solitude and anger. His hair-trigger temper was notorious among his staff. Married and divorced five times, he lived alone in New York, Paris, London, and Rome. He was one of the great financial speculators of the New World, a pioneer of an investment instrument — the hedge fund — that was something of a novelty in the long-ago days when he first began.

In his white shorts and T-shirt, he ran past Paris's famous quayside bookstalls, his Nikes pounding the pavement. Not given to self-examination, he had no idea why he needed to run right now. He saw little connection to the events that had been set into motion today, when he received word he was being sued by the State of New York on civil charges that he had steered business to the Darmond Brokerage in exchange for hot stock offerings.

Still, Prometheus was outraged and more than a little worried. This new suit claimed he directed corporate finance work for InQuox — his public investment firm — to the brokerage arm of the Darmond Bank in return for sweetheart deals on initial public stock offerings — or "spinning," as Wall Street's practice of personally rewarding executives with coveted IPOs was called.

The New York attorney general's complaint demanded he pay a fine of $28 million, which it claimed was the amount of spinning profits made when he sold his IPO shares. That was not all. The asshole wanted another $500 million — preposterous! — for what he said were profits reaped from his sale of InQuox shares. His lawyer read him the news story, since he had not yet received the written complaint: "The shares were ill-gotten due to their being touted to the public by the Darmond's brokerage analysts as part of the scheme."

He had met the attorney general at several Metropolitan Museum of Art parties, which he always attended when in New York. But then, he was on the board of directors, where his Rolodex and, consequently, he were in great demand. He remembered the attorney general as small and sly, his ambition feral.

Every time one of his feet thudded onto the pavement, his muscles complained, and his outrage increased. It was all too much at a time when he needed to concentrate on the new deal he was weaving together in former East bloc countries. It was crucial, providing a beachhead for InQuox where creative financing was still unregulated.

Disgusted and at last tired, Prometheus slowed. He signaled Raoul and Roger, two of his bodyguards, who had been running on either side and a little behind. Their faces were red, and they were breathing hard.

Raoul handed him a bottle of Evian. "Shall I have the car brought, Mr. Hornish?"

"I'll walk." Prometheus — Richmond Hornish — drank and hurled the bottle at Raoul without bothering to screw the lid back on. The water splashed his shirt and the blouse of a woman who was walking past with a little boy. The expression on Raoul's face did not change as the woman shrieked in surprise and pulled the boy close.

Feeling a moment of satisfaction, Hornish turned and stalked back toward his *hôtel particulier.* He banished the noise of Raoul's apologies to the woman and reached out a hand. Roger slapped a plush terry-cloth towel into it. As he mopped his face and neck, Hornish heard his private cell ring. It was attached to Roger's belt. He yanked it off and gave a short, imperious wave. The two bodyguards backed out of earshot.

He took a deep breath. "This is Prometheus."

"Where are you, Prometheus?"

"Paris still. Why?"

"We need a meeting of the entire Coil. My place, London, in two hours."

"I'll be there. What in blazes is going on with the Carnivore's files? I expected the next time you called it'd be to say they'd been located."

"I should think you'd have other things to keep your mind busy. I hear you're in trouble in New York now."

"That? Lawsuits are simply a hazard of doing business. I've been waiting for an update about the files from you, Cronus. Are you trying to run this operation without us?"

"The charges against you are far from minor, as we both know, and there are still the ones in California. I imagine you're having to borrow."

"Possibly, but Hyperion's useless for that now, isn't he?"

Intensely private and exclusive, the Travellers Club was housed in an elegant manse in the heart of the city, just off the Champs-Elysées. Atlas vaguely recalled that a nineteenth-century adventuress — a notorious marquise, whose name he had never learned — had once owned it. In the club's Grand Salon, he nursed a cup of Assam tea at a linen-covered table set against a solid interior wall. The windows were on the far side of the room, lessening the chances of electronic eavesdropping from outside. The ornate salon's other tables and easy chairs were spaced far enough apart to ensure private conversation.

Tall, thin, and intense, Atlas sat curved like a

411

scimitar over his tea, hiding his impatience as he waited for EU Competition Commissioner Carlo Santarosa. Santarosa was crucial, because he could approve Gilmartin Enterprises' projected $40 billion deal to regain its once-dominant position in world construction.

He checked his Timex. The EU bastard was late.

Surrounded by dark woods and the hushed air of privilege, the engineer was imperfectly turned out in his off-the-rack suit, sturdy wing tips, white button-down shirt, and Stanford school tie. There were blue ink stains on the middle finger of his right hand. A calculator and a cell sat near his elbow on the table. Although his fortune was valued at nearly a billion dollars, he hardly noticed luxury. He liked the Travellers Club because it was discreet, not because it was chic; because his privacy was assured; and, most especially, because it impressed those with whom he did business.

He was in his early fifties but already had high blood pressure. His unpretentiousness and apparently relaxed nature hid shrewdness and bottomless ambition. But then, his great-grandfather had built the Hoover Dam, while his grandfather was celebrated as the Atlas Industrialist of World War II, honoring the long line of warships the company's shipbuilding arm had produced under the war's difficult conditions.

His father had topped both when he laid the Alaskan pipeline and doused Kuwait's flaming oil wells after the 1991 Gulf War. When his father chose him from among his three brothers to take over the family empire, Gilmartin Enterprises was the undisputed giant of global contracting. Since then, it had been edged out by hungry newer companies with aggressive interests in services and a willingness to merge.

But Atlas was no financier. He was an engineer who came from a long line of engineers. Like them, he ran Gilmartin Enterprises with a steel hand. Unlike them, he still had made no extraordinary mark on the company. He would admit to no one how deeply this disturbed him. However, that was about to change.

When his cell rang, so much time had passed that he knew the news was bad.

It was Santarosa's assistant, offering apologies. "The commissioner is most sorry, Senhor Gilmartin."

Atlas — Gregory Gilmartin — said smoothly, "Tell him I'm disappointed." Like a scalpel, the forefinger of his free hand drew a sharp line across the tablecloth.

"Senhor Santarosa is equally disappointed," the man said politely in accented English. Santarosa was Portuguese, and so was his assistant. Small people from a small, unimportant country.

Gilmartin allowed steel to show in his voice. "I expect him to make time to have a private conversation tomorrow. Tell him that."

There was a pause of uncertainty. "I cannot —" the assistant began.

Gilmartin's other cell vibrated silently against his chest. He snapped, "Tell him!" He broke the connection. As he surveyed the other guests in the salon, he took his private cell from inside his jacket and turned his back.

"Atlas here."
"Are you still in Paris, Atlas?"
"Of course. What news do you have?"
"We need to meet. Two hours, my house in London."
"Tonight? Why so late, Cronus?"
"It's the situation with the files. We may need to re-evaluate."
"I'm not surprised. When the foundation is weak, the project collapses."
"What is that supposed to mean?"
"I've never been convinced the files existed anyway. It's entirely possible we're chasing a chimera."

It had not been a good year for Ocean. A few doors from the Baroque church of Saint-Louis-en-l'île stood one of his favorite pieds-à-terre, a magnificent town house owned by his automotive company but built by a French duke during the reign of Louis XIV.

Bare-chested and wearing linen trousers, Ocean sat tensely on a Second Empire chair in the high-ceilinged master bedroom, trying not to think. Cecily was singing to herself in the bath, preparing for him. He was a vigorous fifty-five years old, with a full head of black hair, a sloping Prussian nose that Bismarck would have prized, and a stocky build that he never allowed to devolve into fat. He had a charming but implacable will, whether at the most lavish dinner party or in the most competitive boardroom.

414

He had taken his blue pill an hour ago. That was usually more than enough time, but today he wondered. The evening heat pounded the tall windows, making the glass panes seem to vibrate. Above the bed, a plantation fan rotated lazily, and for a few seconds it seemed as if he had escaped to some exotic place in the Far East . . . perhaps to teeming Beijing or colorful Shanghai, where Eisner-Moulton was launching new auto and truck factories, and he could concentrate on the exciting problems of growth.

Two decades ago, he had been Europe's most celebrated wunderkind. He had turned around West Germany's Eisner Motorwerks almost overnight, retooling it from a company that produced clunky, sputtering sedans to one that turned out sleek machines with powerful engines that begged to be driven. After that, his empire had grown rapidly. Dodging economic downturns and leading changes in taste, he had transformed Eisner into an intercontinental power house that produced cars, trucks, and airplanes. In the 1990s, he bought the Clarke Motor Company, the declining U.S. maker of luxury cars, and then merged with truck-building Moulton of France. Today, Eisner-Moulton built vehicles of all kinds and classes around the world.

But now it — and he — were in trouble, largely because he had thought the world economy would continue to boom. Who would have envisioned such a drastic downturn? Worse, that it would last so long?

In January, he'd had to fold the balance of Eisner-Moulton's money-losing electronics subsidiary into other divisions. The cost was a nasty write-off of 1.1 billion euros. In March, he discovered Eisner-USA auto units were draining twice the red ink his accountants predicted. Then came the third blow: In May, he'd had to cut off Koekker Air, the floundering Dutch airplane maker, of which Eisner-Moulton owned 51 percent. As a result, Koekker declared bankruptcy, and Eisner-Moulton faced another write-off, this one a shocking 4.2 billion euros. He had just learned yet another subsidiary, Truckliner America, was expected to post losses of nearly 1 billion euros. A total of some 8.3 billion lost so far, and the year was barely half over.

Ocean jumped up and paced, thinking angrily about Claude de Darmond. He had counted on de Darmond's giving Eisner-Moulton a discreet loan to get past this, so he could diversify into new areas, especially in Eastern Europe. He needed that money. He thought about Citibank's problems with the Justice Department, the money-laundering charges against Bank of America, the internal waffling of Deutsche Bank. Where was he going to find a bank large enough, sensitive enough, and healthy enough —

"Christian," Cecily called, her voice a coo.

Ocean — Christian Menchen — lifted his head. She was shimmying in from the bathroom, blond and swathed in some sort of see-through diaphanous material.

With relief, he felt his heart thump excitedly. She pirouetted beneath the gilt cove ceiling. More than a distraction, she was fascinating, as only the young who did not yet know themselves and their impact could be. As the translucent fabric swirled, he inhaled sharply. There was the tattoo on her left buttock — a curled serpent's tail. He could smell her from where he stood, the scent of musk and violets. In his mind, he saw the five places on her privates where she had applied the costly perfume.

Heat exploded through him, but he did not move. He liked the agony.

She picked up her cloudlike gown, turning, allowing his gaze to follow the blue-green tail that seemed to grow backward from her pink ass, snaking around her hip to her belly, where it swelled into a roaring red dragon tattoo perched just above her blond pubis.

He stared, swallowed hard. His problems evaporated. The curls were pale, barely yellow. He had forgotten how innocent. Like a little girl's.

In three steps, he grabbed her wrists and yanked her close.

She giggled, pretending to try to escape. "*Non, non,* Christian. Oh, you *frighten* me!" She was like a French pastry, smelling of woman's sugar and moistness.

"*Bon,*" he growled. "Be afraid."

She laughed again. He bit her neck. She moaned, and he yanked her head back and covered her mouth with his.

Two hours later, Cecily was drinking champagne and running naked around the room, dressing and prattling. Lying on the large bed, he felt a deep fondness for her. If she had asked for a diamond tiara, he would have considered it. Instead, he knew she was content — even grateful — for the thousand euros he would slide into her purse before she left. He liked that about her, that she was genuinely fond of him.

He felt like himself again. After two intense orgasms, any man would. That was because of another, more pragmatic magic — the blue pill. He did not need it for one, but for two — yes, and well worth it.

His private cell rang. He rolled to the edge of the bed, but Cecily reached his suit jacket first.

"Stop!" he roared.

She froze, wide-eyed, staring with genuine fear. "Christian?"

Naked, he padded toward her. "Never touch it again. *Never.*" He ripped the cell from her hand, punched the ON button, and said softly: "Wait." He pulled out his wallet and told her, "Get the rest of your clothes. I'll call when I need you."

She picked up her remaining things, and he hustled her to the bedroom door, shoving euros into her hand. She lifted her face. He kissed her, again feeling the stirring that was so important to him. He lingered in the doorway as she stepped into her pumps, straightened her skirt, and flipped her golden hair back over her shoulders.

As she headed for the staircase, she gave him a happy wave. He knew her affection was fake. He had known it all along, and now that he was able to reenter his world, he no longer cared. He closed the door and lifted the cell.

"Ocean here. Is that you, Cronus?"

"Yes. We must meet tonight. Two hours, my place in London."

"Tell me what the hell's going on with the Carnivore's files."

"Not much new. We'll discuss it all then."

"Damn right we will. This is a big waste of time. We have to get this problem solved any way we can. Do you agree, Cronus?"

"I should think so. But then, all of us want the files, don't we, Ocean?"

Thirty-Four

Aggravated, César Duchesne limped quickly back to his cab, carrying a strong cup of coffee. His walkie-talkie crackled as he barked orders and listened to the reports from his spies as they wheeled through Pigalle, picking up and dropping off customers attracted to the wild nightlife and drugs, the open sex and neon signs selling the illusion of fun. Increasingly, Pigalle was considered a hip neighborhood by the young. Fools.

"Guignot on the rue Duperré at Fromentin. Waiting for customer. Peugeot continuing on to Douai."

"Trevale," Duchesne instructed, his tone demanding, "you're close."

"Got it."

From south of the boulevard de Clichy up to the top of Sacré-Coeur, he sent one driver after another, following the wrong Peugeots. He'd had one report that was solid, a confirmed sighting of the sports car leaving Belleville — Childs driving, Sansborough in the passenger seat — circling around and down into Pigalle, where it had vanished off the boulevard de Clichy. Since then, nothing.

Duchesne climbed into his taxi, fired up the engine, and raced back into the stream of traffic. For a moment, he had a sense of other cabs, other cities, the excitement of love and purpose wrapped in the perfume of his wife. Berlin. Zurich. Rome. London. New York. Las Vegas. Los Angeles. So many cities. The names rolled off his tongue. He could see each in his mind, but superimposed over all was the face of his wife. The face of a past and joy that was gone, erased with her life, because of the Carnivore's files.

Langley, Virginia

Frank Edmunds shoved his fingers through his hair, frustrated, worried. His people had lost Sansborough. The chaotic streets and stream of humanity in Pigalle had dumbfounded his CIA team. By the time they reached the intersection where the last call from her had been pinpointed, the car was gone, and there was no sign of either Sansborough or Childs on the street or in the shops. Now he had ten men out, looking, on foot and driving, while he waited, helpless, railing. Soon he would have to report to Mr. Jaffa again, and he did not look forward to that.

Paris, France

The feet in the shadowy garage stairwell padded past and continued up toward the top floor. Simon and Liz slid out just in time to see the feet belonged to two men with assault rifles. In the lead was a man reading the screen of an open notebook computer.

"Malko!" Liz whispered angrily. "He's tracking the Peugeot again."

Simon swore. "He must've planted a backup tracker on it!"

As they resumed their quiet flight downward, Simon reached back and took the Uzi from Liz. He listened with barbed pleasure to the frustrated shouts from above as the men discovered his car was empty.

Panting from their six-flight run, they landed at the bottom, where the enclosed area was irregularly shaped and lighted by an overhead bulb. No one waited in ambush, but there was no way out except through a closed fire door.

Simon cracked the door open. His back went rigid, and he closed it quickly. "Malko brought a full team. There are four men on guard, armed to the eyeteeth. We could try to fight our way out, but I should think our chances would be damn slim."

"They've got the firepower to stop us this time." Liz peered warily around a corner that seemed to lead nowhere. "There's another door here, almost out of sight."

Simon followed, and she tried the knob. "Locked, dammit."

Above them, voices debated heatedly. Feet descended the stairwell.

Simon had picklocks in his hand. "My turn."

She stepped away. He tested one picklock after

another as she ran around the corner, jumped, and smashed the light with the butt of her Glock. Darkness enveloped them, then Simon's flashlight glowed on. She returned, took it, and aimed the beam at the lock. His face was intent, completely absorbed. Picking a lock could not be rushed.

Above them, the feet veered off onto another floor, the men searching there. A reprieve, but it would be short. With a tinny rattle of metal, he finally opened the door.

"Perfect timing," she breathed.

They hurried into darkness, but they could not lock the door behind them. The lock was rusted on this side. Simon dropped his gym bag in front of the door. Anything to slow their pursuers. Liz swept the shaft of light around what turned out to be a storage room, revealing haphazard stacks of brooms, shovels, and car parts. The place stank of dirt and grease, and there was no exit. Very bad. Still, she studied the walls closely. The room was far older than the parking garage. The wood paneling was black with age, and the red-brick floor had been pounded dusty pink by many feet. Like a cellar or —

Simon cursed and turned to sprint back to the door. "It's a dead end."

Liz caught his sleeve. "Grab your gym bag and get back here!"

Somewhere beyond the door, people were conversing on walkie-talkies. She could hear voices and buzzes of static. The fire door in the passageway slammed open, and the noise of running feet grew dim, heading into the garage.

She took a deep breath. "There's not much time."

"This is an act of unreasonable trust on my part. They'll be back." Holding his gym bag, he returned.

"They won't find us if we're not here." She directed the light over the wall to the left again and hurried around piles of bald tires to get closer. "I thought I saw something." She inspected the floor and snatched up a rusted metal object, its bent shape resembling an oversize mechanic's grease gun.

He joined her. "What is it?"

She handed it to him. "You tell me."

"Put the flash on it." He examined it. " 'Strewth! It's an ancient Sten gun."

"That's what I hoped." Liz rummaged again. Cheap, rapid-firing, and disposable, the Sten gun was the weapon the British had dropped by the cratefuls to the French Resistance during World War II.

Awed, he turned the rusty relic in his hands. "One of our better inspirations. This one's got a bowed barrel, though, so my guess is someone threw it away right here." He looked at her. "You're hoping this was a transition point."

She picked up a yellowed paper crumbling at the edges. "Damn right. Look, here's more evidence — a wanted poster in French and German for a *maqui*."

"If you're right, we've got another way out."

Liz peered carefully around. During the war, the maquis had created secret places throughout Paris, even in the catacombs and sewers, to meet and plan. Whenever possible, they set up another room first to look like a dead end, so the Nazis would quit searching before they found the real hideout.

Simon studied the ceiling. "Would concealed hinges help?"

She whirled. "Where?"

He was staring up. "See how fancy the ceiling is? Too fancy for a storage place."

She aimed the light where he pointed. The ceiling had ornate wood molding in squares about two and a half feet diagonally. Like the walls and the Sten gun, the ceiling had blackened with time.

Simon took the flash. "Watch the line of the molding. See how it indents a few inches and then straightens out? Two hinges. The way it's built, the hinges are pretty much invisible. Reminds me of the music room in Oaten Place." Oaten Place was in Kent, the family home of their grandmother Childs, née Oaten.

"The squire's secret bedroom? You're right." The family story was that four generations earlier, Squire Oaten fell in lust with his children's music teacher. While his wife and children summered in Portofino, he'd had the clandestine love nest built.

Liz and Simon stacked tires beneath the hinges. She balanced the tires, and he scrambled up. He pressed the wood around the hinges until he felt more than heard the telltale click. He pushed up. The panel creaked and opened. Red and yellow light streaked down. He raised his head carefully.

She whispered, "What do you see?"

"Not much yet. Hold on to the tires. I'm going to jump."

As she steadied the pile, he grabbed either side of the opening and sprang. Catlike and muscular, he pulled himself up almost effortlessly.

As his feet disappeared, she asked, "What's there, Simon?"

His face appeared over the edge, dirty and grinning. "This is good. You're going to love it."

"I'll take that with a grain of salt." She handed up their things.

As he aimed the light down to give her illumination, she rolled the tires back to the stack. Again she heard footsteps and voices in the stairwell. Growing louder.

She ran. "Here I come." Swinging her arms back, she hunched and leaped straight up, her hands extended.

Simon caught her wrists with a strong grip and grunted with the strain.

She grabbed his wrists. Pain exploded from the wound on her arm. She blocked it. *Not now.* And felt that momentary queasiness and fear of empty space, as she dangled helplessly . . . off the sheer cliff in Santa Barbara. His face was strained, neck veins bulging, eyes closed as he pulled her up. She had never seen a prettier sight. With a sudden surge, he lifted her the last six inches and dragged her over the rim.

She flopped like a flounder. "Thanks, I needed —"

Breathing hard, he held his fingers to his lips, set the trapdoor back in place, and crouched.

Gaudy neon lights flashed through the window and across his face.

She pulled herself up to her haunches beside him. Together, they listened.

Voices again, this time directly below. She held her Glock close and gazed at Simon. She recognized the same kind of old, cold fear she always felt while waiting. But as quickly as they had arrived, the voices disappeared. She heard no door closing, but that could be because the door was too far away.

He let out a relieved breath and wiped a sleeve across his forehead. It left a sooty streak. "That wasn't bad."

"It could've been worse." Her adrenaline pulsed like lava.

They looked at each other, exchanging a moment of complete honesty.

"Shit!" she exploded.

He released a pent-up gust of air. "Double bloody *damn!*"

"Shit! Shit! Shit!"

"*Christ,* why did I *ever* think I wanted to do this for a living?"

They inhaled several times, glancing at each other, locked in uneasy truth.

"It's been a long couple of days," she said finally.

"You're telling me. And we still don't know where the files are."

"Or Sarah and Asher."

"What a bloody awful situation."

She sank back and crossed her legs, feeling better after her tantrum. "You say *bloody* a lot."

He collapsed beside her, stretched out his legs, crossed his ankles, and leaned back on his hands. "Only at times like these. You swear a lot, too. You may not have noticed."

"Must be the situation. I need to eat and sleep and never think about death, destruction, and greed again."

"Well" — he shot her a wicked grin — "you've come to the right place." He swung an arm.

Her eyes moved first, then her head. Mirrored panes on the ceiling above the bed reflected its kingly size and its purple velvet coverlet. Little pillows in the shapes of various genitalia were arranged beneath the headboard, which sported a painted rocking horse, noticeably well endowed. Drawings of nude women and men in a multitude of provocative poses decorated the walls. A bidet and toilet were visible through one door, and a small kitchen showed through another, all illuminated only by the loud neon lights that winked in through a single large window.

Liz burst into laughter. "Who would have thought!"

"Imagine the delight of the *maquis*."

"I'm not sure I'm capable."

The trapdoor was beside an oversize dresser. She got to her feet.

He saw what she was doing. "I'll help."

She put her hip into it. "No need. Women have been moving furniture for thousands of years."

He leaned his shoulder against it anyway, and they shoved. When two dresser legs were resting on the trapdoor, Simon checked the bolt on the studio's door and hurried to the window, where he pressed back to the side, out of sight. His chin was brown with beard stubble. Dust coated his hair. His tan sports jacket was filthy. She suddenly wanted to ask how his nose got broken. Instead, she knelt beside his gym bag and took out the three oversize prints of the baron's photo wall.

"I'm going to snatch a bit of time to work." She carried them closer to the window, where the light was best, and sat on the floor.

Thirty-Five

As Simon peered down at the carnival atmosphere of Pigalle, four men stood in a huddle beneath his window, smoothing their jackets, as if assuring themselves they had their pistols. Two more emerged from the garage, carrying automatic rifles close to their sides, where they would be less noticeable. A Citroën sedan filled the garage's opening. It reminded him of the one that passed him as he had sped away from the baron's château.

He described for Liz what he saw. Legs crossed in a lotus position, she studied the three big photos. She looked like a college girl, auburn head bent, intense.

"Find anything?" he asked.

"It's amazing the people the baron consorted with. Everyone from Maria Callas and Aristotle Onassis to George and Laura Bush. Parties, yachting, official occasions, political events, coronations. There's almost fifty years of photos here, and he's in every one. Considering his companions' star quality, my guess is he was showing restraint. He probably could've hung ten times this many." She looked up, her face somber. "And if

Themis and Cronus are of like stature —"

"Exactly. Their photos and the blackmailer's may be there, too. But which ones?"

"Good question." She resumed her scrutiny, muttering to herself.

Simon reported, "Malko's just joined the crew. He's giving instructions. Wish I could lip-read. I thought I recognized that Citroën. He's getting in it and driving off."

Liz's mind was elsewhere. "Both your father and Grey Mellencamp were prominent politicians. If we're right that your father was blackmailed for his vote, and Grey Mellencamp was probably blackmailed for something similar, since he was secretary of state at the time, then the man with the files isn't after just money. That's confirmed by his blackmailing Terrill Leaming, making him take the fall for the baron."

"He wants something else. The 'deal' he was talking to the baron about."

She looked up and considered Simon's profile, the good chin, the determined mouth, then moved her mind back to business. "You wondered at one point whether something besides the publicity for my new shows had made this situation erupt. What if you're right? What if the blackmailer is choosy and blackmails only when he needs some action to make one of his deals succeed?"

"As with the baron? Of course, his attempt there failed miserably, and it failed with Grey Mellencamp and with my father. Three deaths. What we don't know is how many times he's succeeded."

"Exactly. If we're right and he's a Titan, he won't stop easily. He'll still try to put this deal together."

"I agree, but let's not get too far ahead of ourselves. Our main problem's escape. You're dirty enough to have been dragged down a muddy road." As she bristled, he said quickly, "And I probably look as if I've been on a three-week bender. The last thing we need is to draw attention to ourselves. Let's clean up, eat whatever's here, and get out." He headed into the bathroom and closed the door.

"Get out how?" she asked. But he did not answer.

As water rushed in the bathroom, Liz strode to the window. A delivery van with a florist's logo had backed into the driveway, blocking it, while eight men jumped out of the side door. Her stomach knotted. Reinforcements had arrived. Two pairs deployed up and down the block, while another ran into the garage, and the fourth crossed the street. She surveyed the area, viscerally aware Simon and she were the intended prey of a squad of armed hunters who gave every appearance of being well trained, well disciplined, and thoroughly determined.

At the same time, raucous life on the street went on, absorbing the quiet killers into the crowds. On the corner ahead, a mime in whiteface pretended to be a windup tin soldier, while another, sporting a bulbous red nose, nimbly juggled four oversize dildos. Each dildo was a different brilliant color. A throng had gathered, laughing.

But what held her attention were the mimes' white faces. They transported her back to when she was negotiating the coming-in of the Carnivore — in Avignon — disguised as a countrywoman, calling out her wares. When a traveling circus paraded up the street, she joined the crowd to watch as the clowns arrived — tumbling and stopping for exaggerated handshakes. Excited, she pushed her bike closer and clapped her hands. Released, the bike slammed into a white-faced clown dressed like a roly-poly sailor. She smiled at the memory. Almost instantly, the smile turned to grief.

She had no time for that.

In a closet, she found lightweight trousers a little too large, a pullover shirt that was also too big, and a jacket that would do. Everything was black — good for the night. She dressed quickly, wondering about their hostess. She looked through the bureau until she found the answer. She shook her head, smiling wryly at herself, and sat on the floor again with the three big prints. With a yellow Magic Marker from her shoulder bag, she circled the three photos of the baron with Grey Mellencamp. One had been taken within the last decade, and the second looked as if it were from two decades ago, while the third appeared to be even older. She studied the last one, contemplating.

When Simon emerged with a clean face and hands, his jacket slung over his arm, she said, "I have a question for you."

"Let's hear it." He threw his jacket onto the bed, rolled up his sleeves, and went into the kitchen. "Keep talking. I can hear you from here."

"You remember us at Childs Hall?"

Whenever her mother and father were away on "business," she had stayed at Childs Hall in Belgravia, where Simon, their grandparents, his parents, and his stepbrother, Michael — Mick — resided in generational family magnificence. Simon had been a baby when his mother and Sir Robert married. Now that their grandparents and Simon's parents were dead, Mick and his family lived there alone.

"How could I forget? That monstrosity of a dining room table is still there. Might as well be glued to the floor. Never get that whale out the door."

"What about the eucalyptus logs Grandpa imported from North Africa?"

"Every September, several cords still arrive, faithful as a bad debt. Mick's a great believer in tradition. Remember the playroom upstairs?"

"How could I forget?"

"Your dolls are still in residency. Barbie and the whole blasted lot. They're in your cupboard, as if you were going to turn up tomorrow to torment Mick and me. Next thing you know, new chaps'll be queuing up to peer in your windows again, too."

"They didn't!"

"They did, you know." He emerged from the kitchen carrying a long piece of baguette topped by yellow cheese, along with a glass of red wine. He handed both to her. "I made an embarrassment of quid off them. 'Here, boy, go away.' And my absolute favorite: 'Have you seen her naked?' " He smiled. "I sacrificed my youth for you."

"Is that why you kept loitering outside my door? You were hoping to see me undress?" She took a bite of bread and cheese.

"I had become an entrepreneur. I had responsibilities to fulfill."

"You were on your way to being a pimp . . . or a spy." She found herself smiling. "We had a lot of fun. Those where good times."

They paused, catching each other's gazes, and Simon said quietly, "Why'd you think of that now?" He returned to the kitchen.

"I'm coming to that." She eyed the photo thoughtfully. "If we're right that the blackmailer's working on some deal that's not only significant but urgent, then the baron's bank was probably only one piece of it. The deal could involve another company or organization, or a raft of them. It could mean not just funding but meeting government regulations, lining up subsidiaries, all kinds of things."

"You're thinking that there could've been earlier events related to the 'deal.' "

"Yes, more blackmailings that failed. It would've been with someone in a position to cast a vote, or approve a course of action, or make a decision that would've immediately affected the deal. He or she died, or unexpectedly quit, or committed suicide, or voted in a completely out-of-character way, seeming to defy reason." She drank the wine — good *vin ordinaire* — and wolfed down the food.

"What are you getting at?" He reappeared with his own bread, cheese, and wine and resumed his post at the window.

She dusted her fingers, gulped the last of her wine, and joined him, carrying the oldest of the prints. "Do you recognize any of these men?" She pointed to the photo she had circled with the yellow Magic Marker.

He stared. "When was that taken?" He bit off a piece of bread.

"Your youth is showing. I'd say the early sixties, around the time I was born. I'll admit I didn't recognize the three at first either."

Simon studied the photo. "Well, that's the baron and Grey Mellencamp and . . . damn! That's Uncle Henry." Simon stuffed bread and cheese into his mouth.

"That's what I thought." Henry, Lord Percy, had been Sir Robert's mentor. Not a true uncle to either Simon or her, but a beloved grandfatherly figure who had shared Christmases at the Childses' house in London and who often invited the whole family up to his estate in Northumberland for winter ice-skating and summer boating. With his own private petting zoo and hundreds of acres for exploring, horse-back riding, and picnicking, visiting Uncle Henry's place was always an exciting event for a child.

"I shouldn't be surprised," Simon said. "Henry moved in the highest circles."

"Maybe higher than we knew. Is he still alive?'

"Yes, but he's in his mid-nineties at least."

"His estate can't be more than two hundred

miles from Dreftbury, so it's convenient. As I recall, he used to read three newspapers a day and never saw a newsmagazine he didn't like."

Simon nodded. "He kept his finger on the political pulse. Knew everyone, too."

"He might be able to help us figure out what the blackmailer's really after."

"True. But he may not be home. And even if he is, his memory could be dust."

"Call the house. If Clive answers, we'll know Henry's there. Do you remember the number?"

"Of course. Engraved in my brainstem." Simon took out his cell. "I won't say anything, so as not to alarm them. We'll just have to take our chances with the rest."

As he punched in numbers, she studied the street, trying to figure out a way to escape.

Abruptly, Simon broke the connection and grimaced. "Poor Clive. I woke him up. Sounded mad as a hornet, too."

"Good. Clive hasn't changed. With luck, neither has Henry. But we still have the problem of getting out of here intact. How about through the garage?"

"Not unless you want to tackle three well-armed Goliaths. Every once in a while, their cigarette smoke trails out, so I know they're still there. We're cornered. Unless, of course, you've developed an appetite for a shoot-out."

Her stomach clutched. "Some other night. Besides, it's better to get away quietly, so we can go to Henry without dragging trouble with us."

"Being cornered makes that tough." He froze, his eyes wary, his body tense.

She looked down. Two men half-carried, half-dragged a limp man from the garage. Someone had thrown a jacket over the face and torso, but she could see the crisp uniform trousers of the garage attendant. As the pair hurried to a Toyota, the jacket slipped off, revealing his face and a bloody belly wound.

"Dead," Simon observed unnecessarily, his voice brittle.

One of the gunmen snapped up the jacket and draped it over the corpse again. They dumped him into the Toyota's front seat and climbed in on either side, propping him up between them. They closed their doors.

"That's the answer!" Simon dialed his cell again. "This is why one must never give up observing. Situations change."

She surveyed the street. "What answer? What situation?"

Simon pressed his fingers to his lips. In panicked French, his voice spilling with worry and fear, he yelled into the cell, "*Mon Dieu!* It is Terrorists! They are shooting!"

In Pigalle, the police occasionally overlooked questionable activities, but not a murdered man, especially when a citizen reported it as terrorism. As Simon described the Toyota and the florist's van in high alarm, Liz rushed to the closet and pulled out black jeans, a shirt, and a jacket. With luck, they would escape in minutes.

As soon as he hung up, she tossed him the clothes. "Well done! You'd better change fast." She packed the portfolio back into his gym bag and laid the Uzi on its side, completely out of sight. They must not be caught in a police dragnet.

His face was flushed with triumph, but he shook his head. "Our hostess won't have anything to fit me."

"You're in for a surprise." She crossed to the bureau, pulled open a side drawer, and handed him a pair of framed photos attached by tiny hinges. "I found them when I was looking for something to wear."

He angled them toward the street's light. One showed a man dressed in a suit and tie; the other a woman in a long gown. The man was handsome; the woman ravishing.

"Come on, Sherlock," she said. "Tell me what you see."

"You're sure?"

"You bet I am. I've found the clothes to prove it — boy's and girl's. All the same size. Feel like an idiot?"

He studied the photos — the same narrow, straight nose, flat cheekbones, and cleft chin. "They could be brother and sister," he tried.

She hooted. "He's a she. Or she's a he. Talk about sexism. We did this to ourselves. Did my dad ever tell you about the word *assume?*"

He kicked off his shoes. "No, but I have a feeling you will."

As he stripped off his slacks, she printed the word in the dust on the windowsill. "He used to divide it like this." ASS/U.ME. "He'd say, 'Never assume. When you do, you make an *ass* out of *u* and *me.*'"

"Uncle Hal did have a way about him." He took off his shirt.

She turned away. The flash of his legs, the length and breadth of his chest lingered in her mind. Sirens erupted in the distance. He dressed as they listened. It was still not definite they were heading here.

She watched the mimes on the corner, and again the memory of the Cirque des Astres returned. Her parents had used the traveling circus occasionally for cover, as they had that day in Avignon. The posters near her hotel had said the *cirque* was pitched at Le Bourget Airport this week, on the outskirts of Seine-St. Denis. It was a manageable distance — if they could escape Pigalle. At least they had a chance now.

As Simon snapped up his gym bag and rushed to the door, she told him about the circus and how Gary Faust, the owner, might fly them to Northumberland. He had been fond of her mother.

"I like it," he said, although there was tightness around his mouth and eyes. At the door, he opened the bolt and peered out into the hallway.

She slung her bag over her shoulder and took his cell. "I'll call information for the number. Let's get downstairs!"

As they ran, she placed the call.

Thirty-Six

London, England

Under the cover of night, in fifteen-minute intervals, three gleaming black limousines arrived at a stately Georgian house near Berkeley Square. Each deposited a passenger and glided away, and each passenger was met by Cronus's man Beebee, who showed them into the smoking parlor, where the beveled windows were thrown open to the rose garden, and a gentle breeze stirred the brocade drapes.

Scented with the rich aroma of fine Havana cigars, the room was lined with eighteenth-century mahogany paneling, original to the old house. As soon as the last man entered, Beebee vanished, closing the door silently behind. Cronus — Sir Anthony Brookshire — relieved to be home, stood at the bar, serving whiskey, surrounded by his old leather easy chairs and the trophies of his ancestors. Here he felt as much contentment as his sense of urgency over who had the Carnivore's files and the resulting threat to the Coil would allow.

Earlier, when he and Themis had arrived, he

441

had left the younger man, already out of his suit coat and tie, to light his own cigar, while he went upstairs to change into his favorite cardigan and leather slippers. Tonight, everyone was casual. They were alone among themselves, where the intimacy of relaxation was important. It was part of the long tradition of the Coil.

As he changed, he glanced at his wife, Agnes, curled up in their bed with one of her gardening books and drifting toward sleep. He felt nostalgic when he looked at the age lines of her sleepy face that he had watched etch deeper with the years. Nostalgic and a trifle sad. He was growing old. What would his legacy be? Would he be remembered as the man who had failed to protect the Coil and the world he knew from the destruction wreaked by the Carnivore's files?

By the time he was downstairs again, Prometheus and Ocean had arrived and were standing by the bar. Atlas had joined Themis in their usual seats to the right of the fireplace. All were discussing the latest energy crisis.

"Oil prices are excessive. More than thirty-four dollars a barrel," Atlas — Gregory Gilmartin — grumbled in English, the agreed-upon language for meetings. "That's why electricity prices are sky-high, gas stations are closing, and consumers are screaming their heads off. Those OPEC assholes are lining their pockets again, compensating for all the trouble they cause in the Middle East."

Tall and wiry, Gilmartin sat curved over his drink, his morose face radiating gloom. His father, a political as well as an engineering innovator, had turned Gilmartin Engineering into a global power house by planting people high up in governments. A Gilmartin vice president became U.S. secretary of state. Another, based in London, left to head the Tory party's treasury. Similar penetrations had occurred in other world capitals. Eight years ago, when his father died and he rose to lead the closely held multinational, Greg was voted to take his father's place in the Coil.

Sir Anthony picked up his snifter of brandy and took his seat near the middle of the semicircle. Prometheus and Ocean sat to his left. No one mentioned the empty sixth chair — Hyperion's — also to his left. It was symbolic to leave it for the first gathering after a death as an act of respect. Before the next meeting, it would be put against the wall, out of the way, to be returned only when a new Hyperion was elected. Sir Anthony expected it to be Alexandre de Darmond, as Themis had suggested. No one wanted to lose the illustrious de Darmond name and vast banking empire.

He settled back, facing the small, attractive fire that had been lit to increase the room's sense of congeniality, a particularly difficult matter tonight. He could see tension embedded in their faces, and it was not only because of the escalating problems associated with the search for the files. He took a Cohiba from the humidor on the table beside him, rolled it between his fingers, clipped off the end, and lighted it.

In all the decades since the Coil was formed, no one had ever been excised from the group or

443

had tried to leave. They were proud that they had always chosen far too carefully for that. The Coil's secrecy was fundamental, as vital as oxygen, and nothing would or could be allowed to jeopardize it. This was at the forefront of Sir Anthony's mind tonight, because one of the men in this room *had* been chosen in error and must be terminated.

He let his gaze move from face to familiar face as they talked. Which one?

Greg Gilmartin continued his tirade. "Look at what happened in California. Widespread blackouts. Hospitals operating with generators. Not to mention the shambles it made of the state's economy." He waved his cigar like a weapon. "A lot of the poor had to choose between buying food or paying their heating bills. Do they starve, or do they freeze? No one should have to make that choice. What do you think, Richmond?"

Richmond Hornish — Prometheus — was the kingpin behind InQuox and a few other investment vehicles that, when taken together, moved a yearly average of more than $500 million a day. One of the most successful financial speculators of all times, he had just been sued by New York's attorney general. Sir Anthony found the AG's naïveté amusing. Elections were next year. Who did the fool think would finance his campaign if he aggravated a man with the bad temper and influence of Hornish?

Hornish turned his sun-leathered face to Gilmartin. His compact runner's body was taut, seldom at ease. "Oil stocks have fallen into the toilet." His words were laced with the brisk into-

444

nations of New York. "I expect wholesale oil prices to stay high until January first." He paused before delivering the bad news: "Even if the cost of crude settles down, we should plan for the global economy to be sluggish again after that."

Although delivered neutrally, his prediction was grave. It made the four other men glance at one another. They would pass the information to their financial people so they could start pulling back, protecting their interests while taking advantage of market swings.

Themis's graying blond hair looked almost golden in the soft lamplight, but his expression was irritated. "Atlas is right. We've got to pay attention to energy and utilities. Oil prices have always been volatile. Fossil fuels won't last forever. We need to do some long-range thinking about stable, reliable, nonpolluting sources . . . not just for cars, trucks, and boats. Electric power's the lifeblood of industry." Themis — Nicholas Inglethorpe — was the youngest and most impetuous member of the Coil.

Ocean — Christian Menchen — cleared his throat and seemed to examine his cigar. "The depletion of fossil fuels has been grossly exaggerated, as has their deleterious effect on health and the environment. I, for one, expect the internal combustion engine and fossil power plants to survive my great-grandchildren."

With his thick black hair, prominent cheekbones, Prussian nose, and proud bearing, Menchen looked as if he were a relic of the past century. Everyone knew his company, Eisner-Moulton, was going through a contraction, and that he was in mild trouble. Even wunderkinds occasionally stumbled. The enormous automotive kingdom Christian Menchen had created was sound. Besides, he had the shrewd mind of a calculator. He would survive nicely, and he was a valued member of their circle.

Gilmartin crossed his legs and sat back, his expression grim. "You build sports cars and school buses, Christian. You don't know a damn thing about energy, except what you read in the first paragraphs of boring stories buried in the back of your truck magazines. You're just worried about giving up gas engines."

Menchen stiffened. "You're thinking only of your own interests, Greg. That's not what the Coil's about. If something's not good for the world in the long run, it's not a damn bit of good for you or your people either."

"Gentlemen, I believe that's enough." Sir Anthony spoke so sharply that they turned to him in surprise.

The Coil had been founded on a shared vision — that six men at the top of the planet's power elite had a unique opportunity and responsibility. That from their lofty perspective, where the levers of limitless affluence and influence were easily accessible, they could guide the world to peace and prosperity. Compassionate capitalism. Responsible industry. An expansive, wide-ranging view of history and the future, not just the narrowness of self-interest. Politicians came and went, transitory shadows across the face of civilization, but the best in business and banking endured.

The correct six men could make lasting change that would benefit the world as they saw it, and along the way husband themselves and their personal fortunes. That philosophy set them apart from Nautilus, to which all belonged, and where the Coil's original members had met and eventually formed their clandestine group, back in the late 1950s. They had seen a deep need to do more than Nautilus, which thought too often only of creating capital while giving mere lip service to the needs of humanity.

Debate within the Coil was allowed, even demanded. Personal conflict was not. And Brookshire had called this meeting for a specific purpose.

His voice was somber. "I think, gentlemen, it's time to speak of the murder of our esteemed colleague, Baron Claude de Darmond, and our search for the Carnivore's files." He recapitulated the events so far — the murders, the disappearances of Liz Sansborough and Simon Childs, the abduction by unknown forces of Sarah Walker and Asher Flores, and the so-far-fruitless search for the assassin's records.

"Duchesne nearly caught up with Sansborough at the Warehouse in Belleville," he told them. "He now has his network out looking. Simon Childs has joined her. We're still operating on the assumption that she's our best lead to her father's files."

There was a general shaking of heads, an atmosphere of disappointment and, perhaps, some guilt.

"Do you think Hyperion's death is connected

to the files?" Gilmartin asked.

"There's no actual evidence for it," Brookshire said slowly, "but that was my first question when I heard, too, and it would seem to stand to reason." Since the murderer was one of the Coil, he had told no one but Duchesne that the baron had phoned to say he might be able to pass along the name of the blackmailer.

Christian Menchen frowned. "I've never liked any of this. From the moment we set Sansborough up in Santa Barbara, I've been troubled. In a way, we stole her life."

"Or saved it," Themis disagreed. "We gave her a prestigious appointment and an entirely new career she appears to have taken to and enjoys. Whoever has the files might have murdered her if she hadn't been buried in that university."

"But it wasn't *her* life. *Her* choice."

"We all have limited options."

Menchen added soberly, "Look at all the murders since. It's what happens when one plays God. It's a slippery slope . . . paved with good intentions, as they say."

"There was nothing else we could do," Hornish argued. "The files are dangerous. We've seen their power. They must be held responsibly. That's why *we* should have the files."

"That sounds downright Machiavellian," Gilmartin decided. "Perhaps no one should have the files. Simply destroy them."

"In any event, we need to find them before we can destroy them or keep them or bury them in some dark hole," Brookshire said irritably. "We'll decide once we have them. As for Sansborough, it's too late to change her past. Our charge now is to get the situation under control again."

"How do you propose to do that?" Gilmartin demanded. "We don't know where any of them are, for God's sakes. How good is this new man of yours anyway, Tony? This César Duchesne?"

"He was Peter d'Crispi's choice to take over the job on Peter's retirement. Duchesne's list of professional accomplishments is impressive. When poor Peter was injured in that boating accident in the Pyrenees, we needed someone right away."

Gilmartin shook his head. "Just because we trusted d'Crispi doesn't mean Duchesne is on the same level."

As the debate continued, Sir Anthony lighted a second cigar. The smoke spiraled upward, but after a time the robust taste turned bitter in his mouth. He laid the cigar in the ashtray and waited impatiently. When at last they reached the point at which they began — regret for the way events had turned on them, but seeing no other way they could have been handled — he broke in. "So we're in agreement we must continue our search for the files along the same lines?"

He watched each one. Which one would be lukewarm, damn Sansborough's efforts with faint praise?

Inglethorpe exploded. "Dammit, we already made the decision! Why waste more time discussing it? The only question is, What do we do when we get them?"

"The files are too dangerous for anyone else to have," Hornish repeated.

"Granted," Sir Anthony agreed, and dropped his bombshell. "But I think, gentlemen, we must face a danger greater than the files or our blackmailer. That of danger to the Coil itself."

There was complete silence, but Sir Anthony knew that in the back of their minds they had been thinking the same thing. That with Sansborough and Simon Childs completely out of their control and supervision, and Walker and Flores probably in the blackmailer's hands, the future of the Coil itself was in jeopardy, with all that meant for them and their plans for the world's future. For all but one, who did not care.

The Coil had not been founded to cause destruction. Far from it. In fact, one of its first members — Sir Anthony's own father — had been deeply involved in Nikita Khrushchev's rebuilding of central Moscow. When the Cuban missile crisis erupted in 1962, he insinuated himself into advising Khrushchev, eventually masterminding the letter that offered Washington a compromise and led to the Soviets' withdrawal, averting nuclear war.

The previous year, an American member of the Coil made another significant contribution by shepherding the Peace Corps to life. In the late 1970s, the three European members delivered a major strike for democracy in fascist Spain by convincing and bribing Madrid legislators to legalize political parties.

The Coil was indeed on a slippery slope, but Brookshire could see no way off it. The Coil must survive — unknown, undetected, and with its power undiminished. The files must be brought in, but not at the cost of the Coil itself. He, Cronus, knew what had to be done. It was the duty of leadership to make these impossible choices.

His voice was calm as he watched each face for a reaction. "The security of the Coil must come before the Carnivore's files. We will find the files and stop the blackmailer, but not now, and not through Sansborough and Childs. They know that someone has been manipulating them, or they would not be acting the way they are. If they survive, they'll fight us for the files and worse. Each has important connections and could cause vast trouble, not the least of which would be to reveal and destroy the Coil. I see no other option: Sansborough and Childs must be eliminated. After that, the blackmailer will have no further use for Walker and Flores."

There was a profound silence. But beneath it, Cronus sensed relief. They had been worried, all but one.

At last, Richmond Hornish took an audible breath. "Walker and Flores are probably already dead."

Did he know that? Cronus wondered.

"Sometimes sacrifices must be made," Inglethorpe analyzed, "the lesser evil tolerated to eliminate the greater evil."

Was Themis the first yes? Eager to stop the hunt for the files?

"Each is dangerous to us in one way or another," Gilmartin added.

Menchen was the only one who said nothing, only glancing uncomfortably at Sir Anthony and then quickly looking away. *Neutral because he was the blackmailer?*

"Then we are agreed?" Cronus asked. "If so, I will instruct Duchesne to eliminate Sansborough and Childs the moment he finds them."

Hornish gave an abrupt nod. "It's time to cut our losses and move on."

Cronus said, "Prometheus is yes." He faced Gilmartin. "Atlas?"

"It's gone bad. I have to vote yes."

"Themis?"

Inglethorpe muttered, "Yes, dammit."

"Ocean?"

Christian Menchen looked down at his empty palms. He turned them over and seemed to study the backs. At last, he clasped his hands in a knot. "Yes."

Brookshire gazed left and right at the sober faces. He drank deeply of his brandy. "So be it."

PART III

Why rob a bank when you can own one?

— AMERICAN PROVERB

Thirty-Seven

Somewhere in France

A noise like rushing water awakened Sarah Walker from a deep sleep. She had not wanted to sleep. She had intended to stay awake to watch Asher. . . . Her hand reached out. His gurney was warm but empty. The blankets were in a pile.

Her voice was nervous with fear. "Asher?"

"Yup." He was at the portable toilet.

She flung off her blanket, rolled off the bench, bowed her head because of the truck's low roof, and stepped through the darkness, using the wall to keep herself balanced as the big rig swayed around another curve. The tires whined, then resumed their monotonous drone.

"I'm peeing," he said in an irritable whisper. "Geesh."

"Good God, Asher, what are you thinking!"

"Want to help?" A smile in his voice.

In the gloom, she could make out his shadow and the rolling stand that held the bottle of saline solution. One of his hands was braced on the wall of the panel truck.

"You're incorrigible." She smiled to herself.

"I'm finished anyway."

He turned and let her help him back to the gurney. He was remarkably steady, although still bent because of his incision.

"Are you really this strong, or are you pretending?" she asked.

"Pretending. Good at it, aren't I?"

"Yes, dammit. You shouldn't be up again. You could tear things open. You've got so many stitches you look knitted together."

"If I tore a stitch, I'd have blood dripping down my legs. I don't. So I didn't. Want to feel my legs?"

"I'll take your word for it."

He sat on the gurney. In the light that seeped out from around the door that separated them from the driver's section, she could just make out that his shoulders had slumped.

"Want some help lying down?" she asked, feeling sorry for him. "No, don't say it. I'm not going to get into the gurney with you."

"You know me too well." He drifted down onto his right shoulder. He grunted as he landed and rolled onto his back. "Has the truck made any stops?"

"I don't know. I fell asleep, too." She covered him, sat on the bench again, and wrapped her blanket around her legs.

He watched. "I really am feeling better."

"You had your pain pill. That's why you feel better. Go back to sleep."

"I took a leak all by myself."

"And you're to be congratulated. Go to sleep, darling."

She felt more than saw his hand reach out through the darkness. She took it, kissed his palm, and placed it back on his chest. He did not resist.

"I'm going to try to sleep again, too," she told him.

She leaned back and closed her eyes. Her mind was crowded with events of the last few days. With the image of Liz's horrified face in the warehouse . . . with the terror of being kidnapped again . . . with the men who had been killed. Her thoughts roiled with the incomprehensibility of it all, and her chest was knotted with tension. She had no idea where they were. What she did know was these men wore no masks, which meant they were not worried Asher or she would live to identify them.

With a chill, it all came rushing back — the blood, the stench of violent death, the gunfire that had seemed to shake the foundations of the warehouse. The killers had forced Asher and her into a panel truck, Asher's gurney in the middle, wheels locked, between two benches. The woman — a harridan named Beatrice — was in charge. She and the men piled onto the benches and ordered Sarah to the end, far from the rear doors.

The only advantage was the door to the driver was open, and through the windshield she could watch trees, lampposts, and street signs fly past. Judging by the one sign she'd glimpsed, they were headed northeast. Were they being taken someplace to be killed?

Whenever she or Asher tried to speak, every

weapon focused on them. At last, the truck turned into some kind of construction site. Waiting ahead was an enormous big-rig commercial truck. As they slowed, the rear opened and a ramp lowered. The panel truck sped inside, and the gunmen jumped out. When one set a portable toilet between the benches, she and Asher exchanged a relieved look. They were going to be kept alive for a while at least.

The driver closed and locked the door to the front section. As the rear doors locked, too, she jumped up and tried the handles on both. Tied to his gurney, Asher cursed. They were in a mobile jail — sealed inside the panel truck, completely out of sight inside the semi. It was claustrophobic and dark, except for a ribbon of light that seeped from around the door to the driver's section.

She released the straps that bound Asher to the gurney. They held hands and strained to listen as the commercial truck's mighty engine throttled to life. Gears grinding, the big rig circled and sped off. If her sense of direction were accurate, they had left the construction site the way they had entered and turned right, returning to the highway, again heading northeast.

But now she had no idea where they were. Going west to the coast? East toward Belgium or Luxembourg? Had they angled south, and she had missed it? She listened to the incessant whine of the big tires and fought frustration and fear.

Asher cleared his throat. "Do you still have the bag with all the med stuff?"

The semi leaned. They were turning again.

She opened her eyes. "You need to rest. To heal. We'll talk in the morning."

"What we need even more is to figure out how to get the hell out of here. It's better to do it now, at night. We'll have a better chance."

"You're a lunatic."

"Actually, I fibbed. I know you think I'm honest through and through, so it disturbs me to disillusion you. But the truth is, I'm feeling a lot better. Stronger. In fact, much stronger."

She said nothing. Then she saw movement. He was sitting again, fiddling with his hand or wrist.

"What are you doing?"

"I can use the needle from my IV."

She jumped up and grabbed his hand. "No! Asher, darling, don't take it out!"

"Too late. Hey! Watch it! I don't want to stab you by accident. I found the little gizmo to turn off the saline solution. Neat and tidy, that's my motto."

She threw up her hands. "And to think my one big wish was to have you around all the time. *I'm* the one who's nuts!" She forced herself to calm. "Okay. You're well enough that I can't control you, so I guess you're well enough to do a little work. Tell me what you have in mind."

London, England

Amid abandoned crystal snifters and fading cigar smoke, Sir Anthony Brookshire returned to his chair in his study and sat, staring thoughtfully into the last of the fire's angry coals. Tonight's meeting of the Coil had been less than satisfactory. All but one were good men with good intentions, people who recognized the need for pragmatism. A vital balance. Without it, little could be accomplished. They had left a half hour ago for their London homes. Tomorrow was Dreftbury.

And he still did not know which one had the files. The act of betrayal ate at him, acid on his heart. He listened to the quiet of the house, filled with melancholy.

When his special cell rang, he reached for it eagerly. "Yes?"

"I got your message to call." It was Duchesne, his businesslike tone no different whether at midnight or noon. "As I thought, Sansborough and Childs are together, but they've disappeared in Pigalle."

"And the files?"

"No sign yet."

Sir Anthony stifled a groan. "How do you know Sansborough and Childs are in Pigalle?" he asked suspiciously.

"One of my people followed them from Belleville. Don't worry. I have the streets covered. We'll pick up on them again soon. The situation is fully under control."

"The streets covered?" Sir Anthony repeated. "How can you possibly do that? You're not the gendarmerie or the French army." There were times he longed to have Peter d'Crispi in charge again. D'Crispi was perhaps less clever than Duchesne, but he was also far less secretive.

"There are ways," Duchesne said. "My expertise is why you hired me. Have I ever failed?"

"You've been with me only a short time."

"If you want me to pull my people, I will. Perhaps you have a better idea of how to track down Sansborough and Childs."

Hot rage jolted Sir Anthony. César Duchesne had just threatened him, and in it was the implicit contention that they were equals. Sir Anthony prided himself on treating employees with respect. He demanded the same in return.

His fist tightened on his cell. In full control of his voice, he said neutrally, "Are you unhappy with your job, Duchesne?"

César Duchesne knew instantly he had gone too far. Sir Anthony was one of those men who demanded not only obedience but appreciation. As he drove and scanned the sidewalks, looking for Liz Sansborough, Duchesne realized he had allowed his judgment to be clouded by his burning impatience to unmask the blackmailer.

He made his tone conciliatory. "Of course not, Cronus. The work is good. The salary generous. The reason I can't say is that those who help me demand secrecy. If I protect them, I'm able to give you the high standard of return your investment deserves. I hope you can forgive my abruptness."

Sir Anthony nodded to himself. His hand relaxed. "I'm sure it won't happen again. I have two changes in assignment for you."

As Cronus, Sir Anthony was the Coil's clearing house for information. It was his job to shepherd his colleagues through the morass of decisions

461

they faced — everything from choosing which currency markets to support and which oil companies would share in international pipelines to which Third World nation to rebuild and which dictator would remain in power.

It took men with good heads for business to make certain the decisions within reach were handled with the best outcome for all, and if this group were less altruistic than earlier ones, it was because the world had changed and not for the better. During the Cold War, it had been far easier. The enemy was communism, good versus evil, a clear focus. Now there were many enemies, all of whom sapped and abused and chipped away at Western civilization. The Coil could not solve every problem it tackled; that much was obvious. Nor did it always make the right decision — supporting the new U.S. president was an example of that. Still, over the past five-plus decades, the Coil had done its best to make the world a better place.

He felt a wave of nostalgia and quickly admonished himself. Such self-indulgence did no good.

He told Duchesne, "As you know, I met with Themis, Prometheus, Ocean, and Atlas tonight. I was unable to determine who has the files, so I'll need you at Dreftbury. The only explanation I can see for Hyperion's murder is the blackmailer must have put some plan in motion. If we figure out what it is, we'll have the blackmailer's identity."

"Of course. I'll be there. If I may make a suggestion —"

"Yes, what is it?"

"There are certain measures we can take."

As Sir Anthony listened, he began to smile. Yes, Duchesne had his uses. He was a clever, underhanded bastard — just what was needed now.

When they finished, Sir Anthony changed the topic: "As I said, I have a second change in assignment for you." With regret, he described the Coil's new decision. "When your people find Sansborough and Childs again, purge them. You must not fail. If by some miracle they have the files, your orders are still to purge them and, as before, deliver the files to me instantly. In any case, make certain their deaths can't be traced to us."

There was silence. Sir Anthony sensed he had surprised his security chief. He indulged in a smile. If he ever became completely predictable, he might as well be dead.

"Do you have a problem with this?" Sir Anthony demanded.

"Of course not." Duchesne sounded bored. "I was just thinking about Sarah Walker and Asher Flores. Do you want me to liquidate them, too?"

"Yes, of course. If you find them."

"If there's nothing else, I'll get on with it."

Thirty-Eight

Paris, France

As she ran downstairs, Liz tugged Asher's beret to her ears and put on Sarah's glasses. Simon pounded after, slamming his arms into the thin black leather jacket she had found for him. He snapped on his sunglasses and pulled his hair over his forehead. The clothes on Liz were loose and long while Simon's fit him nearly perfectly.

She landed on the first floor and sprinted. He was right behind. At the front door, they hid their pistols and looked each other up and down.

"You're good," he decided. "Can't believe you play a mouse so well." She had that same timid, weighed-down appearance that he had seen in Waterloo Station.

"Just goes to show how little you know me. I'm a retiring creature at heart."

"Your nose just got a foot long, Pinocchia. What about me?"

"*Lout* comes to mind," she said approvingly. "Also *hoodlum*. I was getting tired of that preppy look that you seem to think is the real you."

He smiled. "Thank you." Then the smile vanished. He inched open the door and peered out through the crack.

"Well?" she said.

In answer, he pulled it wider and slid out to the step. She was on his heels. Judging by the strident noise of the sirens, an entire antiterrorist squad was on its way. As the street cleared of anyone with something to hide, a dozen of Malko's gunmen poured into the florist's van. It screeched off, tires screaming.

"My God," she said. "This may actually work."

"Scary, isn't it?"

With enthusiasm, they watched the last two gunmen jump into the back of the Toyota. The driver gunned the engine, and the car exploded off toward the other end of the block. The dead man in the center of the front seat fell forward and was quickly yanked upright as the driver dodged from one lane of traffic to the next.

Only bewildered tourists remained on the sidewalks. As the sirens crescendoed, the old Pigalle buildings with their tawdry fronts and tacky signs took on a desolate air.

Liz and Simon glanced at each other and set off at a steady, ground-eating pace.

He kept a close watch for trouble as she dialed his cell. Any situation could reverse in an instant. When tires suddenly screeched, he spun in time to see the Toyota's door flung open and the body of the garage attendant thud out. With another squeal of tires, the Toyota rammed through the intersection, sending cars reeling, sparks flying. Squad cars pursued, their overhead beacons flashing angrily.

In the other direction, the van full of Malko's gunmen disappeared, successful in its getaway for now.

Simon inhaled, enjoying the moment of freedom. So far, so good. His gaze settled on Liz. His heart throbbed with an odd sensation as he listened to her murmur into the cell in a tone of voice that said "old friend." He wondered whether her plan to get to England was workable. Still, he had nothing else to suggest, and she was determined. He had an unfamiliar willingness to trust her.

When she hung up, he said, "Will Faust do it?"

"Yes, we're in luck. Any problems?"

"Not yet."

As he described with relish how the van and Toyota had turned tail and fled, locals drifted like cemetery ghosts back onto the block. This stretch of the boulevard de Clichy between place Pigalle and place Blanche was thick with peep shows and sex shops as well as live-sex parlors.

Warily surveying the street, Simon and Liz picked up their pace. Blue light spilled out of bars, turning white clothes eerily luminescent. Prostitutes wore Day-Glo gloves and made suggestive gestures, advertising hand jobs. Others flashed knives slipped into garter belts. People queued up to watch violent porn films. The air was filled with the odors of booze and trouble and desperate sex.

With relief, Liz noted no one's attention lingered on her, appraising. With her slouched posture and glasses, she was not only unattractive but uninteresting in the charged scene. Still, she could not shake her apprehension. Alongside her, Simon advanced as if he owned the street, the city, the world. Women cast glances at him over their shoulders, and men looked away.

At the place de Clichy Noctambus stop, they bought tickets and stepped aboard. Advancing down the aisle, they casually inspected faces and sat in the rear. Simon set his gym bag on the floor between them, leaned back, and sighed as the bus ground into motion. He ran his fingers through his hair, pushing it off his forehead, and removed his sunglasses and slid them into his pocket, glad to be finished with the idiotic affectation.

He found himself studying her as she gazed out at the glittering urban nightscape. Her profile was tense, her generous mouth tight. She looked uneasy, as if her mind were far away, someplace only she could know.

As the bus entered traffic, he asked in a low voice, "Is losing Sarah and Asher at the warehouse why you changed your mind and wanted Malko's Glock?"

She glanced at him, then gave a small nod of acknowledgment. He had called her back, and, for him, she had come. "Yes and no. Part of me wanted a gun from the moment I was attacked in Santa Barbara. My first instinct was to kill whoever had tried to kill me. But what does revenge get you but more injured or dead people? Your pain isn't erased. The people who've been hurt or who've died aren't healed or resurrected. Nothing's improved. *You're* not improved. You've acted like them, the evildoers you despise. I don't consider that honorable or smart. Certainly not ethical or moral."

"I'm not sure many people would agree with you."

"What you're saying is *you* don't agree."

"Maybe I am," he admitted.

"Violence has become an all-purpose remedy. I worry about what we're becoming. Where civilization's headed."

"And yet you wanted the Glock."

She sat back, grappling with her emotions, trying to be honest with herself, with him. "There are few people with my training. It'd be hypocritical to ask someone else to save Sarah and Asher, using the excuse that I've got the moral high ground and don't want to be sullied." She gazed at him. "I've got to do it, because I can."

"You hesitated with Beatrice. You weren't sure you could shoot her, were you?"

"No."

His rugged face was kind. "Remember, you're not alone anymore."

"I know." She saw something in him that warmed her, made her feel comfortable. Something she had not experienced in a long time.

His eyes twinkled with a certain amusement . . . and perhaps challenge. "We're partners. Buddies. Pals through thick and thin."

"Sure, the Bobbsey Twins. The Two Musketeers. A lawful Bonnie and Clyde."

They looked away from each other. Soon they transferred buses, heading northeast. She focused on the lessening traffic, on the ubiquitous sea of taxis. Had a tail kept up with them? Found them? Impossible, she told herself, but she watched alertly.

Death was more and more her constant companion. She wondered again as she had thousands of times how her mother could have killed and gone on killing. But she knew the answer; it was just that it had never satisfied her — Melanie had assassinated for her country, for patriotism. For a calling she thought more vital than personal beliefs or squeamishness. When Melanie finally accepted that the Carnivore had been lying to her for years, that they had seldom worked for British or even U.S. intelligence, she never fired a gun again.

Liz shook off a feeling of guilt. Now she was doing what her mother had done — embarking on a path for what she considered a higher cause, this time for Sarah and Asher and to find the Carnivore's obscene files. She had become her mother, or perhaps she had been that way all along . . . which was why she herself had been able to do black work for Langley.

She must stop thinking about it. As the bus's tires hummed, she glanced at Simon. His face was wary as he surveyed the street. She liked the way he sat so easily, nonchalant, big shoulders comfortably back, as if he were relaxed . . . until one looked in his eyes and saw the sharp vigilance.

She whispered, "I've been meaning to ask about Nautilus. Before the garage attendant interrupted us, you were going to fill me in."

He looked around and lowered his voice. "You're right. It's critical you know, especially now. Think moguls and kings, presidents and generals. Think a private alliance between Europe and America that's beyond any mere government."

"*Mere* government?"

"You're getting the picture. All of Nautilus's chairmen have been among the world's elite — a former British prime minister, a former chancellor of West Germany, a former NATO secretary-general, and a former vice chair of the European Commission. That's a fact. The people who attend are at a similar rarefied level — bankers, tycoons, presidents, prime ministers, international statesmen, NATO commanders."

"You need an oxygen mask to breathe at those political heights. If our blackmailer is part of Nautilus, then we really have a hell of a mountain to climb."

"Yes, and we'd better be ready. Their security is formidable, better than most Third World nations. That's another fact."

As the bus pulled to a stop at a red light, she asked quietly, "Just how many people are we talking about?"

"There's a permanent steering committee of about thirty — half Europeans, half Americans — and ninety guests invited to the yearly meeting. They vary, depending on who's in power and who's accomplished what over the last twelve months. There are usually future political stars, too. They're brought in as soon as possible to be educated."

"*Educated?* I don't like the sound of that."

"Of course you don't." He paused. Suddenly it seemed clear that Ada had been wrong about him. In fact, he had been wrong about himself. He had not spent three long years undercover untouched, without thinking about what he saw and learned. "I've heard Tony Blair and Bill Clinton were invited a couple of years before they were elected to national office. George W. Bush apparently wasn't."

"For brainwashing?" When he shrugged, she said, "The bottom line is, they're political and fiscal superstars. Everyone should be able to hear what Nautilus talks about."

"They claim they can't be frank if they're in the public eye."

She snorted with disbelief. "When people don't want you to know what they're saying, be warned. It's usually because they're being more than 'frank.' They're talking about plans they don't want other folk like thee and me to hear." She paused, thinking of Sarah. "I still don't understand why the media doesn't cover their meetings."

Simon scanned the intersection as the light turned green and the bus rumbled through. "When I said tycoons, that included media tycoons. They're like everyone else — they have to pledge not to reveal what's said, who's there, or even that they've been invited. That means they pass the word down to their managers that there's no story. Reporters and freelancers have to make a living, so if their editors tell them there's nothing to write about, they tend to believe them. The only U.S. publications that seriously try to cover meetings are usually on the extreme right or extreme left. The exception is the European press, like the *Irish Times* and *Punch*. They photograph and report on those entering and leaving. I'm sure you've heard the highly sophisticated theory of management that goes like this: Shit flows downhill. This is a perfect example. It all starts at the top, and not even the top crosses Nautilus lightly."

"But some people have? That's encouraging."

"But not always successful. Margaret Thatcher tried in Brussels in 1988. She called the plan for a centralized Europe a nightmare and vowed Britain would never give up her sovereignty or her currency. But a European superstate is a high priority for Nautilus, and Thatcher bloody well knew it, since she attended regularly. So Nautilus worked behind the scenes, arranging for her to be attacked and her supporters coerced and her money to dwindle. Just two years later, in 1990, she was forced to resign."

"That's politics. Hardly unusual."

He shook his head. "Thatcher was no ordinary politico. She was PM, with all the vast dominion and resources inherent in the office, but even she couldn't stand up to them. I know you're going to ask why, so I'll just go ahead and explain. The world's changing. It's globalizing along a commercial path Nautilus has set out. The result is that politicians — including prime ministers and presidents — have less actual power in Nautilus, as well as in their own countries. In fact, two-thirds of Nautilus's core membership is now made up of bankers and financiers and businessmen, not politicians or statesmen. Whether or not you agree with Thatcher's politics, what Nautilus did by bypassing the British public and deciding her political future was despicable. The primary thrust of globalization doesn't have to be profit for the few, but that's what it's become."

As the bus pulled into the station, she said, "It's frightening. But that's the reaction you intended me to have. What if you're wrong about Nautilus?"

He gazed at her, recalling again Ada's accusation that he had no opinions. But he had wanted none then, no problems, certainly nothing to rock the bloody boat. Just to do his job without trouble. Now the boat was capsizing, and he could no longer pretend he did not care.

"I've heard Nautilus called everything from an innocent business network, to an aristocratic think tank, to a conspiracy that runs the world," he told her. "We both know anything that's hidden has intrinsic power. And as your J. Edgar Hoover said, there's something addictive about a secret. Nautilus works too hard to keep the secrecy and the power. If the public's ignorant about what it does that's good, you can bet we're just as ignorant about what it does that's bad."

She felt a sudden chill. "How do you know so much?"

He watched as the bus's door opened and people began to disembark. Either they were partners or they were not. He lowered his voice. "I've been in deep cover, penetrating Nautilus's prime opposition — the antiglobalization movement. The world's structure is shifting from the nation-state to the corporate-state, and it's being encouraged, some say driven, by Nautilus. Which makes it a prime target for the movement, especially since Nautilus meetings are ultrasecret, ultrasecure, by invitation only, never made public, and no media allowed." He glanced uneasily at her. "You understand I shouldn't have told you. You can't breathe a mention."

She did not hesitate. "Simon, if you think you're going to have any job at MI6 when this is over, assuming we survive, you're living in dreamland."

Wounded, he said nothing, weighing her warning. She touched his arm and stood up. He looked around and saw they were the last two people on the bus. He stood up, too. Together they walked toward the exit.

Thirty-Nine

As he followed the florist's van in his Citroën, Gino Malko seethed. He was fighting an unfamiliar sensation — humiliation. He snapped open his cell and punched REDIAL and made a full report without bothering to pull off the street.

He concluded by saying, "The police caught four of our people, but none knows enough to cause us an immediate problem. I phoned the lawyer. She'll bail them out and send them out of France."

Sansborough and Childs had outwitted him damned neatly. It was not only that they had sidelined four men; it was that word of it would spread like a disease. *Malko made a mistake. Malko was outsmarted.* The grapevine always found out.

Childs and Sansborough would pay, and painfully. He could promise that.

"Then I can consider it handled? The four will never talk?"

"It'd be a fatal error," Malko assured his boss. "All have been in the business long enough to know that."

"And Sansborough and Childs?"

"They're isolated and on the run. With the CIA and French police looking, too, something will force them into the open. When it does, I'll be there."

"That may be unnecessary."

His boss's unemotional delivery of surprising changes in plan always gave Malko pause. But then, the man did business with the cold heart of a shark, too. Malko admired him.

"There's a new development?" Malko asked.

"A large one." He described the Coil's decision to terminate Sansborough and Childs. "César Duchesne and his people will take care of it."

Malko objected: "Are you sure it's wise to pull me off? Is he really that good?" He had not met the Coil's new security chief, but he had not met the previous one either. The risk of being sniffed out as a link to the Carnivore's files was too high.

"Duchesne seems smart enough. Besides, I need you in Scotland. Cronus has tumbled. There's no other explanation for why he stopped the flow of information and told us next to nothing when we met tonight. What's good for us is that he's cut off everyone, so he's still trying to figure out which one of us has the files. My biggest risk is at Dreftbury, while I'm trying to put together the deal. If Duchesne loses Sansborough and Childs . . . if they stay alive long enough . . . it's possible they may figure out somehow that I'll be there. This is what I want you to do. . . ."

As his employer elaborated, Malko smiled. When they severed the connection, he sat back, driving automatically as he turned the ideas over in his mind, liking them more and more. As he considered the new direction, he found himself savoring the power of the powerful engine purring in his hands. He liked the quiet strength of the black car, imagining a great hungry panther on the prowl, like the wildcats he had seen in the swamps of Florida in his youth.

Immediately, he discarded the image. Back in Jacksonville, Malko had trained himself to limit his imagination. Much better to rely on facts, not guesses; on what was, not on what might be. He had seen not only family but colleagues destroyed by too much fantasy. After enough kills, longtime enforcers began to see danger in every doorway, and then revenge. Eventually, they slid into too much drink or drugs — or both — and emptied their weapons into enough shadows that either the authorities took them out or another professional did. No one Malko knew in the business lived long enough to retire. His own mentor had died at forty-six in a hunting "accident" outside Fort Lauderdale. Malko had always suspected suicide.

Somewhere in France

As the big semi hurtled through the night, Asher's voice was businesslike. "Did you learn to pick a lock when you were trained at the Ranch?"

"As a matter of fact, I did. But I'm not sure I could still do it." In the murky light, Sarah felt around until she found the paper sack of medical supplies under the gurney.

"Yeah, figures. Good thing I'm still a whiz. When they ditched us in here, I got a look at the door locks. They're wafer-tumbler. I know you won't object if I tell you I need that med sack anyway."

"Why? Are you bleeding where you pulled out the needle?" She located alcohol wipes inside it. "I'm going to make sure you don't get an infection. I'll give you the sack, if you promise not to stab me."

"That's reasonable."

"I thought so." She dropped it on his lap, picked up his left hand, and scrubbed.

"That'll do," he told her, trying to hurry her along. "Thanks."

She said nothing. Finding a stick-on bandage, she applied it, then set his hand gently back into his lap. Immediately, he sorted through the sack. She turned to the IV pole. The saline bag was almost empty, which was a good sign. They had no drinking water, but he would remain hydrated for a while. Yes, the pole's metal parts screwed into one another. At last she found the piece she thought would work.

She released the bolt that held it in place. "How are you doing?" she asked.

"I can use the needle for a pick. It doesn't curve up at the end like I'd like, but I've made a needle work before. The problem is, I need something for a tension wrench. There's nothing in the sack I can adapt for that."

"How's this?" She handed him the small metal

stick she had just unbolted. It was like a miniature flat-headed screwdriver.

"That's my Sarah. Resourceful. Thanks." He moved his legs off the gurney and stood, clasping his hospital gown at the back. "Floor's cold." He seemed to be gazing down at his bare feet.

She knew the truth: He was still having a hard time straightening because of the pain. She wanted to tell him to forget it, get back on the gurney, but she knew he would not do it, at least not yet.

"I'll bet the floor's cold," she sympathized. "Dangerous, too. God knows what's gone on in here. There could be screws, bullets, broken glass, maybe metal shavings down there. I'd say you should watch your step, but it's too dark."

"You're much too cheerful," he grumbled. "I'm going to check out the door in front anyway. I want to know what that light's about."

With misgivings, she grabbed a blanket and followed. They had heard no sound from the driver's compartment since being locked inside. She had tried to peer through the cracks, but they were too narrow. She folded the blanket and laid it on the floor in front of the lock. As the truck swayed into another turn, he braced his hands against the door and lowered himself.

Sarah watched as he assessed the situation. Fortunately, lock picking did not require sight. It required acute hearing and enough practice to sense when the tumblers moved into position. Wafer-tumbler locks were basic and reliable, similar to pin-and-tumbler locks, except there were no pins, just wafer-shaped tumblers that had to be tickled into place for the lock to open. Such locks were common in vehicles, filing cabinets, and lockers, as well as in many padlocks.

"It's a single wafer," he told her. He inserted the makeshift tension wrench and pick, turned the metal stick, and felt around inside the lock with the needle.

Wafer locks were easier because the keyhole was wider. She returned to the IV pole and disassembled it. It took a while. Finally, she had the central pole free of the legs, arm, and other attachments. Carrying it, she padded back to him, pausing whenever the truck lurched.

"How are you doing?" she asked.

"Shh."

She waited patiently, half-hoping he would fail. If he could not get the door open, maybe he would lie down again. Even if he succeeded, they still had no gun, and he would be no match for the first fist slung at him.

"That's it." His voice was almost reverential. "I've still got the touch." He pushed himself up, the blanket in one hand.

"It's ready to open?"

"Yup." He stared at the pole she was holding. "What's that?"

"Our only weapon. Pathetic, isn't it? Why don't we wait until later for this insanity? When I can steal a gun, say, or you can run at least one lap. Then, too, it'd be really good if you had some clothes and shoes."

"Hey, I stood up and peed. Don't forget the importance of that." He grabbed the door handle and paused. Seemed to consider. His voice grew sober. "Don't worry, Sarah. I'm reasonably sure we're alone. I just want to make some progress. Maybe find something useful, or learn something that might help us later. If we're going to get out of this, you're going to have to let me work. I know you're worried, but considering the alternatives, I think we've got to take some risks. If we don't escape, the state of my health may be moot. Okay?"

Under the circumstances, she could hardly deny what he said. "Okay."

He grinned, his white teeth flashing. She could feel him tense, coiled to act. She flattened against the wall next to the door. She nodded. He pulled it open a few inches. She took a deep breath, raised the metal pole, and stared around the corner.

"Empty," she said with relief. She stepped inside the driver's compartment and stared. "Wow."

"What is it?" Asher peered over her shoulder.

"Surveillance monitors. Someone left them turned on. That's where the light's been coming from. There's other surveillance gear here, too."

Above the windshield hung a row of small monitors, alight but showing only the interior of the cavernous semi. There were gauges, dials, screens, and blinking lights.

"Hot stuff," he agreed happily.

"Can we call or radio out?"

"Lemme see." Someone had left a zippered sweatshirt on the front seat. He put it on, zipped it up, and sat, the blanket around his waist and legs. He studied the array.

She found a flashlight inside the glove compartment, climbed out of the panel truck, and played the beam around the semi's interior. Except for the truck, it was empty, no supplies or weapons. Terribly disappointing. She inspected the front end. There were vents, but no way into the tractor cab. She pressed her ear to the divider, but the only noise was the drone of the tires and the rumble of the engine.

She found the rear double doors locked solidly. When she shoved her shoulder into them, she could feel a crossbar on the outside, blocking them. Asher might be able to pick this lock, too, but the crossbar would make escape impossible.

She returned to the panel truck and climbed in behind the wheel. Asher had turned on the overhead light. His face was pale, his black hair wild. There was a waxen look to him, as if he were ready to collapse. Still, his fingers flicked switches, and his gaze swept the equipment.

He glanced at her. "Find anything?"

"Nothing useful. What about you?"

"Not much. The problem is, the cameras and mikes have nothing to read in the semi, so the monitors are blank" — he waved a hand at the overhead screens — "and the listening equipment is silent. There aren't any walkie-talkies or cells, so we have no way to communicate with the outside world. That's the bad news. The good news is, we've got a functioning GPS system."

"That's a start." She leaned around and saw a colored map with a moving arrow showing their route. "We've been traveling all over!"

He nodded. "Northeast to Reims and as far

south as Troyes and Orléans, and now we're heading north again."

"Looks as if we're going to pass just west of Paris. They're keeping us on the move so we won't be found, aren't they?"

"That's the way I figure it. But there is one more good thing — an intercom." He flipped a switch.

The voices of two men sounded from a small speaker. They spoke in French.

"Mecca-Cola?" one asked. "*Merde*. Give me a real Coke any day. It is the only thing the Americans do well."

"You have a kind spot for the Americans?"

As the first Frenchman gave a rough laugh, Sarah turned down the volume. "Those are our chauffeurs?"

There was a glint in Asher's eyes, but it was not from amusement. "Yup. That little exchange makes them seem harmless, but they're not. They're well armed, and they expect to kill us eventually. In fact, they seem to be looking forward to it."

"Just what I wanted to hear. What's holding them back?"

"They're waiting for the order. They did get one call, but it wasn't on a speaker phone, so I couldn't hear the other end of the conversation."

"Their boss?"

"Something like it. No name, naturally."

They hunched near the radio, listening, hoping the men would say something useful. Five minutes later, they had learned only that the pair was hired recently. They wondered about the identity of the man who hired them but had decided the pay was good enough that they were not as curious as they might be.

"Is he just their boss, or is he higher up?" she asked.

"No way to know yet."

She studied Asher. His skin color had bleached to chalk white. "You've done enough. It's my turn. I'll take the first shift."

"You don't mind?"

"Oh, Asher. You can be such a dope. The situation's bad enough already. Get the hell back to the gurney. Rest. Take care of yourself. You're scaring me to death."

He started to push himself out of his seat and stopped abruptly. "We're slowing."

As he sank back down, a long stream of French oaths burst into the cabin from the speaker. "What an asshole!" one man bellowed indignantly.

The other sounded resigned. "He does what he's told, same as us."

Silence. Sarah and Asher waited. The only sound was an occasional curse.

Finally, one of the men said, "There it is. See?"

"Big fucker, isn't it?" the other grumbled.

As the truck continued to slow, engine noises somewhere ahead grew in intensity — louder and louder, throbbing. Asher took Sarah's hand and squeezed it.

"Jet engines?" Sarah asked, worried.

"Yeah." He looked at her. Her eyes were dark, vigilant, and trying not to show her anxiety. "Sounds like it."

Forty

Paris, France

Liz and Simon transferred buses. He dozed, his head falling against her shoulder. Beyond the Périphérique, the suburb of Seine-St. Denis was dark in the long hours of early morning. Occasional lights showed in businesses where all-night cleaning crews still labored.

A mile before Le Bourget Airport, they left the bus. A cab cruised past, followed by another. The first carried a passenger, but the second was empty. It pulled alongside, offering a ride. She turned away, coughing into her hand.

"Merci, non," Simon told him. As the cab drove on, he asked. "Did you recognize him?"

"Not this time."

"Awfully convenient he showed up right here, right now." He shook his head, angry. "We're shying at shadows, like nervous cats."

"Be glad. It's a defense mechanism. If we stop, we're in trouble."

A wind came up, rustling the trees and evaporating the sweat from their skin. At this hour there were no other pedestrians, and the

485

roadsides were dark and eerily still. Periodically, they ducked into yards and side streets, where they paused to make certain they were not being followed.

Finally they continued briskly on, and Simon chuckled.

"What are you thinking about?" she asked. She liked to watch him walk, the long strides, the jaunty spring as he rolled off the pads of his feet.

"Malko, in the alley. He didn't have a chance, once you'd spotted him."

"I'm not sure that's a compliment."

"Sure it is. Women are underestimated most of the time. There's an advantage to that, if you use it. And you do."

"It also gets me into trouble when I don't recognize it."

"Are you talking about Santa Barbara? About the dean and your boyfriend?"

He felt a surge of jealousy. He wondered what Kirk Tedesco had been like. Why in God's name had she ever gone to bed with him? He did not know she had, but he suspected it. She was an adult. She was alone. We all made mistakes. Before he could stop himself, Viera's face appeared in his mind. He felt the stroke of her fingers, saw the happy glint in her gaze. He tried to banish her before he resaw her death. But the image was faster than a thought . . . there — the bright flames fatally swallowing her.

"That can be another trait of women — trust," she said. "I trusted Kirk because I liked him and enjoyed his company. I never questioned his lightweight scholarship or suspected he and the dean were informing on me." Her voice exuded irritation. "I was an idiot."

"More likely, your controllers were very good."

"No. I wanted an idyllic life so much that I set myself up to be taken. I'll never forget the thrill of learning I'd won the chair. It gave me a sweet excuse to stop chasing Langley, and it was like the Good Housekeeping Seal of Approval for what I'd do next."

Simon asked gently, "Do you regret getting your Ph.D.?"

She paused. "I love teaching. The TV series grew out of my interests, and I cared — care — deeply about that, too."

"You want to go back?"

She saw Santa Barbara in her mind. Her house was secluded high up in the Santa Ynez Mountains and overlooked the city. From there, she had a breathtaking panorama of red-tiled roofs and palms that spread down to where the lush land dropped into the aqua-blue sea. The city lay across a rising plane between the ocean and mountains, as if cupped in a gentle hand. Exotic flowering plants thrived in the mild climate — hibiscus, bougainvillea, mariposa lillies, birds-of-paradise.

All of a sudden, she felt deeply lonely. A cavern opened inside her — cold, empty . . . familiar.

Something had been missing there. Something she could not quite describe and had managed to ignore by keeping herself busy with university work, committees, classes, the TV series, karate — even Kirk — all gifts wrapped in the town's sleepy beauty. As she recalled Kirk's good-natured laziness, loneliness swept over her, leaving her chilled, despite the summer night. She had trusted him. He had betrayed her.

She did not look at Simon. "People go to Santa Barbara to forget or to dream. I went to forget. I don't know what I'll do when this is over. What about you?"

"It's not a question I think about. I'm an MI6 lifer."

"Saying it that way makes it sound like a prison sentence."

He glanced at her, surprised. "That's not what I meant."

"Here's some free advice from your resident shrink: Pay attention to people's little jokes, especially about themselves. It's that sneaky unconscious again. Those bouts of self-deprecating humor often hint at far deeper truths than we intend . . . or want anyone to see, especially ourselves."

There was no hesitation. "Agreement number two: You don't psychoanalyze me, and I won't ask how, if you're so smart, you acquired a humbug boyfriend like Kirk."

An angry retort shot to her lips, then she laughed. "Touché. I'm humbled, sir. I will close my *DSM-IV* and crawl meekly away from my lectern."

"Good tactic."

He smiled, she smiled back. They continued silently onward. Traffic continued to ease. Trees loomed black against the starry sky. Her mind was tumultuous, thinking ahead.

"I've been mulling what you said about Nautilus," she told him. "It's not just the blackmailer we'll be looking for at Dreftbury; it's Themis and Cronus and anyone else with a Greek code name. If we can identify them, we'll narrow our search."

He nodded. "Obviously, we're going to have to do without a data or statistics expert. Still, we should study the documents I photographed as soon as possible. Together, we may know more than we realize."

"I agree. How much time do we have before Nautilus starts?"

"People will begin arriving around four or five this afternoon to check in, get drinks, play a round of golf. There's an opening banquet with a speaker around eight o'clock. The first presentations and panels start at eight a.m. Saturday. Tomorrow. The last are late Sunday night."

"And security?"

"It's usually a mixture of private and public. Nautilus hires an A-list firm like Kroll or Wackenhut. Then, depending on the country, local police or military forces or both support it. We can count on the security being tight and in place by daybreak."

"Wonderful."

"Nautilus knows what it's doing. Right now, you can be certain the entire resort is closed to the public and that regular guests have been sent packing. It's Nautilus's routine to do that, just as they always choose each resort carefully — either owned by or somehow in the control of a member of Nautilus."

She sighed. Then felt a surge of energy. "There's our circus."

It had set up on the airfield's tarmac, near the parking lot. The big top billowed in the wind, a white sailing ship beneath a black sky of high, bright stars. Off to the side, the trailers of performers and roustabouts were parked, a ramshackle assemblage with an occasional newer vehicle among the dilapidated. The Cirque des Astres had never been particularly lucrative and apparently still was not.

On the other side of the tent, the buildings of Le Bourget Airport rose in the night, large and blocky. Grass and pavement extended around them. Famous as the landing site of Charles Lindbergh's historic flight across the Atlantic, the old airport was no longer a major terminus. It still handled freight and business flights, the semiannual Paris Air Show, and other exhibitions and events, including this circus.

All was quiet, somnolent. The night helped hide their goal.

It had been seven years since she last saw Gary Faust. A former French Resistance leader, he would be in his eighties now. His French mother and American father had founded the circus in their youth. Then, during World War II, Gary had used it as a front for his ring of spies and saboteurs, members of the fabled Resistance. For his brave work, he was awarded the Légion d'Honneur, the Croix de Guerre, and the Médaille de la Résistance. A hero of France.

As they rounded the tent, she saw the plane in the moonlight, ghostly, almost an apparition. It was a 1940 Westland Lysander, one of only two in the world still flying.

"Is that it?" Simon asked, staring at the high-winged monoplane. His low tone revealed his skepticism. "Can it still get off the ground?"

"Gary says she flies like a dream." When local ordinances allowed, he took families up for free rides. The flights were good advertising, of course. But more than that, Gary loved to pilot the geriatric craft, giving others a taste of the precariousness and strange exhilaration of a long-ago war.

Simon shook his head. "Looks as if someone built it in their basement out of tinfoil and school paste. How's that going to carry us across the Channel?"

"Watch how you talk about my girl," said a very French voice in English. "She is easily insulted. If you want her to take care of you, you must show respect." The man who stepped out of the plane's shadows had an easy gait. He was bulky and erect, dressed in dark gray coveralls and a cap, goggles dangling from his neck.

He took Liz by both shoulders, kissed her on both cheeks, and pushed her back, still holding on as he peered through the moonlight. "So, you are well?"

"I've had a glass of wine." She smiled. "Cheese and a baguette."

"That is all any of us can ask, eh? Who knows what tomorrow brings?"

"I'm glad to see you, Gary."

"And I, you. I am sorry about your mother's death. But perhaps it is just as well. She was tormented. That father of yours!" He released her and crossed himself. "I speak ill of the dead." He crossed himself again and chuckled. "After all these years, it still seems not to have harmed me. Why do I worry?" He turned. "You are Simon? Melanie's nephew?"

They shook hands. "Good of you to help us," Simon told him. The old fighter's hand was dry and strong. "Liz tells me you have the perfect plane for our —"

"Say no more." Gary pressed a finger to his lips. "Decades ago, I learned it is better to not know the detail of a mission unless I am to lead it. You are young, Simon, which means you are worried. No doubt you have never seen a miracle in flight like this one." He patted the Lysander's wing. "You must relax and trust. She and her sisters ferried your F Group people into France and sneaked many of your downed fliers home again. The Free French used her as a spotter plane, and she brought arms and supplies to us *maquis*. Why could she do all this? Because she flies slow and low to ground, and she can land and take off in the most inaccessible places. That is necessary for where we go tonight."

Simon studied the plane suspiciously. "You have room for both of us?"

"I had her rear gun taken out and the seat enlarged forty years ago, after I bought her in a war-surplus sale. All this time, she has easily carried two passengers."

"That would be us." Liz climbed up on the wing.

"*Oui,* that would be you. Hurry along, Simon. I must get you there long before dawn so I can return here unseen." He raised his face and seemed to taste the night. "We go to a field I know in Northumberland. It's on the farm of a friend from the old days. The past and our advancing ages cement those of us who survived." As soon as Simon climbed up, Gary followed. "This is an important assignment, *hein?*"

"Very," Liz told him.

"*Bon.* Then we fly."

Langley, Virginia

In his office, Frank Edmunds swore into the phone. "Damn. Not a sign, then?"

"We located the Peugeot in a private parking garage in Pigalle. Sansborough and Childs must've pulled it off the street not long after you sent me to find them. Anyway, we checked the Peugeot and the garage, but there was nothing to tell us where they went. But listen to this, Frank: The street's crawling with antiterrorist forces. They stopped four guys who were trying to get away, and now they're searching everywhere. The only good thing was all the noise and fuss attracted our attention. But then they came back to search, and we had to get out fast, before they identified us. Talk about bad luck."

Edmunds suspected luck had little to do with it. In fact, the antiterrorist raid smacked of Sansborough or Childs. It was becoming obvious that others were after them, and whoever it was could have cornered them in the garage. Reporting terrorist activity would have been a clever way for the pair to scare off the attackers and escape at the same time. At least, that was what made sense to him.

In any case, Sansborough and Childs had slipped through Langley's net again. For someone who was supposed to be loony tunes, she seemed to have a lot on the ball. More and more, he wondered whether Jaffa could be wrong. What if her report was real? What if she was sane?

There was only one way to find out. "Okay. Keep your men on it. Sansborough and Childs are probably disguised, but what are we if we can't see through a disguise? Have you traced her arrival in Paris and where she went after that?'

"Couldn't, Frank. Know why? Because there's no evidence she ever came to Paris or France at all. Not a damn trace."

Edmunds's unease grew. "What about Asher Flores and Sarah Walker?"

"That's another weird story. Flores really was in Paris but under his own name, so it makes no damn sense that he's in black cover. Anyway, I found out through my contact in the gendarmerie that Flores and his wife are registered at the Hôtel Valhalla, paid up a week, until Sunday. But this morning, a corpse was found in their closet. This is what the cops know: Walker was in and out before that, but no one's seen her since. No one's seen Flores since Tuesday night. The cops are getting ready to issue arrest warrants, if they haven't already. That's as far as I've gotten."

"Keep digging, Jeff." Edmunds's stomach churned. He could feel an attack of heartburn starting. "Into all of them. Into everything! And find Sansborough, dammit."

"Are we still supposed to wipe Sansborough and Childs?"

Edmunds hesitated. Swearing under his breath, he reached for his Prevacid.

"Frank? Are you there?"

"I'm here." He swallowed the pill, drank more water, and sighed. "Hold off. We'd better find out what the fuck's going on for sure before we go to extreme measures."

He ended the connection and punched in the first number of Walter Jaffa's extension. And stopped. Was Sansborough's outrageous story true after all? She might have done the Company some harm years ago because of her father, but before that, she was one of their own.

He slammed down the phone. Until he found out a lot more, he would not report this to Jaffa.

Forty-One

Northumberland, England

From the air, the moon cast a silver veil across the wild border valley of the North Tyne River. The small plane flew over thick woods and dramatic moorlands and isolated ridges of wind swept heather. As Simon watched, Gary Faust piloted the plane along the river to a sprawling farm, where he brought it in for a gentle touchdown . . . until the tires hit the rudimentary runway. The plane jumped and rattled. Still, the old *maqui* had been right: It could land on a postage stamp.

Liz awoke, yawning and stretching, and they taxied toward the farm house. At the end of the strip, Faust turned off the Mercury radial engine.

"Nice landing," Simon said as they climbed out.

"*Oui,* and you are relieved to be safely on terra firma," the Frenchman observed, not bothering to hide his amusement. Simon had been on alert the whole way.

"She surprised me," he said. "She's as sturdy as you said."

Liz stared, remembering his tension when she suggested flying to England. "You don't like to fly — at all."

He shrugged, shot her an embarrassed grin, and they hurried off, Faust between them. Scattered trees and bushes moved, wavering with the black wind. Above them, charcoal-dusted clouds raced across the starlit sky. Simon noticed that Liz, too, was surveying the house and outbuildings. The likelihood of having been followed was remote. Still, neither could — or would — relax.

Faust had phoned ahead and discovered his friend Paul Hamilton, a decorated RAF pilot from the war, had left in his De Haviland Humming Bird for an air show in Kent. Still, Hamilton said they could borrow his Jeep. Faust located a key hidden behind a window box of red geraniums by the kitchen door. He stepped inside and returned, handing keys to the Jeep to Liz.

She thanked him. "Is that Bellingham?" she nodded at a sprinkling of lights. If so, the roadway along it was the B6320, which also ran past Lord Henry Percy's estate.

"*Oui*, that it is." He turned to Simon. "Good-bye, son." He shook Simon's hand and took Liz's shoulders again, quickly kissed both cheeks, and wheeled off. "Good luck." His voice trailed back, carried on the wind.

Liz and Simon ran to the garage and pulled open the door. Inside were a Jeep and a motorcycle. They climbed into the Jeep, and she backed it out. He found a map in the glove compartment. It had been twenty years since she'd visited Henry. Ten years since Simon had. She sped the Jeep onto an asphalt road and then to the country highway, where she turned south, skirting the lazy river and the dense forests of Northumberland National Park. The roadway was nearly deserted.

"This time, we can be certain we're not being tailed," she told him.

"Except by the phantoms of the Border Reivers."

"You're reminding me of Henry's colorful stories."

He smiled and peered around, as if looking for the feuding farmer-bandits who had raided crops and animals for centuries on either side of the English-Scottish border. The earls of Northumberland — Henry's family, the Percys — had ruled like kings in those lawless days.

She smiled, too, suddenly feeling lighthearted. They had lost their hunters, and she indulged in a sweet sense of optimism. Somewhere, Sarah and Asher were alive, she promised herself, waiting for Simon and her to find the files and them.

At last, Simon spotted a mass of boulders that looked like a reclining man. Called the Sleeping Drunk among locals but described in tourist brochures as the Reclining Sage, it signaled the beginning of Baron Henry Percy's estate. She turned the Jeep onto the familiar drive, which pointed straight ahead like an arrow. But now it was so overgrown with trees that the branches scraped the sides of the Jeep like bony fingers.

"I don't remember this," she said.

"I don't either. Odd that Clive would let it get out of hand. He was always so fastidious."

With the moonlight cut off by the canopy of growth, the tunnel was black. She flicked on the Jeep's bright lights and sped through, passing a glen with a stream where they had picnicked as children. At last, the arbor disappeared, and they had a clear view of the Moorlands — the rambling manor house that had always been Henry's country home, until he finally retired and turned over his investment interests to a handful of nephews and nieces. At that point, the Moorlands became his full-time residence, except for excursions to Africa and the Far East and the occasional anthropological trip to Las Vegas. Henry, Lord Percy, was an old-fashioned, tight-suspendered Englishman who liked the occasional adventure. Or at least he had.

She parked at the side of the big house, in the shadow of a grape arbor.

"The zoo is gone," Simon said as he climbed out. He walked away from the Jeep and stared across to where corrals and picturesque sheds had housed zebras and Andean goats and llamas, as well as other exotic animals. Now there was simply a field. The riding stables still stood north, but there were no horses in sight.

"I don't smell manure," she said.

"Neither do I. The horses are gone, too."

The lawn was tidily clipped, and summer flowers bloomed in planters along the stone walkway. The stone mansion itself seemed in good repair, and the two ancient oaks she remembered from her childhood towered in front, taller, wider, more stately than ever. Still, the building and grounds had the feel of gentility grown tired.

As Simon and she strode around the drive and onto the front walk, she scooped up the *Times* and saw it was the early Friday edition. "Here's a good sign. He's still addicted to at least one newspaper."

"Let me see that."

Simon stopped before the massive single door, took it from her, and opened one page after the other of the first section, holding each up to the moonlight, until she realized what he was looking for.

She swore and took the second section from him. But he was the one who found it — four photos, two news items. She leaned into him, feeling nervous, anger growing as she stared: The photos were of her, Sarah, Asher, and Mac, who, according to the caption, was a New Jersey businessman named Aldo Malchinni. One story covered London CID's hunt for her in connection to Patricia Childs's murder, while the other one described the Paris police's search for Sarah Walker and Asher Flores for questioning in the murder of Malchinni. The story noted she and Sarah were cousins and almost identical in appearance.

"Oh, hell," she breathed.

"This could be very bad for you tomorrow. Maybe you shouldn't go to Dreftbury with me. We don't —"

Abruptly, lights blazed on above the door, illuminating the walk and drive. She slid her hand into her shoulder bag and gripped her Glock, and Simon slipped his under his jacket, to his Beretta. They looked at each other.

"A bit jumpy, aren't we?" she said.

He nodded, withdrew his hand, and folded the paper. "We'll have to get rid of this."

"Who's there?" It was not Clive's voice.

They said their names. Seconds later, the door opened.

Henry Percy received them in the library on the first floor, a Douglas tartan over his knees where he sat in a wingback chair, although Liz and Simon had been waiting in the foyer and had not seen him come downstairs. While there, Simon had stuffed the newspaper behind the antediluvian umbrella stand.

Now Clive knelt at the fireplace in a blue robe, slippers, and pajamas, and poked a small blaze. His wizened face glanced occasionally up at the baron as if to be sure he was well. Clive was nearly as old as Henry and had shrunk, although he appeared as spry and irritable as ever. But by his stiff back and glowering gaze, he clearly objected to the visit. Another servant — Richard — stood across the book-filled room, arms politely at his sides, also in robe and slippers, waiting to be needed. More than a half century younger than Henry and Clive, he had met Liz and Simon at the front door.

"Lizzie! Simon!" Henry stretched out his hands, parchment skin freckled with age spots. "How good to see you. We won't mention the beastly hour. I'm certain you wouldn't be here

501

unless it was important."

His face was longer and thinner than Liz recalled, but mostly unlined, despite his more than nine decades. His sparse white hair was brushed neatly back. His most remarkable feature was still his thick, beetling brows, now silver. Beneath them, his gray eyes were almost colorless, although they retained a piercing quality that at one time could shoot fear into rivals or peer gently into a child's most heartfelt cares.

"It *is* important," Liz assured him. "But it's also wonderful to be with you again." She took one hand and kissed his sunken cheek.

Simon took the other. "You're looking grand, Henry. Thanks for letting us impose."

Henry beamed. "No imposition at all. Tea, Clive. Something hot and pleasant. Oolong, I think."

"I shouldn't suppose they'd like sandwiches, sir." Clive glowered. "Cook must be awake. Impossible to miss the fuss. She'll cut off the crusts."

"Sandwiches?" Simon said. "That would be excellent. Thank you, Clive."

Liz said, "May I give you a kiss, for old times' sake?"

Clive frowned but presented his right cheek. Liz leaned toward the small man and pecked the wrinkled skin. There was the briefest of smiles, and he was gone.

World War II hero, former MP, diplomat, and international businessman, Henry, Lord Percy, was a direct descendant of the fourth Lord Percy, the first earl of Northumberland, who died in

1409. It was his son, Henry, who had so distinguished himself in battle at the age of twelve that he was designated Hotspur and immortalized nearly two centuries later by Shakespeare in *King Henry IV* and *King Richard II*. Before he died, Hotspur had a son out of wedlock with a girl in Wark, to whom he gave his name. This irregular line of Percys thrived, becoming tradesmen and local officials and eventually going off to London to make their marks. The current Henry's grandfather had bought this old mansion south of Wark, bringing the family home again at last.

"Sit, sit." Henry lengthened a finger at a leather-covered settee across from him.

Liz and Simon sank onto it. The fire crackled, and on the mantel, a Victorian clock ticked. The ceiling was at least sixteen feet high, the walls below lined with wood shelves packed with leather-bound volumes. The air smelled of oiled leather and the inviting fire.

Henry looked at the man at the door. "Richard, be polite and leave."

"But Clive said —"

"I'm still in charge." Henry's voice was dry and had a slight tremble, but his firm delivery had the finality of a guillotine.

Liz and Simon exchanged a glance. Henry's mind was operating fine.

His jaw muscles clenching, Richard inclined his head and walked out.

Liz watched the door close. "Henry, we have a situation —" she began.

But Henry raised a gaunt hand, stopping her. His gaze was sharp, accusatory, as he said, "I saw a story about you on the BBC, Liz. Did you kill Tish Childs?"

She blinked, surprised. "Of course not! You know I could *never* do such a thing!"

His chin stuck out. "You were CIA. Obviously, you could have."

"It's got nothing to do with skill, dammit. You know that. You know *me*. Tish was tortured and murdered. How could you even think I'd do such a horrible thing!"

She glared, and he glared.

The ticking of the clock seemed to grow louder. She would not look away.

He seemed to see something that decided him. His shoulders relaxed. "I had to ask. People change." He gave a tired smile. "Here you come in the middle of the night, waking my household. It had to be serious. I thought perhaps —"

"You were wrong."

"Yes, I can see that. Put it up to a feeling of mortality. Advancing age can make one afraid. I wager you never thought you'd hear me admit that." He leaned forward on his elbows. "Really, Liz dear. I'm sorry."

There was moistness in his eyes.

With a burst of compassion, she leaned forward, too, and patted his hand. "I adore you, Henry. Always have, always will. It's forgotten."

Simon cleared his throat. "Well, glad that's over. And glad you're sitting down, Henry. We do have a situation. Bugger of a hornet's nest. Are you up to hearing it?"

The old man settled back into his chair. "Wouldn't miss it. It's been a long time since anyone's brought me something dicey."

"It begins with Father. His suicide."

Darkness swept across Henry's face, and his mouth tightened. From the extensive Childs and Percy families to the top of parliament, it was well known that the powerful Henry Percy treated Sir Robert as if he were the son he never had.

"I never understood why Robbie did it," Henry said. "Those were bloody damn lies about him and call girls."

"Mother and he were too close for that." Outrage shot from Simon's eyes.

Henry nodded, angry. "But afterward, a lot of his so-called friends hinted to the press he'd been philandering for years." His lip curled. "That's just one problem with politics these days — an insatiable desire to appear to be 'in the know.' Let's hear about this hornet's nest of yours, children. Perhaps there is something I can do."

Le Bourget Airport, France

César Duchesne sat low in his taxicab, his cap pulled down to his eyebrows, the window open. As he slouched behind the steering wheel, he alternately dozed and snapped awake the instant the night sounds altered. He was resting while at the same time staying on guard. The habits of a lifetime were useful.

Of course, it was possible the pilot of the plane would stay with Sansborough and Childs, wherever he had taken them, but Duchesne doubted it. The man had a circus to operate. More likely, he would return quickly, hoping no one had missed him.

As Duchesne had predicted to Cronus, one of his drivers had finally spotted Sansborough and Childs — this time as they approached the place de Clichy. After that, a fresh three-man taxi team with night-vision surveillance had taken over, following as the pair rode the bus, transferred, disembarked the last time, and walked. Basil called with the news they had met some old man, gotten into his plane, and flown off.

Now Duchesne waited alone, his taxi parked in the shadow of the big top. A breeze ruffled the tent's canvas sides. Ropes clattered against poles. As he listened, his mind drifted back over the years to happier times, when he was young and powered by outrage. When he thought life would turn out far differently, and happiness was possible. A dark sadness washed through him, followed by bone-deep rage. With his usual steely will, he banished the emotions.

He sat impassive, alert. When at last the drone of a small plane sounded far away in the west, he watched the craft approach and land and roll toward the billowing tent. The pilot was alone. No Sansborough or Childs.

Duchesne remained where he was, patient, almost unfeeling. The plane stopped, and the former *maqui* climbed down, unarmed. His movements were slow, arthritic, different from the smooth agility that had been reported to Duchesne. Duchesne stepped out of the taxi and limped toward him, his right foot dragging.

In the pewter moonlight, the pilot saw Duchesne. He recoiled, and his gaze fixed on the Walther in Duchesne's hand.

Duchesne gestured at the taxi and ordered in French, "Get in."

"And if I say no?"

"You've lived a long life already. Perhaps that's enough for you. Otherwise, we will talk. You will tell me where you took them."

The old man's gaze remained steady, as if searching Duchesne's eyes for a clue to his will. After a moment, what he saw made his back slump. He gave a short nod and climbed into the cab.

Forty-Two

Northumberland, England

As the minutes ticked past, Liz and Simon alternated, bringing Henry up-to-date. Clive arrived with the promised tea but forgot the sandwiches. He returned with them five minutes later. Everyone ate. With his usual astuteness, Henry asked questions until at last he fell silent, thinking. Simon wandered to the fireplace, where he leaned against the mantel. Liz paced restlessly, pulling back the drapes to stare out at the black night.

At last, Henry emerged from his trance. He shook his white head in disbelief. "I had no idea your father was the Carnivore, Liz. When I think of all the years he came up here with your mother and you . . . I never would've guessed. It's shocking. Utterly shocking. And he left behind a detailed record that someone's been using for blackmail? Outrageous! Of course you're determined to find the snake who has the files. He must be stopped." He hesitated, and his voice grew thick with emotion. "And then there's Robbie. What a tragedy to lose such a fine statesman, one who did so much good. His wiping out that scum who was killing little boys was obviously the right choice."

Liz and Simon exchanged a look of surprise.

Henry did not notice. "As for the three Titan names . . . alas, I have no idea. Cronus, Hyperion, and Themis — right? Sounds like a club, but whether they're related to Nautilus is far beyond my scope."

"Is there any way you can help us figure out who they are?" Liz asked.

"I think not. I've never been good at that sort of data sifting. Now I'm going to change the subject. Give you a little history lesson. . . . Do you recall the tale of the Robsons and the stolen sheep?"

Liz shook her head. "Sorry."

"North Tynedale, right?" Simon said.

"Exactly." Henry peered off into space, as if he could see those long-ago days. "This is what my father told me. . . . One dark night, the Robson men sneaked across the border into Liddesdale. They were excited to find an entire flock belonging to the Grahams. So of course they brought them home to Northumberland. But what the Robsons didn't know was the sheep had scabies. It spread like wildfire into their own flocks, and they were furious. Without another thought, they stormed back to Liddesdale, grabbed seven members of the Graham family, and hanged them. Then, to make certain all of the clans got the point, they left a note. It went something like this." With a lilting accent, he recited, " 'The neist time gentlemen com to tak the schepe, they are no te' be scabbit!' "

Simon nodded soberly. "What's mine is mine, and what's yours is mine, too. I see your point. Yes, that's what some people believe of Nautilus. They're like the Border Reivers, treating the world as if lines — whether moral or political or geographic — are irrelevant. Whatever Nautilus wants, it will manipulate, legislate, or take outright."

"Baldly put, Simon. But yes, I've heard that, too. For years. But when people are on emotional rampages, their accusations are often hyperbolic. That was never what Nautilus was intended to be, and I doubt it is today. It's important you understand what you're so easily dismissing as a monolithic organization of too much secrecy and power. Nautilus's roots are deep . . . going all the way back to before World War Two, to a Polish émigré named Josef Retinger. He was a spy, but also far more."

"Retinger?" Liz said and looked at Simon.

He shook his head. "I don't recognize the name either."

"No reason you should. He was one of those gentlemen agents who slid in and out of the shadows. A murky character, rumored to have worked for everyone from the Freemasons to Vatican potentates, from the Mexican to the Spanish governments. No one knew what he was for or against until the war, when he came out against the Nazis. At that point, Whitehall recruited him, and he ran spies for us across Europe. Damn good at it, too. In fact, Liz, his status grew so great that all he had to do to meet with your President Truman was pick up the phone. But then, he'd been significant in the Allies' victory."

"That's impressive," Liz said. "But what does he have to do with Nautilus?"

"Picture this situation," Henry told them. "Three long years after the war, in 1948, Europe was still digging out of the rubble. Hundreds of thousands wandered the streets because they had nowhere to go. It wasn't just that they were without a home, but without a country. Without a future. It was . . . heartbreaking. Many starved — adults and children. Anti-Americanism swept the Continent, and torrents of people joined the Communist party. Retinger was afraid Europe would erupt in war again, but this time it'd be devastating because it'd be nuclear. So he went to top businessmen, ex–military men, and politicians — the gray eminences of postwar policy, as the press called them — and convinced them Europe's survival was at stake. A handful met for the first time in 1952, around a lowly Ping-Pong table in a small Paris apartment."

"Secretly, I assume," Simon said, "to keep the Communists in the dark."

"Primarily, yes."

Liz had been studying the nonagenarian. He held his head high against his wingback chair, and his gaze had that incisive quality she recalled. Although his hands and voice trembled with age, there was an edge to him that spoke of passion and knowledge and vision. For years, she had heard of Henry Percy's exploits, but in the most general way . . . adviser to British prime ministers and foreign heads of state . . . investments that straddled commerce and continents and kept him apprised of people's needs as well as their yearnings for life's material things. All cloaked in natural modesty. But perhaps also in deft understanding of back room power, like Averell Harriman or David Rockefeller, who had shaped so much of modern America's political history — and Europe's, too.

Suddenly, she knew what she was sensing . . . why he spoke with such authority. "You were there, Henry. Weren't you? You were invited to that meeting in Paris around the 'lowly' Ping-Pong table."

Simon looked up quickly, staring first at her, then at Henry.

Henry gave a simple nod. His expression was somber. "Few recall how close Europe came to being another totalitarian satellite of the Soviet Union. It was a grave time. But also exciting. We knew we were at a historical turning point, and because we saw the peril, it was our duty to act. For centuries, emperors and kings had tried to unite Europe by means of war. We knew it had to be done, but with no more large wars. They're simply too expensive, too devastating, and few people profit. Along with that, we envisioned a peacefully integrated Europe . . . a closer cooperation with America . . . and the death of fascism and communism. The meeting went well, so we held a more formal one two years later at a resort on France's north coast called L'Hôtel Nautilus."

"So that's why the name Nautilus," Simon said.

Liz's mind was elsewhere. "The CIA must've been part of it. Bill Donovan, too. Their primary mandate was to work with groups and individuals to stop the spread of communism." Wild Bill Donovan had been OSS and helped found the CIA.

"Yes, of course. He and Allen Dulles were most helpful, and the CIA became one of our top funders. But now that the Cold War's over, it plays a lesser role. As for your accusations about Nautilus today, Simon, you're looking too much on only one side of the equation. Yes, we focused on unifying the industrialized world. Globalization, as you call it. That's because history has taught us that if nations are left to their own devices, they remain territorial, and wars are inevitable."

"I'm definitely in favor of no more war," Liz said, "but there have been one hell of a lot of 'small' wars in the last fifty years. Nautilus didn't stop them."

"But perhaps Nautilus likes some of those wars," Simon said.

Henry looked sharply at Simon. "What do you mean?"

Simon peeled away from the fireplace. He sat again, crossed his legs, and studied Henry. "Perhaps Nautilus considers little wars necessary when oil or territory or some other profit is to be gained. One of the rare exceptions was Europe's split from the United States when it attacked Iraq. But that disagreement had more to do with who'd control the spoils and wield political power in the aftermath than it did with the ethics of the invasion."

Liz paused in her pacing. "If Nautilus has so much influence, why doesn't it stop al-Qaeda and some of these frightening terrorist states?"

"Nautilus takes the long view," Simon theorized. "Al-Qaeda and the rest are fringe problems it'd like to solve immediately but can't because terrorist leaders are fanatics and don't respond to the usual incentives — you can't bribe them, because all they want is to kill their 'enemies.' That means us. Besides, in the long run, fanatics don't really matter to Nautilus, because terrorists and terrorist states play only a marginal role in the globe's economy. As the planet gets more economically unified, they'll be crushed, or they'll get the right 'religion' and turn capitalist."

"Economically unified?" she asked. "What are you talking about?"

Henry cleared his throat. "All right, Simon, I listened politely. Now it's my turn. Two people can look at the same forest and perceive utterly different scenes. One sees grim shadows — an eerie place full of danger — while another sees bright light filtering down through the trees. Where you see shadows and darkness, I see light and hope." He looked at Liz. "Simon's referring to the fact that one of Nautilus's first creations was the European Common Market, back in the 1950s."

"The Common Market was a Nautilus idea?" Liz said. "The little Common Market that grew into the big European Union?"

"Our idea, and we nursed it through, with a healthy result: Europe's uniting at last, without a single shot being fired. Now there's talk of a United States of Europe, while you in North America have NAFTA. It's likely there'll be a Pacific-Asia free-trade zone in the next decade, too, with Japan or China as the base country."

Simon scowled and explained, "Liz, this isn't altruistic. Nautilus is carving the planet into economic hemispheres because it benefits business. If what I hear is accurate, in a couple of decades, Nautilus plans to push through a single currency for the United States and Europe."

She said instantly, "It'll never happen."

"That's what people said about the euro ten years ago," Simon countered. "Even five years ago. Bad prediction."

"Simon's right," Henry said. "In fact, the *Wall Street Journal* ran an article recently saying that if the euro could replace the French franc, the German mark, and the Italian lira, then a new world currency could easily merge the U.S. dollar, Europe's euro, and the Japanese yen. It's a sound idea. We'd have world money, a world central bank, and stability. But that will happen only when the United States shifts its focus from international military leadership to international political leadership."

Simon said stubbornly, "If Nautilus's version of globalization is so wonderful, why has poverty increased everywhere? Why are more than half of the world's one hundred largest economies not nations but corporations? Multinationals are so global and so powerful that they manipulate government policies all the time."

Henry spread his hands, palms up, in a gesture asking for understanding. "Don't listen to the doomsayers. Nautilus is no feuding Reiver clan. It was created to make the world a safer, better place. That's why we worked so hard to rise above nationalism. The more unified the industrialized world is, the less chance there'll be for war, disease, poverty, and illiteracy. And, yes, the more money will be made by everyone."

"I like a lot of your goals," Simon said. "But your methods aren't working. The IMF and World Bank are impoverishing entire —"

Liz interrupted, "We're not going to resolve this tonight." She hurried around the settee to stand between the two men. "You're looking tired, Henry. Besides, Simon and I have more work to do. We told you earlier we think the blackmailer's planning some new deal that'll climax at Dreftbury. Can you give us some insight into it?"

"I remember now." Henry's voice was fading, but his gaze remained alert. "As a matter of fact, at about the time Robbie died, the chancellor of Germany resigned over some minor slush fund. Also, I think there were a number of U.S. congressmen from the left and right who announced they wouldn't run for reelection around then, too. You say Robbie was being blackmailed for his vote on some trade issue. Whatever it was, the others might have had some clout in it as well."

"What about lately?" Liz asked eagerly. "Have you seen anything unusual happening with someone who's in a high enough position to make a difference?"

Henry rubbed his chin. "I think so. A month, perhaps two months ago, EU Competition Commissioner Franco Peri died suddenly of a heart attack in Brussels. What was odd was that he'd had no history of cardiac problems."

"That's right," Simon said. "He was young, early forties. Very unexpected. Was there anything unusual about the person who succeeded him?"

"On the contrary," Henry said. "Carlo Santarosa had been talked about for some time as the best choice when Peri's term ended. Since no one else was obvious, and Santarosa was amenable, the process was orderly and swift. He's taken over smoothly."

They fell silent. Suddenly Liz understood. "Maybe that's it!"

Simon scowled. "What?"

"Yes, what?" Henry said.

"Don't you see?" Liz said, excited. "The blackmailer could've counted on the obvious candidate getting the job!"

"Bloody damn, you're right," Simon said. "If the blackmailer has something on Santarosa, and his deal has to go through the EU Competition Commission to be approved —" he stopped. "Does Santarosa have that kind of power, Henry?"

Henry folded his hands. "Actually, yes. His people research and make recommendations, but he decides. The EU Commission is still rubber-stamping him."

"Will he be at Dreftbury?" Liz asked.

"His predecessors were, so no doubt he's planning to." His eyes were heavy.

Liz studied Henry. "You look as if you're falling asleep, Henry. Being up this late can't be good for you. Please go back to bed. You've helped us a lot. Would you mind if we stayed on a few hours?"

"Of course not. Perhaps you'll both rest, too. I believe Clive is preparing the family suite. You can have your old rooms. Simon, would you please open that door?"

Again the long finger stretched out, pointing. On the other side had been Henry's den. But when Simon opened it, he saw it had been converted into a bedroom. Beside the bed stood a wheelchair, which explained why they had not seen him walking downstairs. He had been asleep here.

"Bring her to me, will you?" Henry asked. "I call her Dodd, after another border family. Reliably colorful, the Dodds. Wheelchairs are such a bore. One tries to make them as interesting as possible." As Simon rolled it toward him, he asked Liz, "Will you check on Clive and the suite? His memory is fading. I've had to hire a larger staff to cover for him. Perhaps you noticed the grounds need care." Henry shrugged. "Clive doesn't want to retire, and I won't make him. So some things are left untended."

"Here we go," Simon said. He helped Henry into the wheelchair. The old baron was light as an autumn leaf.

"I'll say my good nights now." He beamed. "It's been grand to see both of you. Lively, like old times. But if you're gone by breakfast, I'll understand. And if you don't come to your senses and agree with me, Simon, I'll understand that, too. Perhaps I've been some help. Be careful, you two. I suppose Nautilus could have gone bad, but I hope not. I most sincerely hope not."

Alone in his bedroom, the silence of the stone manse enfolded Henry Percy like an old friend. As he sat in his wheelchair, he held his cell and listened for the voices of his ancestors. These days, he thought about Hotspur often — honored warrior, misunderstood politician — and mourned his early death, not yet forty. And here he himself was, nearing the century mark. Some died too young; others lived too old.

He shook his head, warning himself not to let nostalgia carry him off his path. He had too much brimstone and savvy to have reached "too old." More than the young people upstairs would ever know. He was retired, not dead.

"Silent, are you?" he said into the hushed air. "Nothing to say? Does one sacrifice the individual for the masses? Or is life so sacred that no one may be sacrificed, no matter the cost to others? What have you learned from the other side of the grave?"

He waited for an answer to his long-standing moral dilemma. When the silence grew painful, he placed the call. Sir Anthony Brookshire answered, but Lord Henry Percy talked.

"This is Cronus. What in God's name have you done, Cronus? Are you mad? How dare you cross me like this?"

"What?"

"You heard me, Cronus. Simon Childs and Liz Sansborough are my family, and you bloody well know it. Did you think I wouldn't find out? Did you think I'd do nothing when I did? How dare you set her up! *And don't tell me you're not behind the reactions of MI6 and Langley. You have one chance, and I give this to you only because I sponsored you. Call off your goons. Simon and Liz are under my protection. If they chase you straight into your grave, your people are not to touch one hair on their heads. The files are her father's. That means she inherits. If she finds them, they're hers."*

"The blackmailer as good as killed Robbie."

"Robbie's dead. There's nothing we can do for him. Besides, we both know that's beside the point. You want the files for yourself!"

"No, Cronus. You're utterly wrong. This isn't for me. It's for the Coil. It's what's best for all of us!"

"Rubbish! I forbid it. Do you hear me?"

"I should think so, Cronus. You've made yourself perfectly clear."

London, England

In the hallway outside his bedroom, Sir Anthony Brookshire slowly lowered the cell from his ear.

The old bastard. He was retired! How could he have found out?

Instantly, he knew, because there was only one logical answer. He dialed his cell. "I've discovered where Sansborough and Childs are!"

Forty-Three

Northumberland, England

Clive was gone by the time Liz and Simon arrived on the second floor and walked to the back of the house. The door to the family suite was open, and a squad of muscular young men were pulling off dustcovers and putting things in order. Within minutes, everyone was gone, and a calmness settled over the large living room. Two doors on either side opened into bedrooms. Ahead were soaring windows. Liz and Simon went to them and gazed out at the fishpond and apple orchard, silvery in the moonlight. She looked up at the night sky, at the stars twinkling far away in foreign universes.

Liz turned back to savor the familiar room. "It hasn't changed."

Despite the dark-wood wainscoting, the room was cheerful. Brilliantly hued tapestry covered the chairs and sofas, while pillows in more bright colors lay about on straight chairs and the floor. Every floor lamp and table lamp was ablaze. The rugs were simple — each a solid blue, but in different shades. Tables for lunches and games were scattered about. An old-fashioned reading table stood in front of the end window, where Liz had done homework over spring holidays.

Emotion welled into her throat. "I didn't realize how much we meant to Henry."

He nodded soberly. "It's like a time capsule. Does make one feel guilty. But on the other hand, we had many good times here. That's what he wanted. Scrabble and gin rummy and laughter."

"Hide-and-seek. Remember when Mick got locked in the trunk?"

He chuckled. "Was bloody annoyed about that, he was."

She grinned. "Mick was annoyed a lot. *We* annoyed him." She set her shoulder bag on the floor next to the reading table and headed for the liquor cabinet. "Here's something different — it's unlocked." She pulled open the door and studied the bottles. Only for a moment did she consider making her usual martini. She rubbed her hands. "Ah, yes. Cragganmore. Who could resist?" She picked up the bottle of single malt. Little known abroad but highly respected in Britain, Cragganmore came from a small distillery high on the Spey River in Scotland.

"I'll have a wee dram." Simon sat at the reading table with his gym bag and removed his portfolio. "Didn't your father drink Cragganmore?"

"Yes. Good memory."

"You developed a taste for it, too?"

"Uh-huh. Let's not probe any more into how

similar I am to my parents. I've done enough ag-
onizing about that over the past few days to last
several lifetimes." She found two glasses, poured,
and walked them to the table. She handed him
his glass.

"You won't hear me disagree." He held it up to
the light.

The whiskey was the rich color of gold. He
touched the heel of his glass to the rim of hers. In
that gesture, traditional in the Childs and
Sansborough families, he saw a world of commu-
nication distilled, their shared history, their critical goal now.

Her gaze was sober. "To Sarah and Asher. May
we find them safe and quickly."

"And may Santarosa lead us instantly to the
bloody damn blackmailer!"

As they drank, she made herself pay attention
to the whiskey. It was full and sweet, mouth-
filling. Not a note off-key. There was a touch of
astringency in the finish that somehow made it
even more satisfying.

She sat and looked at Simon. He was not truly
handsome. His features were irregular, and of
course his misshapen nose destroyed any refine-
ment to his face. She remembered his un-
dressing in Pigalle. How his muscles had
rippled. His long limbs were sleek, like a runner's. He had a tan down to his bikini line.
There was something freewheeling about him,
from his thick hair and penetrating blue eyes to
the casual way his body moved. He had always
drawn people to him, but he was not as natural,
as unguarded now. Something had made him

take on personality traits to hide himself.

She asked, "What's happened to you since the last time we met?"

"What?"

"The last time I saw you, you were easygoing, open. Not hiding out. You were different."

"You expect me to remember that long ago?" He gave a small smile to buffer not answering.

She studied him, wondering what the truth was.

He changed the subject. "How's your arm?"

"Fine. Hardly hurts at all." True, or maybe she was just too tired to notice.

"Right. Let's see whether we can find some meaning in the photos." He arranged the three big prints of the baron's wall left to right. "It might help to tell me more about those Titans you mentioned."

"Sure. Their names were Atlas, Cronus, Hyperion, Ocean, Prometheus, and Themis. Atlas was the one who carried the world on his shoulders. Cronus was the leader. Hyperion was the father of the sun, the moon, and the dawn. I suppose one could push the analogy for Baron de Darmond and say he could *buy* the sun, the moon, the dawn, and probably all the stars in the galaxy, too. Ocean was the river that encircled the earth. Prometheus was the savior of humanity. And Themis was usually translated as Justice."

Simon scowled. "Justice? There was certainly no justice in what they did to you."

"People are resourceful when it comes to justifying their actions. Anyway, we know Hyperion was Baron de Darmond. Look, here's a fourth photo of

Mellencamp." She dug out her yellow Magic Marker and circled it as she had the three others.

"In this one, the baron and he are with your president and France's prime minister. In the second, they're with John Sloane, Paige Powell, the international financier Richmond Hornish, the Italian ambassador Edward Cereghino, and Christian Menchen, the fellow who runs the car company."

"Who are Sloane and Powell?"

"Hotshot journalists from the BBC. They did a miniseries about the financial interdependence of Europe and the United States a couple of years ago. Four of the people they interviewed were de Darmond, Hornish, Cereghino, and Menchen."

"Okay, the journalists aren't going to be high enough up the food chain for the Titans, but Menchen runs Eisner-Moulton, right?"

He knew instantly where she was going: "Eisner-Moulton owned that warehouse where Sarah and Asher were held."

"My mother always said there was no such thing as a coincidence."

Simon took lined paper from the table's drawer and wrote:

The Titans

Baron Claude de Darmond
  ("Hyperion," deceased)
Grey Mellencamp
  (maybe "Themis," deceased)
Christian Menchen — Eisner-Moulton
  (potential member)

He said, "Here's a photo with Mellencamp, the baron, Nicholas Inglethorpe, and some other fellow. Do you recognize the background?"

"Forget the background." There was excitement in her voice. "I don't think I got around to telling you that I tried everything to find out who gave the order to cancel my TV series. Finally, I climbed so high up the corporate totem pole that I reached the office of the man whose company owned the network."

He stared. "Inglethorpe?"

"Yes! He runs InterDirections, which owns Compass Broadcasting as well as a slew of newspapers, radio stations, and other media companies. Compass spent a lot of time and money on my series. It made no sense they'd kill it. I left a message to talk to Inglethorpe, but of course he never got back to me. And there's another connection. He was on the Aylesworth board with Mellencamp and succeeded Mellencamp as chairman. Which meant he was chairman when the board awarded me my chair."

"Inglethorpe has to be a Titan." He wrote the name. "Who's the other chap?"

"Another American. Gregory Gilmartin of Gilmartin Enterprises. They're huge in international construction. They do defense production, too — tanks, airplanes."

Simon pointed. "See those big trees behind them? Those are redwoods. That carving is an owl, the symbol of the Bohemian Grove group. They meet in the redwoods north of San Francisco."

"I remember reading an article about them. A

low-profile, all-boys camp where men go to act like jackasses and bond. But a lot of power and shoulder rubbing, too. Are you saying that if the baron and Inglethorpe were at the Bohemian Grove together and they're both Titans, then Gilmartin may be a Titan, too?"

"Guilt by association. Shaky ground, but in this case, we should consider it."

She frowned. "That connection's tenuous. Gilmartin's not as active as Mellencamp or Baron de Darmond were, or as Christian Menchen and Nicholas Inglethorpe are now. Gilmartin's quiet, reserved. His father was the flamboyant one."

"Yes, but he's influential not only in the private sector but in government circles. When MI6 needs to insert someone into the Middle East, we often go in as engineers or technicians for Gilmartin, or as employees in one of their hotels. The company's always building somewhere — because they're so big, they can underbid almost anyone. They put up hotels to house their staff, then they charge the government for housing. That's how their hotel chain started. Of course, once the deal's made, they give a kickback to local officials and apologize that it's all going to cost more than they first thought. You'd think the public would figure it out."

"Okay, add his name, but put two question marks after it."

As he wrote, she sat back and stretched. "Let's look at the files you photographed."

Huddled together, they studied the financial statements and letters. Every time they saw the name of one of the men on their list, Liz high-lighted it. At last, they came to a letter recommending an investment in prefabricated pubs.

"Thomas Brookshire?" she said. "Why do I know that name?"

"Tom Brookshire's my age. The letter says this is his first company. He can't be a Titan, for God's sake."

Liz pointed to the letterhead. "It's from his father. Didn't Sir Anthony and Lady Agnes have dinner once or twice a year with your parents?"

"Right. He was chancellor of the Exchequer, and now he's an EU commissioner. He's held various portfolios in Tory governments for decades."

She read the letter again, looking for hidden meanings. She sat up abruptly and pointed to the lower left-hand corner.

"Simon, look!"

He frowned. "All right, so old Tony Brookshire doodled one of those Slinky toys that kids like. Or maybe a pinwheel. Or it could be a coil of rope or a snake's coil. So?"

She was already digging through her bag. "Here it is." She brought out the crumpled paper with the dean's address from Santa Barbara and described finding it on the ground after she and Mac had put the corpse into her car trunk.

"You think the paper fell out of the janitor's clothes?" he asked.

She started to nod but stopped. Her eyes narrowed. "That's what Mac said, and it seemed logical. I figured I'd missed it when I searched the body. But what if it fell out of Mac's pocket instead, when he leaned into my trunk? Mac worked for the kidnappers. The Titans. Their emblem or sign could be this squiggle or coil."

"Coil?" Simon's pulse quickened as he remembered. "There's something else. I remember now. . . . When the baron was telling the blackmailer off, he said he'd fight him at Dreftbury. Then he threatened him: 'I'll even tell the Coil that you're the one.' The *Coil*. That's what this mark is, and I'll bet that's what these Titans call themselves — the Coil!"

"You could be right. The inside of a nautilus shell is a spiral —"

"A coil!" He tapped Brookshire's letter. "And it's the key to this puzzle!"

It took only seconds. They found ten more photo prints with the same symbol, always in the lower left-hand corner, always small and written lightly in pencil. Easily erasable. They were also in the same hand, as if the baron were marking which documents would receive his special attention. Each was a request or application for a loan or investment, or for backing for a large stock or bond offering. Some were linked directly to the living names on their list — Brookshire, Gilmartin, Inglethorpe, and Menchen. Others were from partnerships in which one of these men was involved, while a few were from companies downstream from the parent, subsidiaries that one of the men ran or in which he had a financial interest. Several letters and applications included two or more of the names. The sweep of multinational alliances was staggering.

Simon was excited. "Until now, we've been guessing and deducing. With the Coil symbol, we have confirmation about Sir Anthony and the others. That leaves us needing the last member. Let's take a look at those four photos again."

They returned to the pictures Liz had circled in yellow. The second had showed Baron de Darmond, Mellencamp, the two journalists — Sloane and Powell — Italian ambassador Edward Cereghino, automotive wunderkind Christian Menchen, and the legendary financier Richmond Hornish.

Liz said, "Didn't we just read about Hornish?" She sorted through the prints. "Yes. Here's the letter from him. Hornish wanted the bank to help guarantee a new securities instrument." She looked up. "He's the international speculator who almost destroyed Malaysia's economy by betting against their currency."

"Right. Malaysia and six other countries. Now he's making showboat charity donations — buying computers for kids in Latvia, funding a free university in Bulgaria, promising college scholarships to every kid who graduates from one of Chicago's inner-city schools. *Shazam* — his face on the cover of *Time* magazine, awards from churches and temples, and a shot at the Nobel Peace Prize. He's buying himself respectability. I'd believe his sincerity a lot more if he weren't still up to the same dirty business. To hell with the people who starve because of his greed."

She tapped the discreet coil on his letter. "This

proves it. He's the final one."

"Agreed." He snapped out a clean sheet of paper and wrote the names alphabetically.

The Titans

1. Brookshire, Sir Anthony — EU commissioner & politician.
2. Gilmartin, Gregory — Gilmartin Enterprises, international construction.
3. Hornish, Richmond — InQuox & investment vehicles, speculator & investor.
4. Inglethorpe, Nicholas — media & communications empire, including InterDirections, which owns Compass Broadcasting.
5. Menchen, Christian — Eisner-Moulton, automobiles & transportation.

As they studied the list, the room receded. The silence extended.

"The blackmailer is one of them," she said, her tone reverent because they had reached this moment at long last. "But which one?"

Forty-Four

Somewhere in northern Europe

In Asher's weakened condition, there had been no way they could fight their transfer from the truck to what turned out to be an anonymous Learjet. The only improvement in their situation was clothes for Asher — sweatpants, shoes, socks, and a shirt, plus the jacket he had found in the truck.

Once he was dressed, Sarah's demands that he be carried to the jet and up the stairs were ignored. By the time they were aboard, he was white as snow, drenched in sweat, and gritting his teeth. He fell into a seat, and she gave him extra pain pills.

Enraged, she stayed awake, listening. The jet sat on the tarmac two hours before finally taking off for a short flight. There were four men — two armed escorts, and the pilot and copilot, who never left the cockpit. From their occasional conversations, she learned Asher and she were being kept alive only until some important deal was closed.

In the dark hours before daybreak, the jet

landed in a rainstorm so drenching she could not make out landmarks or signs. They were blindfolded and transferred again, this time to some kind of powerful sedan driven by a man named Malko, who was obviously in charge. The car plowed through driving rain and rolling thunder and a harsh wind that shook all of them. Malko swore as he fought to keep the car on the highway.

At last, the noise abruptly stopped, and so did the car. Its big engine sounded almost docile as it echoed inside some kind of shelter. Sarah found Asher's hand, but before she could squeeze it, he squeezed hers. There was comfort in a known love, and hope, despite the overwhelming odds.

The men yanked her out of the car. She could hear Asher's being pulled out, too.

"Be careful of him!" she said angrily. "He's been shot!"

"Too bad," said a disinterested voice.

Hands hustled them down steps and into an enclosed space colder than the driving wind that had met them at the jet. The storm continued to rage outside, but there was another sound — surf?

When a heavy door clanged shut, Sarah ripped off her blindfold. "Asher?" The darkness was thick. The room stank of mold and damp stone.

"I'm here." His voice came from somewhere to her right, sounding of pain and exhaustion and — very unlike him — not trying to hide it. Still, there was fight, too. "Wherever the hell we are, it's near the ocean. Listen to those waves pound. They're louder than the rain or the thunder," he said.

"Big waves hitting big rocks below us. We must be on a cliff."

As soon as her eyes adjusted, she saw they were in a small empty room. Cold sea air blasted in through two barred windows high in the wall. Asher had slumped on the floor. There was no source of heat, but two canvas cots stood side by side.

"We need to get you warmed up," she said.

"You won't get an argument from me. I'm colder than an extra-inning night game at Candlestick."

She took his chilly hands and pulled as he struggled up. He leaned on her and she helped him to the nearest cot.

She picked up blankets. "Three for each of us. I guess they don't want us to freeze to death, at least not yet. But they don't want us to be comfortable either."

His breathing was labored. "I better lie down before I fall down."

She folded two blankets and spread them on the cot. He collapsed onto them, his teeth grinding against pain. She covered him with a third blanket. With his clothes, she hoped it would be enough. Bone-weary herself, she turned to the second cot.

She prepared it the same way and crawled in. "Where do you think we are?"

"Europe still," his shivering voice responded. "Far enough north that it's cold. Not a long-enough flight to be a summer night in San Francisco."

She nodded into the gloom. Asher did not know how to despair or give up. "Maybe it's Elsinore," she suggested. "Hamlet's castle in Denmark."

This time he did not answer. She listened to his teeth chatter, worrying he was too cold and too tired and near shock. She reached out and found his shoulder. He was shivering uncontrollably. Afraid, she jumped up and spread her blankets over him.

"S-s-sorry, Sarah."

"No need to be, darling." She slid quickly under the blankets. "I just wanted an excuse to be close anyway."

Worrying, she wrapped herself around him. When he said no more, she knew how badly off he was. A lump thickened her throat. She kissed his icy ear and held him. At last, his shivering ceased, and he fell asleep, his breath a ghostly mist above their faces.

Northumberland, England

Simon said, "Every time I look at Tony Brookshire's name, I feel queasy. Disgusted. He's an old friend of the family, for God's sakes. How could he keep tabs on you in Santa Barbara and kidnap Sarah?" His expression dark, he sipped his whiskey.

"If the baron's files are any indication, they do favors for one another," Liz said. "Look at how many of the same boards they sit on. They're already working together officially, so it's not much of a leap to think they work together privately as well — consulting, informing one another, making mutually advantageous deals."

"You're right. But there's more — Brookshire's the only one in public service. The five others run multinationals richer than most small nations, and not one of them is in the same industry. So if they've decided to cooperate, their sweep and power are vast."

She sat up straighter. "Does that ever sound like the ancient Titans! And look what they did with *their* power. . . . They laid out rules, delivered punishments, and handed out rewards so the world would move in a direction they conceived and where they remained in charge."

"I don't like the sound of that. *Their* vision. *Their* control." Simon poured second glasses of whiskey.

"Democracy dies behind closed doors." She repressed a shiver and packed the photo prints back into Simon's portfolio.

As Simon put logs into the stone fireplace, he said, "If Nautilus's meetings are secret, the code names indicate the Coil's are even more so."

"Afraid so." She turned off lamps and settled onto the sofa, watching him thoughtfully as he built a fire, enjoying his company but wishing it were under happier circumstances. Wishing Sarah and Asher were with them.

At last, the fire burning strongly, he sat beside her, crossed his legs, leaned back, and threw an arm across the back of the sofa away from her. With his other hand, he cradled his glass to his chest. The shadowy room was warm and the fireplace comforting. The aroma of burning pine drifted toward them.

Modern humans were still cave dwellers, she decided, yearning for light and heat . . . atavistic, especially when threatened.

In the firelight, his hair was the color of rich mahogany. His nose seemed larger and more slapdash than usual. His head rested back as he stared into the fire. She liked the way the planes of his face were almost vertical, rounding down into his square jaw. His lids looked heavy and his face worn. He was spent, drained, and allowing himself to show it.

She kept glancing at him, seeing something new each time, as if she were just discovering him. Finally, he sighed. It was not only a weary sound, but vulnerable.

It all crowded in on her — from his sudden appearance in the storage locker outside London to their flight here to visit Henry, never had he seemed vulnerable. Only headlong and impatient and often irritatingly right. She tried to see the little boy in him now but could not. No more than she could see the girl she had once been. She was an adult now, and so was this tired man weighed with responsibility. She felt drawn to him, as if she could sit here with him forever.

"I'll tell you a secret, but you'll have to tell me one, too." He rolled his head to the side and peered at her, a quizzical expression on his face. "General's Permission."

It was a children's game they had played, named after their great-uncle, Gen. William Augustus Childs, who had died at Dunkirk. His brooding portrait hung with others along the staircase at Childs Hall. The rules were simple: No lies, no excuses, and no dares. Always played in a closet with the lights out, where the secrets once spoken were left behind as soon as the door opened and they returned to the world.

"We're not wrapped up in blankets in the closet with Mick," she said.

He drank. "So?"

"All right. The general gives you permission to speak."

He sat his glass on his knee. "You asked what had happened to me since I last saw you. A few years ago, I was sent into Bosnia to extract an asset. We'd had word his cover was blown." He paused, his voice thickened. "My legend worked fine, but I said something inadvertently. . . . I was young and stupid, chasing a woman I'd met on the train."

"Let me guess. She was a Juliet agent. Under the circumstances, expected."

He did not look at her. "Beautiful, of course. I made her instantly. The problem was, I decided to play her."

She waited.

"My cover was as a UN agricultural expert. I had money, so I fed her on the train, got her drunk, and tried to pump her. But she slipped me a mickey. Don't know to this day what it was or how she did it. Of course, I was carrying passports for the asset and his family, a miniature camera to take their photos, and glue to paste them in. After I passed out, she found all of it in the special compartment in my carry-on, but that wasn't enough to tell her his identity and where they'd be waiting. But when I was trying to worm information out of her, I'd mentioned a bombed salt factory in Tuzla. I finally woke up when the train slammed to a stop because guerrillas had ripped up the tracks. It threw me into the seat ahead, and I busted my nose." He shook his head, disgusted, angry. "She was gone. By the time I got to the factory, our asset was dead. So was the whole family. Executed, bullets to the head. Just lying there. Even his baby."

She inhaled. "You felt you'd caused it."

"Bloody damn right I did. Hubris. Fucking hubris. Why didn't I just lose her when I got to Tuzla? I could have. But no, I was going to get something from her first. The hero. Instead, she walked away clean with six British passports and enough of a clue from me that an entire family was wiped out." Deep lines riddled his face. He looked a decade older, and the hand that held his drink trembled. He peered down at the whiskey, drained it, and stood up. "Want another?"

"I'm fine."

She watched him stalk to the liquor cabinet and pour. He went to the window, pulled back the drape, and gazed out at the night.

At last, she spoke to his back, "You haven't forgiven yourself."

"What I did was unforgivable."

"And so you decided not to care anymore?"

"Of course I care. I just don't get too involved."

"Well, you're involved now. And you might as well forgive yourself. You can't fix it. You can't bring them back. When you quit making mistakes —"

"I know. I'll be dead, too. The problem was, I knew better."

"It changed your life. That might not be so bad. You learned something. I'll bet you've never made a mistake like that again." She studied his rigid posture. Finally: "Your chief's furious with you. She's trying to send you to Florence. Something must've happened in Bratislava, too, didn't it?" She recalled the headlines she had seen — the demonstration that turned lethal. "That young woman who immolated herself . . . you were there, undercover. What was her name?"

"Viera. Viera Jozef." He heaved a sigh and turned. His face was stricken.

"You knew her."

"Rather well." From across the room, he related the story. "I don't understand why she did it."

"Or why you didn't guess and stop her. But this time you really are clear, Simon. In Tuzla, you made a tragic mistake that you'll live with the rest of your life. That's piggybacked onto all the other errors you make every day just because you're alive. All of us make them. Then Viera killed herself. That made her loss even deeper for you."

"I don't need a psychologist."

"No. But you could use a friend."

He gave a brief smile. "Perhaps you're right. Partly, I feel guilty because I didn't love her. If I had, I might've seen what she was up to."

"Now you're bringing out the old crystal ball.

There's no way you can predict that. Are the murders of that family in Tuzla why you never got your nose fixed?"

"A reminder." He rubbed a finger along it. "Every time I look in a mirror." He turned his head away.

"Extreme, but understandable. For whatever it's worth, I forgive you."

He glanced at her. Gave a small smile. "Believe it or not, it helps."

She smiled in return. "Not only that, I forgive you for using me as a business, back when we were young."

He returned to the sofa, drank deeply, and leaned back heavily. "I've never told anyone about Tuzla. Of course, MI6 knows. I was sidelined on a desk until I convinced them to send me into the antiglobalization movement. HQ needed someone, and I had the requisite skills. I suppose I was trying to redeem myself."

"Three years is a long time to give up everyone and everything, including your own identity. I'd say you'd done something useful and fine."

She liked the compassion she saw in Simon. Admired it. She felt vaguely guilty for having assumed he was a lightweight. She could hear her father's voice. *Never assume.* The room was filled with the warmth and fragrance of the fire and with an oddly serene sense of intimacy. There was that feeling about him again, the trust, the attraction.

"My turn," she said.

"The general gives you permission to speak."

"It's nothing as dramatic as yours. Did you

hear how my father died?"

"Never could ferret it out. Hush-hush and all that." He shifted on the sofa again so he could watch her. She wore no makeup, her skin scrubbed clean back at their Paris hideout. Her face was spectacular — large eyes and generous mouth, high arching brows, and of course that mole beside her lips. But now as he looked at her, each feature seemed more delicate than dramatic. The way her eyelashes brushed down when she lowered her gaze. The single silky curl that rested against her jaw. The blush of weariness on her cheeks. She had been kind to him just now. She had listened. It had been years since he had wanted to talk honestly about himself — or anyone had really wanted to hear.

She was saying, "After the failure of Bremner's scheme, all of us were sure the Carnivore was dead, but Sarah tracked him to Sicily, near where his grandmother was born. He'd been living there, holed up with his books. Mother told me later he'd returned there occasionally over the years because he felt an affinity for the land and the people. Anyway, Sarah believed he should be brought in to be debriefed, because he'd promised he would, and because she didn't trust him to stay retired. She didn't tell me. Only Asher knew. They arranged with the CIA to helicopter them and some troops to his estate. What they didn't know was he'd rigged his house and land. When he saw them, he set off a string of underground explosions."

"That's how he died?"

She gave a slow nod. "Sarah said it was horrible. Like a series of earthquakes. Anyway, there wasn't even a body for a funeral, and I'd lost my last chance to see him. When Sarah told me, I didn't speak to her for months. I was furious because I thought — I still sometimes think — that if I'd been there, he wouldn't have done it. But then Mom died, and I was alone. What a mess. Of course, Sarah was right to try to bring him in, but she should've told me. I think she was worried I wouldn't agree."

"He didn't give himself up in Paris with your mother, even after you made the arrangements."

"I know. I think about that, too. So when Mom died, I realized I had to get on with my life, and I apologized to Sarah. We owed her for what she went through with Bremner, and I owed her again for my anger." She frowned, fell silent.

"There's something about it that's still bothering you."

"My husband. He . . . he was violent, too." She hesitated. "He'd go through dark periods, and he'd hit me. It was only later that I figured out it didn't matter what I said or did. That he'd always find some new excuse to beat me."

His hand clenched on his glass. "You *let* him beat you?" And realized that was where the story about her father had been heading.

"It's more complicated than that. I know . . . who'd believe I was a battered wife, right? Tough Liz. Karate-trained Liz. CIA Liz. But I never reported him, and I never fought back. I wonder whether there was something in the air when I was growing up that enabled me to live with his violence. Children sense things, but they don't have the words to express the unsaid. It's the thousand-pound gorilla hulking around the family room that everyone ignores. Oddly, I knew I'd never let anyone else treat me that way. Then, of course, he died. So I lost the chance to develop some backbone and leave him."

"Did you tell anyone?"

"Maybe some of the guys at Langley guessed." She glanced at him. "I went through therapy while I was getting my doctorate. That helped. I can give you all the jargon for it, the analysis, but who cares? In the end . . . I allowed myself to be his victim. And no, I don't think I 'loved him too much.' I quit loving him in there somewhere, but I was too damn stupid and needy to do anything about it."

"And you're still not at peace with it."

"Apparently not. Since I just told you." She gave a wan smile.

"Are you feeling your mortality right now?"

"You bet I am. God knows what today will bring."

"Nothing like trying to make up for one's mistakes at one blow, right? We're a pair. I liked you a lot as a kid. I think I like you even more now."

"Thank you. It's mutual."

"Are you as tired as I am?" he asked, his voice low and intimate.

"Maybe. Probably. I have an alarm on my watch. I'll set it, and we can sleep for a couple of hours. Then we should leave for Dreftbury and make plans."

He checked the hallway outside and locked the door. As she placed one more log into the flickering flames, she decided she liked the sense of safety in this room . . . in Henry's house. They met at the sofa. She sat, and he sat beside her again. Closer. Hesitantly, he took her hand. She let him, then his in both of hers. His skin was warm and dry, the muscles and tendons powerful. They leaned back, still holding hands, as the fire flickered and spat, and fell quickly into troubled sleep.

Henry Percy detested the fact that the younger servants kept the fire high in his new bedroom all night. Still, July was often cold here, and at his advanced age, the chill could easily carry him off. He did not intend to die just yet. The problem was that the heat often made him fall asleep in his wheelchair as he read.

He groaned and stretched to ease the pain in his shoulder. What had awakened him? He remembered dreaming of his motorcycle, the old army bike he had brought with him from the war nearly sixty years ago. Or had it been a dream?

He frowned and listened but heard nothing. Yet . . . had a motorcycle come to a stop somewhere nearby? As a faint click sounded in the silent room, he immediately felt a quick draft of air, there and gone. He whirled his wheelchair around, staring at the long drapes that covered his French doors. Had they moved?

His pulse raced, and fear shot through him. His gun was in his bedside table. He was half out of his wheelchair when a man stepped from behind the drapes.

"Good evening, Baron." He aimed his pistol.

Henry Percy stared at the weapon, then raised his gaze to the man's face. "You!"

Forty-Five

As the noise of a motorcycle engine stopped abruptly, Liz forced herself awake, her eyes still closed, not sure what she had heard. She listened to the mutterings of the old timbers in Henry Percy's mansion, aware of Simon beside her on the sofa. Her head lay on his shoulder, his cheek resting against the crown of her head. She wanted to stay here forever. He smelled good, irresistible, like walnuts and raisins with a soupçon of fine malt. She listened to his light snore, a heavenly sound, and turned to nuzzle his shoulder . . . until she recalled —

Her eyes snapped open. Had there been an engine — a motorcycle — that had quit before it reached the house? She settled back, considering. Maybe one of Henry's servants had returned from a tryst. Or maybe one of the gardeners had arrived early for work. She waited for whispers, giggles, voices, a door closing. Nothing. But then, Simon and she were at the back of the house, on the second floor. Anything that occurred at the front or in the main rooms or even in the kitchen was difficult to hear.

Judging by the flames crackling in the fireplace

and the darkness of the night, they had not slept long. She was not sure she had even heard the engine. The truth was, she was on edge, her mind roiling. That was the real problem. She tried to relax, but her thoughts returned to their long conversation with Henry about Nautilus and his role in it, then finally moved on to their deducing the five remaining members of the Coil.

She wondered about them . . . the respect their names evoked internationally. Their towering wealth and influence. The dry-lipped awe of those struggling to reach the same exalted career heights.

Yet they had treated her like a rat in an experiment, and they had murdered Kirk and the dean and the dean's wife. How could they? The easy answers were greed and ambition for her father's files. But that was unsatisfactory, superficial. Repulsed, she recalled what Sophocles wrote in *Oedipus Rex*: "God keep you from the knowledge of who you are!" That was it: The ancient Greek playwright had known the human soul — that the ultimate judge and jury was oneself. To keep a high opinion of themselves, people rationalized away their less-than-stellar deeds. The more they rationalized, the better they became at it. And the greater the evil they could justify.

She repressed a shudder. Simon seemed to sense her unease. He pulled her closer — and a single gunshot shattered the silence.

It was like a knife through her heart. "Simon!" She shook his arm.

He was already awake. "Damn! What . . ."

"A shot." She disentangled and ran to the high windows.

He was at her side. "Did you hear anything else?"

The fishpond and forest looked untouched, full of deep shadows as the moon sank toward the horizon. Nothing was out of place. Simon opened the window.

"Before the shot," she told him, "there might have been a motorcycle engine."

"A motorcycle and a single gunshot could mean a poacher." He listened, but there were only the dawn songs of insects.

"Maybe." She crossed the room and grabbed her shoulder bag.

He followed and snatched up his gym bag. "You think it's someone after us."

"If I'm wrong, we can always come back and finish our nap."

"We're going to have to wait for that, I should think."

All business, he checked his pistol, and they hurried to the door.

Liz cracked it and peered out. "No one." Her voice was tight.

He pressed it open wider and gazed through the space beneath the hinges toward the opposite end of the dimly lit hall. "No one this way either."

She flung the strap of her bag across her chest. The Glock in both hands, she slid out. He followed with his Beretta, the handle of the Uzi jutting conveniently from his bag. Silence. Liz nodded toward the short end of the hall. He nodded, agreeing. They sprinted along the carpet, passing portraits of Henry's stern-faced ancestors. At one time, family and friends had filled the suites and rooms in this wing every weekend. Now the emptiness resounded.

The corridor ended at a back landing. At the arched opening, they studied the elaborately carved staircase that curved up and down. No movement. No sound. The silence was eerie, like the hush before a thunderstorm. They left their cover and glided down the stairs, then stopped abruptly when they heard four or five sets of feet padding across a wood floor.

"That's no poacher," Liz whispered. "They're in the house."

Before Simon could agree, a violent fusillade exploded from the front. Windows shattered. Bullets whined and thudded. There was the noise of ripping wood and the loud pinging of rounds striking metal. Instantly, people inside returned fire.

"We've brought them down on Henry!" she said.

"Damnation!" Simon reached the first floor in one jump.

Liz was on his heels. They raced down the hall, slid inside the foyer, looked carefully both ways, and started across.

A fusillade smashed in, fracturing window-panes and puncturing the massive front door. The noise was deafening. Wood splinters flew like arrows. Liz and Simon dived onto the marble floor and covered their heads.

As soon as the firing paused, they crawled

around glass shards and across to the parlor, where three servants in pajamas huddled beside windows, their hands shaky as they held a motley collection of shotguns and ancient bolt-action rifles. The low moon filled the room with gray light and eerie shadows. Another short round of shots blasted inside. A painting crashed to the floor. A wooden lamp splintered. When the firing paused again, the men rose up to shoot wildly out the windows and duck back.

Liz and Simon hurriedly crab-walked to Henry's servant Richard, hunched like a praying abbot beneath his window.

"Who are they?" Liz asked. "How many?"

"I don't know." His face was half in shadow, making him look far older than when he had invited them into the mansion. He turned in alarm as another volley sounded. "A dozen. Maybe more. Well armed."

"Where's Henry?" Simon asked worriedly.

"In his bedroom with Clive, sir."

As another shot slammed through the window, Richard flattened against the wall. Window glass exploded like glinting ice. He waited, darted up to fire out wildly, and fell back, his face twitching with fear.

More isolated shots followed, pinning everyone down, riddling the walls. As the servants returned fire, Liz and Simon scuttled back to the foyer and down the hall to what had once been Henry's den and was now his bedroom. The door was open.

Liz froze, shocked. "Oh, no!" Her throat tightened, and she fought a sudden ache behind her eyes.

"Henry!" Simon's quick intake of air sounded like a gasp.

Lord Percy lay on his back in a pool of blood, motionless, his face bone white, his gray eyes staring upward. Sitting cross-legged next to him, Clive wrung his hands and muttered under his breath. From the French doors, where the drapes had been pushed back, dingy moonlight illuminated them.

Liz and Simon ran to him. Clive looked up, his grizzled cheeks streaked with tears. They knelt, and Clive gently closed Henry's eyes. Sharp pain pierced Liz's heart and lingered. Instantly, shots detonated somewhere outside, and bullets screeched in through the panes of the French doors, spraying glass.

Clive started to rear up, but Simon yanked him down to the floor.

"Stay here!" he ordered, clamping him flat.

More bullets rammed into an upholstered chair. Goose down burst out in a white cloud. Other gunfire crashed into distant walls — the east wing. There was the sound of a door's being battered open there.

"They're coming inside!" Clive looked around frantically and tried to sit up, but Simon held him down. "They want *you*," Clive said. "Go. Hurry!"

Liz resisted. "No. We can't leave you. We —"

"He's dead," Clive insisted tearfully. "You can't help Lord Henry. And if you're not here, they may leave us alone!"

Running feet sounded in the east wing. His memory might be bad, but Clive was right. There was no way the untrained servants with their sporting weapons could hold out. There were too many attackers — and too many servants to be saved — for Liz and Simon to force a better result.

Clive rolled away and sat up. "Go! Now. Please! So we can surrender!"

Liz and Simon exchanged a look. They leaped up and ran back down the hall as the gunfire outside halted suddenly, indicating the invaders were likely inside. The lull was Liz and Simon's only advantage. They sped past the curved staircase and into the cross corridor at the rear of the house as shouts erupted from the foyer. Feet thundered after them.

They slammed through the rear door and tore around to the grape arbor and their parked Jeep. In the lead, Liz vaulted into the driver's seat. Simon tumbled in on the passenger side. The engine sputtered, then started.

As the first two attackers stormed out of the house after them, Liz gunned the engine and screeched the Jeep in a sharp J-turn, fishtailing until her tires gripped the cobblestones and the vehicle straightened out.

As she raced the Jeep past the shadow-drenched front lawn, Simon yanked the Uzi from his bag and leaned out the window. She glanced at him once, caught his implacable expression. In the moonlight, beads of sweat glinted on his forehead.

"Here they come!" he warned, voice taut. The

killers were ghostly shadows, legs pumping as they chased the Jeep and raised their weapons. "Looks like at least a dozen."

"On foot?"

"So far."

"We'll outrun them then." With a jolt of adrenaline, she floored the accelerator.

But they could not outrun bullets. A volley crashed into the Jeep's tail and screamed past their windows. The horrible noise penetrated to her marrow. Simon squeezed off a burst and ducked inside just as a shot detonated his side-view mirror. Pieces exploded into the air and pinged against the door.

"A tad close, that." His voice was grim and breathless.

"Too close!"

She bit back fear as Simon ducked out and fired again. Still, the bombardment from their hunters was lessening.

"Are we out of range?" she asked hopefully.

Simon fell into the front seat again. "Yes. Their bullets are going wild." He stared back over his shoulder through the shattered rear window, watching.

She nodded silently and eased up on the accelerator. She glanced up at the rearview mirror, glimpsing a dark-clothed figure who paced alone ahead of the pack of gunmen, his movements radiating anger and frustration. Her breath seemed to freeze in her lungs when she thought she saw a limp. She ripped her gaze away to concentrate on keeping the hurtling Jeep on the dark, narrow drive that led back to the country road.

"Do you see a limping man back there?" she asked anxiously. "The limp should be on the right side."

"Yes. It's on the right. Didn't the man at the Eisner-Moulton warehouse have a limp?"

She nodded. "I think he's the one who dropped the jacket with the Cronus note inside. I didn't get a good look at him then, and I don't dare try now. Do you see any signs of a car?"

"Yes! Here comes one now!" A van had paused beside the hunters, and they had jumped inside.

Pulse pounding, Liz killed the lights as she sped the Jeep into the tunnel of brush and overgrown trees. They might as well have been inside an inkwell. The only light came from her dashboard. Branches screeched against the Jeep's sides. Simon seized the door handle, holding tightly. The towering vegetation blurred past like a long brushstroke of black paint. Behind, headlights pierced the night ominously, searching.

Simon said nothing, tension radiating from him like heat from an oven. She stared ahead, her eyes aching with the strain of trying to see the road. It was as straight as a bullet's path, or at least that was what Henry had always said. She gripped the steering wheel, unconsciously leaning forward, trying to spot . . . waiting . . . there it was. A break in the trees! The faint shine of the stream. The glen!

But at this heightened speed . . . still, it did not matter. She had little choice.

"Hold on!"

She slammed the brakes and yanked the steering wheel. The wheels banged on rocks as the vehicle thudded blindly over the roadside and dropped, throwing them against their seat belts. She held the steering wheel tightly while letting the vehicle find its own way as it smashed saplings and rolled over rocks. She controlled it enough to keep it upright and still moving in the general direction and . . . there were the headlights again, glowing through the trees as if a monster were out looking for them with searchlights.

"There!" Simon pointed to a leafy horse chestnut tree.

"They won't see the stream from the drive," she said, turning the wheel, "unless they kill their headlights."

"Unless they know where to look."

"That thought doesn't make me happy."

With a queasy feeling, she braked and yanked the steering wheel once more, nosing the Jeep under the tree. Branches draped themselves across the rear, cloaking it. The front pointed at a sixty-degree angle to the spring. She killed the engine.

They were not only silent but completely hidden. Simon reached out. She took his hand. With his other hand, he covered hers. They lifted their heads, listening. The growl of the engine approached, and the illumination brightened. They stared back. She found herself holding her breath. *Breathe, dammit.*

Up on the drive, a large van charged past, its engine so powerful it could not help but advertise itself with its immense, smooth strength. In an abrupt Doppler effect, the noise level dropped.

And the immediate danger was gone, red tail-lights soaring onward.

She inhaled deeply. "Did you see what kind of van it was?"

"Not a prayer. Much too fast. But it was big enough to hold the dozen men who were chasing us." He watched the taillights disappear. "You're a hell of a good driver."

"Thanks. I like to drive." She added, "Usually."

They sat like two automatons, the sound of the rushing stream in their ears.

At last, he said, "They'll be back, and we have to decide what to do. We can't drive out the way we'd planned. They might be waiting for us."

"We've got one advantage — the Jeep." She turned on the engine. "Four-wheel drive."

He knew instantly what she had in mind. "You want to use the stream bed?"

"Why not? Unless it's changed, it's a gentle descent."

"What the hell. I don't remember any boulders. Let me know when you want me to spell you."

She touched the accelerator, and the vehicle rolled into the water. The tires bumped and bounced. The left front wheel landed heavily in a hole, and a wave of dark water splashed up over the fender.

As low-hanging branches scraped along the top, he saw her glance at him. Her dark eyes glowed like a feral animal's, dangerous with worry.

"What is it?" he said immediately.

"If I'm right that the man with the limp works for the Coil, then everything's changed." She paused, her gaze on the treacherous streambed. "Up until now, the Coil's been protecting us against the blackmailer, because it wanted us to find the files for them. This attack proves they've changed their minds. Not only the blackmailer wants us dead — they do, too. And if they worked on Henry before they shot him, they'll know we're on our way to Dreftbury. They'll be waiting."

Forty-Six

The drive down the streambed took nearly three hours, although the distance was only a little more than a mile. They jumped out four times to roll oversize rocks out of the way. As sunrise rose in brilliant pink and gold above the treetops, Liz saw a shortcut. She drove up over the bank, across a shady meadow where grazing deer scattered like bird shot, and then back into the stream. Shortly after Simon took over the wheel, a waterfall appeared ahead. Liz got out and walked along the bank, guiding him as he maneuvered the Jeep down one jarring lip of rock to another, seven in all. Then a tire went flat.

By the time the vehicle emerged at the country highway, it was soaked, the paint was chipped, the body battered, and they felt shaken to the marrow. And they were wet. But no one had followed, and no one waited in ambush.

Jubilant, they used a blanket from the back to dry themselves and set their socks and running shoes on the backseat for the sun to dry. Once more on a real road, Liz accelerated, and the sturdy Jeep headed south. The ride felt smooth as a sheet of glass. Stands of trees towered against the morning sky. White sheep grazed in green fields. Traffic was sporadic in this sparsely populated area.

Still, her voice was tense when she asked, "Do you see anything?"

He was sitting with his back to the door, Beretta in hand. His face was craggy and determined as he watched behind. "Nothing yet," he said.

"*Yet.*"

"We mustn't ever assume again we're safe from them."

That word again — *assume*. Her jaw tightened, and she nodded. "Do you think it was through Gary that the Coil found us?"

"He's the most logical source."

"That feeling in Paris I had of being followed, even while we were going to the airport . . . I must've been right. Somehow they tracked us to him. Then they made him tell where he'd flown us. I hope they didn't kill him." Her voice sounded dead. She blinked back tears, thinking of Henry's broken body. And banished his murder and her worry about Gary Faust. "We need information about Dreftbury."

"I've been thinking the same thing. A cybercafe would do the trick."

"Good. We can check out the EU Web site, too, to see whether we can figure out which of the Coil members has a deal pending with Carlo Santarosa's commission."

He gave a cold smile. "Yes. I like that." His fist tightened on his Beretta.

She glanced at him. "How are you planning to get into Dreftbury?"

"Use one of my MI6 IDs." Nautilus would be a magnet for foreign agents, which meant Britain's counterintelligence arm, MI5, would be there. But there was little love lost between MI5 and MI6, and the chance MI5 had been told of his new status was remote. MI6 considered MI5 drones; MI5 thought MI6 snobs. In Simon's opinion, both were right. "I'll be an expert on antiglobalization organizations and eavesdropping. MI5 will resent me like the Black Plague, but they'll be glad for me, too."

"That might work. I'm going to need one of your MI6 IDs, too."

With Simon navigating, his gaze never at rest, they continued on toward the small town of Hexham, where they picked up the A69 west. Liz watched the traffic and the rugged countryside as they passed red sandstone villages and castles that had once guarded the border. They were in Cumbria now, which had a history of feuds and warfare as long and violent as Northumberland's, dating back before the Romans.

At Carlisle, she took the Jeep off the highway. Once a simple outpost of Hadrian's Wall, Carlisle had grown into a city of more than 100,000.

"If you'll look into cyber cafés, I'll pump gas," she told him.

"For you, anything." He smiled.

She smiled back and pulled into a petrol station. While she filled the tank, he made calls at a phone kiosk. As she paid, he bought a local map, and soon they were back in the Jeep. He directed her south into the city. The café was in an area of little shops on a picturesque street. Their socks and shoes were dry. They dressed. As they left the thrashed Jeep, she adjusted Asher's beret and put on Sarah's glasses.

Breakfast odors of bangers and baked tomatoes and fried eggs wafted from a traditional diner. It was midmorning. Still, people crammed tables, gossiping.

Next to the diner stood the cybercafe — Byte Me. Simon checked the sidewalk as she opened the door. They stepped into noise and the aroma of rich espresso. The decor was hard-surfaced and techno, with a lot of chrome and white paint. Businesspeople, students, and geeks and freaks of all persuasions sat at some twenty terminals, cups and mugs at their elbows, gazes riveted to screens. Each terminal had a small printer.

In a distant corner was an espresso bar, and above it hung a wide-screen television. A BBC news program was on in full living color. Since the network had carried the story about her yesterday, it was possible it would still be broadcasting it.

Swearing under her breath, Liz tugged the beret down to her ears and hurried to the only free terminal, where she angled the chair so she could sit with her back partly to the TV. Instantly, she punched in Shay Babcock's code and went to work. She might have little time, if she were recognized. The terminals were just a few feet apart — too close.

Simon took in the situation with one troubled appraisal. At the espresso bar, he ordered two lattes and two hard buns with cream cheese. He laid his last twenty-pound note on the table. A necessary expenditure, if it worked.

"Can't break that." The man had sleep in his eyes and irritation in his voice.

"Not a problem. Say, would you mind switching to CNN? Addicted to it, as it were." And at this early hour, CNN would be covering world news and sports, far less likely than a UK station to run a story about the search for Liz Sansborough.

The man was staring at the cash.

"Oh," Simon said, as if remembering, "and do feel free to keep the change."

That did it. The fellow's eyes slitted, the money vanished, and CNN appeared. Simon watched the room. When his order was ready, he rejoined Liz. Her profile was tense. He pulled up a chair and sat close.

"Thanks," she whispered. "Anything?" She drank the latte.

"Five copies of the *Times*. Fortunately, none look opened. We may get lucky."

She glanced uneasily around.

"Want to go back to the Jeep?" he asked. "I can do this alone."

Her brows shot up. "No way. My disguise has been fine so far."

"Then let's get to work. What have you found?" He sipped his latte.

"This is the EU Web site. I'm checking the Competition Commission. Here's Santarosa. Thought you'd like to see what the commissioner looks like."

Carlo Santarosa had a wide Mediterranean face, with dusky skin, narrow dark eyes, and the sort of mouth that could easily be sweet or cruel, depending on circumstances or whim. His hair was pepper gray, and he wore wire-rimmed glasses.

"He doesn't look as if he'll roll easily," Simon decided.

"Our blackmailer may have a tougher time than he's anticipating." She clicked a hyperlink. "Competition cases are posted, so we're lucky. I'm in the section on antitrust and cartels — you know, when companies collude instead of competing, and how the commission controls anticompetitive agreements. What I found almost instantly was Eisner-Moulton, in a nasty case where it's accused of illegally controlling car and truck prices throughout Europe. Christian Menchen's named specifically."

"That sounds bad."

"Very. His multinational's swimming in red ink and closing plants and selling off subsidiaries. The one bright spot has been European sales. If the decision goes against him, profits will plunge, which will hurt him on several fronts, including making it difficult to borrow money to offset debt. The company's huge. It'll survive. But if this continues, Menchen may be out of a job, and Germany's not known for its platinum parachutes the way the United States is."

"Is he our blackmailer?"

She shot him a grim look. "He's a good possibility. So much depends on who he is. What he fears. What he wants. Assuming Menchen has the files, he could look at this as a chance not to be missed. All he has to do is blackmail Santarosa into deciding in Eisner-Moulton's favor, and a lot of his personal as well as business problems vanish."

"He sounds like the blackmailer. But common sense tells me we need to make sure we haven't missed anyone." The computer next to him was free at last. He moved over and signed on, using one of his covers.

They worked quietly, drinking their lattes.

"Here's your old nemesis — Nicholas Inglethorpe," Simon said at last. "In the mergers section." The Competition Commission was the one-stop shop for merger control in the EU. "The commission is weighing whether to demand his multinational divest itself of its six-billion-dollar stake in pay-TV operator SkyCall before it's allowed to buy Grossblatt of Poland, because Grossblatt owns one of Inglethorpe's biggest competitors — Polska-Storrs Media. It'd be the largest forced divestiture ever."

"Inglethorpe's multinational is having financial problems, too. The lousy world economy's hurting everyone. I remember reading he wanted to expand into the old East bloc. If he were counting on SkyCall, and Santarosa makes him divest, he'll reel."

"That makes two of the Coil who could be our blackmailer."

They exchanged an uneasy look and resumed searching. Liz stayed in her chair, keeping her face in her screen, but an hour later, Simon left to buy two more lattes.

When he returned, he drank slowly. "Here's the East bloc again." He kept his voice low. "This time it's Richmond Hornish and his flagship charity project — computers he's selling below cost to every school in Bulgaria. The commission is investigating whether he's been granted interest relief, which, it claims, distorts competition."

"Are they saying Hornish may be taking kickbacks?"

"Basically, yes. If the report concludes he is, and Santarosa sanctions the report, the scandal will blast Hornish out of the running for the Nobel Peace Prize. He's devoted the past five years to trying to undo his reputation as a financial mercenary and prove he's worthy of it."

"He's got a lot to lose then. He could be the blackmailer, too."

Simon nodded, and they returned to their investigation. They had read through the entire site and were just about to quit, when Liz saw Gregory Gilmartin's name.

"I'd forgotten about Gilmartin Enterprises' merger with Tierney Aviation. But then, it's already been approved in the United States by the SEC. I had no idea the EU had to okay it, too. Both are American companies. Why is Europe involved?"

"Because both do serious business here," he said, "so SEC approval isn't enough. Our Competition Commission isn't like your SEC — it can't break up companies that abuse their market power, and it can't force them to divest. Once a merger's approved, the commission has little recourse to stop monopoly. Its real control is beforehand, so that's why it investigates, no matter what the SEC has said. Then Santarosa decides."

"This merger's colossal. A forty-billion-dollar coup. It's so big, it'll make Gilmartin-Tierney one of the largest multinationals in the world and skyrocket Gregory Gilmartin's reputation ahead of his father's and grandfather's. I recall reading that they were legendary, but he's been a corporate wallflower so far."

Simon sat back and stretched. "So now we know the bad news — four of the Coil have reason to blackmail Santarosa. No clear-cut answer, dammit."

"It's surprising so many have actions waiting for his decision. Still, I imagine it's impossible to conduct international business these days without stumbling into regulatory agencies."

"You're right. Globalization's all about free trade, so corporations can move money, factories, and investments anywhere in the world to find the cheapest labor and materials, the most lucrative markets, and the best tax shelters. So every time they cross a border, they risk new rules and regulations. Part of the fallout from that is international trade agreements are destroying the ability of governments to govern. In fact, they're becoming subsidiaries to financial markets . . . to bonds and stocks and investments, not to what people need."

"You mean food and shelter."

"Yes, and clean water and an education. The

EU's fighting to control corporations, but as long as profit is capitalism's primary goal, multinationals will keep striving for it, and they'll continue to run afoul of the Competition Commission. In the end — unless globalization becomes less about wealth — I think the multinationals will win."

"And the public will lose. That's depressing as hell," she said.

"The only progress we made here was to eliminate Brookshire, because he's a politician. Naturally, he's the only one with no deals pending before Santarosa." He studied her. "You've been sitting here nearly two hours. Want to take a break while I look into Dreftbury?"

"Sure. Thanks."

At the espresso bar, she ordered two regular coffees while a windblown CNN reporter on location in Glasgow listed the attendees expected at the G8 on Monday. When Liz returned to the terminal with the coffee, Simon had not moved, but four sheets of paper lay on the table beside him, facedown.

"Thanks." He took his coffee. "What do you remember about Dreftbury?"

She sat. "The resort is beautiful — rolling hills, trees, and links golf courses. The hotel's on a high knoll, built on the remains of a castle. There's a long drive leading up to it, very dramatic. You can see the hotel and parts of the golf courses from the road."

"That helps." He turned over four printouts. Across the top of the first page was the announcement:

THE DREFTBURY HOTEL,
GOLF LINKS, AND SPA
A LUXURY RESORT
RENOWNED FOR ITS
    OPEN CHAMPIONSHIP TOURNAMENTS

He arranged the four pages to form a rectangle. "Here's a map of the grounds. It's big — nearly eight hundred acres." The central hotel had two arms reaching back and jutting around to form something of an upside-down pi — π, plus there were several outbuildings, as well as roads, trails, and areas for other sports.

With a finger, she traced an arm of land that jutted into the sea. "One of the links extends over this peninsula. The cliffs are high and sheer, and in some places there's almost no beach. I remember Mom and I tried to go wading, but there was no way."

Woods encircled the perimeter of the vast property and made occasional sorties onto the grounds. Dreftbury was bookended by the sea and the highway, which ran from Ballantrae and Loch Ryan in the south to Troon and Symington in the north.

"I couldn't find any information about who's staying in which room." He pointed. "But here's the main entrance from the road, and here's the service entrance. As I said, security will be heavy — local constabulary and probably Glasgow police and Scotland Yard, too, and of course a private company. Dreftbury could be a target of choice for terrorists this weekend, which means MI5 will be there as well. We can count on the grounds being completely patrolled. Entering won't be easy, even for us."

With a chill, she nodded. "I know. It's brains and cunning all the way."

"Let's get out of here. We've got to create the movie of our lives."

Forty-Seven

Somewhere in Northern Europe

Sarah awoke with a start, although the noise of surf rhythmically pounding rocks had softened, which meant it was probably low tide. Morning light slanted down through the barred windows, coloring the air dusky rose as it illuminated the walls, floor, and ceiling, all of which were built of red sandstone blocks that looked centuries old. Restless, worried, she eased away from Asher, who seemed to have slept soundly once he was warm. She walked around their prison, looking for a way to escape, but the sandstone blocks appeared solid.

She was examining the door, which was heavy, iron bound wood, when she heard the metallic screech of a bolt being pulled. She stepped back quickly, and the door opened. Standing there was one of the men from last night. He held an AK-47 rifle in one hand and thrust a paper sack forward with the other. Beyond him was a narrow stone corridor with a low ceiling, typical of medieval castles.

"Sandwiches." He gave the room only a perfunctory scan.

She kept her gaze casual as she studied him. His brows were thick, and his face lopsided. His expression radiated boredom. He held the rifle loosely. A cell dangled in a leather case from his belt.

"Thanks," she tried. "Is it a nice morning?"

He stared at her as if she were out of her mind and stepped back.

"Hey," she objected, "is this all? We're hungry."

"Eat or not." He swung the door closed, and the bolt slid home.

"Food?" Asher inquired from the cot. He sat up.

His voice was stronger than last night. Even from across the cell, his eyes looked clear. His curly black hair was crazed, but his coloring was normal. He sat with his feet firmly on the floor, his back erect. He looked fine, except for tightness around his jaw and eyes. Dappled sunlight from the high windows played across his hawklike face.

She sat on the cot beside him, and they ate cold egg and bacon sandwiches and shared a bottle of water. Ever since the guard had arrived with food, she had been mulling a plan. "I might see a way out of here, but do you feel well enough to help? It'd involve a fight."

Asher's eyes hardened into black agates. "Talk to me."

"We need a big, sharp rock. Something that looks menacing. When the guard comes back, you stand with the rock raised, as if you're going to attack. Since they seem to want to keep us alive — for a while at least — his first response should be to knock you down, probably with his rifle. So you'll be far enough away that he'll have to run at you. That's where I come in. I'll be flat against the wall, beside the door. When he blasts through, I'll kick the rifle out of his hands. You grab it while he goes for me."

Asher's face fell. "Holy heaven, Sarah. What makes you think a plan that simple has a chance?"

"The guard does. He's bored out of his skull. He's going through the motions because he thinks we're no threat."

Asher considered the idea. "Among the top risks are that his orders have changed, or that you can't actually hit the rifle hard enough to make him let go. Are you sure you're still good enough at karate to pull this off? I mean, it's been a long time."

She said coolly, "I do more than research and write while you're gallivanting around the world."

He decided saying no more was wise, since his absences were a sore point with her. He felt a twinge of guilt, because he should have known about the karate. He looked across at her. Her face was streaked with dirt, and she had that pissed expression that meant no quarter given. He had always liked that about her.

He was just about to mention it, when she said, "Plus, there's the issue of whether you're strong enough. Because even if my plan works, we still have to get out of whatever this place is, and that may mean running."

Asher nodded. "I can ignore the pain."

"Unless it gets so bad you pass out."

"Not going to happen," he assured her.

But both knew it could. Still, they had no other options. They finished eating and went to work, checking the walls for a loose rock large enough to make the guard react.

By afternoon, sunlight warmed their stone cell, and the briny scent of the sea filled the air. Sarah had found two cracked blocks of stone, but neither she nor Asher had been able to pry them from the wall. There was nothing in the room to help them, and the guard might return any moment.

"I've been thinking carefully about this," Asher announced. "I believe we're not in Elsinore. Personally, I believe we're in Scotland, on the coast."

"Good heavens, why?" She sat back on her heels and stared. He often did this to her — surprised her with deductions, without bothering to explain first.

"Couple of reasons. First, people are playing golf out there. I've heard some snatches of conversation. Golf is Scotland's national sport. Second, we weren't in the air long enough to go anywhere far. And third" — he grimaced, trying to explain — "this place *feels* like Scotland. Rain in the air. A scent of heather. The pounding sea. High cliffs. A streak of coldness even though it's July. And then there's this old castle — Scotland's full of them. Of course, I could be wrong."

But she could tell he did not think he was. The

best agents had what was unscientifically called gut. Using a combination of experience, genes, and boldness, they sensed or intuited answers or actions that often turned out to be uncannily correct.

"You're probably right," she decided. "But I don't see how that helps us."

"Yeah. I was afraid of that." He was just about to predict a rainstorm, when there was another voice outdoors, but this was near enough to be almost clear.

She lifted her head. "You hear him?"

"It sounds like the guy who drove us from the plane last night."

"Malko. Can you make out what he's saying?"

"No. I —"

She ran to the cot they had not used. It had a welded metal frame, with stained canvas stretched across. She propped it against the wall at about a thirty-degree angle.

"Come here and brace it, will you?"

"Sure." He was there in an instant.

As he leaned into the cot, holding it in place, she hurried to the other wall, ran back, and scrambled up to the window, where she grabbed the bars and tucked her feet between the canvas and the frame.

"What's he saying?" Asher asked.

"Shhh."

Now she knew what Malko looked like — sturdy and muscular, dressed in an expensive business suit. He had one of those long, ordinary faces that was forgettable. The kind of man easily lost in a crowd, an advantage for a janitor. He wore sunglasses and was talking into a cell as he walked alone down below, along the cliff. He gazed around as if the manicured grounds hid hordes of adversaries. He showed no signs of nervousness, just the high alertness of the professional. Beyond him spread the sea, gray and churning from last night's storm.

". . . in Alloway," Malko was saying. "Of course, everything will be ready there. You don't have to worry, sir. There's plenty of time. I'll get the message to his assistant. You can count on me." There was a pause, then his voice grew soft, and she strained to hear. "Thank you, sir. Yes, thank you."

As he severed the connection and dropped the phone into his pocket, Malko turned to face out to sea, his shoulders square. She had an odd sense about him, as if he were an eager killer dog whose master had just stroked him well.

Abruptly, he turned and strode off around the building, purpose in every step. When he was out of sight, she slid down the cot and told Asher what she had learned.

"Isn't Alloway in Scotland?" she finished. "That's where Robert Burns was born. You must be right about where we are."

He nodded. "When you were looking at the sea, did you see any islands?"

"As a matter of fact, I did. It must be an island, but it looks like a big fat rock. Or a big round loaf of bread."

"Ah! That's got to be Ailsa Craig. Now we're getting somewhere. We're on the Firth of Clyde, in southwest Scotland. I was here a few years ago, passing through to Glasgow. So let's get the hell out of here. If this is a golf resort, then there have to be cars. I'm ready to escape, aren't you?"

Dreftbury, Scotland

The A77 highway skirted the Firth of Clyde and curved up among undulating green hills where brown-and-white Ayrshire cattle grazed in the lacy shade of great-limbed pines. Simon was driving a new Land Rover, while Liz watched for exit signs for Dreftbury. He checked his rearview mirror often.

Every time she looked at him, she had a strange sense. At some point during the last forty-eight hours, he had ceased being an artifact from her childhood. Now he sat next to her in disguise — dirty blond hair, sunglasses, a cheap sports jacket, and a polyester tie. With his broad face and oversized nose, he could be an undertaker — or a government agent. She doubted anyone, even his closest friends — if he still had any — would recognize him.

"You're looking at me," he said.

"You're not blushing."

"Should I be?"

"I was simply admiring the new you."

"Oh." He flashed her a grin.

Using one of his aliases, he had rented the Land Rover outside Dumfries, where they abandoned the Jeep. In town, they bought two prepaid cells and clothes and hair coloring and found an inn, where they paid for the night but stayed just long enough to clean up, bleach their hair, and change. She still had euros left over from Sarah's wallet, which she split with him. With the instant camera from his gym bag, they took each other's photos, and he doctored two MI6 credentials he carried. She became Veronica Young, and he, Douglas Kennedy.

Finally, they returned to the A75, following it west to Stranraer on the huge inlet of Loch Ryan, where they turned north onto the A77.

"I'm excessively impressed by your disguise, too," he told her. "Nothing like being seen with a gray-haired sex pistol."

"Excuse me?"

"What did you expect? You've got the hair of a seventy-year-old but the face of a college girl. And that black pantsuit is too proper to be believed. Just the right combination for certain kinds of sexual fantasies."

"You're messing with me."

"Only a little."

"You're ignoring all of the wrinkles I applied so carefully."

"It's easy to."

Traffic grew thicker and slowed as he drove around a long bend. She scanned the area. Ahead to their left, on a hill above the sea appeared a stately white building with pillars and arches and a red-tiled roof.

"There it is. That's it — the Dreftbury hotel." Liz nodded, wondering what they would find there.

The resort's famous links spread on either side, a perfect carpet of vivid green, spotted with pot bunkers and bordered by a high, ragged rough of blowing coastal grasses. A few golfers swung at balls while the sun glinted out from gathering storm clouds. Black shadows snaked across the landscape.

As she studied it, memories came back to her — the grand salon, the bar with the congenial stone patio overlooking the firth and the valley, elevators, long hallways with crooks and side halls, and the way servants had hovered.

Simon hit the brakes. The traffic ahead slowed, the average speed dropping to less than thirty miles an hour.

"What happened?" Liz looked around as the road straightened.

"There's the answer." He fought memories of Viera and that last violent night in Bratislava. "The antiglobalists are here in force."

They now had a sweeping view not only of the magnificent hotel but all the way down to the base of the hill, where a two-lane country road was also snarled with traffic. Dreftbury's high stone wall fronted the road. Slowed by security checks, limousines with smoked windows queued up at the main entrance, while trucks and delivery vans waited in single file at the service gate.

But across the road from this orderliness were shouting ranks of demonstrators, thousands of them, lined up five and eight deep behind saw horses and cordons monitored by uniformed police. Dressed in casual clothes and wearing backpacks, the massed protesters pumped signs up and down. Above them, on the crest of a hill, was their command station, where a cadre of men and women orchestrated the protest's progress, binoculars to eyes, walkie-talkies to ears.

"Turn on the radio," Simon said tersely. "I see reporters and cameras."

As she searched for a news station, he told her about the antiglobalists' frustration that the mainstream media seldom took their charges and complaints seriously. That they felt marginalized, voiceless, unheard.

"I'm not surprised they're here," he explained. "I'd warned my boss something was brewing. They've been looking for a way to open the public's eyes, and Nautilus is a natural target. Whether they can force it nationally . . . even internationally —"

Liz interrupted, "There's the exit sign to Dreftbury."

She found a station and turned up the volume. As Simon sped off the highway and around onto a country road, a newswoman reported, her voice raised, ". . . at the very exclusive Dreftbury resort."

On the radio, car engines revved and idled, people shouted orders, while others chanted slogans. The din was unrelenting.

"We're standing across from an estimated three thousand demonstrators," she continued. "Some are sending aloft a huge flamingo pink balloon in the shape of a pig. They seem to have a sense of humor — it's labeled CAPITALIST PIG EQUALS HOT AIR. More agitators arrive by the hour. They dart under the barricades and rush to Dreftbury's two entrances but are arrested before they can force their way inside. Then the police pack them into lorries and send them off to jail. Inspector Hepburn, of the local constabulary, declares there have been no injuries, but he urges the public to stay away. Standing here, we can only agree. We've never experienced such congestion and chaos in so small an area. At the service entrance, Glasgow's string orchestra was ordered off its bus and told to remove all their instruments for inspection. They were most unhappy, but no one is exempt from being searched. Now we're walking toward the limousines, where we'll speak with some of the guests. They're the planet's elite, according to the protesters, and they're here to conspire about how to run the world over the next year."

Her voice faded and suddenly rose. "Stand aside, young man. We are Edinburgh radio. You are *not* the police. How dare you! You really *can't* stop us. Mister! Mister!" They could hear someone tapping on glass. *"Roll down your window so we can talk!"*

Liz lowered the volume as Simon braked. They were approaching the tangle of traffic that crawled in front of the Dreftbury resort.

"At least we've reached the stone wall," she said.

"Look inside that stand of trees."

As the Land Rover rolled forward, bumper-to-bumper with the car ahead, she studied the dense timber edging Dreftbury's grounds. A leashed German shepherd stepped out, head high, quickly followed by his handler, who was dressed in combat black and carried an automatic rifle. The armed man and trained dog were policing the perimeter. Soon she saw more men, more dogs.

Her rib cage tightened. "Daunting," she said. "Private security?"

He nodded. "Thought you'd like to know."

Asher seldom worried. It was not his nature. For him, worry felt more like a sense of heaviness, of uncertainty. But from the moment Sarah was kidnapped, his guts had been in twisted knots. That was how he knew he was worried. Their reunion in Paris had relieved him at first, because she was alive. After that, it was all downhill again. She was still in danger, and he was still out of commission.

Her plan could work, but the rock they needed had not materialized, although they had carefully inspected three walls and were now on the fourth. They searched for flaws and tugged at any irregular protrusion.

Then with a suddenness that stunned him, a chunk of ragged red stone about six inches wide and a foot long popped out a few inches.

With a simple tug, Asher held it in his hands.

She watched, her eyes as wide as pizzas. "You found a piece. It's perfect!"

He did not answer. He was staring into the hole.

The metallic rasp of the door's bolt being thrown made them wheel and stare.

"Take that rock over there, quick," she said. "Get ready to pretend you're going to attack him!"

"No! *Wait*. Emergency change of plans. Go to

the door and make nice. Do *not* kick or clobber him." He jammed the rock back into the wall. Brushing sand from his hands, he hurried to the cot and collapsed. The door swung open.

She was there, waiting. "Thanks," she told the same armed man as before.

Lack of interest had deepened on his irregular features. He still carried the rifle and wore the cell phone attached to his belt. He grunted, handed over two more bottles of water and another paper sack, and left. Again the door closed solidly and the bolt slammed home.

Asher smiled. "Nice." It pleased him that she occasionally did what he asked.

She whirled. "Whatever you found in that wall better be a miracle."

Forty-Eight

As soon as Sir Anthony Brookshire checked in, he went straight to his suite, disgusted by the mobs of crazed agitators who were obviously intent on ruining what should be a quiet working weekend of ideas and consensus. Dressed in his favorite corduroy jacket with the leather elbow patches, he stood at his window, hands clasped behind, gazing down into the valley, where the idiots milled and screamed.

He felt an odd numbness, as if time had sped past too quickly. Something had gone wrong somewhere. Was he no longer in step with the future?

"I've spent my life trying to understand how the world works," he ruminated. "What makes civilization. What overarching meaning is behind our triumphs and failures, our ability to find happiness and to endure sadness. Since we're all part of the same world, the same species, it seemed sensible that we act like it. To be against globalization is to want to turn back the clock. To believe the earth is flat. To believe in fairies and witches, and to pray to pagan gods." He sighed.

When there was no response, he turned. He

did not like where his path was heading, but he could see no way off. Standards must be upheld, and one must stay the course. In the end, endurance was perhaps the greatest virtue.

"What do these demonstrators want?" he demanded.

César Duchesne had been standing just inside the door. Dressed in a tan knit shirt and tweed jacket and brown slacks, he wore a yellow assistant's badge clipped to his front pocket, although he continued to function as Coil security.

"To re-create the IMF and World Bank," Duchesne said. "To end all Third World debt. To put a one percent tax on speculative financial transactions worldwide in order to raise a trillion-dollar fund for underdeveloped countries to direct their own growth. To bring to a Nuremberg-style trial those they hold responsible for the new global economic disorder and vast shift of wealth from the poor and middle class to the already rich."

"Is that all?" Brookshire said bitterly, tired of those with neither the wisdom nor experience to see the complexities involved. They worried about their own survival, not the world's. Petty and unproductive. His voice rose. "They're ignorant, and they hold on to their ignorance as if it were a talisman or some religious relic. They're bloody fanatics. If they want change, they need a realistic understanding of the modern world!" He paused, sighed. "Is there any particular reason they're harassing us right now?"

"To expose Nautilus. Force you and your guests onto the international stage. To lift the curtain, if you like. They want substantive inquiry."

"Do they, now? They're not going to get it by acting like spoiled children. Shouting, jumping up and down. Look at them. They're having fits like two-year-olds." He turned back from the window and sat. Gloomily, he studied his security chief. He forced himself to calm down to return to business. "Is Henry Percy dead?"

Duchesne inclined his head respectfully. "As ordered."

"And Sansborough and Childs?"

"They escaped ahead of my people."

"What! Duchesne, I'll — !"

Duchesne interrupted quickly. "There's more. They've deduced not only that the blackmailer was behind the death of Franco Peri a few months ago but that the execution was a ploy to speed Carlo Santarosa into taking charge of the Competition Commission. I think they're right. They believe the blackmailer needs Santarosa's approval for some action. Henry Percy told them he thought it likely Santarosa would be at Dreftbury."

Sir Anthony placed his elbows on the arms of his chair, steepled his fingers, rested his chin on top, and studied his security chief, who remained standing, his posture seemingly relaxed. Still, Sir Anthony thought not. For the first time, he saw hints of worry, of anger. *Good.* He needed Duchesne to be fully motivated, to be more wary, more clever than ever, because Duchesne had indeed brought something useful.

Sir Anthony said, "You think they'll come here

to use Santarosa to find the blackmailer. You're probably right. Once Sansborough went on the run, who could've predicted she'd get as far as she has? Of course she'll come here. I assume you've set a trap to catch both Sansborough and Childs, as well as the blackmailer."

Duchesne described his precautions and his ambush.

Sir Anthony made a few modifications.

As soon as he was alone, Sir Anthony pushed himself out of his chair. He had been a hunter his entire life, and he knew and enjoyed firearms. He had owned his first rifle at eight, his first shotgun at fifteen, and his first handgun at sixteen. From a bureau drawer he removed his favorite Browning.

Before he left London, he had cleaned and loaded it. He did not expect to need it, but a wise man took precautions. As he hefted the weapon, he caught sight of himself in the mirror, his thick silver hair brushed back, his large head, his cheeks baby pink and freshly shaved, his chin jutting forward, his clothes natty in the way of old money. His beefy, athletic build. And the stern look of sagacity he had spent a lifetime cultivating. Yes, he was Old World, but woven through it was both pragmatism and idealism. He remembered what Plato had told the Athenian democracy: The penalty for not participating in political affairs was to be ruled by one's inferiors.

Under the roiling gray sky, Simon grabbed his gym bag, and Liz took her new shoulder bag. They left the Land Rover parked at the side of the road and advanced through the no-man's-land between the agitators, who waved their signs and shouted, and the security forces, who clasped their weapons and glared. The air stank of ozone and sweat. It was well past five o'clock, and the long caravans waiting to enter Dreftbury had shortened. Still, it was much faster to walk in.

As they passed the service entrance, policemen used dogs to sniff vehicles while security frisked drivers and checked loads. One poured out a carton of milk; another sliced open a package of frozen peas. They were probably looking for small weapons or Semtex. At the same time, four elderly protesters scrambled under the barricades and rushed across the road toward the gate, white hair and wrinkles shining in the afternoon sun. Security clasped their weapons and raced to intercept.

"This reminds me of Bratislava the night Viera set herself on fire," he said uneasily. "After that, people rioted." Through his sunglasses, he scanned the crowds, assessing the tension. There were a few faces he recognized — the usual teachers and laborers, housewives and students, speaking German, Polish, Slovak, Czech, English.

"I'm not surprised." Her gaze moved with his, her senses on high alert. "Rioters can never win, you know."

"No way they'd believe that. Look at those old people. They're not giving up."

Police handcuffed the elderly quartet and shoved them toward a paddy wagon. They smiled grimly, almost as if they were off to a party.

She said, "They aren't rioting. Protesters start

by wanting to make things better, even if their idea of 'better' isn't. They want a positive revolution. But rioting's not revolutionary. It's reactionary, and it always ends in defeat. The only payoff is an immediate emotional catharsis. That's followed by a sense of futility, because the coin of whatever power they felt in the beginning is spent. The next step is helpless rage."

"Is that the wisdom of Professor Sansborough?"

"Actually, it's from Martin Luther King Jr. Of course, I'm paraphrasing. But look at the faces of the agitators and then at the cops. Look at their body language. They're mirror images of one another, seething with moral outrage."

"So if it's really senseless, why do people riot?" Simon scanned security and the demonstrators. That was when he spotted Johann Jozef, Viera's brother. Burly, not quite six feet tall, he held aloft a placard in English:

MAKE THE GLOBAL ECONOMY WORK
FOR THE PEOPLE WHO DO THE WORK!

Johann's face was twisted with anger. Sorrow showed in new crevices around his mouth. On his chest, he wore a plastic badge that displayed a photo of Viera, smiling. Simon's breath caught in his throat.

"A lot of it is herd mentality," she said. "The power of the mob. But it's also because they feel as if they have to do *something*. It's like when some mentally ill people bang their heads against a wall or bite themselves. They desperately need to feel something, anything. The catharsis of feeling something. Naturally, people who are trying to right a wrong or improve a situation grow frustrated. And they may never get what they ask, and maybe they shouldn't. The danger comes in a situation like this, when there are so many of them. The frustration of not being heard grows, the tension multiplies, something happens, and they riot. They get their catharsis, even though it's not the way they want it. After that, there's a lull. Then the tension can build again."

"That's depressing as hell."

She peered up at him and adjusted her sunglasses. "What's happened? You've seen someone, haven't you?"

"Viera's brother is here." He described Johann and turned away. To look at anyone long enough invited them to look back. He doubted Johann would recognize him in his disguise, but he could take no chance.

"He's furious," she decided.

"Viera martyred herself, and already she's off the front pages. Maybe he's beginning to comprehend that you've got to stay alive to make a difference."

As Liz and Simon approached Dreftbury's swank entrance gates, a security man inspected luggage in the trunk of a limo while another stood at the driver's open window, matching passports to a list of invitees. A Doberman pulled his handler around the car, sniffing tires and the undercarriage.

Across the road, the chants and shouts of the

protesters grew louder, more urgent, and the breakouts through police lines became bolder and more frequent. Troubled, Simon studied the chaos. As if to reflect the violent mood, the threat of rain filled the air, rising above the stink of diesel fumes, the clouds burgeoning into huge thunderheads. He remembered a saying: In Scotland, it's either raining, or it's just rained, or it's about to.

"There's our man." Liz kept her expression neutral. "You have my cell number memorized?"

"I do. You remember mine?"

She nodded, visualizing her Glock, packed at the top of her shoulder bag within easy reach. Simon wore his Beretta in a holster under his jacket, while the Uzi was zipped into the gym bag. The prepaid cells were their way to communicate.

Simon gave a single nod. As they expected, an MI5 man was inside the gate and off to the side, inconspicuous, except to those who knew the signs — the casual posture as he leaned against the gate house, almost out of sight; the bored look as the sunglasses observed every face and vehicle; the slightly lopsided cut of the jacket, tailored to hide the pistol under his arm; and — above all — the isolation. Security was giving him a wide berth. A mistake. The agent should have told them to act normally, chat him up as if he were one of their own or a civilian.

Liz's muscles tensed as a stout guard, Bull Pup rifle cradled in the crook of his arm, turned. He had just cleared one of the limos. As it glided away toward the hotel, she exchanged a quick look with Simon, acknowledging the movie had begun.

They readied their credentials.

"May I help you?" There was a weary politeness in the guard's voice; it had been a long day. But his gaze was sharp as it swept first Simon, then Liz.

"Indeed you may," Liz said coolly, the English accent quickly returning.

They showed their MI6 credentials low and close, where no one else could see.

"I need to speak with the chap over there," Simon said, and nodded.

There was hesitation as the guard weighed the situation.

Liz did not like that. "Sorry we can't tell you more," she said conspiratorially. "You understand."

To make sure he got the point, she opened her purse, showing her Glock, as she put away the ID.

At the same time, Simon pulled back his jacket to return his credentials to an inside pocket, displaying his holstered Beretta.

That did it. The guard looked from one to the other. He blinked, waved them through, and studiously ignored them, feeling part of something big.

Liz let out a long stream of air.

Simon smiled pleasantly as they approached the MI5 man. He put on his best Oxbridge accent: "Need a chat with your chief, old man."

MI5 kept his gaze on the gate. "The both of you?"

"You MI5 nosers need a dose of bloody reality," Liz snapped indignantly.

MI5 stiffened just enough for her to know she had made a hairline crack in his enameled superiority. When necessary, even MI5 had to lower itself to work not only with MI6 but with women.

"Names?" he said. "Invitation numbers?"

"Kennedy, MI6," Simon said. "This is Young, MI6. Don't be tiresome."

A long-suffering sigh. "Let's see, then."

They displayed the IDs. After a glance, MI5 returned his attention to the gate and spoke inaudibly into his breast pocket. There was a tiny speaker in his ear.

"You'll be met at the hotel," MI5 said, dismissing them.

Hiding her relief, Liz nodded as if thanking a doorman. They climbed the drive, passing golf links and immaculate topiary bushes. Armed guards strolled the paths.

"I thought that went well." She brushed sweat from her forehead.

"One more to go."

At the top, a woman with a clenched jaw was waiting, hands on hips. She wore the blue jacket and Dreftbury crest of a golf pro, but in her ear was another tiny speaker.

"What the bloody hell are you doing here?" she demanded, glaring.

"Antiglobalization beat," Simon said kindly. "Wire-snooping and electronics."

Liz explained, "HQ sent a few more of us than needed to watch the chaps down on the road.

Chief thought we should offer assistance."

"Well, well." MI5 was pleased to take advantage of MI6's disorganization. "My lucky day. You nanny our phone and electronics setup, and I can move mine onto regular security. MI6 to the rescue, eh?"

She described the monitoring closet and handed them green badges, indicating security. Every chief of detail always needed extra agents, and no one liked to be stuck in a tiny room doing surveillance all day. They had counted on that. While Liz went to look for Santarosa, Simon would report to the wiretap center to find out Santarosa's room number as well as the room numbers of every member of the Coil.

Forty-Nine

"A tunnel?" Sarah peered into the dark space in the prison wall where Asher had pulled out the chunk of red sandstone.

"Yup. Sure looks like it," Asher said.

There was a passage about three feet high, with a trace of dusky light far ahead. She removed the rest of the broken block and tugged out three whole ones. To annoy the guards, she stacked the heavy blocks in front of the door.

"I'll go first," she told him. "We don't know what's ahead."

"You've got claustrophobia."

"That makes it all the more interesting. You're feeling better, but there's no shame in saying no. That first piece of rock you pulled out has a sharp point that'll get their attention. We can go back to my original idea."

"I adore you, Sarah. You're the love of my life. But I don't believe in heaven, so we've got to get out of this mess alive. This is a better shot."

She nodded, took a deep breath, and stuck her head and shoulders into the opening. The stink of dirt and mold assaulted her, and her chest tightened. *You can do this.* She crept inside, focusing on the dim light ahead, and put one hand, then the other, in front of her. As she forced herself to leave the cell behind, the rough walls of the tunnel seemed to squeeze around her. *Breathe. Crawl. Breathe. Crawl.*

Within two minutes, she heard Asher follow. "Are you okay?" she asked.

"Never better." But his voice was strained.

At last, the illumination increased, the tunnel curved, and she saw a spattering of sun rays. There was a whiff of fresh ocean air. She inhaled, grateful.

Asher smelled it, too. "Maybe there *is* a heaven."

Excited, she crawled faster. The tunnel narrowed, but the light beckoned. As she neared the end, she saw a small boulder blocked the opening, but sunshine trickled in around it, plant roots acting like sieves. She listened for voices or other sounds that would tell her someone was nearby. Birds sang. Insects buzzed.

Asher was breathing right behind her. "I'm here."

"Pain bad?"

"It's tolerable."

"Uh-huh. Okay, you stay where you are."

She broke off small roots and scooped away dirt. When she had cleared an opening about six inches wide next to the boulder, she peered out. They were on a grassy slope dotted with bushes, just steep enough she did not want to risk losing control of the boulder and drawing attention to them. She hesitated, realizing that as soon as they left here, they would be on the run. Hunted. She had a hollow feeling, as if they had come full circle, back to the sort of irreconcilable danger that had brought them together in the first place.

"Is everything okay?" he asked.

"Wonderful."

She rotated on her butt and used her feet to push dirt until she made a hole about two feet wide and high. Immediately, she slithered out, gulping fresh air, and rose into a crouch. Dark clouds gusted across the sky, filtering ominous light down onto the land.

She was on a bank to the side and below their two barred windows. As it turned out, their cell was partially underground, probably once part of a medieval cellar. The rest of the stone walls vanished into the slope. Atop was a modern building, no more than a century old. Very large, with white walls and a red-tile roof and another wing that also jutted toward the sea on the north side, closest to the cliffs. Where they were appeared to be a little-used area of the property.

Warily, she studied the structure directly above. There was a solid line of reflecting windows on the first floor — an indoor pool? On the three floors above were regular windows that stared out like vacant eyes. Fortunately, she was so close to the wall she would be difficult to see, if anyone was looking.

"Sarah?" His questioning whisper seemed to float toward her from far away.

"You can come out now." She moved aside and described the terrain.

He grunted and wriggled through. But he was wider than she, and his shoulder grazed the boulder. It rolled. Pulse pounding, she threw herself onto it, but it hurtled away, carrying her. She fell off, a sharp ache in her chest. Pulled by gravity, it sped down the decline, bouncing with increasing speed.

In seconds, Asher was hunched beside her. "Goddammit." He watched as it crashed through bushes. "Sorry. You all right?"

"Fine. Just pissed that I couldn't stop it." She pulled herself up onto her heels.

Tensed, they waited as the boulder noisily thumped and rolled. Birds stopped singing. The land fell silent. Finally, it slammed into a thicket of gorse and stopped. The sudden quiet filled her ears. They stared at each other and waited. Still, there was no sign anyone had heard or was yet aware of what they were doing.

She jumped up. "I heard car engines around to the left. I feel inspired to escape. Are you well enough to do some hot-wiring?" She offered her hand.

He took it and climbed to his feet. "Does a fox lick its paw?" He looked gravely into her eyes. "They haven't got us yet."

"And they won't." She hurried around the corner and onto a flagstone walk that skirted the south wing.

As she rounded another corner, she stopped, stunned, and quickly darted behind a large topiary bush shaped like an elephant. She peered out again. At a port cochere, uniformed hotel ambassadors offered white-gloved hands to passengers climbing out of backseats, while above the drive, men and women in expensive clothes, drinks in hand, peered over a balustrade. Sarah followed their gazes down to a road, where a protest was in full progress. Shouts and voices amplified by bullhorns drifted up the hill toward her.

When Asher caught up, he was holding a fist-sized rock and panting. He had that determined expression that could turn deadly in an instant. His black eyes widened as he took in the sight. "Where the hell —"

"Shh. Listen." She pointed above them, indicating two men who had just leaned over, apparently to see the demonstration better.

"Do they have any idea what they're screaming about?" asked one. "A clue? Even half a brain?" Impatient, irritated, he spoke with a sharp Chicago accent as he slung his suit jacket over his shoulder. He drank his martini.

His companion explained, "Alas, they are deluded. To them, we are the destroyers of nations." His accent was French. He wore a golf shirt and immaculate linen slacks and sipped from a highball glass.

The first man snorted. "Is that it? Fools. Fifty years ago, there were only seventy countries. Now there are more than two hundred. Does that sound like we're destroying nations?"

"You know what is said about leaders. When one is out in front of the herd, the view is better. The problem is, one's back is rather exposed."

The two men laughed.

"It is good to see you, Walter," the second said. "Must we reserve these reunions only for Nautilus?"

As the pair moved back out of range, Asher stared at Sarah.

"Nautilus?" Asher said. "Do you know about Nautilus?"

"No. Should I?"

"Oh, man. Oh, man. This is something. Really something. Serious. How did we end up here? Somebody in Nautilus must have the files!"

"What in heaven's name is Nautilus?" Sarah asked.

But Asher had already moved on. "Okay, this does make sense. We would've been brought here if the guy with the files is a player. Nautilus always meets someplace that's owned or controlled by a member or by a government friendly to Nautilus, so they can dictate security." His head turned, studying, remembering. "According to the hotel uniforms, we're at Dreftbury. That's a hotshot resort, not a government place. And that means someone in Nautilus owns it, or one of his or her companies does."

"I give up about Nautilus. You can explain it later. But if the files are involved, and we're here, then it seems to me something major is about to happen."

"It won't be here," he reminded her. "In Alloway. Remember, Malko said Alloway. That's inland, near Ayr. We need to get to Alloway."

"You're probably right, but how? The security here is in overkill. There's no way we can steal a car. Plus, we've got no ID, and we look more like terrorists than we do like trustworthy people. No one's going to believe us."

Dirt streaked her crumpled trousers and shirt

and tailored jacket. He badly needed a shave. His beard grew in so fast that his jaw was the color of tar.

As she dusted herself off, he contemplated his grimy sweatpants.

"If we had a cell, you could call Langley," she told him. "I'm going inside to steal one. Don't let anyone see you. The way you look, they'll arrest you in a heartbeat."

"Yeah," he said morosely. "You're right." Then with a sudden movement, he pulled her close and kissed her. "Be careful. I don't want to lose you again."

Enormous and elegant, the hotel lobby gave off a hushed air of privilege. As Simon vanished into the north corridor, carrying his gym bag, Liz repressed a profound sense of peril. She wiped all expression from her face, took off her sunglasses, put on Sarah's glasses, and stiffened her spine as she stepped back against a wall, hoping that the blackmailer was not already in some back room with Santarosa. And that she and Simon would not be found out either by the killers who worked for the Coil or those employed by the blackmailer.

But when people sauntered past and caught sight of her security badge, they looked through her or away from her. Good. With luck, she was now officially invisible, to attendees at least.

She surveyed the lobby. The Venetian chandeliers and French parquet floor gleamed. Registration clerks wore starched uniforms in the colors of Scotland's saltire flag, the oldest in Europe —

white on azure blue. Across the expanse, guests sporting midnight blue badges lounged on settees around generous coffee tables, where drinks in handblown glasses and goblets caught the sunlight that streamed in through tall French doors, fading and brightening as dark clouds rolled past. At opposite ends of the lobby were the two corridors that extended into the north and south wings, where she remembered elevators, meeting rooms, guest rooms, banquet rooms, the spa, and assorted other opportunities for edification and relaxation — and ambush.

Oriented, she gazed at the faces around her, instantly recognizing most. There were tycoons and statesmen, presidents and generals, just as Simon had said. But no Carlo Santarosa. Excitement swept through her as she spotted Richmond Hornish, the powerful financier, and Gregory Gilmartin, the construction czar, in intimate conversation at a distant window. She waited another minute. When neither looked up, she moved to the Balmoral Café and surveyed the sprinkling of people drinking coffee and eating snacks.

"Think of this as a retreat," Leslie Cheward, the Canadian who ran the largest shipbuilding firm in the world, was explaining to the new president of Sweden. "Nautilus provides a rare chance to exchange information and ideas without having to censor ourselves. If that seems exclusive, so be it. Would you rather we met on either side of a battlefield with automatic weapons in our hands and war on our minds?"

When she did not see Santarosa, she hurried to a hand-lettered sign that related the weekend's events. There was an opening banquet at eight o'clock tonight, with an after-dinner talk by software king Bob Lord about investing in electronics. On Saturday and Sunday, seminars began at 7:30 a.m. and did not finish until 10:30 p.m., with one-hour breaks for breakfast, lunch, and dinner. Topics were serious — Turkey's role in the Middle East, Asia's poor economy, the effects of NATO expansion, state-sponsored terrorism versus freewheeling terrorism, that sort of thing. Whatever else they were, Nautilus attendees appeared to be here to work.

Her face neutral, she crossed the lobby to the wood-paneled Culzean Bar. Staff with orange badges hurried past on errands. Inside, drinkers complained about the demonstration. Again, no Santarosa. He was not on the veranda either or inside the gift shop. Kilts hung in the window and from display racks.

She opened the door to leave, again worrying they had missed the blackmailer's dirty work. And stepped back. For a moment, she had a sense of utter dread: Malko was skirting the lobby, walking with quiet purpose, almost unnoticeable. Mid-thirties, dressed in a gray suit, he wore a green security badge like hers.

But Malko could lead her straight to the blackmailer. She slid her hand into her bag and clutched her Glock. When he turned into the south corridor, she followed.

On the wall behind the registration desk hung two oval mirrors in ornate gold frames. Each offered one-way viewing. In the office on the other side, César Duchesne received reports and monitored a tracking device as he secretly observed the lobby. Liz Sansborough's disguise was good. With her gray hair brushed severely back, she looked like a guard from some high-security prison. He admired her chameleon qualities. It had taken him nearly five minutes to make her. He checked the Walther in his holster, gave a grim smile, and slipped out the door.

Fifty

After carefully checking the corridor, Simon entered a utility closet, where an MI5 agent sat hunched over a computer, earphones on, listening in on the hotel's phone lines and extensions. MI5 looked up instantly, hand on the weapon on his hip, but Simon already had his credentials out. One swift look, and MI5 was back at work.

A cable from his computer hooked into a multicolored bundle of cables that ran through a metal box on the wall. The oversize green screen displayed a grid of two hundred white squares. Inside each was a room or office number and the surname of the occupant. As the counterespionage agent listened to the conversations, the hot-button software silently searched all lines for words like *gun, weapon,* and *kill* in more than a hundred languages. If the software — called BlackWash — found any, the miniature printer would spew out pertinent information — phone numbers, locations, a transcript — while the computer stored everything, including the audio, on its hard drive.

Three squares flared fiery red. MI5 immediately touched one, listened, and it turned yellow. He touched the second, again listened, and it, too, turned yellow. He touched the third, with the same result. He was scouting for threatening tones of voice or nonsense conversations that might indicate coded messages.

He looked up. "I've been expecting you."

"Ready for a break?"

MI5 might dislike MI6, but not this time. He stood. "You know how to handle the equipment?"

"Absolutely."

Without a backward glance, he hurried out, and Simon sat and ordered the software to print the room plan. On his way to relieve the MI5 technician, he had stopped at the reception desk and learned all members of the Coil had arrived, each late because of the turmoil. Santarosa had shown up less than a half hour ago. Simon put on the headphones and touched a new red light. ". . . at table seven tonight," a man's voice said in German. "Kroner will be there, too. Let's catch a drink. . . ."

Simon disconnected and studied the squares on the screen, quickly identifying the rooms of Commissioner Santarosa and the Coil — Brookshire, Hornish, Inglethorpe, Menchen, and Gilmartin. None was alight. Disappointed, he dialed Santarosa's room.

An annoyed voice said, "Santarosa."

"Oh, so sorry, old man," Simon said innocently. "Seems I have the wrong room."

The receiver slammed down in his ear. Carlo Santarosa was angry, edgy about something. An appointment with a blackmailer perhaps? Or since the blackmailer was unlikely to tip his hand until face-to-face, just an appointment with a man he did not want to meet because he intended to turn him down?

He dialed Brookshire's room. This time, he broke the connection the moment the receiver was lifted. He dialed Hornish next.

Tense, jumpy, Sarah moved quietly along the south hall, dodging people as they appeared from meeting rooms and offices and what looked like a distant lobby. She recognized three — NATO's supreme allied commander, the new female head of Germany's power house Bundesbank, and the extraordinarily wealthy prime minister of Italy, who was also the current EU president. All were accompanied by assistants and were deep in conversation. She stared after them, wondering again what Nautilus was.

But that would have to wait. As soon as she found a bathroom, she washed up and used the cloth towels to damp-mop her clothes. Then she was off again, listening at doors, opening them when there was no sound, and gliding inside to check desks, tables, and chairs, looking for a cell, fighting discouragement. Surely someone had left one behind somewhere.

In a windowless staff room, she worked her way down the row of employee lockers. No cells, and one locker was locked. *What the hell.* She used a butter knife to jimmy it. On the shelf were paperbacks, candy, toiletries, condoms, and cigarettes, but no phone. There was a man's shirt and sports jacket, too. She felt the pockets. Empty. But when she moved the jacket, she saw a belt hanging from the same hook. She stared. Attached to the belt was a holster encasing a big Colt .45. Unbelievable. Wonderful! But not loaded.

She checked it — recently cleaned and oiled. She rummaged through the bottom of the locker, found a box of ammo, loaded the cannon, and raced back to check the rest of the lockers. When she came upon a padded cloth bag full of knitting yarn and needles, she dumped out half and lay the Colt inside.

And paused for a few seconds to marvel that something good had happened. But she still needed a cell.

At the door, she listened. Another door was closing. She opened hers a few inches. It was the guard with the AK-47, the one who had brought them sandwiches. Her heart leaped with hope: His cell still dangled from his belt. She took out the Colt, waited for him to pass, and prowled after. He was heading around toward the rear, where the corridor paralleled the wing and then angled back to the main hall.

She had been there already. As he disappeared around the corner, she broke into a quiet run, warily following.

At the same time, Liz headed into the south corridor, which turned out to be a discouraging thicket of meeting rooms and offices off side hallways. Predatory, almost invisible, Malko drifted past a stand of wooden telephone booths and crossed to a side hallway. As he vanished, Liz's heart seemed to stop. She did not want to lose him. She yanked out her Glock and ran. At the corner, she paused, weapon extended, and slid around.

He was gone again. But where? She strained to listen, heard footsteps ahead. A door closed somewhere. Pulse accelerating, she sprinted to the corner. Again she raised her weapon in both hands and rolled around into the next hall.

And froze. Fear shot through her, and her temples throbbed as she stared into the barrel of a huge Colt .45.

Then she saw who held it. Her heart soared. "Sarah!" she whispered.

Emotions ricocheted through Liz — relief and excitement and utter amazement. There are moments when time really should stand still. When if the world were fair or even halfway right, you should be able to extend for eternity that surprising sense of the miraculous, coupled with inordinate gratitude. Sarah was alive, and, somehow, she was here.

Liz drank in the sight of her. "My God, Sarah. I could've shot you!"

"Liz? Is that you?"

Sarah stared at the gray hair, the lined face. But the voice was right. So were the eyes and the shape of the face. The last three days swept over her, the maddening frustration and bottomless fear . . . the sight of Liz in the warehouse, the agony on her face . . . and, later, the worry Liz would be destroyed by the forces that had been manipulating Asher and her.

609

She found herself grinning, saying irrelevantly, "You're wearing my computer glasses!"

They smiled deeply into each other's eyes, acknowledging in only a few seconds one of those natural friendships that was impossible to articulate and the love and trust that bound them.

Then they remembered where they were. What they were doing. Both looked quickly up and down the corridor.

"Let's get out of sight so we can talk!" Sarah said quickly.

Liz was already listening at the door to the next room. She nodded and opened it slowly. As soon as she peered inside, her Glock came up.

Looking over Liz's shoulder, Sarah saw the bored guard with the thick brows and irregular face. He had found an empty conference room in which to relax and was pulling out a chair, *Hustler* magazine thrown onto the table next to his rifle.

He scowled. "What are —"

And noticed Sarah. He grabbed for his AK-47. A gunshot would bring security instantly. Liz dropped her shoulder bag, ran straight at him, and delivered a stunningly fast *morote-zuki* two-handed punch to the chest. He staggered back but hoisted the Kalashnikov, forcing Liz to stop.

Desperate, Sarah leaped onto the desk. As he swiveled to face this new threat, she shot a *mae-geri* snap kick to his chin. His head cracked back, and he toppled against a side table. In an instant, Liz was there. She supported him so he would collapse quietly to the carpet, unconscious.

"That was close," Sarah breathed.

Liz snapped up his weapon. "I'll say. You know him?"

Sarah jumped down. "He's the reason I had the Colt aimed when you and I ran into each other." She described the guard's role in the prison in which Asher and she had been held under the hotel.

"Asher's here, too? Thank God!"

Sarah unsnapped the guard's leather pouch and removed the cell. "He's hiding out front, waiting for me. This is what I wanted." She held it up. "Asher's going to phone Langley for help." She turned it over and swore. The keyboard was cracked.

"He must've crushed it when he landed against the table."

Two pieces fell into Sarah's hand. "Damn! Do you have one I can borrow?"

"Yes. Let's take care of this guy before he wakes up, and I'll give it to you."

"Good. And you can tell me what in God's name is going on. I don't know much more than it's about your father's files."

As Liz quickly filled her in about Santa Barbara, Simon Childs, Nautilus, the Coil, and the blackmailer, they stripped off the cords that held back the drapes on the two windows and tied the guard. While Sarah described her captivity with Asher, she and Liz used a scarf from Liz's shoulder bag to gag the man.

"Langley must have someone here undercover," Liz said, "considering the history with Nautilus and the high level of the attendees. Thank God, because Langley will listen to Asher, and we need help. You mentioned Malko brought you here. He's the one I was looking for when you and I met. I'd hoped he'd lead me to the blackmailer."

"Now I know why he wanted to keep us alive — in case he needed us as a weapon against you and Simon. I overheard a conversation he had with his boss. It may make sense to you." She repeated it.

"Alloway?" Liz said. "That's definitely what Malko said?"

"Yes. He was making preparations for something important in Alloway. If you're right about Santarosa, maybe the blackmailer plans to meet him there."

"But it doesn't make sense. Too far away. Too inconvenient. Why go to all that trouble when both men are here already?" Liz closed her eyes. Where had she seen that name? In her mind, she was back in the lobby, studying the schedule of seminars. They were held in rooms with the names of Scottish places, villages, inns. "The Alloway *Room*. That's it!" She pulled out her cell and dialed.

"Where the deuce have you been, Liz! I've been trying to call —"

"I turned off my cell because I was following Malko."

"You tracked him? Now that has possibilities! And?"

"I lost him, but I have better news. Sarah and Asher are not only alive, they're here. In fact, I'm with Sarah now. Asher's going to phone Langley, so

612

with luck, we'll have help in unmasking these bastards. She overheard Malko phoning his boss. It sounds as if Malko's made some kind of special preparation to meet in Alloway, but I doubt he meant the town. Unless you've got better intel, my guess is the blackmailer's setting up the meet with Santarosa in the Alloway Room."

"Damn impressive. Tell Sarah thanks. On my end, I can report Santarosa's still in his suite, or he was ten minutes ago. He's been here in the hotel not quite an hour, so I doubt he's had any meetings yet."

"Where are the Coil members?"

"Not in their rooms. Except Brookshire. Hold on just a minute. . . . Yes, I see there's a schedule here, as well as a map. Okay, the room next to the Alloway is the Tam o'Shanter. Nothing's programmed for either place tonight. I'll set up a listening post in the Tam o'Shanter, so you and I can make sure we've got the blackmailer in the Alloway and not just some poor sod who's stumbled into the wrong room."

"Give me directions. We'd better get there damn fast."

Sarah and Liz quickly dumped the unconscious guard in a linen closet Sarah had found during her search for a cell. As Liz hurried off to meet Simon, Sarah took Liz's cell and headed in the opposite direction, toward the side door that would take her outdoors to Asher and his all-important call to Langley. But as she moved down the hall, Malko stepped from an office. His head turned left and right. Heart thumping, she darted into a writing room.

When she peered out again, Malko was

prowling off to where the corridor dead-ended. Were she and Liz wrong? Was the blackmailer here, not in the other wing, waiting in the Alloway Room?

As Malko disappeared, she sprinted after, troubled. The wing ended in a T, where there was a glassed-in swimming pool and spa. When she reached it, there was no sign of him. The aromas of expensive massage lotions and suntan oils drifted through the air. She approached the glass carefully. The pool was Olympic-size, with diving boards at the far end. More important, the entire area was empty, although a gentle ripple ruffled the water's perfect blue surface.

The Colt felt heavy in her hands. She raised it, reminding herself to keep her legs springy, her walk even and stable. She advanced along the windows, studying the water. It smoothed slowly, the surface growing glassy. Something had caused that ripple. Something like a rush of air from a door's rapid opening and closing.

Worry crowded her. She had not fired a gun in years — not since Bremner. . . .

She stopped the thought and opened the door. Chlorine-tinged air enveloped her. She stepped inside and pulled the door closed silently. The pool's surface crinkled again, but less this time. To her far right, steam rose from a hot tub.

To her left past the diving boards and beyond another glass wall were elliptical trainers, stationary bicycles, and treadmills, all lined up like oversize toy soldiers. She could see no one inside. On that wall were three doors — one into the exercise room, one labeled STEAM ROOM, and the third labeled OFFICE.

If Malko had come this way, he must be inside one of them. The office seemed most likely. She fervently hoped he was there with his boss, and that she would either recognize him or hear something to identify him. She padded forward, tight with tension. At the exercise room, she peered carefully through the glass windows. Empty. And stepped toward the steam room. There was a glass oval in the door. She looked through. The steam was not on; the air clear. The wood benches were deserted.

That left the office. She gripped the doorknob and turned. *Locked. Where —?*

"How nice we should meet again." It was Malko, behind her.

She froze, listening to the door of the steam room swing back into place. Cursing herself, she realized he must have been hiding directly beneath the glass oval, where she would not spot him — unless she opened the door.

She thought all this in a flash, heard his voice, and reacted.

"Put down your weap—" he began.

She whirled, stepped forward, and slashed up her foot in another *mae-geri* kick aimed at his chin. He dodged, rebalanced, and shot a side-thrust kick into her shoulder that sent her spinning across the floor and told her she was greatly outmatched.

He ran after and swept up her weapon. She jumped back up. Too late. He kicked again, this time connecting with her chin as a blinding flash of lightning illuminated the pool and a loud burst of thunder cracked the air.

Her neck snapped. Black pain radiated through her entire body. She pitched sideways into the cold hard softness of water. Enveloping her. Choking blackness surrounding her as thunder rolled and exploded again, sundering the heavens.

The summer rainsquall poured down as Asher crouched in the thick cover of the topiary bush. Soaked, he glanced at his watch, wondering what was taking Sarah so long, worrying about her.

Three times, he had been forced to burrow deeper into cover as private security passed uncomfortably close. Now as the thunder and lightning split the boiling black clouds, the noise from the protesters suddenly seemed to turn ugly. Asher peered cautiously out from the sodden topiary elephant and down at the distant road. The giant fuchsia balloon in the shape of a pig whipped and twisted in the wind, looking more like a feeble, frightened piglet. Despite wrapping themselves in sheets of plastic, the activists were drenched, and their faces were taking on an angrier look.

According to snippets of conversation he had overheard, it must have been a discouraging day for them. They had not breached the police ranks, nor had they stopped a single person from entering, despite having thousands of protesters in attendance. What had begun as triumph was turning into bitter defeat. Asher could almost feel their frustration escalate and their mood darken, although the rain had stopped.

Then he saw provocation: Counterprotesters had arrived.

A car drove slowly, almost arrogantly, along the long line of wet, aggravated activists. Its driver and passengers made obscene gestures. A second car followed at the same stately pace. Its occupants repeated the gestures and shouted slogans of their own so loudly that they floated up to the hotel.

"Go home, assholes!"

"Losers! Losers! Losers!"

That car was followed by another.

It was too much. A bolt of indignation seemed to shoot through the throngs. With a mighty roar, the thousands of agitators seemed to rise up together and charge, slamming into all three cars, heaving them up, and hurling them onto their sides as easily as if they were toys. Then the crowd rolled in a tidal wave toward the police and private guards.

Convinced the threat was over, the security forces were so surprised that they were overwhelmed before they could reach any weapons except truncheons. Their lines broken, they fell back in splintered groups as the triumphant protesters stormed through the gates and over the walls like a conquering army assaulting a hated castle.

Everywhere on the grounds, security guards, staff security, and police abandoned their posts and barreled down the slope as protesters battled the first ranks of regrouped but completely outnumbered police, pushing them upward.

Asher slid back out of sight, waiting for security to pass. When he reemerged, he was completely alone. With a pang of fear, he wondered again where Sarah was, but at the same time his cool gaze came to rest on the rows of limos and tradesmen's vehicles in the parking lot. Statistically, there had to be at least one cell in there somewhere. Considering the popularity of car phones these days, maybe there were a dozen. He ordered his feet to move faster than his wound wanted. Grabbing his side, he decided he would give himself a few minutes to investigate. Then if Sarah were not back, he would go find her.

Fifty-One

As Liz hurried into the lobby, she was surprised to see guests picking up their drinks and rushing to the tall French windows to peer down the hill. Anxious voices in a variety of languages sounded throughout the room. Security people in street clothes and uniforms seemed to emerge from everywhere, pulling out weapons as they converged on the doors. The stream of humanity moving in a single direction said something momentous had happened, but with so many people at the windows, there was no way Liz could look, too.

She changed directions and sprinted out through the passage between the bar and gift shop to the veranda. A few last raindrops fell noisily and ricocheted up, dampening her trousers. She edged in between two women at the balustrade. One held a hand to her mouth, her brows arched in horror. The other took a long drink from her glass of malt.

"They are insane," the first decided in Italian. "Mad!"

"There are so many of them," said a man on her other side, also in Italian, "that it doesn't matter whether they know what they're doing."

"How many do you think?" asked the woman.

"At least five thousand," Liz answered in Italian, her tone worried. "Perhaps more." As the two looked at her, she pointed to her security badge and backed away before they asked questions. "Must go."

She paused again. The river of agitators poured over the wall and started up the hill, while at the same time the vastly outnumbered security forces with their dogs and weapons flooded out to intercept them. Liz felt the hair on the back of her neck stand on end. Unless a miracle happened, she could see no good outcome for anyone.

And what would this mean for the blackmailer? She wondered uneasily whether he would ignore his meeting with Santarosa and fade into dangerous anonymity again. No, she decided. He had no choice now. He must go ahead. For him, the deal was so critical he had already risked his place in the Coil and killed for it. Whatever its rewards, he expected them to endure far beyond the events of this weekend.

With a sense of renewed urgency, she ran inside, crossed the echoing lobby, where even the registration clerks were craning to see out the windows, and hurtled into the north wing. Office doors were standing open, the desks inside deserted, as if a wind had blown through — or word of the demonstrators' assault on Dreftbury.

But the farther she ran, the less impact she saw. Soon phones rang and voices answered behind closed doors. A man in a phone booth cooed to his girlfriend. Another stepped from an elevator, straightening his suit. He wore an orange staff badge.

The Alloway and Tam o'Shanter rooms were in the tangle of side corridors near the end, on the outside of the wing. She sped into the maze, reading room numbers, recalling Simon's directions. Prints of Scotland hung on the walls, and heather stood in tall vases on narrow tables. She turned two corners and stopped at the Tam o'Shanter. As she reached for the knob, a wave of nervous excitement rushed through her.

EU Competition Commissioner Carlo Santarosa had arrived from the other direction and was advancing on the Alloway. His dusky face showed sharp irritation.

Without a glance at her, he knocked once, pulled open the door, and announced, "I can give you ten minutes, no more. There's trouble with the demonstrators — a riot! And I must return to my people. What is this vital evidence you claim will convince me?" The door closed abruptly.

Smiling grimly, eager to hear from Simon who the blackmailer was, she opened the door to the Tam o'Shanter and hurried inside. And stopped. Her breath solid in her chest. Her blood icy with fear.

"Simon!" He lay on the floor, eyes blinking as he struggled back toward consciousness. A bruise was purpling on his cheek. She looked up, enraged, eyes burning, and stared across the room.

Malko was aiming an Uzi at her heart. "Congratulations, Sansborough. You've found me."

EU Competition Commissioner Carlo Santarosa felt ill. He sank into the chair in front of the computer screen.

"So, Commissioner, have you seen enough?"

Santarosa could barely speak. "Where did you get that information?" His voice was wispy with fear.

"Your onetime employee, the Carnivore, kept business records, and I managed to acquire them. Fully detailed records, I might add, with names, dates, all parties involved, and payment details. You'd be amazed at his clients, who engaged him often for quite good and moral reasons. Still, it's murder for hire, isn't it? Your career and reputation won't survive such a revelation. But then, I can't imagine anyone's would."

Santarosa wiped a shaky hand across his forehead. His face felt greasy with sweat. "Just because I approve your merger doesn't mean the commission will agree."

"Of course it will. This is in your hands. Not only my future but yours."

Santarosa hunched over as if his stomach hurt. "You give me no choice. I can't bring shame to my wife, my family, my —"

In the room next door, Gino Malko rose from his chair, Simon's gym bag in his hand. He set it on the table beside him. Behind him, French doors framed a flagstone walk. In the distance, the sea was an angry swatch of muddy brown and green. Black thunderheads still billowed.

There was a faint rumble of sound, as if from many voices.

"Your cousin had an unfortunate loss of memory," Malko told her. "He seemed to think you were still in Paris. Hand over my Glock. I've missed it."

Liz stared at him. "You bastard. How did you find us?"

"The Glock." His face was impassive. "Finding you was no trouble. I have access to every security camera in the hotel, since my employer owns it. You look surprised. Didn't see the cameras, did you? High-tech, the size of pinheads, and buried in the molding where the walls meet the ceilings. As for your disguises, they're good, of course. But since I've studied both of you now, it's impossible you'd get past me for long."

Inwardly, Liz swore as she desperately tried to think of a ruse, some quick move, a clever trick that could reverse the situation. At the same time, her mind was working over something he had said . . . something that was important. . . .

"Throw me the gun," Malko ordered. "Or I'll kill him. By now, you know I mean that. Glocks don't go off on their own. I want it far away from you."

Liz tossed the Glock to the floor, where it landed between Simon and Malko. She hoped Simon was alert enough to roll over and grab it. But Malko kicked it away. His Uzi swung between her and Simon, covering them, as he squatted, retrieved the Glock, and stood again. He knew exactly what he was doing, a janitor of skill, always protecting himself with distance. He dropped the pistol into the gym bag and grabbed the handles.

He gestured with the Uzi. "Help him up. He's ready."

"Where to?" She took three quick steps and knelt beside Simon. She would bide her time, wait and watch. She would figure out something. She must.

"Just get him on his feet."

"Simon? Can you hear me?"

"Get him up!"

She tugged at Simon's arm. He swore. She stood and pulled. He shook his head and swore again, but his eyes opened.

"I've got to quit doing this," he muttered. "Bloody Christ."

Malko had moved around them, Uzi unwavering. Passing the French doors, he went to a connecting door and knocked.

A voice inside said, "Yes?"

Malko opened it. "Are you finished, sir? I have them. They're unarmed."

"Santarosa's gone. Bring them in."

Liz tugged Simon's arm over her shoulder and lifted. He stood up, his feet gaining firmness as they moved slowly to the open doorway. As she helped him, her mind was far away, trying to remember something Malko had said . . . something about his employer owning the hotel. It was important.

With a jolt, she suddenly knew. Of course. Her jaw clenched, and unconsciously she held Simon tighter. She remembered something he had told her. . . . Yes, if she were right, the blackmailer not only owned Dreftbury but also a vast chain of other resorts and hotels, many built originally to house his construction workers. She knew now who he was. The deal he wanted Santarosa to approve was worth more than the annual budgets of most nations, as large as the gross national product of Hungary.

Sir Anthony Brookshire and César Duchesne rushed down the hallway, rage in every step Brookshire took. The two men were almost identical in size and age, both just under six feet. Still, where Sir Anthony had a large head with a full head of silvery hair and was slightly muscular, his security man had a shaved head and was solid-looking and athletic. Sir Anthony wore his classic jacket, while Duchesne's tweed hung loosely, as if it had been fitted on an overweight plumber. The difference between class and breed, Sir Anthony decided. He wondered how Duchesne had hurt his leg. It dragged slightly as he walked. A disfigurement.

"You're sure Santarosa's in the Alloway?" Sir Anthony demanded. As he thought about the blackmailer again, his gorge rose, livid at how the traitor's arrogance had threatened the Coil. He could take no chance it would happen again.

"As we agreed, I dropped a tracking device into Santarosa's pocket when he arrived. I was able to do that with Prometheus and Ocean, too, but Themis and Atlas sent their assistants to register, and I never saw them. After Santarosa checked in, he circulated through the lobby and stopped briefly in the bar. Then he went to his room. He left a little while ago and went directly to the Alloway. Neither Prometheus nor Ocean is there, so either Themis or Atlas is the blackmailer. That's when I called you."

"So the bastard is finally cornered," Sir Anthony growled. "He'll have the Zip disc with him, since he may need it to 'convince' Santarosa. Take it from him immediately and give it to me."

"And if he won't turn it over?"

"He must. You understand."

Duchesne inclined his head. "What will you do with the disc?"

"That's none of your goddamned bloody business."

They turned into another corridor. "There's the room," Duchesne said.

As Liz supported Simon, she looked desperately around, trying to see something that would help them escape. But Malko had their weapons, and he stayed out of range. Although he was walking better, Simon was still not himself.

She listened as ice clinked into a glass in the other room. "Gregory Gilmartin," she called. "You have my father's files."

"Yes, I do."

In his cheap suit, the engineer appeared in the doorway, thin and lanky, with the intense expression of the driven. His analytical gaze took in the situation with a single sweep. He turned back into the room and drank from the highball glass as Liz helped Simon to the door.

"But we're going to make it appear as if not only do you have the files but you're willing to kill and die for them." He waved a hand, beckoning them in. "Don't bother to hope Santarosa will say anything later. He has far too much to lose." He took out a green Zip disc and tossed it onto the table, then he sat in front of a top-of-the-line IBM ThinkPad, whose monitor was divided into four windows, each displaying views of the hall outside the room. Two figures stood there. He closed the top and drank again.

Liz's gaze returned quickly to the disc. She stared at it hungrily. "Is that it?" she asked before she could stop herself.

He gave a cool smile. "You're a fool if you think I'd ever let it get beyond my reach, particularly here." He ejected a Zip disc with the same green label from the computer and put it inside his jacket pocket. "Malko, they're here. Let them in. Carefully. Do you have a weapon for me?"

Malko handed him Simon's Beretta. As Gilmartin aimed it at them, Malko hurried to the door.

Fifty-Two

With César Duchesne beside him, Sir Anthony Brookshire slowed, reading the names on the doors until at last the Alloway Room appeared, the letters engraved on a shiny brass plate. He stroked his jacket, where his Browning was stored in the holster under his armpit, and stopped. He lifted his head, listening. The roar of voices outdoors was coming closer. Somewhere, glass broke.

"I'll wait here," he announced. "You go in first. Kill all of them. With luck, this blasted riot will cover for it."

Duchesne's quiet, untroubled expression cracked for a moment. Outrage lashed out, red-hot, scalding. "No." He turned on his heel and left.

Shocked, Sir Anthony opened his mouth to bellow, order him to stop, come back, do as he was told. But suddenly the door swung open. A solid-looking man in a gray suit and sharp gray eyes stood there.

Behind the man, a voice called, "Come in, Cronus. How did you find us?"

Sir Anthony hesitated. This was not what he planned.

The man in the gray suit lifted an Uzi and pointed it at him. "Now."

Chest tight with anger, Cronus stalked inside. He recognized the voice. "Damnation, Atlas. Stop this. What in God's name are you thinking? I knew it had to be one of us. Look at the hell you've put the Coil through! Doesn't loyalty mean anything anymore?"

"You haven't answered my question. The engineer in me is curious. Of course I expected you to pin me down eventually. Still, how did you find us?" He gestured with the Beretta from where he sat. His Timex watch showed beneath the sleeve of his cheap dress shirt.

Malko closed the door and turned into the room, the Uzi slowly panning Sir Anthony, Liz, and Simon.

Sir Anthony still glared at Atlas. "Duchesne planted a tracker on Santarosa."

"Ah, sweet." Gilmartin nodded approvingly. "I see Duchesne deserted you. I'd always thought he wasn't as good as you claimed. As for how I knew you were here, I used the security cameras, of course. Our meeting is a perfect example of the power of technology. But there's one thing it can't substitute for, and that's intelligence. What you've done is unintelligent, Tony. You can't win every battle, and you've pushed this business with the files much too far. I left all of you alone for five years, except for the occasional but necessary deal that my other resources couldn't bring into line. But I think you'll agree my merger with Tierney Aviation is worth more than a little trouble. After all, we're talking more than forty billion dollars."

As the tension in the room mounted, Liz alternately watched the standoff between the two men and looked out the French doors, which were about thirty feet to her right, where a group of protesters dashed past, picking up rocks that lined the flower beds and dropping them into backpacks. She glanced at Simon. He had stopped swaying. She helped him to a side chair near the gym bag, which sat on the floor where Malko had left it when ordered to open the door. From where she stood, she could see the handle of a pistol. Perhaps Malko's, now that he had the Glock.

Sir Anthony was saying, "What you mean is that you'll have a monopoly on avionics."

"I sincerely hope it'll be a monopoly. That's where competition eventually leads, isn't it? A fight to the economic death until only one company — one man — is left standing. Look at the consolidations constantly going on. What other purpose is there? Certainly not competition. Besides, you'll notice the SEC approved my merger. Santarosa and his EU people were acting like terrified nuns, legs crossed before the act."

Sir Anthony clasped his hands at his back, and his chin jutted forward. His entire posture radiated disapproval. His gaze fell upon the Zip disc. He looked at it longingly.

The construction magnate shook his head. "No, Tony. It's not yours. Don't pretend you're shocked. I could tell last night you'd guessed the blackmailer was one of us. You just hadn't figured out which one." His lips twisted in disgust.

"Climb down from your Olympian throne, *Sir* Anthony, KCB, or whatever the hell knighthood those initials stand for. Do you think money is why *I* do everything? The reason *I* joined the Coil? For God's sakes, such naïveté." He waved the Beretta. "You're slime, Tony. All of you are slime. I'm not like you. I don't need more wealth, and I never used the files to extort money. My job is to make a *difference,* as my father, my grandfather, and my great-grandfather did." He paused, his satisfaction evident. He was enjoying the attention, what he perceived as respect. "I won't be just the largest construction company in the world, I'm on the way to being the largest in aeronautics as well. I'll take civilization not just into the jungle and up to the mountaintop but into space, too. *That's* why I did it."

Sir Anthony said softly, gently, "You needed to make a mark as big as they did. Poor Greg."

Simon seemed to rouse himself. Liz studied him as he shifted on the chair and looked around alertly. She put her hand on his shoulder and used a finger to draw an arrow pointing at the French doors. He turned slightly, saw the demonstrators, watched them collecting rocks, then looked up at her. She gazed down at the gym bag. He followed her line of sight. She hoped he remembered that she was no longer a reliable shot.

Gilmartin snapped, "I'm making a contribution."

"Really?" Simon said instantly, proving he was alert enough to follow the conversation. "If your merger made no profit, would you still want it?"

631

"That's not the point," Gilmartin said, outraged. "Of course it'll make a handsome profit. Anything of value does."

Sir Anthony had been watching the agitators for some time, the groups rushing back and forth, collecting rocks. He stalked forward, his cheeks hot, his anger barely under control. The weight of his responsibilities felt very heavy, the crushing failures and disappointments of the search for the files an indictment of his leadership. He thought about the Browning in the holster under his jacket again. Since he had not detected Atlas's lack of moral compass, Atlas would ruin the Coil completely. He could see that clearly now. Atlas would expose the Coil, bring down the authorities, end whatever future good it could offer the world. Only he, Cronus, should have the files. Only he could be trusted with the terrible secrets within. He had guessed this but had not yet been willing to admit it. Now he had no choice.

He accused, "You're not what the Coil's about, Atlas. You've hurt us badly. You've pushed us into behaviors . . . actions . . ."

"You mean setting up Sansborough?" Gilmartin said, rising angrily from his chair. "You mean murder? You old hypocrite. No one *made* you do anything! You are what you are and have always been. All of the Coil is! And so is Nautilus. If you were really so altruistic, would you have done any of it? No! *I'm* the honest one. I know the way the world works, and I don't hide behind illusions. You're out of date and out of step. You're —"

Liz squeezed Simon's shoulder. Quickly, he glanced across the long meeting room and out the French doors, saw the maddened faces, the fists swinging back, the rocks hurling. There was a sudden explosion of noise, of glass panes breaking, shattering, singly and simultaneously, cascading and reverberating throughout the wing and into the huge old hotel.

At the same time, rocks and glass crashed into the room, striking the podium and blanketing the far end of the conference table. Fresh air gusted in afterward, cool, smelling of rain. Suddenly, gunshots thundered outdoors, too.

As Greg Gilmartin whirled to look, Sir Anthony smiled coldly to himself, amused that neither Gilmartin nor his man had thought him sufficiently dangerous to search for a weapon. But then, that was Greg. Too arrogant or perhaps too hungry to assess a situation accurately. Definitely not the man his father was. He must be stopped. Permanently.

All of that passed through Cronus's mind in an instant. He yanked the Browning from under his jacket just as Simon dived a hand into his gym bag and Liz sprinted toward Malko. One second later, Gilmartin turned back, realized what was happening, and yanked up the Beretta to aim.

Sarah's mind swam, flickering on the edges of consciousness. Nausea and achiness seemed to flow through her veins. Her chin and neck hurt. She forced herself to remember: Malko had kicked her in the chin and knocked her into the water.

Groaning, she opened her eyes. Tried to grasp where she was.

There was a coffee table, a lamp, a couch. Farther off, a door. She was in a hotel room, where Malko had tied her to the chair. But everything was different. The lamp, a chair, and a low table lay on their sides beside the window, under a glittering blanket of glass. Rocks sat on top of the mess. She heard gunshots and shouts. Other pieces of furniture were upright still. She studied the door, saw it was horizontal. . . .

That was it. She was lying on her side, still tied to the chair, a boulder next to her. Now she recalled it all — a howling noise, shouts, bullhorns, the hail of rocks, the explosive shriek as a boulder hurled through the glass door, the shocking impact as she fell. Then emptiness, nothing.

Bitterly, she complimented herself. Very clever. Oh, yes, so clever that she had allowed Malko to fool her with an obvious old trick like hiding directly beneath a window. At least he still wanted her alive, if only for a short time. She pushed away fear and rolled her head to look at more of the room. But her cheek slapped floor tiling, and new pain radiated out. Her mind swam again. It seemed to her the horizontal door opened and feet floated into the room, moving sideways. A man's pants and athletic shoes.

Her chest tightened, and her lungs squeezed with fear. But she kept her voice steady. "Decided to kill me after all, Malko?"

The man said nothing. His legs limped around her.

She tried to twist to look up at the face, but he

was too close. She fought pain. Then he was behind her. "Malko?"

Gino Malko was behind Sir Anthony and to the side, listening with genuine respect to his employer. He had never had one as rich or as powerful. For Malko, every word of praise from Mr. Gilmartin had been a gold ingot, to be deposited in his inner savings account, security against the cold winds of poverty and chance. Malko saw nothing unusual about old Sir Anthony's movements, and Sansborough was simply an irritation he would deal with in time. Instead, his gaze locked on the real threat — Simon Childs, at the hand coming out of the gym bag with his pistol.

Simon saw that Sir Anthony's grip on his weapon was steady, the gun trained on Gregory Gilmartin. With luck, they would kill each other.

Malko swore and raised the Uzi. Too late.

The gunshots were almost simultaneous, the noise volcanic.

Simon's bullet caught Malko in the heart. Blood erupted, misting the air pink. Malko's Uzi exploded, the bullet bursting into a vase, detonating it like a hand grenade.

At the same time, Sir Anthony's first shot went into Gilmartin's white shirt and the second into his throat.

Gregory Gilmartin toppled forward, his eyes wide, his finger convulsing on the trigger of his gun and sending a single bullet into the expensive carpet. Blood geysered from his wounds.

In the room, there was a second of shock, as if the world had tilted. The three left standing —

Liz, Sir Anthony, and Simon — were motionless, as if stillness would make the horror acceptable. The hot stench of blood stained the air, while dust from the shattered window floated gently in layers above the corpses of the two men.

Liz moved first, sweeping up the Uzi from Malko's lifeless fingers. She pointed it at the Coil's leader. "Put down your gun, Sir Anthony. Or would you prefer to be called Cronus?"

Sir Anthony blinked. Oddly, he remembered something George Eliot had written. He had read the book — *Adam Bede* — one languid summer in Paris: *Our deeds determine us, as much as we determine our deeds.* He believed in the future. He had lived his life in that passionate pursuit, and as much as he hated it, he saw clearly everything had led up to this moment. He sensed he had somehow, somewhere made a profound mistake, and that was an admission he could not abide.

Sir Anthony turned swiftly, his finger pulling the trigger.

But Liz had seen the movement and guessed what he intended. She squeezed off a burst. The Uzi's bullets punctured Sir Anthony's firing arm and slashed into his chest. He jerked up to his toes. His gun fired wildly into the ceiling. As plaster dust showered down, coating the room in white, he rotated, his eyes soft with relief. He fell hard to the floor.

As she stared down, an odd silence filled Liz's ears. She felt a sharp stab of failure. And then soaring elation that she was alive. That Simon was alive. She looked at him. He was peering worriedly at her. She smiled, gave a brief nod.

Joy flashed across his face. He threw an arm across her shoulders, pulled her close, and kissed her cheek. She wrapped her arms around him and held him tightly, as if all of life were encapsulated in this moment.

The door opened. Instantly, they released each other and whirled, their weapons raised.

"Sarah!" Liz sighed a long stream of air and lowered the Uzi.

"Thank God!" Simon lowered his pistol.

Sarah walked carefully into the suite, as if she were either weak or injured. She was followed by an older man with a cap on his head. Liz realized she might have seen him around the hotel, one of the many anonymous security people who wore green badges. But as he drew next to Sarah, Liz saw that he limped on his right side. Simon noticed it, too. They exchanged a knowing glance.

Sarah was staring at the carnage. "My God, Liz. What happened?"

"In a minute," Liz said. Then she looked directly at the man: "Who are you? You've been helping us, haven't you?"

"César Duchesne," he said simply in a low voice that hinted at a growl. "It was my job, until Brookshire told me to kill you." His gaze was focused on the green disc on the table. "Is that it?"

She had a strange desire to trust him. "No. It's in Gilmartin's inside pocket. It's mine now, though."

"Yes, it is."

"Duchesne found me," Sarah explained and

smiled at him. "Malko tricked me in the pool area. He knocked me out and tied me up."

"Liz! Simon!"

They turned quickly at the sound of the familiar voice. Stunned, Liz grinned with relief. "Henry!"

"Yes, it's me. Turned up like a bad penny." Lord Henry Percy hobbled into the room, pushing a walker. His old face scanned the bloodbath, and his mouth tightened. He was almost erect, a towering figure, the way she remembered him before his wheelchair.

"You're all right then," he decided, his keen gaze scrutinizing Simon and her and then moving to Duchesne as if to be sure who he was. "Duchesne said you would be. I'm sorry about the trouble at the house. I was worried you might actually check me for a pulse, but Clive handled it well, I thought. Duchesne said you must believe we'd really been attacked. That it was critical to your continuing the job."

"Henry!" Simon said, disgusted. "You bastard. We thought you were dead! What are you doing here?"

Again the look at Duchesne. "He brought me so I could explain to the police when the time came, you see." He peered down at Sir Anthony's body. "I can't believe it. Tony turned out to be such a stupid chap." He shook his head.

Sarah was studying Liz and Simon and seemed to see something. "Asher found the agent Langley assigned here," she told them. "They'll be up shortly. Henry, we should leave. You need to talk to them, set the stage."

He frowned, nodded, and followed her out the door. As they left, Duchesne limped to Gilmartin, knelt, patted him down, and stood, the Zip disc in his hand.

"That's the right one," Simon said instantly.

Duchesne did not glance at him. He went to Liz and handed it to her, his gaze downcast.

With a chill, she stared at it. "Thank you."

"I think we should burn it," Simon told her. "No one should ever have that sort of power again." He gazed at her, waiting for a response.

She said nothing, watching Duchesne as he silently limped toward the door. With a queasy feeling, she studied his gait. Then, as he stepped outside, she had her answer: The limp vanished, and he walked normally, strongly, with a spring in his step. He turned his head quickly, looked directly into her eyes, and gave a wry smile. The door shut, and he was gone.

Raw emotion flooded her.

Simon frowned, studying her intense expression, the hard lines around her mouth.

"What is it?" he said. "Something else happened. Is it the Zip disc? Would you rather not destroy it?"

She seemed to come out of a trance. She turned and stared up at him. Her face was stricken, but there was also rage and fear there, too.

"I don't have the disc, Simon," she told him.

"Yes, you do —"

She shook her head violently. "No. Duchesne switched discs. He gave me a fake one. He left with the real one."

Simon's voice rose. "You didn't stop him? *Why?*"

"Because I recognized him. He's had more plastic surgery, and he's on steroids again. But it was him. I've seen him make that sort of switch before. Then he dropped his limp. I wonder how long he's been working for Sir Anthony. My guess is, he's been following me all along, probably since before I moved to Santa Barbara."

Simon's blue eyes darkened. There was anguish in his tone. "Tell me I'm wrong. Tell me I don't know who you're talking about."

Her throat tight, she avoided his gaze. "The disc belongs to him. No, don't look at me like that, Simon. I couldn't expose him." She turned away. "He's my father. Duchesne's the Carnivore."

Epilogue

Madonie Mountains, Sicily

In the distance, the weathered town of Gangi clung to a sharp slope below the sun-dried peak of Monte Marone. The snaking streets and the sandstone steps that connected the medieval town's levels were invisible from where Liz hiked down a hillcrest. All she could see of it now was the sea of red-tiled roofs faded over the centuries to the color of exhausted flesh. Earlier today, she had gone into Gangi, asking for her father by name and by three of his aliases — Alex Bosa and Alessandro Firenze and César Duchesne. She showed a drawing of what he had looked like at Dreftbury.

In his proper black suit, the mayor proudly assured her he knew personally everyone in this remote area but did not recognize the face or names. Of course, the Mafia capo did not either, and neither did the carabinieri. Shopkeepers and housewives knew nothing, had seen nothing.

For her, time had run out. It was September, and she had been in Sicily nearly a month, going first to the beautiful resort city of Cefalù on the northern coast, because it was the ancestral home of the Firenzes and the Bosas, from whom her father, she, and Sarah were descended. That was where he had secretly built a villa, retired, and supposedly died.

When she found no clue there, she moved inland along the SS286, searching to the east and west among the isolated farms and villages that dotted Sicily's wild central mountains. Some villages were so small they appeared on no map. According to rumor, Bernardo Provenzano, the Cosa Nostra's brilliant *capo di tutti capi*, the "boss of all bosses," was hiding somewhere among them. Provenzano had avoided police capture for forty years. This being Sicily, the only unusual aspect of his disappearance was the remarkable duration. The capo before him — his friend Salvatore Riina, known as "the Beast" — had hidden for a mere twenty-three years before finally being caught in 1993.

Liz gave the town of Gangi one last suspicious look and turned off into a *cortile* that fronted a tumbledown stone building, weathered and gray. In the dirt courtyard stood a dozen tables covered by crisp, blue-checked cloths, waiting for the night's crowd. She had learned that people gathered here from miles around to eat, drink, and gossip after a day in the fields and olive groves. Sometimes it was called Il Santuario; other times, Il Purgatorio. The owner of the *ristorante*, who had an encyclopedic memory, was allegedly connected.

The door was open. From the doorway drifted the odors of garlic, spicy tomato sauce, and wine.

She put a pleasant smile on her face and stepped into cool darkness, hiding her eagerness. The stone building was very old, with small windows that gave little light. But the room was large. In it was only one person.

"Signore Aldo Cappuccio?" she asked.

A man stood behind a wooden bar. The top was worn smooth by decades of elbows and glasses. He opened his hands over it, palms up, and smiled in return, the gracious host.

"Buon giorno. Che cosa desidera?"

Short and wiry, he was around fifty years old, with a black mustache, a swarthy complexion, and green Sicilian eyes. She saw no sign of a weapon. In the dusky room, he looked like a good-natured imp, not a man who commanded respect on both sides of the law. Still, there was something about his face. It was a mask, she decided.

She smiled broadly. *"Buon giorno. Il vino della casa, per favore."*

He cocked his head as if to hear better. *"Basta così?"*

"Sì, grazie."

"Buono. You're developing a Sicilian accent," he decided, continuing in Italian as he reached behind for the house wine. "You're English, yes? Welcome to my home."

As he poured three inches into a simple glass, he kept glancing at her.

Curious, she glanced back. "I'm English and American. Live in California now." She picked up her wine, leaned against the bar, and scanned the room, controlling her excitement. Since

Dreftbury, every time she approached a doorway, every time she walked down a street, every time she met someone new, she wanted to shake them, ask them, *Do you know my father? Have you seen him?*

"You've come a long way," he said.

While Cappuccio's place appeared near ruin from the outside, the room was gracious, filled with fine antiques, expensive fabric-covered chairs, varnished tables, and old photos in heavy frames. The clothing in the photographs told her they had been taken long ago. Beside them was a tranquil fresco of angels with pipes and harps. It was far older than the photos.

She picked up her glass and walked toward the fresco. "Gaspare Vazzano?"

"*Sì*. You know Vazzano's work?" He left the bar and followed.

"I know he painted a lot of frescoes around here, but I thought they were mostly in churches. Your place must date back to the sixteenth century." Vazzano was born in the mid 1500s in Gangi, where she first had seen his work.

"No one knows for certain exactly when, but yes. Here, the years run together." He snapped his fingers. "There. That's my life." He snapped them again. "And yours. We have a saying that life's not a gift, it's a surprise, and death is never a surprise, but it's often a gift. This is a hard land. A hard country with hard rules and even harder customs. You know my name, *signorina*. It's only fair I know yours. *Come si chiama?*"

"Elizabeth Sansborough." She sipped her wine. It had a rough coat to it, a taste of good local grapes but not aged enough. "I'm looking for my father." She took out the drawing from her backpack and handed it to him, watching his expression. "He may be using the name Bosa or Firenze. Those are family names. Perhaps even Duchesne."

"So?" He stared down at it a long time, expressionless. At the square face and bald head and even features. When he raised his gaze, it was to study her again. There was knowledge in those eyes. He made no effort to hide it.

Breath seemed to catch in her throat. "You know him, don't you? *Where is he!*"

He shrugged. For a flash, she saw beneath the mask. He was a man who calculated risks. For whatever reason, he had decided there was little this time.

"He was a Bosa, Don Alessandro Bosa. Yes, that's what he was called. There are changes in his face." He tapped the drawing. "He was reading *The Leopard*." He stared into space. "Ah, yes. 'Bare hillsides flaming yellow under the sun.' He quoted it to me, because he'd come from Cefalù to see our summer."

"Where is he now?" She kept her tone neutral, but her heart was racing with excitement, with hope.

He frowned. "Didn't you know? He died. Someone dynamited his villa, and it killed him. Several years ago. Maybe eight. A big event like that, word spreads."

"I heard he'd survived."

He shook his head. "Who could've survived that?" He handed back the drawing. "Drink your wine. Don't be upset. How long have you been looking?"

"I heard he reappeared recently."

"I see only with my eyes, hear only with my ears. I have no magical powers. I've told you what I know." He returned to the bar, no longer interested.

She watched his straight back and thin, ropy shoulders as he rounded the counter. He was a man who had managed to create some kind of neutrality in a country where old grudges and simmering passions exploded with ease.

"You haven't seen him lately?" she demanded.

He made a dismissive gesture. "It's what I told you. He's gone. Dead. Not alive . . . even to you. Go home. You won't find him here. Why do you persist in looking for what no longer exists? If he's really alive, he doesn't want to be found. If he's dead, give him his peace. Go back to California. Find your own life. Leave his memories here, where they belong. Respect him enough to make your way without him."

She glanced away. The lined, formidable face of an old Sicilian woman in one of the photos caught her eye. As she stared at it, an odd relief swept through her. She felt comforted.

Then she looked back. Her gaze bored into him. "You haven't see him?"

"No!" He threw up his hands. Then calmly: "I have customers who'll be here soon. Sit. Drink your wine. I have work." He pulled up bottles of red wine from somewhere beneath the bar and stacked them behind it, against the wall.

She walked to the bar and set down her glass.

"Quanto costa questo?"

He told her the euros. She left them next to her wine and walked out into the long shadows of twilight.

The wind was dying down at last. As she crossed the courtyard, she took off her straw hat and rubbed her forearm across her brow. Immediately, it was wet again. The rainy season had not yet begun. All day, hot sirocco winds from North Africa had blasted across the parched hills and valleys, sucking the last molecules of moisture from people and land. Astoundingly, tempers were seldom short. After being conquered and reconquered for three thousand years, Sicilians accepted acts of God and nature with equanimity.

Three middle-aged men strolled in from the road, laughing, cigarettes dangling from their lips, and sat at one of the outside tables. Signore Cappuccio emerged and, without a look at her, asked what they were drinking.

She hiked away, passing a grizzled goatherd, his dog, and a herd of mangy goats. As night approached, the wind changed directions, coming from the north. She lifted her face, finding relief in its coolness. The lonely sound of a car engine carried clearly from the east through the quiet mountains. She checked her watch. Yes, he was on time.

Eagerly, she climbed another hill and stood there waiting as sunset painted the western horizon the brilliant colors of the oranges and lemons for which this region had once been known. Now half the residents of a decade ago were gone to the cities of Europe in search of work. People had told her over and over how empty their mountains were — only the old, the lazy, and the drunk remained. Globalization had struck even here, stealing the young and leaving their elders to pine. Like the seasons, globalization was inevitable. The only question was whether its leaders would push it forward with the least damage to the voiceless or with the greatest profits to themselves.

As she stared out over the darkening hills and valleys, her memory returned again to her father. In her mind, she saw him clearly, leaving the Dreftbury hotel room. She could have called his name, revealed him, fired a round over his head. But she had not, because he had been the one to walk away. After that, she had waited almost a month, a dull pain near her heart. Then she went in search with a desperate, hopeful longing to find him, his love.

Behind her, the pickup pulled off the road. She turned and ran to the door. "Come look at the sunset with me. Did you learn anything?"

Simon's craggy face smiled at her, his thick hair shiny in the waning light. "A few things," he told her, climbing out. "How about you?"

As they walked back toward her spot on the hill, she told him, "I met an interesting man. If anyone knows whether Papa's here somewhere, it'd be him. But he believes Papa's dead. So I think Papa's probably not here."

He nodded. "None of my people turned up anything about Jack O'Keefe or any of his compadres, including Elaine and George Russell.

O'Keefe's got to be in his seventies by now, so he could've died quietly somewhere in his sleep."

"Or he could be alive. With Papa." It was through O'Keefe that Sarah had sent the message that had trapped the Carnivore at his Cefalù villa.

Simon shrugged. "True. But if O'Keefe were active, I think we'd know."

She had been wrong to assume that MI6 would not want Simon back. As for Sarah and Asher, they had returned to Paris, determined to finish their vacation. Gary Faust was alive and healthy, still flying his Westland Lysander wherever the circus pitched its tent. She and Simon had replaced Paul Hamilton's Jeep and sent a cash donation to the studio apartment in Pigalle for clothes and food. The agitators arrested that day at Dreftbury were quickly bailed out, represented by lawyers hired by an umbrella group that was bringing together the disparate branches of the movement, hoping to make it more effective by taking it mainstream.

And so life went on, too often filled with interest, not passions. For a few brief days, Nautilus was in Europe's spotlight, and the nature of the group — whether sinister or benevolent — was an issue discussed in barrooms and boardrooms and even a few bedrooms. Then another small war broke out somewhere, and British and American soldiers in Iraq came under fire, and the news value of the still-clandestine organization plummeted.

As it turned out, the vanished César Duchesne was the only outside witness to the Coil's bloody plot. The authorities had found Henry Percy's information intriguing, but only as background. As for the damage to his mansion caused in the fake attack, he had laughed, saying he had enjoyed the adventure, and after all, what was money for but to have a good time occasionally? Gregory Gilmartin's brother, the second eldest, had assumed the reins of the family construction empire and was pressuring EU Commissioner Santarosa to render a favorable decision in the merger with Tierney Aviation.

It was no surprise Richmond Hornish, Nicholas Inglethorpe, and Christian Menchen did not turn against one another but instead brought in their lawyers. The Coil would continue, shaken but resolute. They lived by their own golden rule: He who has the gold makes the rules.

When Liz reached the crest of the hill, she gestured at the seamless panorama of rolling hills draped with shadows, their tops burnished with the radiant light of the setting sun. It was one of those moments she wished would extend forever, standing there with Simon, looking out at a world that seemed unsullied.

He took her hand, raised it to his lips, and kissed her fingers. She leaned against him, her side to his, as they continued to stare out, soaking up the wild beauty.

"Have you decided?" she asked.

"Yes. I'm going to Santa Barbara with you."

She pulled away. She looked into his eyes, saw a weariness that had been growing since July. She kissed him, and he kissed her back, lingering.

"I can't do it anymore," he told her at last,

stepping back. "Somewhere while I was in MI6, I got lost. It's such a bore, but it's the truth. I want to find out what else there is."

"I'm glad you'll come. Very, very glad. And I feel the same way. That's why I have to keep teaching. The students give me hope."

"I know." He tugged on her hand, pulling her close again, and they resumed their watch. "The best is, we'll be together." The sun had dropped below the hill. The sky was red.

"Did you see that?" she asked.

"No. What?"

"Across on the next hill. A flash of light. It's gone now."

"Probably a bicyclist, or maybe a shepherd with some metal on his knapsack. We should go. It's a long drive out to Cefalù."

She nodded, and he swung his arm across her shoulder, holding her close as they walked to the pickup.

She slipped her arm around his waist, her body matching the rhythm of his. "Did you know that Gangi has a pagan festival? The Christians don't much like it, of course. It's called the Sagra della Spiga, and there's a procession of the old gods — Pan, Bacchus, and Demeter, the fertility divinities. When I was in town, a man at the Bongiorno palace told me Monte Alburchia may be the site of an ancient fertility temple built by the Greeks."

"The Greeks? I'd forgotten they'd gotten this far inside Rome's territory."

"Curious, isn't it? Wherever humans go, we take our gods, in one form or another."

As they continued to talk in low, intimate voices, a man rose to his haunches on the hill opposite, where Liz had seen the flash of light. He had been lying on his belly under the leafy branches of an olive tree, using a powerful directional microphone as he listened and watched through binoculars. For an instant, he had worried he would be discovered. But the moment passed, because Liz was involved in Simon and the future. This was good; what he wanted.

He ran a hand over the new growth on his head. Soon his hair would be full again, thick and gray. He repressed a wave of yearning to be with his daughter, packed away his equipment, and hiked off into the night.

Author's Note

About eight years ago, during research I stumbled upon one of those paragraphs that are the lifeblood of a novelist. It mentioned a yearly meeting of powerful world leaders that called itself the Bilderberg Group. I was intrigued. Unlike the VIP-bristling World Economic Forum, which usually gathers in Davos, Switzerland, and Allen & Co., which is legendary for its low-key, high-level summits in Sun Valley, Idaho, the Bilderbergers were a complete unknown to me.

For good reason. As it turned out, the elite organization not only shuns publicity, it forbids it. Or as the Toronto *National Post* explained later, on May 24, 2001, "The conferences are held under absolute secrecy and tight security, with no media coverage allowed."

But back in 1995, I had no idea what I faced. I dived in, setting up shop in the library, hunting through thousands of U.S. newspapers, magazines, and books. I'm a researcher. I know how to find the most arcane data, but I was stymied, until I discovered *Spotlight*, a right-wing populist newsweekly based in Washington, D.C., which claimed to have reported Bilderberger's annual assemblies for more than two decades. Taking away *Spotlight*'s extreme political and emotional spin, but figuring in its on-the-scene photos, lists of attendees, and lists of yearly venues dating back to 1954, I began to believe the Bilderberg Group might not only be real but an idea for a book.

The test came a year later, when *Spotlight* predicted Bilderberg would hold its next covert confab at a luxury resort outside Toronto. I ordered the *Toronto Star* and held my breath. On June 6, 1996, I had confirmation at last from a mainstream news source: "The Bilderberg Conference of 120 world business and political leaders is unfolding in secrecy," the *Star* reported, "just as they planned" at the Canadian Imperial Bank of Commerce's leadership center at the former King City Ranch.

That night, I enjoyed a large glass of excellent pinot noir in celebration.

Over the years, as I wrote other novels, I continued to research the Bilderbergers — a hobby, perhaps an obsession. As a result, in *The Coil*, the Nautilus Group is based loosely on the Bilderberg Group. Both have headquarters in The Hague, both were named for the hotels in which they first officially met, and both employ extreme security, color-coded badges, and sniffer dogs. But after that, the facts diverge. For instance, I have no information or knowledge that a diabolical inner circle such as the Coil exists within Bilderberg.

I'm pleased to report that because of the doggedness of some journalists and protesters and the vast resources of the Internet, news coverage of the group is widening. In fact, London's *Sunday Times* jokes that Bilderberg meetings are "the world's greatest networking opportunity," while Portugal's *The News* refers gravely to the group's members and guests as "the world's unelected leaders."

In a tongue-in-cheek article, *The Guardian* of England and Wales points out, "It is, according to some, a sinister shadow world government dedicated to seizing control of the levers of the global economy. So why . . . put Lord Carrington's picture at the top of this column? He runs [Bilderberg] along with Henry Kissinger and David Rockefeller, billionaire owner of New York's Chase Manhattan Bank. . . . What will they discuss? Don't know. There are no statements, no sound bites, no photo calls. . . ."

The Atlanta Constitution seems to think it has a better handle on the situation: ". . . the Bilderbergers say the required pledge of delegates not to discuss what goes on at their meetings is simply to provide a private, informal environment in which those who influence national policies and international affairs can get to know each other and discuss, without commitment, their common problems."

Still, with media giants like Donald Graham of *The Washington Post* and billionaire bankers like Edmond de Rothschild and auto tycoons like Jurgen Schrempp of DaimlerChrysler and politicians with global clout like James D. Wolfensohn of the World Bank and Donald Rumsfeld of the

U.S. Department of Defense in attendance . . . the Bilderbergers continue to hold my interest.

They may just be talking shop, but the clandestine nature of their gatherings provokes all sorts of reactions. As *The Financial Times* once pointed out, "If the Bilderberg group is not a conspiracy of some sort, it is conducted in such a way as to give a remarkably good imitation of one."

Its current secretary-general, Martin Taylor of WH Smith, says he's done his best to increase its openness, according to the *Sunday Times*. But then, the minutes of its meetings have been secret for the past half century, which likely hinders that goal. When *Time* magazine analyzed the top six "Business Power Camps" in its July 20, 1998, issue, it awarded exclusivity ratings. Ten meant the most exclusive. Only one group rated it — the Bilderbergers.

For more reading, I suggest two books originally published in Britain:

MI6: Inside the Covert World of Her Majesty's Secret Intelligence Service, by Stephen Dorril, published by the Free Press in 2000.

Them: Adventures with Extremists by Jon Ronson, published by Simon & Schuster in 2002.

Gayle Lynds
Santa Barbara, California
August 18, 2003

Acknowledgments

Several years ago, Liz Sansborough took up residence inside my mind. She'd played a pivotal role in my first novel, *Masquerade*, but that wasn't enough for her. She wanted her own book, her own story. So she lingered, contemplating her future, making me increasingly uneasy as I waited. What would happen to her? Her life had been suffused with violence. Both parents were international assassins, now dead. Her CIA husband was tortured and killed in the field. She was CIA, too, and loved the work. Or thought she did. But all of us change. Sometimes we learn. Now Liz wants out. She wants peace. For herself, for the world. In this new violent millennium, perhaps impossible. But she must try.

Liz returns to school to earn her Ph.D. in the psychology of violence. . . .

Because the examination of violence from its most subtle to its most bloody permeates *The Coil*, I turned to friend and colleague Lucy Jo Palladino, Ph.D., who in earlier books led me in explorations of Asperger's syndrome, cellular memory, and conversion disorder. As always, her guidance was revelatory, providing an insider's view of violent people and acts and cultures.

For information about assassins, MI6, the CIA, and the globe's underbelly of crime and espionage, I thank several sources who must remain unnamed and in particular fellow author Robert Kresage, founding member of the CIA's Counterterrorism Center.

Paris, France, played a major role in *The Coil*. For advice, photos, and translations, I am indebted to Christine McNaught and novelist Len Lamensdorf for their selfless help.

Editing is that mysterious but crucial art form that in rare instances elevates a work above the author's vision. Most of us start with a blank page and a dream. Somewhere along the line, the pages fill, and the dream is overpowered by the words, scenes, chapters, sections. I was saved from that by Keith Kahla, editor extraordinaire, who knew better than I the novel inside *The Coil*. With deep appreciation, I thank him for his insight and wisdom, his nights and his weekends, and the unfettered access to his highly creative brain.

My husband, novelist Dennis Lynds, is both editor and collaborator, a constant source of feedback, revision, and ideas. My gratitude to him is boundless, as it is to my literary agent, Henry Morrison, and my international agent, Danny Baror, and my former webmaster, Brandon Erikson, and my new webmaster, Greg Stephens.

I've been blessed with a spectacular new publishing family at St. Martin's Press, including

Sally Richardson, Matthew Shear, George Witte, Matthew Baldacci, John Murphy, James Di Miero, Joan Higgins, John Cunningham, Jennifer Enderlin, John Karle, Dori Weintraub, Steve Eichinger, Harriet Seltzer, Christina Harcar, and Jerry Todd. I'm most appreciative for all of their help and support.

And finally, no book comes to life in isolation. My gratitude to Barbara Toohey, Paul Stone, Julia Stone, MaryEllen Strange, James Stevens, Theil Shelton, Philip Shelton, Kathleen Sharp, Elaine Russell, Monika McCoy, Kate Lynds, Deirdre Lynds, Fred Klein, Randi Kennedy, Steven Humphrey, Melodie Johnson Howe, Bones Howe, Nancy Hertz, Gayatri Chopra Heesen, Julia Cunningham, Ray Briare, Katrina Baum, Vicki Allen, and Joe Allen.

About the Author

Gayle Lynds is the author of the *New York Times* bestselling thriller *Masquerade*, as well as the novels *Mosaic* and *Mesmerized*. With Robert Ludlum, she is the author of three of the bestselling Covert-One novels, *The Hades Factor*, *The Paris Option*, and *The Altman Code*. After a varied career including stints as a journalist, an editor, and at a military think tank where she had top-secret clearance, Lynds is now a full-time writer. She lives with her husband, novelist Dennis Lynds, in Santa Barbara, California.

The employees of Thorndike Press hope you have enjoyed this Large Print book. All our Thorndike and Wheeler Large Print titles are designed for easy reading, and all our books are made to last. Other Thorndike Press Large Print books are available at your library, through selected bookstores, or directly from us.

For information about titles, please call:

(800) 223-1244

or visit our Web site at:

www.gale.com/thorndike
www.gale.com/wheeler

To share your comments, please write:

Publisher
Thorndike Press
295 Kennedy Memorial Drive
Waterville, ME   04901